**Susanna Gregory** was a police officer in Leeds before taking up an academic career. She has served as an environmental consultant, worked seventeen field seasons in the polar regions, and has taught comparative anatomy and biological anthropology.

She is the creator of the Matthew Bartholomew series of mysteries set in medieval Cambridge and the Thomas Chaloner adventures in Restoration London, and now lives in Wales with her husband, who is also a writer.

Also by Susanna Gregory

*The Matthew Bartholomew series*

*The Thomas Chaloner Series*

# SUSANNA GREGORY

# THE SANCTUARY MURDERS

THE TWENTY-FOURTH CHRONICLE OF
**MATTHEW BARTHOLOMEW**

sphere

SPHERE

First published in Great Britain in 2019 by Sphere

1 3 5 7 9 10 8 6 4 2

A CIP catalogue record for this book
is available from the British Library.

ISBN 978-0-7515-6265-1

Typeset in ITC New Baskerville by Palimpsest Book Production Ltd,
Falkirk, Stirlingshire
Printed and bound in Great Britain by Clays Ltd, Elcograf S.p.A.

Papers used by Sphere are from well-managed forests
and other responsible sources.

Sphere
An imprint of
Little, Brown Book Group
Carmelite House
50 Victoria Embankment
London
EC4Y 0DZ

An Hachette UK Company
www.hachette.co.uk

www.littlebrown.co.uk

In loving memory of
Ethel, Audrey, Gertie, Food (Ada), Dusty,
Florrie, Sybil, Olive and Ma
and for
Hen, Hulda, Molly, Mabel, Hazel and Harriet

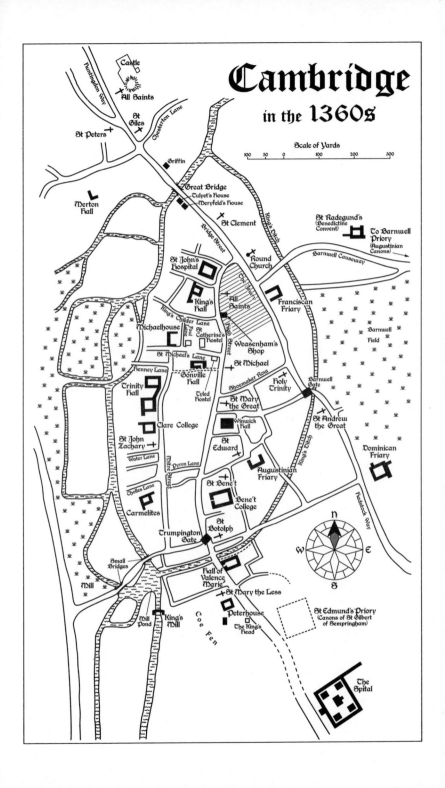

# PROLOGUE

*Sussex, March 1360*

Robert Arnold, Mayor of Winchelsea, had many flaws, but chief among them was an inappropriate fondness for other men's wives. His current lover was Herluva Dover, the miller's woman. She had agreed to meet him at a secluded spot near the sea – on a little hill that afforded excellent views in all directions, thus reducing the chances of them being caught.

Herluva was plump and buck-toothed, so Arnold was not sure why she had caught his fancy. Perhaps it was to spite her husband, Valentine Dover, whom he detested. Or maybe he was just running out of suitable prey and Herluva was the best of those who had not yet succumbed to his silver tongue and roving hands.

Although there was a little hut on the hill, Arnold had chosen to entertain Herluva outside that day. It was a beautiful morning, unseasonably warm, and the scent of approaching spring was in the air. The heather on which they lay was fragrant with new growth, while the sea was calm and almost impossibly blue. A solitary gull cried overhead, but their hideaway was otherwise silent. Arnold sighed contentedly, savouring both the tranquillity and the giddy prospect of what Herluva was about to provide.

Then she spoiled it all by sitting up and blurting, 'What is that? Look, Rob! A whole host of boats aiming for the river—'

'The grocers' ships,' interrupted Arnold, leaning over to plunge his face into her ample bosom. It smelled of flour and sweat – a not unpleasing combination, he

1

thought serenely. His next words were rather muffled. 'They are due back any—'

'I know the grocers' ships.' Herluva shoved him away and scrambled to her feet. 'These are different. *Look* at them, Rob.'

Frustrated and irked in equal measure, Arnold stood. Then gaped in horror at what he saw: a great fleet aimed directly at Winchelsea. His stomach lurched. It had been more than a year since the French had last come a-raiding, and he had confidently informed his burgesses that it would never happen again – that King Edward's immediate and ruthless reprisals in France meant the enemy would never dare attempt a repeat performance.

He recalled with sickening clarity what had happened the last time. Then, the invasion had been on a Sunday, when Winchelsea folk had been at their devotions. The raiders had locked the doors and set the church alight, and anyone who managed to escape the inferno was hacked to pieces outside. The slaughter had been terrible.

'Stop them, Rob,' gulped Herluva. 'Please! My children are down there!'

But Arnold was paralysed with fear as memories of the previous attack overwhelmed him – the screams of those roasted alive in the church, the demented howls of the attackers as they tore through the town, killing and looting. He dropped to his knees in the heather, shaking uncontrollably. He had never seen so many boats in one place – there were far more than last time – and he knew every one would be bursting with French marauders, all intent on murder, rape and pillage.

'Rob!' screeched Herluva. 'For God's sake, *do something*!'

Arnold pulled himself together. 'Sound the tocsin bell,' he ordered shakily. 'Then take your little ones to the marshes. They will be safe there. Hurry, woman!'

'What about you?' she demanded suspiciously. 'What will you be doing?'

'I have a plan to send them packing,' he snapped, looking out to sea so she would not see the lie in his eyes. 'Now go! Quickly, before it is too late.'

He watched her scamper away, but made no move to follow. By the time either of them reached the town, it would be far too late to organise any kind of defence. Besides, he knew what happened to those who challenged raiders, so why squander his life for no purpose? It would be better to hide until the attack was over, then take command once the enemy had gone. It was then that a man with good organisational skills would be most useful – arranging for the dead to be buried, the wounded tended, and damaged properties repaired.

He crouched in the heather and watched the ugly, high-prowed vessels reach the mouth of the river, where they furled their sails and rowed towards the town. On a gentle breeze, he heard the first frantic clang of bells, followed by distant howls of alarm as the residents of Winchelsea realised what was about to happen. He could picture the scene – people racing in all directions, rushing to barricade themselves inside their houses, rounding up missing children, loading carts in the wild hope of escape.

Like the last time, the French could not have picked a better occasion to attack. It was market day, so wares would be laid out for the taking, while half the town was in church, listening to a special Lenten sermon by the priest. Arnold's eyes narrowed. Was it possible that they had been told when to come by spies?

France was not only at war with England, but with herself, and two years before, a small group of displaced Frenchmen had taken up residence in Winchelsea. They were tolerated because they were generous to local charities, never did anything to offend, and regularly professed a love of all things English. But were they decent, honest folk eager to adapt to their new lives, or were they vipers in the nest? Perhaps *they* had sent messages home, saying when

Winchelsea would be most vulnerable. Arnold had suggested as much after the last raid, but the miller, Val Dover, had dismissed the accusation as false and mean-spirited.

Arnold allowed himself a small, grim smile of satisfaction. But who had been right? *He* had, and the current raid was the price of Dover's reckless support of strangers. He decided that as soon as the crisis was over, he would announce his suspicions again, and this time the foreigners would pay for their treachery with their lives.

He watched the first enemy ship reach the pier. Armed figures swarmed off it. A few brave townsmen raced to repel them – two invaders went down under a hail of kicks and punches – but a second boat joined the first, then a third, a fourth, a fifth, until the tide was impossible to stem. Then it was the defenders who were overwhelmed by sheer force of numbers. In the river, ships jostled and collided as their captains struggled to find a place to land their howling, blood-crazed passengers. Then came the first wisps of smoke.

Unable to watch more, Arnold went inside the little hut and closed the door.

Hours later, when the sun had set and the shadows faded into darkness, Arnold started to walk home. He arrived to sights even worse than he had feared. The dead littered the streets, and the dying wept, cursed and begged for help as he picked his way through them. He coughed as smoke billowed from the inferno that was the guildhall, and its heat seared his face. Then someone grabbed his arm. He yelped in terror, then recognised the soot-stained, bloodied face of his old rival Val Dover.

'You told us we were safe,' the miller rasped accusingly. 'We believed you. It was—'

'It is not my fault,' snapped Arnold, wrenching free. 'Blame the spies who told the French that I was in Rye today, thus leaving no one to mount a proper defence.

*They* are the ones responsible for this outrage, not me. I was appalled when I came home to find—'

'You? Mount a defence?' sneered Dover. 'And what is this about spies? I hope you do not aim to accuse our settlers again. They are our friends.'

At that moment, a gaggle of invaders swaggered past – stragglers, drunk on stolen wine, who were in no hurry to follow their compatriots back to France while there was still plunder to be had. Yelling for Arnold to follow, Dover plunged among them, cudgel flailing furiously. Two stalwart defenders could have defeated them with ease, but Arnold was too frightened to help, and only watched uselessly from the shadows.

When Dover was dead and his killers had lurched away, Arnold hid, vowing not to emerge again until the last enemy ship had sailed away. While he waited, he became increasingly convinced that someone *had* sent word to the French, telling them when to come. He scowled into the darkness. It *was* the settlers – their gratitude for Winchelsea's friendship was a ruse, and they had betrayed their hosts at the first opportunity. Well, *he* would not sit back while they profited from their treachery – he would round them up and hang them all.

But what if Dover was right, and they were innocent? His heart hardened. Then that was too bad. He needed a way to deflect the accusations of cowardice he knew would be coming his way, and the settlers would provide it. His mind made up, he hunkered down until it was safe enough to show his face.

*Cambridge, late April 1360*

'The French are coming!'

Isnard the bargeman's frantic howl attracted a sizeable audience, and folk listened agog as he gasped out his report. Then they hurried away to tell their friends and

5

families, adding their own embellishments to the story as they did so. By the time the news reached the castle, Sheriff Tulyet was startled to hear that a vast enemy horde was marching along the Trumpington road, and would be sacking Cambridge within the hour.

'They landed on the coast and headed straight for us, sir,' declared Sergeant Orwel, delighted by the prospect of a skirmish; he had fought at Poitiers and hated Frenchmen with a passion. 'They heard about the great riches held by the University, see, and aim to carry it all home with them. We must prepare for battle at once.'

Although small in stature, with elfin features and a boyish beard, Tulyet was one of the strongest, ablest and most astute royal officials in the country. Unlike his sergeant, he understood how quickly rumours blossomed beyond all truth, and was disinclined to fly into action over a tale that was patently absurd – particularly as he knew exactly how Isnard had reached the conclusions he was currently bawling around the town.

'I had a letter from the King this morning,' he explained. 'Rashly, I left it on the table while I went to Mass, and I came home to find my clerk reading it out to the servants. Unfortunately, Isnard happened to hear – he was there delivering firewood – and he seems to have interpreted His Majesty's words rather liberally.'

Orwel frowned his mystification. 'What do you mean, sir?'

'The first part of the letter described how several thousand Frenchmen attacked Winchelsea last month,' began Tulyet.

Orwel nodded. 'And slaughtered every single citizen. It was an outrage!'

'It was an outrage,' agreed Tulyet soberly. 'And although many people *were* killed, far more survived. In the next part of the letter, the King wrote that the marauders went home so loaded with plunder that it may encourage them to come back for more. Somehow, Isnard took this to mean that they *will* return and that Cambridge is the target.'

'And it is not?' asked Orwel, disappointed to learn he was to be cheated of a battle that day. 'Why did the King write to you then?'

'As part of a country-wide call to arms. We are to gather every able-bodied man aged between sixteen and sixty, and train them in hand-to-hand combat and archery. Then if the French do mount a major invasion, he will have competent troops ready to fight them off.'

'A major invasion?' echoed Orwel eagerly. 'So we might see the French at our gates yet? We are easy to reach from the sea – you just sail a boat up the river.'

'Yes,' acknowledged Tulyet, 'but the enemy will opt for easier targets first, and if they do, we shall march there to fight them. Personally, I cannot see it happening, but the King is wise to take precautions.'

Orwel was dismayed by the Sheriff's predictions, but tried to look on the bright side. 'I suppose training new troops might be fun. Does the order apply to the University as well? Most of them are between sixteen and sixty.'

Tulyet nodded. 'Which means we shall have a lot of armed scholars and armed townsfolk in close proximity to each other, which is never a good thing. Let us hope Brother Michael and I will be able to keep the peace.'

'Why bother?' asked Orwel, scowling. 'Most of them University bastards are French – I hear them blathering in that foul tongue all the time. Fighting them would be a good way to hone our battle skills *and* deal a blow to the enemy at the same time.'

'Most scholars are English,' countered Tulyet sharply. 'They speak French because . . . it is the language they use at home.'

It was actually the language of the ruling elite, while

7

those of lower birth tended to stick to the vernacular. Tulyet just managed to stop himself from saying so, unwilling for Orwel to repeat his words to the garrison. Soldiers already resented scholars' assumed superiority, and reminding them of it would not be a good idea.

Orwel continued to glower. 'They live in England, so they should learn English. I do not hold with talking foreign.'

'No,' said Tulyet drily. 'I can see that.'

Orwel regarded him rather challengingly. 'Will you tell Brother Michael to stop them from strutting around in packs, pretending they are better than us? Because they are not. And if the French do invade and the University rushes to fight at their side, we shall beat them soundly. No scholar is a match for me and the lads.'

'Underestimate them at your peril,' warned Tulyet. 'Some trained as knights, while others are skilled swordsmen. They are a formidable force, which is why the King has included them in his call to arms.'

'*We* have knights,' Orwel pointed out stoutly. 'And all of them are better warriors than any French-babbling scholar.'

Tulyet saw he was wasting his time trying to reason with such rigidly held convictions, and only hoped the belligerent sergeant could be trusted not to provoke a fight. Relations between the University and the town were uneasy at best, and it took very little to spark a brawl. A taunting insult from a soldier to a student would certainly ignite trouble.

'We shall have two more knights by the end of the week,' he said, to change the subject. 'The King is sending them to help us drill our new recruits. Sir Leger and Sir Norbert, both veterans of the French wars.'

Orwel was delighted by the news, although Tulyet was full of trepidation. He knew exactly what the newcomers would be like – vicious, hard-bitten warriors whose experiences on the battlefield would have left them with a deep and unbending hatred of all things French. The townsfolk would follow their example, and friction would follow for certain. He heartily wished the King had sent them to some other town.

At that moment, there was a commotion by the gate – Isnard was trying to force his way past the guards. As the felonious bargeman never entered the castle willingly, Tulyet knew there must be a very good reason as to why he was keen to do it now. He indicated that Isnard should be allowed inside.

'I came out of the goodness of my heart,' declared Isnard, all bristling indignation as he brushed himself down. 'But if you do not want to hear my news, I shall go home.'

'My apologies, Isnard,' said Tulyet mildly. 'Now, what did you want to tell me?'

'That there has been a murder,' reported Isnard gleefully. 'Of a *French* scholar named Baldwin de Paris. He was a member of King's Hall, a place that is well known for harbouring foreigners, traitors and spies.'

'And so it begins,' sighed Tulyet wearily.

# CHAPTER 1

*Cambridge, early May 1360*

It was noon, and the bell had just rung to tell the scholars of Michaelhouse that it was time for their midday meal. The masters drew their discourses to a close, and the servants came to turn the hall from lecture room to refectory, carrying trestle tables from the stack near the hearth and setting benches next to them.

Most Fellows were only too happy to stop mid-sentence and rub their hands in gluttonous anticipation, but one always needed a nudge to make him finish. This was Doctor Matthew Bartholomew, who felt there was never enough time in the day to teach his budding physicians all they needed to know. He was regarded as something of a slave driver by his pupils, although he genuinely failed to understand why.

'Enough, Matt!' snapped Brother Michael, tapping his friend sharply on the shoulder when the first two more polite warnings went unheeded.

Michael was a portly Benedictine and a theologian of some repute. He was also the University's Senior Proctor, and had recently been elected Master of Michaelhouse – although what had actually happened was that he had announced he was taking over and none of the other Fellows had liked to argue.

Under Michael's auspices, College meals had improved dramatically. Gone was the miserable fare of his prede-cessors, and in its place was good red meat, plenty of bread and imported treats like raisins. He considered food a divine blessing, and was not about to deprive himself or the scholars under his care of God's gracious bounty.

As he dragged his mind away from teaching, Bartholomew was astonished that it was midday already. He had been explaining a particularly complicated passage in Galen's *De semine*, and as semen held a special fascination for most of the young lads under his tutelage, they had not minded running over time for once.

'Are you sure it is noon, Brother?' he asked, startled. 'I only started an hour ago.'

'*Four* hours ago,' corrected Michael. 'I appreciate that you have much to cover before you leave us for a life of wedded bliss in ten weeks, but you should remember that even your lively lads have their limits. They look dazed to me.'

'Transfixed,' corrected Bartholomew, although it occurred to him that while *De semine* might have captured their prurient imaginations, he was less sure that his analysis of purgative medicines, which had taken up the earlier part of the morning, had held their attention quite so securely. Indeed, he was fairly sure a couple had dozed off.

'Well, you can continue to dazzle them this afternoon,' said Michael, drawing him to one side of the hall, out of the servants' way. 'But make the most of it, because tomorrow morning will be wasted.'

Bartholomew frowned. 'Will it? Why?'

Michael scowled. 'Because William is scheduled to preach on the nominalism–realism debate. You *know* this, Matt – we have been discussing ways to prevent it for weeks. But my predecessor agreed to let him do it, and William refuses to let me cancel.'

Father William was the College's Franciscan friar. He was bigoted, stupid, fanatical and a disgrace to the University in more ways than his colleagues could count. Unfortunately, he had been a Fellow for so long that it was impossible to get rid of him, as the statutes did not list dogmatism and unintelligence among the crimes for which an offender could be sent packing.

'You should have tried harder,' grumbled Bartholomew, hating the thought of losing an entire morning to the ramblings of a man who knew even less about the subject than he did.

The dispute between nominalists and realists was deeply contentious, although Bartholomew failed to understand why it evinced such fierce passions. It was a metaphysical matter, revolving around the question of whether properties – called universals – exist in reality or just in the mind or speech. Even those who did not really understand it felt compelled to make a stand, with the result that a lot of rubbish was being spouted. William was a worse offender than most.

'"Tried harder"?' asked Michael crossly. 'How, when William threatened to sue me for breach of contract if I stood in his way? Yet I shall be glad of a morning away from the lecture hall. I have a lot to do now that I am Master of Michaelhouse *and* Senior Proctor.'

'You mean like hunting whoever murdered Paris the Plagiarist?'

Paris, an elderly French priest, had caused a major scandal the previous term, when he had stolen another scholar's work and passed it off as his own. In academic circles, this was considered the most heinous of crimes, and had brought great shame to King's Hall, where Paris had been a Fellow. Someone had stabbed him ten days before, but Michael was no nearer to finding the killer now than he had been when it had first happened.

'I suspect the culprit acted in a drunken rage,' the monk confided. 'He was no doubt sorry afterwards, and aims to get away with his crime by keeping his head down. I shall not give up, of course, but the trail is stone cold.'

'You have no leads at all?'

'There are no clues and no witnesses. It was a random act of violence.'

'Not random,' said Bartholomew, who had been particularly repelled by what Paris had done. Academic integrity was important to him, and he thought Paris had committed an unpardonable offence. 'I imagine he was killed for being a fraud, a liar and a cheat.'

'His killer may be someone who feels like you,' acknowledged Michael. 'But *I* think he was struck down because he was French.'

Bartholomew blinked. 'You consider being French worse than stealing ideas?'

'Most townsmen do. The Winchelsea massacre ignited much anti-French fervour, as you know. The last few days have seen the rise of a ridiculous but popular belief that anyone with even remote connections to France will applaud what happened in Sussex.'

Bartholomew grimaced, aware of how quickly decent people could turn into a mob with unpalatable opinions. 'Of course, our own army is no better. I saw them run amok in Normandy once, and it was an ugly sight.'

'Hush!' warned Michael sharply. 'Say *nothing* that might be considered pro-French, not even here among friends. Emotions run too high, and folk are eager to roust out anyone they deem to be a traitor.'

'No one can accuse me of being unpatriotic,' grumbled Bartholomew. 'Not when I shall squander an entire evening practising archery tonight – time that would have been much better spent teaching.'

'It would,' agreed Michael. 'But shooting a few arrows will not save you from the prejudices of the ignorant.'

Reluctantly, Bartholomew conceded that the monk was right. 'Townsfolk glare at me when I go out, even ones I have known for years. I am glad Matilde and Edith are away.'

Matilde, the woman he was going to marry, had gone

to fetch an elderly aunt to their wedding, and had taken his sister with her for company.

'I wish I was with them,' sighed Michael. 'Of course, that would leave Chancellor de Wetherset unsupervised. I like the man, but he should let *me* decide what is best for the University, and it is a wretched nuisance when he tries to govern for himself.'

Bartholomew smothered a smile. Over the years, Michael had manipulated the post of Senior Proctor to the point where he, not the Chancellor, wielded the real power in the University. The last two incumbents had been his puppets, implementing the policies he devised and following his edicts. But the current holder, Richard de Wetherset, bucked under Michael's heavy hand.

'He ran the University well enough when he was Chancellor before,' Bartholomew said, not surprised that de Wetherset had his own ideas about what the office entailed.

'Yes, but times have changed since then, and I do not want him undoing all the good I have done. For example, he disapproves of me compromising when dealing with the town – he thinks we should best them every time, to show them who is in charge. He believes the only way forward is to fight until we are the undisputed rulers.'

'And have sawdust in our flour, spit in our beer, and candles that smoke?'

'Quite! Of course, none of it would be a problem if Suttone was still in post. Why did he not talk to me before resigning as Chancellor? I would have convinced him to stay, and then there would be no great rift opening between us and the town.'

'Depose de Wetherset,' shrugged Bartholomew. 'You have dismissed awkward officials in the past, so I am sure you can do it again.'

'It is tempting, but no,' said Michael. 'Not least because it would mean another election, and I am tired of fixing those. De Wetherset is not a bad man or a stupid one. We worked well together in the past, and I am sure we can do it again. He just needs a few weeks to adjust to my way of doing things.'

While the servants toted steaming pots and platters from the kitchens, Bartholomew looked around the place that had been his home for so many years – something he had taken to doing a lot since Matilde had agreed to be his wife. Scholars were not permitted to marry, so he would have to resign his Fellowship when he wed her at the end of term. He loved her, but even so, he was dreading the day when he would walk out of Michaelhouse for the last time.

The College comprised a quadrangle of buildings around a muddy courtyard, with the hall and the Fellows' room – called the conclave – at one end, and two accommodation blocks jutting from them at right angles. The square was completed by a high wall abutting the lane, along which stood a gate, stables, sheds and storerooms. It had grounds that ran down to the river, and included an orchard, vegetable plots and a private pier.

Michaelhouse had never been wealthy, and bad luck and a series of unfortunate investments had resulted in it teetering on the verge of collapse more times than Bartholomew could remember. However, now Michael was Master, things had changed. New benefactors were eager to support a foundation with him at its helm, and his 'election' had attracted not just generous donations, but powerful supporters at Court, which combined to ensure the College a much more stable and prosperous future.

He had also appointed two new Fellows. The first was Bartholomew's student John Aungel – young, energetic and eager to step into his master's shoes. The second was Will Theophilis, a canon lawyer who had compiled a popular timetable of scripture readings entitled *Calendarium cum tribus cyclis.* Theophilis was ambitious, so Michael had also made him his Junior Proctor, which he promised would lead to even loftier posts in the future.

Michael had raised the College's academic standing as well. He had written several sermons that were very well regarded in theological circles, while Bartholomew had finally published the massive treatise on fevers that he had been compiling for the past decade – a work that would spark considerable controversy if anyone ever read it. No one had attempted it yet, and the only comments he had received so far pertained to how much space it took up on a bookshelf.

But these were eclipsed by a stunning theosophical work produced by John Clippesby, a gentle Dominican who talked to animals and claimed they answered back. Michael had wasted no time in promoting it, and the College now basked in its reflected glory.

Clippesby's thesis took the form of a conversation between two hens – one a nominalist, the other a realist. Although an eccentric way of presenting an argument, his logic was impeccable and the philosophy groundbreaking without being heretical. The whole University was gripped by the 'Chicken Debate', which was considered to be the most significant work to have emerged from Cambridge since the plague.

The two new Fellows filled the seats at the high table once occupied by Master Langelee and Chancellor Suttone. Master Langelee had gone to fight in France, where he was far more comfortable with a sword in his hand than he had ever been with a pen; Suttone had resigned the Chancellorship and disappeared to his native Lincolnshire. Bartholomew missed them both, and had liked the College more when they were there. Or was he just getting old and resistant to change?

'Do you think Michael will excuse me tomorrow, Matt?'

The voice that broke into his thoughts belonged to Clippesby, who cradled a sleeping duck in his arms. The Dominican was slightly built with dark, spiky hair and a sweet, if somewhat other-worldly, smile.

'Tomorrow?' asked Bartholomew blankly.

'Father William's lecture,' explained Clippesby. 'He will attempt to explain why he thinks realism is better than nominalism, and I do not think I can bear it.'

One of William's many unattractive traits was his passionate dislike of anyone from a rival Order. He particularly detested Dominicans, and was deeply jealous of Clippesby's recent academic success. His determination to ridicule the Chicken Debate was why he had refused to let Michael cancel his lecture – he believed he could demolish Clippesby's ideas, although he was wholly incapable of succeeding, and would likely be intellectually savaged in the process. Bartholomew was not surprised the kindly Clippesby was loath to watch.

'I am sure Michael will understand if you slip away,' he said. 'I hope to miss it, too – with any luck, a patient will summon me.'

Clippesby wagged a cautionary finger. 'Be careful what you wish for. It might come true.'

'What might come true?' asked Theophilis, coming to join them.

The new Junior Proctor had long black hair parted in the middle, and a soft voice that had a distinctly sinister timbre. Bartholomew had disliked him on sight, which was unusual, as he tended to find something to admire in the most deplorable of rogues. He considered Theophilis sly, smug and untrustworthy, although Michael often remarked how glad he was that the canon lawyer had agreed to be his deputy.

'We were discussing wishes,' explained Clippesby, laying an affectionate hand on the duck's back. 'Ada here expressed a desire for a large dish of grain, but when one

17

appeared, greed made her ill. Now she is sleeping off her excesses.'

'Goodness!' murmured Theophilis, regarding the bird askance. 'Perhaps she should have enrolled at King's Hall instead – that is the College noted for overindulgence, not ours. Incidentally, have you thought about the questions I raised last night – the ones about Scotist realism and the problem of universals?'

He often asked the Dominican's opinion on philosophical matters, although he demonstrated a polite interest in the answer only as long as Clippesby was within earshot; once the Dominican was away, he mocked his eccentric ways. This duplicity was another reason why Bartholomew had taken against him.

'Things have a common nature indeed!' he scoffed when Clippesby had gone. 'What nonsense! He should be locked up, where he can do no harm.'

'If you really think that,' said Bartholomew icily, 'why do you spend so much time with him?'

Theophilis shrugged. 'It amuses me. Besides, there is no harm in making friends, even with lunatics. But speaking of friends, I have been invited to St Radegund's Priory tomorrow, to hear a nun pontificate on sainthood. I have permission to bring a guest, so would you care to join me? It will allow you to escape William's tirade.'

Bartholomew flailed around for an excuse to decline, as even listening to William was preferable to a jaunt with Theophilis. 'I may have patients to attend,' he hedged. 'You will be better off asking someone else.'

'Perhaps another time, then,' said Theophilis, all amiability.

Bartholomew hoped not.

A short while later, the bell rang to announce that the food was ready to be served. The students aimed for the body of the hall, while Michael and his five Fellows stepped on to the dais – the raised platform near the hearth where the 'high table' stood. The Master's chair occupied pride of place in the middle, with benches for Bartholomew, Clippesby and Aungel on his right, and William and Theophilis to his left.

Michael waited until everyone had reached his allotted place, then intoned a Grace. It was neither too short nor too long, and each word was beautifully enunciated, so that even William, whose grasp of Latin was questionable, could follow. As Michael spoke, Bartholomew reflected on the other Masters he had known during his tenure – dear old Kenyngham, who had been overly wordy; the smarmy Wilson cousins; and Langelee, whose Graces had been brief to the point of irreverence. Michael did everything better than any of them, and he wondered why he and his colleagues had not elected him sooner.

When the monk finished, everyone sat and the servants brought the food from behind the serving screen. There was bread – not white, but not rye bulked out with sawdust either – and a stew containing a good deal of meat and no vegetables, just as Michael liked it. As a sop to Bartholomew's insistence on a balanced diet, there was also a small dish of peas.

Meals were meant to be eaten in silence, with no sound other than the Bible Scholar's drone, but Michael considered this a foolish rule. Students spent much of the day listening to their teachers, so it was unreasonable to expect them to stay quiet during meals as well. A few were monks or friars, used to such discipline, but most were not, and needed to make some noise. Moreover, many were eager to discuss what they had learned that day, and Michael hated to stifle intelligent conversation.

The students were not the only ones who appreciated the opportunity to talk. So did Bartholomew, because it allowed him to collar Aungel and issue yet more instructions about how the medical students were to be taught

19

after he left. He was about to launch into a monologue regarding how to approach the tricky subject of surgery – physicians were supposed to leave it to barbers, but he liked to dabble and encouraged his pupils to do likewise – when his attention was caught by what Theophilis was saying in his slyly whispering voice.

'The Chancellor granted the stationer special licence to produce more copies of the Chicken Debate this morning. All profits are to go to the University Chest.'

Michael gaped his shock. 'But de Wetherset cannot decide how and when that treatise is published, and he certainly cannot pocket the proceeds for the University! They belong to Clippesby – and, by extension, to Michaelhouse.'

'He told me that Clippesby had agreed to it,' explained Theophilis. 'The Vice-Chancellor arranged it with him, apparently.'

He glanced at the Dominican, who was feeding wet bread to the two hens he had contrived to smuggle into the hall. As a relative newcomer, Theophilis still found Clippesby's idiosyncrasies disconcerting. The other Fellows were used to animals and birds joining them for dinner, although Bartholomew had banned rats in the interests of hygiene and cows in the interests of safety.

'Well, Clippesby?' demanded Michael angrily. 'Did you treat with Vice-Chancellor Heltisle behind my back?'

Heltisle was the first ever to hold the office of Vice-Chancellor, a post de Wetherset had created on the grounds that the University was now too big for one man to run. De Wetherset was right: it had doubled in size over the last decade, and involved considerably more work. Appointing a deputy also meant that Michael could not swamp him with a lot of mundane administration, as he had done with his puppet predecessors – a ploy to keep them too busy to notice what he was doing in their names. De Wetherset passed such chores to Heltisle, leaving him free to monitor exactly what the monk was up to.

Clippesby nodded happily. 'He told me that the money would be used to build a shelter for homeless dogs. How could I refuse?'

Michael's expression hardened. 'Your dogs will not see a penny, and you are a fool to think otherwise. Heltisle loathes Michaelhouse, because we are older and more venerable than his own upstart College. He will do anything to harm us.'

Clippesby smiled serenely. 'I know, which is why I added a clause to the contract. It states that unless the kennel is built within a week, he will be personally liable to pay me twice the sum raised from selling the treatise.'

The other Fellows gazed at him in astonishment. Clippesby was notoriously ingenuous, and was usually the victim of that sort of tactic, not the perpetrator.

'And Heltisle signed it?' asked Michael, the first to find his tongue.

Clippesby continued to beam. 'I do not think he noticed the addendum when he put pen to parchment. He was more interested in convincing me that it was the right thing to do.'

Michael laughed. 'Clippesby, you never cease to amaze me! Heltisle will be livid.'

'Very probably,' acknowledged Clippesby. 'But the dogs will be pleased, and that is much more important.'

'I hope you do not expect me, as Junior Proctor, to draw Heltisle's attention to this clause when the week is up,' said Theophilis uneasily.

'I shall reserve that pleasure for myself,' said Michael, eyes gleaming in anticipation.

For the rest of the meal, the monk made plans for the unexpected windfall – the gutters on the kitchens needed replacing, and he wanted glass in the conclave windows before winter.

While Michael devised ways to spend Clippesby's money, Bartholomew studied Theophilis. Because Michael had given him his Fellowship and started him on the road to a successful academic career, Theophilis claimed he was in the monk's debt. In order to repay the favour shown, he had offered to spy on the Chancellor and the Vice-Chancellor on Michael's behalf. It was distasteful, and Bartholomew wondered yet again if Michael was right to trust him.

'Heltisle will not have fallen for your ruse,' warned Father William, a burly, rough-looking man with a greasy halo of hair around an untidy tonsure. His habit had once been grey, but was now so filthy that Bartholomew considered it a health hazard. 'He will have added some clause of his own – one that will make us the losers.'

'He did not,' Clippesby assured him. 'I watched him very closely, as did the robin, four spiders and a chicken.'

'Which chicken?' demanded William, eyeing the pair that pecked around Clippesby's feet. 'Because if it is the bird that expounded all that nominalist nonsense, then I submit that its testimony cannot be trusted.'

'*She*, not it,' corrected Clippesby with one of the grins that made most people assume he was not in his right mind. He bent to stroke one of the hens. 'Gertrude is a very sound theologian. But as it happens, it was her sister Ma who helped me to hoodwink Heltisle.'

This was too much for William. 'How can a debate between two fowls be taken seriously?' he scoffed. 'It is heresy in its most insidious form. You should be ex-communicated!'

Clippesby was a firm favourite among the students, far more so than William, so there was an instant angry growl from the body of the hall. Aungel, so recently a student himself, rushed to the Dominican's defence.

'Many Greek and Roman philosophers used imaginary conversations between animals as a vehicle to expound their theories,' he pointed out sharply. 'It is a perfectly acceptable literary device.'

'But those discussions were between *noble* beasts,' argued William. 'Like lions or goats. But Clippesby chose to use hens.' He virtually spat the last word.

'Goats?' blurted Theophilis. 'I hardly think *they* can be described as noble.'

'What is wrong with hens?' demanded Clippesby at the same time.

'They are female,' replied William loftily. 'And it is a fact of nature that those are always less intelligent than us males.' He jabbed a grubby finger at Gertrude. 'And do not claim otherwise, because I saw *her* eating worms the other day, which is hardly clever.'

'But *you* eat worms, Father,' said Clippesby guilelessly. 'There is one in your mouth right now, in fact – it was among the peas.'

There followed an unedifying scene during which William spat, the chickens raced to examine what was expelled, Clippesby struggled to stop them, and the students howled with laughter. Aungel joined in, while Theophilis watched in tight-lipped disapproval. Michael could have ended the spectacle with a single word, but he let it run its course, feeling it served William right.

'How do you like University life, Theophilis?' asked Bartholomew, once the commotion had died down and everyone was eating again, although no one was very interested in the peas. 'Are you happy here?'

'Yes – I enjoy teaching, while spying on the Chancellor and his deputy for Michael is pleasingly challenging. However, the tension between scholars and the town is worrisome.'

'Relations are strained at the moment,' acknowledged Bartholomew. 'But the hostility will subside. It always does.'

'Perhaps it has in the past, but that was when Michael was in charge,' said Theophilis, pursing his lips. 'Now we have de Wetherset, who has a mind and opinions of his own. For example, Michael wanted to pass an edict forbidding scholars from speaking French on the streets, but de Wetherset blocked it, which was stupid.'

Bartholomew agreed. 'It would have removed one cause for resentment. However, in de Wetherset's defence, there are a lot of scholars who do not know English – and tradesmen will not understand them if they speak Latin. I understand his reservations.'

Theophilis lowered his voice. 'De Wetherset wants to rule alone, like he did the last time he was Chancellor. He chips away at Michael's authority constantly, so that Michael grows weaker every day. Moreover, Heltisle supports him in all he does, which is why de Wetherset created the post of Vice-Chancellor, of course – for an ally against Michael.'

'De Wetherset will never best our Master,' said Bartholomew confidently. 'So it does not matter if he has Heltisle to support him or not – Heltisle is irrelevant.'

'I hope you are right, because if not, de Wetherset will take us to war with the town, and I fear—' Theophilis broke off when a soldier from the castle hurried in and a student conducted him towards the high table.

'You are needed at the market square,' the man told Bartholomew breathlessly. 'Bonet the spicer has been murdered, and the Sheriff wants your opinion about it.'

It was not far from the College to the market square, where Jean Bonet occupied a handsome house overlooking the stall where he sold his costly wares. He had lived in Cambridge for many years, but his nationality had only become a problem since the Winchelsea massacre and the King's call to arms. He lived alone, and was reputed to be fabulously wealthy.

Bartholomew arrived at the spicer's home to find three men waiting for him. One was Sheriff Tulyet, who owed at least part of his shrieval success to the good working relationship he had developed with Michael. He had been horrified when Suttone had resigned, lest the new Chancellor proved to be less amenable. He was right to be concerned: relations had grown chilly with de Wetherset at the helm, despite Michael's efforts to keep matters on an even keel.

Tulyet was dwarfed by the two knights who were with him. They were Sir Norbert and Sir Leger, sent by the King to oversee the town's military training. The pair were much of an ilk – warriors who had honed their trade in France, with the scars to prove it. Sir Norbert was larger and sported an oily black mane that cascaded over his shoulders. He was a dim-witted brute, never happy unless he was fighting. His friend Leger was fair-headed and a little shorter, but far more dangerous, because he possessed brains to go with his brawn.

'You took your time,' Norbert growled when Bartholomew walked in. 'No doubt you would have been faster if it had been a scholar who asked you to come.'

'Perhaps he just does not want to help us solve the murder of a Frenchie,' shrugged Leger slyly. 'Who can blame him?'

'I came as quickly as I could,' objected Bartholomew. He did not care what the two knights thought, but Dick Tulyet was his friend, and he did not want him to think he had dallied.

Tulyet indicated the body on the floor. 'We believe this happened last night – the alarm was raised when no one opened his shop this morning. Clearly, he has been stabbed, but can you tell us anything that might help us find out who did it?'

Bartholomew was sorry the spicer had come to such an end. There had been no harm in him, and he had been careful to keep a low profile once the town – and the University, for that matter – had decided that anyone even remotely foreign should be treated with suspicion and contempt. He was on the floor of his solar, and had been trying to run away when his attacker had struck – the wound was in his back, and his arms were thrown out in front of him. Bartholomew glanced around carefully, reading the clues in what he could see.

'The killer came while Bonet was eating his supper,' he began. 'There is no sign that the door was forced, so I suspect he answered it in the belief that whoever was calling was friendly.'

'He was clearly no warrior then,' said Norbert in smug disdain. 'Or he would have known to consider any visitor a potential threat.'

'No, he was not a warrior,' said Bartholomew coolly. 'And I cannot imagine why anyone would kill a peaceable old man. However, I can tell you that the culprit is a coward of the most contemptible kind – the same kind of vermin who has no problem slaughtering unarmed women and children in French villages.'

Tulyet stepped between him and the knights when hands went to the hilts of swords.

'What can you tell us about the wound, Matt?' he asked quickly, to defuse the situation before there was trouble. 'Was it caused by a knife from the dinner table?'

Bartholomew shook his head. 'Bonet was killed by a blade with two sharp edges – a dagger, rather than a knife.' He nodded to a bloody imprint on the floor. 'It lay there for some time after the murder, which probably means the killer left it behind when he fled the scene of the crime. Who found the body?'

Tulyet sighed. 'Half the population of Cambridge – they burst in en masse when it became clear that something was amiss. My sergeant did his best to keep order, but

Bonet was French, so his home was considered fair game for looters. His servants say all manner of goods are missing, and the murder weapon must be among them.'

'You will never find it then,' said Norbert, giving the impression that his sympathies lay firmly with the English thieves rather than the French victim. 'The culprit will know better than to sell it here, so you should consider it gone permanently.'

'We have asked for witnesses,' added Leger quickly, seeing Tulyet's disapproving scowl. 'But no one saw a thing – or at least, nothing they are willing to admit.'

'Because Bonet was a Frenchie.' Norbert was about to spit when he caught Tulyet's eye and thought better of it. 'Cambridge folk think as I do – that the world is a better place without so many of them in it.'

'Then go outside and ask again,' ordered Tulyet sharply. 'Because Bonet was not just some "Frenchie" – he was a burgess who lived among us for years. I want his killer caught and hanged.'

'Even if a scholar did it?' asked Leger deviously, and smirked. 'The Chancellor will not approve of you executing his people. It will likely spark a riot.'

It was not a discussion Tulyet was about to have with them. He glared until they mumbled acknowledgement of his orders and slouched out. Bartholomew breathed a sigh of relief. The solar was spacious, but Leger and Norbert overfilled it with their belligerently menacing presence.

'They might be good at teaching archery,' he told Tulyet, 'but they are always trying to pick quarrels with scholars, and one day they will succeed. Then we will have a bloodbath.'

'I know,' sighed Tulyet. 'But Leger is clever – he makes sure all their aggression is couched in terms of patriotic zeal, thus making it difficult for me to berate them. They are a problem I could do without, especially as de

Wetherset seems intent on destroying all that Michael and I have built.'

'Perhaps the situation will improve when the horror of Winchelsea fades in everyone's mind,' said Bartholomew, sorry to see the lines of strain in his friend's face. 'We cannot hate France and all things French for ever.'

'I think you will find we can,' said Tulyet wryly, 'so do not expect a lessening of hostilities anytime soon. But tell me more about poor old Bonet. You say he was killed with a dagger. So was Paris the Plagiarist. Do we have a common culprit?'

'I cannot say for certain, but it seems likely, given that both were French. Will it serve to unite town and University, do you think? We have lost a scholar and you a burgess.'

'Unfortunately, what Norbert said is true: most towns-folk *do* think the world is a better place with fewer Frenchmen in it. Ergo, I do not see us joining you on Bonet's behalf, or your scholars standing with us to catch Paris's killer.'

Unhappily, Bartholomew suspected he was right.

# CHAPTER 2

'Two weeks,' grumbled Michael the following morning. The scholars had attended Mass, broken their fast and then the Fellows had repaired to the comfortable room adjoining the hall that provided them with a refuge from students. 'You and I were in Suffolk for *two weeks* over the Easter vacation, and we returned to find our entire world turned upside down!'

He was talking to Bartholomew, who sat by the fire with him. Three other Fellows were also in the room: William was by the window, practising the lecture he was to give that day; Clippesby was on the floor, conversing with an assortment of poultry; and Aungel was at the table reading an ostentatiously large medical tome, one specifically chosen to show his colleagues that he took his new teaching duties seriously. The last Fellow, Theophilis, had gone to St Mary the Great to spy on the Chancellor for Michael.

Bartholomew cast his mind back to the tumultuous fortnight that he and the monk had spent in Clare, where they had learned that Cambridge was not the only town plagued by murderers and people with grudges. It had only been a month ago, but felt longer, because both had been so busy since – Michael with his new responsibilities as Master, and Bartholomew determined to make the most of his last term in academia.

'Not all the changes have been bad,' he said. 'You have made improvements—'

'Yes, yes,' interrupted Michael impatiently. 'There is no question that I am a fine Master, and if I ousted William we would easily be the best College in the University.

However, I was referring to Chancellor Suttone and his inexcusable flight. How *could* he abandon us without so much as a backward glance?'

'We should have predicted that his terror of the plague might override his sense of duty. He was obsessed with the possibility of a second outbreak.'

Michael glared into the flames. 'He still should have spoken to me before resigning. When I think of all the trouble I took to get him in post . . .'

'I imagine he went then precisely *because* you were away – if he had waited, you would have talked him out of it. He never could stand up to you.'

Michael continued to scowl. 'I shall never forgive him. And it is not as if the Death *is* poised to return. There have been no rumours of it, like there were the last time.'

'Actually, there have,' countered Bartholomew soberly. 'In the Italian—'

'No,' interrupted Michael. 'I will not allow it to sweep among us. Not again.'

Bartholomew raised his eyebrows. 'And how will you stop it exactly? Or have you set your ambitions on more lofty roles than mere bishoprics or abbacies, and aim to play God?'

Michael glared at him. 'I was thinking that you and I have the authority to impose sensible anti-plague measures this time – setting up hospitals, separating the sick from the healthy, and burning infected clothing. Working together, we could defeat it.'

Bartholomew knew it was not that simple. 'It would be—'

'Of course, it is Heltisle's fault that we have de Wetherset as Chancellor,' interrupted Michael, more interested in University politics than a disease that might never materialise. '*He* was the one who forced an election the moment Suttone slunk away. Everyone else wanted to wait until I got back.'

'He must have been within his rights to do it,' Bartholomew pointed out. 'Or you would have contested the result.'

'Being legal does not make it acceptable,' sniffed Michael. 'And as Senior Proctor, I should have been here. I imagine Heltisle wanted the post himself, but when he realised no one would vote for him, he encouraged de Wetherset to stand instead. Then he demanded a reward, so de Wetherset created the post of Vice-Chancellor for him.'

Bartholomew had known Heltisle, who was also the Master of Bene't College, for years, and had always disliked him. He was arrogant, dangerously ambitious, and made no secret of his disdain for the way Bartholomew practised and taught medicine. Their mutual antipathy meant they avoided each other whenever possible, as encounters invariably ended in a spat. Unfortunately, Heltisle's new position meant Bartholomew was now obliged to deal with him more often than was pleasant.

'It is a pity he and de Wetherset are friends,' he mused. 'De Wetherset was a lot nicer before poisonous old Heltisle started whispering in his ear.'

'Heltisle is poisonous,' agreed Michael. 'Fortunately, he is not clever enough to be dangerous. The man who *is* dangerous is Commissary Aynton. *Commissary* Aynton! Yet another sinecure created without my permission!'

Bartholomew blinked. Calling Aynton dangerous was akin to saying the same about a mouse, and any teeth the new Commissary might possess were far too small to cause trouble. Indeed, Bartholomew was sorry that the bumbling, well-meaning Aynton had allowed himself to be dragged into the perfidious world of University politics in the first place, as strong, confident men like Michael, Heltisle and de Wetherset were sure to mangle him.

'There is no harm in Aynton,' he argued. 'Besides, he has no real power – it is Heltisle who will rule if de

31

Wetherset is ill or absent. All the Commissary does is sign documents.'

'Quite!' said Michael between gritted teeth. '*Sign documents.* And what do these documents entail? Agreements pertaining to money, benefactions or property; the appointment of officials; the giving of degrees; and the granting of licences to travel, preach or establish new hostels. All were matters handled by me until *he* came along.'

Bartholomew was astonished. 'You let de Wetherset take those privileges away from you and give them to someone else?'

Michael's scowl deepened. 'I did not "let" him do anything – I returned from Suffolk to find it had already happened. I shall take it back, of course, but not yet. I will wait until Aynton makes some catastrophic blunder, then step in and save the day.'

'*If* he makes a catastrophic blunder. He is not a fool.'

'No, which is why I say he is dangerous. I call the three of them – de Wetherset, Heltisle and Aynton – the triumvirate. I am sure their ultimate goal is to oust me completely. Fortunately, I have a secret weapon: Theophilis is an excellent spy and wholly loyal to me. The triumvirate have no idea that he tells me everything they do or say.'

'I hope you are right about him,' said Bartholomew. 'Because he makes me uneasy.'

Michael dismissed the physician's concerns with an impatient wave of a hand. 'He owes all he has to me – his Fellowship, his appointment as Junior Proctor, and a nice little benefice in York that pays him a handsome stipend for doing nothing.'

'We have met colleagues who bite the hand that feeds them before,' warned Bartholomew, thinking there had been rather too many of them over the years.

'Theophilis is not a viper,' declared Michael confidently. 'Besides, I have promised to make him Chancellor in time – which will not be in the too-distant future if de Wetherset continues to heed the dubious advice of Heltisle and Aynton over sensible suggestions from me. But enough of this. Tell me about Bonet. Dick says he was killed by the same culprit as Paris.'

'Probably, although we cannot say for certain without more evidence. Why? Will you explore his death as well as Paris's?'

Michael nodded. 'The town will not approve, of course, just as scholars will resent Dick looking into Paris. All I hope is that one of us finds the killer before there is trouble over it.'

A short while later, Bartholomew returned to his room, which he shared with four medical students. They were rolling up their mattresses and stowing them under the bed when he arrived, and he reflected that this was something else that had changed since Michael had become Master. Before, a dozen lads had been crammed in with him, which meant no one had slept very well. One of the monk's first undertakings had been to convert the stables into a spacious dormitory, so conditions were far less crowded for everyone. Matters would improve further still when the new wing was built. This would be funded by the new benefactors he had secured – three wealthy burgesses, the Earl of Suffolk, four knights and a host of alumni who remembered their College days with great fondness.

'Do we really have to listen to Father William this morning?' asked Islaye, one of Bartholomew's senior students. He was a gentle lad, too easily upset by patients' suffering to make a good physician. 'I would rather study.'

'We can do that while he is ranting,' said his crony Mallett, who was not sympathetic to suffering at all, and saw medicine purely as a way to earn lots of money. 'He will not notice.'

'Sit at the back then,' advised Michael, overhearing as he walked in. He sat so heavily on a chair that there was a crack and Bartholomew was sure the legs bowed. 'If he suspects you are not listening, he will fine you.'

The students gulped their alarm at this notion, and hurried away to discuss tactics that would avoid such a calamity. Through the window, Bartholomew saw William walking towards the hall, carrying an enormous sheaf of notes that suggested he might still be holding forth at midnight.

At that moment, Cynric, Bartholomew's book-bearer, arrived. The Welshman had been with him for years, and although he rarely did much in the way of carrying tomes, he was a useful man to have around. He acted not only as a servant, but as bodyguard, warrior, burglar and spy, as the occasion demanded. He had saved Bartholomew's life more times than the physician cared to remember, and was a loyal friend. He was also deeply superstitious, and his hat and cloak were loaded down with talismans, charms and amulets.

'Does a patient need me?' asked Bartholomew, hopeful for an excuse to go out.

Cynric nodded. 'Chancellor de Wetherset – the fat pork he ate for breakfast has given him a griping in the guts. I know a couple of spells that will sort him out. Shall I—'

'No,' gulped Bartholomew, suspecting Cynric meant the Chancellor harm. The book-bearer had been affronted when de Wetherset had replaced Suttone with what he considered to be indecent haste, and had offered several times to help Michael oust him. 'I am coming. Where is he? At his home in Tyled Hostel?'

The University had eight Colleges and dozens of hostels. The difference between them was that Colleges had endowments to provide their occupants with a regular and reliable income, so were financially stable, whereas hostels tended to be poor, shabby and short-lived. Tyled

Hostel was an exception to the rule, and was both old and relatively affluent. It stood on the corner of St Michael's Lane and the high street, and had, as its name suggested, a roof with tiles rather than the more usual thatch. It had six masters and two dozen students, and was currently enjoying the distinction of being home not only to the Chancellor, but to the Commissary as well – de Wetherset and Aynton both lived there.

'He is in St Mary the Great.' Cynric turned to Michael. 'He wants you as well, Brother. The cheek of it, summoning you like a lackey! Shall I tell him to—'

'Now, now, Cynric,' tutted Michael. 'I am sure he meant no offence.'

'Are you?' muttered Cynric sourly. 'Because I am not.'

'Besides, it will allow me to miss William's lecture,' Michael went on. 'There is nothing worse than listening to a man who has no idea what he is talking about. I do enough of that when Heltisle and Aynton regale me with their opinions about University affairs.'

He and Bartholomew began to walk across the yard, where a dozen chickens – including Clippesby's two philosophers – pecked. They met Theophilis on the way. The Junior Proctor handed Michael the Chancellor's morning correspondence with a flourish.

'I took the liberty of briefing the beadles, too,' he said gushingly. 'To save you the trouble. Your time is too precious for such menial tasks.'

Beadles were the small army of men who kept order among the scholars.

'Thank you,' said Michael, scanning the letters quickly and deciding that none held anything important. 'You had better go to the hall now. William will start in a moment.'

The Junior Proctor regarded him in dismay. 'You expect *me* to be there? I assumed you would spare me such horrors.'

'I wish I could,' said Michael apologetically. 'But someone needs to supervise. Matt and I are summoned to St Mary the Great, Clippesby has a prior appointment with a pig, and Aungel is too junior. You are the only Fellow left.'

'But I was going to St Radegund's Priory,' objected Theophilis. 'One of the nuns is going to preach about sainthood, and I invited Aynton to accompany me. He will be disappointed if I tell him that we cannot go.'

'Then I am afraid he must bear it as well as he can,' said Michael, unmoved, 'because you are needed here. Now, remember – seat all the Dominicans at the back, where they cannot hit the speaker, and separate the Franciscans from the Carmelites. Keep your wits about you at all times, and be ready to intervene if the situation looks set to turn violent.'

'You think a lecture on theology will end in fisticuffs?' gulped Theophilis, alarmed.

'Only a man who has never heard William sounding off would ask *that* question,' muttered Michael as he walked away.

Although it was May, the weather was unseasonably warm. Unusually, there had been no snow or frost after January, and the first signs of spring had started to appear before February was out. By April, the countryside had exploded into leaf. Farmers boasted that they were more than a month ahead of schedule, and predicted bumper harvests. It was so mild that even the short walk from the College was enough to work up a sweat, and Michael mopped his face with the piece of silk that he kept for the purpose.

Cambridge was attractive if one did not look too closely. It boasted more than a dozen churches, each a jewel in its own right, and a wealth of priories, as most of the main religious Orders were represented – Franciscans,

Dominicans, Carmelites, Austins and Gilbertines. And then there were the eight Colleges, ranging from the palatial fortress that was King's Hall to little Peterhouse, the oldest and most picturesque.

There were also two hospitals. One was St John's, a venerable establishment that accommodated some of the town's elderly infirm. The other was a new foundation on the Trumpington road named the Hospital of St Anthony and St Eloy, although everyone usually just called it 'the Spital'. It was to have housed lepers, but incidence of that particular disease had declined over the last century, so it had opened its doors to lunatics instead.

The high street was pretty in the early summer sunlight, the plasterwork on its houses glowing gold, pink, blue and cream. There was a busy clatter as carts rattled to and from the market square, interspersed with the cries of vendors hawking their wares. Above it all rose the clang of bells, from the rich bass of St Mary the Great to the tinny jangle of St Botolph, calling the faithful to prayer.

Despite the beauty, Bartholomew sensed a darkly menacing atmosphere. So far, the heightened tension between town and University had been confined to words and the occasional scuffle, although everyone knew it would not be long before there was a full-scale brawl. The College that bore the brunt of the town's hostility was King's Hall – massive, ostentatiously wealthy, and home to the sons of nobles or those destined to be courtiers or royal clerks. By contrast, Michaelhouse was popular because Bartholomew treated the town's poor free of charge, while Michael ran the choir, a group of supremely untalented individuals who came for the free bread and ale after practices.

'I hope there will be no trouble while the nuns are here,' the monk said, watching a group of apprentices make obscene gestures at two Gonville Hall men, who had rashly elected to don tunics that were currently fashionable in France. 'I hope to secure a couple of abbesses as benefactors, so I shall be vexed if they witness any unseemly behaviour.'

Bartholomew regarded him blankly. 'What nuns?'

Michael shot him a weary glance. 'The ones who are here for the *conloquium*. Do not pretend to be ignorant, because I have spoken of little else since the Bishop's letter came.'

'Our Bishop?' asked Bartholomew, vaguely recalling that a missive had arrived, although it had been some weeks back, so he thought he could be forgiven for having forgotten. Moreover, Michael had been the prelate's emissary for years, keeping him informed of what was happening in the University, and the Bishop was always writing to thank him. As a result, letters bearing the episcopal seal were nothing out of the ordinary.

'Of course our Bishop,' said Michael crossly. 'Surely you cannot think I would arrange such an event for another one?'

Gradually, Bartholomew remembered what Michael had told him about the *conloquium*. It was a once-in-a-decade event, when leading Benedictine nuns gathered for lectures, discussions and religious instruction. He recalled being surprised that Michael had agreed to let it happen in Cambridge, given that he had his hands so full already. He said as much again.

'I did it because the Bishop is on the verge of recommending me to the Pope as his successor,' explained Michael. 'I cannot afford to lose his goodwill by refusing to let a few nuns get together, not after all my dedicated grovelling these last ten years.'

'I suppose not,' said Bartholomew, amused by the naked ambition. 'But if I recall aright, the *conloquium* was supposed to be in Lyminster Priory this time around.'

'It was, but Lyminster is near the coast, and the King

felt it would represent too great a temptation for French raiders. He is right: not only would there be rich pickings for looters, but high-ranking delegates could be kidnapped and held to ransom.'

'Would the Dauphin risk such an assault? We have his father in the Tower of London – a father who will forfeit his head if the son attacks us again.'

'You can never trust the French to see sense, Matt. *Our* King certainly does not, or he would not have issued the call to arms. Anyway, His Majesty wanted the *conloquium* held inland, so our Bishop recommended St Radegund's. I agreed to organise everything, and the delegates began arriving a fortnight ago. It has gone well, and will end in just over a week.'

'St Radegund's,' mused Bartholomew. 'Was there nowhere more suitable to hold it?'

He phrased the question carefully, because that particular foundation had been the subject of several episcopal visitations, after which even the worldly Bishop had declared himself shocked by what went on there. The present incumbent was irreproachable, but the convent's reputation remained tarnished even so. Ergo, it was not a place *he* would have chosen for a gathering of the country's female religious elite.

'It has a large dormitory, a refectory big enough for everyone to eat together, and a huge chapel for their devotions. The Bishop was right to suggest it – it is the perfect venue.'

As the monk had elected not to understand his meaning, Bartholomew let the matter of the foundation's dubious past drop. 'How many nuns are here?' he asked instead.

'Two hundred or so – the heads of about fifty houses and their retinues. St Radegund's cannot accommodate them all comfortably, so I put ten in the Gilbertines' guesthouse and twenty in the Spital. The lunatics were not very pleased to learn they were to have company, but it could not be helped.'

'You brought two hundred women here?' asked Bartholomew in disbelief. 'In term time, when we have students in residence?'

He did not need to add more. Women were forbidden to scholars, but it was a stricture few were inclined to follow, especially the younger ones.

'They are nuns, not ladies of the night,' retorted Michael. 'Besides, the delegates have a full schedule of interesting events, so are far too busy for romantic dalliances. The only ones you will see in town are those going to or from their lodgings with the Gilbertines or at the Spital.'

'Yes, but some of these "interesting events" are open to outsiders – Theophilis was invited to a lecture. Moreover, it is unreasonable to expect these women to go home without seeing something of the town.'

'Then I shall encourage them to leave promptly – hopefully *before* they witness anything unedifying, especially the ones I aim to make Michaelhouse benefactors.'

'Good luck with that! Mischief is in the air, and has been ever since we heard about Winchelsea and the King ordered everyone to train to arms. Not to mention the murders of Paris the Plagiarist and now Bonet the spicer.'

'Yes,' acknowledged Michael unhappily. 'There will be a battle sooner or later, despite my efforts to prevent one. All I hope is that these rich – and hopefully generous – nuns do not see it.'

St Mary the Great was the University's centre of power, as all its senior officers worked there. It was a handsome church, occupying a commanding position on the high street, and was the only building in the town that could accommodate every scholar at the same time.

The largest and most impressive room should have

been the Chancellor's, but Michael had appropriated that years before, leaving the University's titular head with a rather poky chamber near the back door. De Wetherset had tried to reclaim it while Michael was in Suffolk, but the beadles were devoted to their Senior Proctor and refused to allow it. Thus Michael's domain remained his own.

Bartholomew glanced through its door as he and Michael hurried past. It was sumptuously decorated, with wool rugs and fine furniture. It had two desks, both set to catch the light from the beautifully glazed windows. The ornate, oaken one was Michael's, piled high with documents bearing the seals of nobles or high-ranking churchmen. The other was Junior Proctor Theophilis's, neat to the point of obsessional.

By contrast, de Wetherset's room was dark, plain and smelled of damp. It was also cramped, as the Vice-Chancellor and Commissary worked there, too – Michael had declined to oust his clerks and secretaries to make room for the newly created officials, claiming that de Wetherset should have considered such practicalities before appointing anyone.

'Ah, here you are,' said de Wetherset, as Michael strutted in without knocking. Bartholomew hovered on the threshold, uncertain whether to follow suit, but the Chancellor beckoned him inside. 'Good.'

He was a solid man of late-to-middle years, whose physical strength was turning to fat. He had iron-grey hair, small eyes, and wore Tyled Hostel's uniform of a dark green academic tabard, which fitted him like a glove. Although he seemed honourable, there was something about him that had always made Bartholomew wary. Perhaps it was the aura of power that emanated from him, or his sharp, sometimes unkind tongue. Regardless, he was not someone the physician would ever consider a friend.

41

He had been Chancellor for years before the stress of the post had forced him to resign. To recover, he had gone on a pilgrimage to Walsingham, and had returned bursting with vitality. He claimed his good health was a miracle, although Bartholomew suspected he had just benefited from fresh air, regular meals and plenty of exercise. He had bought a pilgrim badge when he had reached the shrine, which he always wore pinned proudly on his hat.

As usual, the men he had appointed were with him. Tall, haughty, elegant Vice-Chancellor Heltisle was immaculately clad in a gold-trimmed gipon with his uniform tabard – in Bene't College's royal blue – over the top. His shoes were crafted from soft leather, and he wore a floppy hat that most townsfolk would automatically assume was French. He had always been wealthy, but additional funds had come his way after he had invented a metal pen. These had quickly become status symbols, with scholars scrambling to buy them, even though they were indecently expensive. Matilde had given one to Bartholomew, although he had found it more trouble than it was worth and never used it.

Commissary Aynton was a stooped, gangling man with a benign smile and dreamy eyes, so that Bartholomew sometimes wondered if he was fully aware of what was going on around him. His clothes were expensive, but he wore them badly, so he always looked vaguely disreputable. Bartholomew liked him because he often made discreet donations of medicine for the poor, something Heltisle would never do.

'I am glad to see you, Bartholomew,' said de Wetherset, one hand clasped to his paunch. 'Do you have that remedy for a griping in the guts? I thought I was cured of my delicate innards – this is the first trouble I have suffered since Walsingham.'

'Do not trust *him* to give you relief, de Wetherset,' said

Heltisle nastily. 'You should have sent for Rougham. He is a much better physician, and does not waste time washing his hands with such irritating regularity.'

'Oh, come, Heltisle,' chided Aynton with a pleasant smile. 'Matthew has a rare skill with griping guts, as you know perfectly well. Or were you the only member of your College who did not swallow his remedy after the feast that made everyone vomit?'

Heltisle's red face provided the answer to that question, but he was not a man to recant, so he went on another offensive to mask his discomfiture. 'If you are going to physick him, Bartholomew, hurry up. We are busy, and cannot wait for you all day.'

Bartholomew was tempted to leave there and then, but de Wetherset was looking decidedly unwell, and the physician was not in the habit of abandoning those who needed him. He indicated that de Wetherset was to lie on a bench – the Chancellor probably had indigestion, but it would be remiss not to examine him before prescribing a tonic.

'These nuns, Brother,' said Aynton, watching Bartholomew palpate the Chancellor's ample abdomen. 'Are you sure it was a good idea to bring them here? I have heard alarming stories about what St Radegund's was like in the past.'

'You mean when it was a delightful place to visit?' asked Heltisle with a leer that made Bartholomew dislike him even more. 'As opposed to now, when it is full of women who only want to pray? Of course, you had no right to arrange a *conloquium* here, Brother. It should have been de Wetherset's decision.'

Michael regarded him coolly. 'No, it should not. First, St Radegund's does not come under the University's jurisdiction. Second, de Wetherset was not Chancellor when the Bishop made his request. And third, the Bishop approached me because the delegates are from my own Order.'

Heltisle sniffed. 'Well, do not blame *me* if our students

take advantage of the fact that thousands of nubile young ladies lie within their grasp.'

Michael laughed. 'There are only two hundred, and few are nubile.'

'Nor are they within anyone's grasp,' put in Bartholomew, not liking the notion of someone like Heltisle marching out there in the hope that he would receive the kind of welcome he had evidently enjoyed when standards had been different.

Heltisle rounded on him. 'And you would know, of course. You have no right to be a scholar while you have a woman waiting to wed you.'

'He breaks no statute – not in the University and not in Michaelhouse,' retorted Michael sharply. 'And do not accuse him of enjoying illicit relations, because Matilde is away.' He turned away before Heltisle could argue and addressed de Wetherset, who was sitting up to sip the tonic Bartholomew had poured. 'Why did you send for me, Chancellor?'

'To discuss the call to arms,' explained de Wetherset, some colour returning to his plump cheeks. 'The town has two knights to monitor its training, but we have no one – our scholars just arrive at the butts, loose a few arrows and go home. We need someone who can teach them how to improve.'

'Cynric,' said Aynton, smiling at Bartholomew. 'He is a very good archer, and I am sure you will not mind lending him out. Beadle Meadowman will help.'

'Not Meadowman,' said Michael immediately, loath to lose his favourite henchman when he was needed to prevent brawls.

'Nonsense,' stated Heltisle. 'He and Cynric will oversee matters, and your Junior Proctor can record the name of everyone who attends. Then we can identify those who think they are too important to sully their hands with weapons, and inform them that they are not.'

Michael concealed his irritation at such presumptuousness with a show of indifference. 'Very well. Of course, I shall expect you three to be the first in line, setting a good example.'

'Then you will be disappointed,' declared Heltisle, 'because we have hired proxies – men from the Spital, who are mad and therefore not expected to answer the call themselves.'

'*My* proxy is not a lunatic,' said Aynton hastily. 'He is a scholar from King's Hall – a Fleming, who is exempt on the grounds of being foreign. I dared not hire a madman, lest he forgets whose side he is on and attacks his friends. I do not want that on my conscience!'

Michael raised his eyebrows. 'I hate to break this to you, but the option of hiring proxies is only available to certain priests. You are not—'

'It is available to anyone who makes a suitable donation to the King's war chest,' countered Heltisle smugly. 'Several of my Bene't colleagues will follow my example, although I imagine no one at Michaelhouse can afford it.'

Michael's smile was tight. 'We could, but none of us will, because it reeks of cowardice and elitism. I advise you to reconsider, lest you win the contempt of your fellow scholars.'

'Not to mention the resentment of townsfolk,' put in Bartholomew. 'They will not take kindly to the fact that the wealthy can buy their way out of their military obligations.'

'Who cares what they think?' shrugged Heltisle. 'Our fiscal arrangements with the King are none of their business. Besides, it is inappropriate for high-ranking members of the University to engage in such lowly activities. We have our dignity to consider. It is—'

He was interrupted by Cynric, who appeared silently at the door – so silently that Bartholomew was sure he had been listening. The book-bearer gave no indication as to whether he was pleased or alarmed by the plans being made for his future, and his expression was carefully neutral as he addressed Michael.

'You must come at once, Brother. There is a situation at the Gilbertine Priory.'

'What kind of situation?' demanded Heltisle. 'And please direct your remarks to the Chancellor. He is in charge here, not the Senior Proctor.'

'Of course he is,' said Cynric flatly, and turned back to Michael. 'Apparently, it is ablaze, and as you have lodged some of your nuns there, I thought you should know.'

# CHAPTER 3

Bartholomew, Michael and the triumvirate hurried into the high street to gaze at the plume of greasy black smoke that wafted into the air to the south.

'That is not the Gilbertine Priory,' said de Wetherset. 'It is further away.'

'Some farmer, clearing land, probably,' said Heltisle dismissively.

'It is the Spital!' exclaimed Michael in alarm. 'I have nuns lodged there, too – a score of ladies from Lyminster Priory.'

'One convent sent *twenty* delegates?' asked de Wetherset in surprise. 'That is a lot.'

'The largest by a considerable margin,' acknowledged Michael, his face pale. 'And one of them is Magistra Katherine de Lisle.'

'De Lisle?' mused de Wetherset. 'Is she any relation to our Bishop Thomas de Lisle?'

'His older sister,' replied Michael tautly. 'She is scheduled to speak at the *conloquium* today, so hopefully she will have left the Spital already, but—'

'Then go and make sure,' gulped de Wetherset. 'The Bishop will never forgive us if his sister is incinerated at an event organised by an officer of the University.'

Knowing this was true, Michael began to hurry along the high street. Bartholomew fell in at his side, because everything was tinder-dry after the long spell of warm weather, and he wanted to be sure the blaze represented no danger to the town – only fools were unconcerned about fire when most buildings were made of timber and thatch. Cynric followed, and so did the triumvirate.

47

'We cannot have you telling the Bishop that we skulked here while the Senior Proctor and his Corpse Examiner rescued his beloved sister,' called Heltisle. 'We know the kind of sly politics you two practise.'

A few years before, Bartholomew had objected to the number of bodies he was required to inspect out of the goodness of his heart, so Michael had established the post of Corpse Examiner. The duties entailed determining an official cause of death for any scholar who passed away, or anyone who died on University property. Bartholomew was paid threepence for each body he assessed, all of which was spent on medicine for the poor. However, he wished Michael had chosen a less sinister-sounding title for the work he did.

'Speaking of sly politics, Heltisle,' said the monk coolly, 'I understand you struck a deal with Clippesby over the sale of his treatise.'

Heltisle smirked. 'And there is a contract to prove it – signed with one of my own metal pens, in fact – so do not try to renege. And if you claim he is mentally unfit to make such arrangements, then he should not be in the University. You cannot have it both ways.'

'I cannot wait to see his face when he realises he has been bested by Clippesby,' murmured Michael, walking more quickly to put some distance between them. 'I must find a way to depose him, as he is a dreadful man. Even so, I would sooner have him than Aynton – at least Heltisle does not try to disguise his vileness with cloying amiability.'

'Perhaps I can shoot him while I show scholars how to use a bow,' suggested Cynric. 'An arrow in the posterior will teach him a little humility.'

'Please do not,' begged Bartholomew, afraid he might actually do it. 'He would claim you acted on our orders, and we do not want Michaelhouse sued.'

The plume of smoke seemed no closer when they

reached the Trumpington Gate, where the sentries were gazing at the smudge of black that stained the sky.

'It *is* the Spital,' said a soldier to his cronies, 'which is no bad thing. The place is haunted, and I shall not be sorry to see it go up in flames.'

'He is right,' Cynric told Bartholomew and Michael, as they hurried through the gate. He considered himself an expert on the supernatural, and was always willing to share his views with the less well informed. 'It stands on the site of a pagan temple, see, where human sacrifices were made.'

'It does not!' exclaimed Bartholomew, although he should have known better than to argue with Cynric. The book-bearer's opinions, once formed, were permanent, and there was no changing his mind.

'You do not understand these things, boy,' declared Cynric darkly. 'Building that Spital woke a lot of evil sprites. Indeed, it may even be them who set the place afire.'

'Then let us hope Heltisle has the right of it,' said Michael, 'and it is just a farmer burning brush in order to plant some crops.'

'Regardless,' said Bartholomew, fearing it was not, 'we should hurry.'

Five high-ranking scholars and Cynric, trotting three abreast along the main road south, was enough to attract attention, and folk abandoned what they were doing to trail after them, sure an interesting spectacle was in the offing. They included both scholars and townsfolk, who immediately began to jostle each other. Isnard the bargeman and his cronies were among the worst offenders, and Bartholomew was concerned – with only one leg, Isnard was vulnerable in a scuffle, although he never allowed it to prevent him from joining in.

'I feel like the Piper of Hamelin,' grumbled Michael.

'Followed by rats.' His eyes narrowed. 'And four louts from King's Hall, who have chosen to don clothes that are brazenly French. They have done it purely to antagonise the likes of Isnard.'

'It is working,' said Bartholomew, aware that the bargeman had fixed the haughty quartet with angry eyes. 'I had better send him and his friends home before there is a spat – the King's Hall men have swords.'

For which we have His Majesty to thank, he thought sourly. Scholars were forbidden to bear arms in the town, but this stricture had been suspended by royal decree until the French threat was over. King's Hall, which had always been warlike, was delighted to arm its scholars to the teeth.

Bartholomew knew Isnard and his cronies well, as all were either his patients or members of the Michaelhouse Choir. They had never been particularly patriotic, but the raid on Winchelsea had ignited a nationalistic fervour that verged on the fanatical. It would be forgotten when some other issue caught their attention, but until then, they were affronted by anything they deemed to be even remotely foreign. They met in disreputable taverns, where they nurtured their grievances over large flagons of ale.

'No,' snapped Bartholomew, seeing Isnard prepare to lob a handful of horse manure at the scholars. 'If you make a mess on their fine clothes, they will fight you.'

'Then they should wear English ones,' retorted Isnard sullenly. 'Right, lads?'

There was a growl of agreement, the loudest from a soldier named Pierre Sauvage. It was an unusual name for a man who had never ventured more than three miles outside Cambridge, but his mother had once rented her spare room to an itinerant acrobat from Lyons. Sauvage was so touchy about the possibility of having foreign blood that he was rabidly xenophobic. He told anyone who would listen that he had signed on at the castle purely because he wanted Tulyet to teach him how to kill Frenchmen.

'Too right,' he declared. 'They have no right to strut around looking like the dolphin.'

'He means the Dauphin,' said Isnard, evidently of the opinion that the physician was unable to deduce this for himself. 'Who we hate because it was *his* army what invaded Winchelsea and did all those terrible things. Is that not so, Sauvage?'

Unfortunately, his indignant remarks were overheard by the scholars from King's Hall, who immediately swaggered over. Bartholomew shot an agonised glance at the smoke – he did not have time to prevent quarrels when he should be making sure the blaze represented no threat to the town.

'Sauvage, Sauvage,' mused one. 'I think we might have a Frenchman here, boys. Shall we slit him open and see what is inside?'

'Go home,' ordered Bartholomew, cutting across the outraged response Sauvage began to make. 'All of you. There will be nothing to see at the Spital.'

'No?' demanded the scholar archly. 'Then why are you going there?'

Bartholomew thought fast. 'Because the inmates have contagious diseases for me to treat.'

'Lord!' gulped Isnard. 'I never thought of that. Come on, Sauvage. The Griffin broached a new barrel of ale today, and it would be a pity to let it go sour.'

He swung away on his crutches, and most of his cronies followed. The scholars stood fast, though, so Bartholomew began to describe some of the more alarming ailments he expected to be rife in the Spital, and was relieved when the King's Hall men edged away and began to saunter back the way they had come.

'Follow them,' he told Cynric. 'Make sure they go home

51

– preferably without goading any more townsfolk into a spat along the way.'

By the time Bartholomew caught up with Michael, the monk and the triumvirate had passed the Gilbertine Priory with its handsome gatehouse and towering walls. Beyond it, the road was in a terrible state. There had been heavy rains the previous month, and carts had churned it into ruts. These had dried like petrified waves when the weather turned warm, so anyone hurrying risked a twisted ankle or worse. Bartholomew and his companions were obliged to slow to a snail's pace, leaving Michael fretting about the nuns.

The Spital stood on what had, until recently, been nothing but scrubland. It comprised five buildings within a perfect walled square. In the centre was a hall that had a large room for communal eating below and a dormitory above. A chapel jutted from its back, placed to catch the rising sun at its altar end. The other buildings were in each of the four corners: a kitchen and accommodation for staff; a substantial guesthouse; the stable block; and a large shed-cum-storeroom.

The Spital's gates were always closed, as not everyone was happy about lepers – or lunatics – living near the town, and the founders were cognisant of security. However, the gates stood open that day, as access was needed to the brook that ran along the side of the road for water. The scholars looked through them to see the blaze was in the shed – a temporary, albeit sturdy, structure used to store building materials. Smoke billowed through its reed-thatched roof, although the fire was so far contained, as there were no leaping flames.

'The nuns are safe,' breathed Michael in relief, seeing a black-robed gaggle near the stables. 'Thank God!'

As everyone inside the Spital was busy with the fire, and no one came to greet them, de Wetherset began to relate its history to Aynton, who was a relative newcomer to the town.

'A man named Henry Tangmer founded it to atone for sins committed by his niece. What was her name, Brother? I cannot recall.'

'Adela,' supplied Michael, who remembered her very well. 'She is dead now, God rest her soul, and we have a leper hospital.'

'I am no physician,' said Aynton, 'but I do know that one does not meet many lepers these days. So why did Tangmer dedicate his wealth to helping them, of all people?'

'Lepers, lunatics, they are all the same,' said Heltisle with a dismissive shrug. 'Folk who cannot be allowed out, lest they infect the rest of us with their deadly miasmas.'

'Lunacy is not contagious,' said Bartholomew, not about to let such an outlandish claim pass unchallenged. 'Nor are many kinds of leprosy.'

'Regardless, the sufferers are still pariahs,' retorted Heltisle, 'so it is good that they are locked away, out of sight and mind.'

'That is a terrible attitude towards—' began Bartholomew hotly.

'I have heard that Tangmer's wife is very good at curing diseases of the mind,' said de Wetherset, cutting across him. 'She uses herbs, fresh air and exercise, by all accounts.'

'Does she?' asked Bartholomew, immediately intrigued.

'Do not tell me that you have never been called out here,' said Heltisle, then smiled superiorly. 'But of course you have not. The inmates may be mad, but they will not want to be tended by a man who loves paupers and who insists on washing his hands at every turn.'

Bartholomew ignored him, knowing this would annoy him far more than any riposte he could devise on the spur of the moment. He asked de Wetherset to tell him more about Mistress Tangmer's unusual therapies, but the Chancellor had had enough of the Spital.

'They have the blaze under control,' he said, watching two servants use fire hooks to haul down patches of smouldering thatch, where they could be doused with water. 'The Bishop's sister is safe and there is no danger to the University. I am going home.'

He, Heltisle and Aynton began to walk back the way they had come, Heltisle grumbling about the wasted effort. Bartholomew and Michael lingered though; Michael wanted to speak to the nuns, while Bartholomew's interest was piqued by the Spital's innovative-sounding treatment of lunacy and he hoped to learn more.

'I asked Tangmer to show me around when I arranged for him to take my nuns,' said Michael. 'But he refused, lest my presence upset his patients.'

'It might,' said Bartholomew. 'However, a fire will be far more distressing. I wonder how the Tangmers will deal with it.'

He watched the people inside, trying to distinguish patients from staff. Most were busy with the fire, although two distinct groups were not: the nuns, and a dozen respectably dressed individuals with children, who stood near the hall. Curiously, there was none of the frantic yelling that usually accompanied such crises, and the whole operation was conducted in almost complete silence. It was peculiarly eerie.

'Of course, the nuns should be at the *conloquium*,' said Michael, watching them crossly. 'Magistra Katherine is due to lecture there shortly, and the other delegates will be wondering what has happened to her.'

Bartholomew frowned. 'I thought you put twenty ladies here. I only count nineteen.'

Michael looked around wildly. 'The Prioress – Joan de Ferraris! *She* is missing!' Then he gave an irritable tut of relief. 'There she is – in the stables. I might have guessed. She has always preferred horses to people.'

He nodded to where a massive woman, who would stand head and shoulders above her sisters, was soothing the animals. She looked rather like a horse herself, with a long face, large teeth and big brown eyes. She had rolled up her sleeves to reveal a pair of brawny forearms.

'She is an excellent rider,' Michael went on, and as he had lofty standards where equestrianism was concerned, Bartholomew supposed she must be skilled indeed. 'And she single-handedly built her priory's stables, which are reputed to be the best in the country. I should love to see them.'

'But is she a good head of house?' asked Bartholomew, aware that riding and stable-building were not especially useful skills for running a convent.

'She is stern but fair, and not afraid to delegate tasks she feels are beyond her. She can also repair roofs, clean gutters and chop wood. Her nuns like her, and Lyminster is a happy, prosperous place, so yes, she is a good leader. But I had better go and pay my respects.'

He and Bartholomew started to walk towards them, but were intercepted by three men – Sheriff Tulyet and his two new knights, who were stationed just inside the gates.

'Tangmer has asked us to keep sightseers out,' explained Tulyet, raising a hand to stop the scholars from going any further. 'He says they frighten his inmates.'

'They do not look overly concerned to me,' said Michael, although Bartholomew was aware of being eyed by the group near the hall. 'They do not look particularly mad either.'

'Insanity is not something you can diagnose at a glance,' said Tulyet. 'At least, that is what Tangmer told me, when I suggested much the same.'

'How dare he use us as free labour,' growled huge, black-haired Sir Norbert. 'We are not servants, to be ordered hither and thither. We are friends of the King.'

'You offered your help,' said Tulyet drily. 'And this is how Tangmer chose to deploy it. It is your own fault for recklessly putting yourself at his disposal.'

'*I* know why he wants everyone kept away,' said fair-headed Sir Leger sourly. 'Because madmen are exempt from the King's call to arms, so are eligible for hire as proxies. Several scholars have already been here, clamouring to buy substitutes, and Tangmer aims to put a stop to it.'

'By "scholars" he means Chancellor de Wetherset and his henchman Heltisle,' put in Norbert, and spat. 'Cowards!'

'Speaking of cowards, have you made any progress with finding whoever dispatched Bonet the spicer?' asked Michael.

'None,' replied Leger. 'The killer left no clues, and there are no witnesses. Ergo, I am not sure we will ever—'

'That man is on fire!' interrupted Tulyet urgently, and stepped aside. 'Your services will be needed, Matt. If Tangmer complains, tell him *I* let you in.'

By the time Bartholomew arrived, the burning man had smothered the flames by rolling in the grass, saving himself from serious injury. One arm was scorched, though, so Bartholomew sat him down and applied a soothing salve. Grateful for his help, the man began to chat, saying he was Tangmer's cousin, Eudo. He was enormous by any standards, larger even than Sir Norbert, and reminded Bartholomew of a bull – powerful, unpredictable and not overly bright.

'Everyone who works here is a Tangmer,' Eudo said. 'Henry and Amphelisa have no children, but his father had six brothers, so he has uncles and cousins galore. Lots of us were eager to come and work for him.'

Bartholomew had been told this before, and remembered that the policy of kin-only staff had caused great resentment in the town – there had been an expectation of employment for locals, and folk were disappointed when none was offered. Worse, the Tangmers declined to socialise outside the Spital, which, along with them refusing visitors, had given rise to rumours that it was haunted and that all its patients were dangerously insane.

'Do you like Cambridge, Eudo?' Bartholomew asked conversationally.

Eudo shook his massive head. 'I used to go there to buy candles – before we started making our own – and there was always some spat between students and apprentices. I think it is a violent little place, so I try to avoid going there.'

'You are not obliged to practise your archery, like the rest of us?'

'Cousin Henry arranged for us to do it here instead, which is much nicer than rubbing shoulders with brawlers.'

When he had finished tending Eudo's burns, Bartholomew started to walk back to the gate, but was intercepted by the founders themselves – Henry and Amphelisa Tangmer.

They were a curious pair. Tangmer was a heavyset, rosy-cheeked man who could have been nothing but an English yeoman. His wife was an elegant lady in a burgundy-coloured robe, who smelled strongly of fragrant oils. To Bartholomew's eye, her facial features and casual grace were unmistakably French, and with sudden, blinding clarity, he understood exactly why they discouraged visitors. It was a sensible precaution in the current climate of intolerance and unease.

'Thank you for helping Eudo,' said Tangmer, stiffly formal. 'But we can manage now. The shed is lost, but it was due to be demolished anyway, so it does not matter. All it means is that we shall have to build our bathhouse a bit sooner than we anticipated.'

'Bathhouse?' asked Bartholomew, immediately interested.

Amphelisa smiled. 'We feel cleanliness is important in a hospital.'

Bartholomew thought so, too, although he was in a distinct minority, as most medical practitioners considered hygiene a waste of time. He opened his mouth to see what else he and Amphelisa might have in common, but Tangmer cut across him.

'The children love to play in the shed, and I imagine one knocked over a candle. But the blaze is under control now, so if there is nothing else . . .'

'I saw children by the hall,' fished Bartholomew. 'Are they patients?'

'No, but we believe madness can be cured faster when the afflicted person is surrounded by his loved ones,' explained Amphelisa. 'We encourage our inmates to bring their families.'

'Does it work?' asked Bartholomew keenly.

Amphelisa was willing to discuss it, but her husband cleared his throat meaningfully, so she made an apologetic face. 'Perhaps we can talk another time, but now I must soothe those who are distressed by the commotion.'

'I can help,' offered Bartholomew. 'A decoction of chamomile and dittany will—'

'We have our own remedies, thank you,' interrupted Tangmer, polite but firm. 'And now, if you will excuse us . . .'

He took Bartholomew's arm and began to propel him towards the gate, but stopped when there was an urgent yell from Eudo, who had returned to help with the fire.

At the same time, a flame burst through the roof in a slender orange tongue.

'Let it burn,' Tangmer called. 'It will save us the bother of knocking it down later.'

Eudo turned a stricken face towards him. 'But I heard something. I think someone is still inside!'

Loath to get in the way while the Spital's people effected a rescue, Bartholomew returned to Michael, Tulyet and the knights. The nuns also kept their distance, other than the mannish Prioress Joan, who abandoned the horses and strode forward to see if she could be of any use. Meanwhile, all the inmates raced towards the shed and began to hammer on it with their fists.

'Stop! Get back!' shouted Tangmer in alarm. 'You will hurt yourselves. Eudo is mistaken – no one is inside. Is that not right, Goda?'

He turned to a woman who stood nearby. She was so small that Bartholomew had assumed she was a child, especially as she wore a bright yellow dress – an unusual colour for an adult – but Michael murmured that she was wife to the vast Eudo, leading the physician to speculate, somewhat voyeurishly, about the difficulties their disparity in size must generate in the marriage bed.

'Of course it is empty,' Goda said irritably. 'The door was ajar, and the fire had not taken hold when I first saw the smoke. Anyone inside would have walked out then.'

'Well, the door is closed now,' said Prioress Joan, peering at it through the smoke. 'So perhaps we had better open it and have a look inside.'

'I ordered it shut after Goda raised the alarm,' explained Tangmer, 'to contain the blaze and make it easier to put out. But I can assure you that no one is—'

'There!' yelled Eudo, cocking his head to one side. 'Voices – a woman's.'

59

Bartholomew suspected the big man was mistaken, as the fire had been going for some time, belching smoke at a colossal rate. It was unlikely that anyone was still alive inside.

'I heard it, too!' shouted another of the staff, his face tight with horror. 'We have to get her out. Open the door! Quick!'

'*No!*' howled Bartholomew, darting forward to stop him. 'The door is smouldering – open it, and the fire will explode outwards, greedy for air. Is there another way in?'

Tangmer shook his head, his face pale. 'All we can do is to hurl water at the flames until they are extinguished, and hope we are in time. Everyone – remove your shoes and fill them from the stream over the—'

'Shoes will not suffice,' snapped Prioress Joan. 'Sheriff – set the men in a chain between here and the brook. Amphelisa – round up the women and children and send them for buckets. Well? What are you waiting for? *Move!*'

The urgency of the situation had caused her to lapse into French, the first language of most high-born ladies who held positions of authority in the Church. Bartholomew began to translate, sure few Spital folk would understand, but most immediately looked at Tulyet and Amphelisa, suggesting that they had.

'But we do not have more buckets,' gulped Amphelisa. 'We have already used—'

'Then bring pots and pans,' barked Joan. 'Anything that holds water. Master Tangmer – take your elderly lunatics and the smallest brats to the chapel. They are in the way here.'

'If there is no other entrance, we will have to make one,' said Bartholomew urgently. 'At the back, where the fire burns less fiercely.'

'Good thinking,' said Joan. 'Come with me and choose

the best place.' She jabbed a thick forefinger at one of the inmates, a dark-haired, wiry man with angry eyes. 'You, bring us an axe. The rest of you, human chain and water *now*!'

She hitched up her habit and strode to the back of the shed, managing a pace that had Bartholomew running to keep up. They arrived to find smoke oozing between the planks that formed the walls. Bartholomew put his hand to one and found it was cool – the flames had not yet reached it. He heard the faintest of moans. Eudo was right: someone *was* inside!

He grabbed a stone and pounded the wall with it, to reassure whoever was inside that help was coming. Joan did likewise, although her blows caused significant dents.

'Where is that lunatic with the axe?' she demanded in agitation. 'Hah! Here he is at last. Where have you been, man? To buy it in town?'

'I did not know where to look,' snapped the man, bristling. 'And my name is Delacroix. I am no man's servant, so do not address me as one.'

'Keep your bruised dignity for later, *Delacroix*,' said Joan acidly, grabbing the hatchet from him and swinging at the walls with all her might.

Splinters flew. Then the massive Eudo arrived with the biggest chopper Bartholomew had ever seen. In three mighty swipes, he had smashed a head-sized hole.

Bartholomew darted forward to peer through it, blinking away tears as fumes wafted out. It was impossible to see anything inside, and it occurred to him that who-ever was in there had probably suffocated by now. Then he glimpsed movement. Someone was struggling to stand, and he had a brief impression of a bloodstained kirtle and a bundle shoved at him. He saw golden curls. The bundle was a child.

'Stand back!' he yelled, and indicated that Eudo was to hit the wall again.

61

More wood shattered. Then Delacroix snatched Joan's axe and began a frenzied assault that had no impact and prevented Eudo from working. Bartholomew tried to stop him, but Delacroix fought him off. Then a fist shot out and Delacroix reeled backwards.

'Put your back into it before it is too late,' roared Joan at Eudo, wringing her bruised knuckles. 'Hurry!'

Eudo obliged, and the hole expanded. Joan struggled to clamber through it, careless of the smoke that belched around her. She was too big to fit, obliging Bartholomew to haul her out again. She emerged smouldering, her wimple alight. Eudo threw her to the ground and rolled her over, whipping off his shirt to smother the flames.

'No, help *her*!' she snarled, pushing him away. Her face was streaked with soot, her habit was rucked up to reveal two powerful white thighs, and her wimple was in a blackened, unsalvageable mess. 'The child!'

Bartholomew thrust his arms through the hole. Immediately, something was pushed into them. He pulled hard. There was an agonising moment when clothes snagged on the jagged edges, but Eudo drew a knife and hacked the material free.

Leaving Eudo and Delacroix to rescue the woman, Bartholomew and Joan carried the child away from the smoke. Her eyes were closed and there was no heartbeat. Bartholomew began to press rhythmically on her chest, pausing every so often to blow into her lungs. Nothing happened, so he did it again. And again, and again.

'No!' snapped Joan, when he stopped. 'Do not give up. Not yet.'

He did as he was told, and was on the verge of admitting defeat when the child's eyes fluttered open. She sat up and began to cough.

'Praise the Lord!' breathed Joan. 'A miracle!'

She fetched Eudo's discarded shirt and wrapped it around the girl, although it was Amphelisa who took the dazed child in her arms and crooned comforting words.

Bartholomew turned his attention back to the shed. Its roof was a sheet of orange flames, and groans and crashes emanated from within as it collapsed in on itself.

'What of the woman?' he asked hoarsely.

'We could not reach her,' rasped Eudo, whose face was ashen. 'It was Mistress Girard, God rest her soul.'

# CHAPTER 4

The next morning dawned cool, damp and wet. Bartholomew fancied he could smell burning in the misty drizzle from the still-smouldering Spital shed, although this was impossible as it was too far away. His sleep had teemed with nightmares, so he had risen in the small hours and gone to the hall to read. But even Galen's elegant prose could not distract him from his thoughts, so he had spent most of the time staring at the candle, thinking about the fire.

By the time it was out, the rubble had been far too hot for retrieving bodies, so Tulyet, whose responsibility it was to investigate, had asked him to return the following day to examine the victims. A roll call had revealed five people missing – the rescued girl's parents, uncle, aunt and teenaged brother.

The bell rang to wake the scholars for Mass, so he went to the lavatorium – the lean-to structure behind the hall, built for those interested in personal hygiene. Until recently, only cold water had been available, but Michael liked the occasional wash himself, and had ordered the servants to provide hot as well. It was an almost unimaginable luxury.

Bartholomew stank of burning, so he scrubbed his skin and hair vigorously, then doused himself with some perfume that someone had left behind. He wished he had used it more sparingly when it transpired to be powerful and redolent of the stuff popular with prostitutes. He started to rinse it off, but the bell rang again, this time calling scholars to assemble in the yard, ready to process to the church. He left his soiled clothes in the laundress's basket, and sprinted to his room for fresh ones, wearing nothing but a piece of sacking tied around his waist.

'You had better not do *that* when you are married,' remarked Theophilis, watching disapprovingly. 'Not with a woman about.'

Bartholomew was tempted to point out that Matilde was unlikely to mind, but held his tongue lest Theophilis thought he was being lewd. Back in his room, he donned a fresh white shirt, black leggings and a clean tabard. Then he forced his feet into shoes that were still wet from fire-drenching water, and hurried into the yard.

Michael was already there, hood up to keep the drizzle from his immaculately barbered tonsure. His Benedictine students stood in a small, sombre cluster behind him, while Bartholomew's medics formed a much noisier group near the hall. Aungel was with them and they were laughing. When he caught the words 'chicken' and 'debate', he surmised that they were reviewing William's attempt to debunk Clippesby's thesis the previous day.

Clippesby and Theophilis were by the gate, so he went to join them. The Dominican was kneeling, and Bartholomew thought he was praying until he realised he was talking to the College cat. Theophilis listened carefully as Clippesby translated what the animal had said, then rolled his eyes, mocking the Dominican's eccentricity. Bartholomew bristled, but William strode up before he could take issue with him.

'I have a bone to pick with you, Matthew,' the friar said coolly. 'Your students kept asking questions during my sermon yesterday.'

'Of course they did,' said Bartholomew, aware of Theophilis sniggering. 'They have been trained to challenge statements they deem illogical or erroneous.'

William's scowl deepened. 'My exposition was neither, and the next time I give a lecture, *they* will not be invited.'

Bartholomew was sure they would be delighted to hear it. Then Aungel approached.

'Yesterday was great fun, Father,' he declared enthusiastically. 'I have never laughed so much in all my life. The best part was when you claimed that all robins are nominalists, because they know the names of the worms they eat.'

'I never did! You tricked me into saying things I did not mean.'

'We did it because it was so easy,' said Theophilis in his eerily sibilant voice. 'And our students learned one extremely valuable lesson: to keep their mouths shut when they do not know what they are talking about.'

'But I *do* know what I am talking about!' cried William, aggrieved. 'I am a Franciscan theologian, and my understanding of the realism–nominalism debate is far greater than that of Clippesby's stupid chickens.'

'In that case, Father,' said Theophilis slyly, 'perhaps you should debate with them directly next time. You might find Ma and Gertrude easier to defeat than the students.'

William narrowed his eyes. 'You want me to appear as mad as Clippesby! Besides, all his hens look the same to me. How will I know which are the right ones?'

Theophilis regarded William warily, not sure if he was serious, while Bartholomew laughed at them both.

'Audrey has just mentioned something interesting,' said Clippesby, indicating the cat. Bartholomew was glad he never took umbrage at William's insults, or the College would have been a perpetual battleground. 'She was hunting near the Spital just before dawn, and she saw what appeared to be a ghost – a spectre that undulated along the top of the walls.'

The Dominican often went out at night to commune with his animal friends. When he did, he sat so still that he was all but invisible, which meant he frequently witnessed sights not intended for his eyes. Unfortunately, he invariably reported them in a way that made them difficult to interpret.

'You mean you saw a *person* on the wall,' said Aungel. 'Who was it? A townsman trying to get inside to see the charred bodies? A lunatic trying to escape?'

'It was a white, shimmering shape, which rippled along until it vanished into thin air,' replied Clippesby. 'Audrey has never seen anything like it, and she hopes never to do so again.'

'Are you sure she was not dreaming?' asked Bartholomew, hoping Clippesby would not mention the tale to Cynric, or they would never hear the end of it.

Clippesby nodded. 'She recited prayers to ward off evil, and ran home as fast as her legs would carry her.'

'What was she doing out there in the first place?' asked Theophilis suspiciously. 'It is not safe, given the unsettled mood of the town.'

'She went to make sure that no horses were involved in the fire,' explained Clippesby. 'Burning would be a terrible way to die.'

'It would,' agreed Bartholomew soberly. 'As five hapless people have discovered.'

Eventually, the last student emerged yawning from his room, and Michael led the way to church. This was something else that had changed since he and Bartholomew had returned from Clare. The two of them had spent years walking side by side, talking all the way. Now Michael was obliged to be in front, leaving Bartholomew with William, who was not nearly such good company. Aungel and Theophilis were next, followed by Clippesby and any animal he had managed to snag. The students tagged along last, those in holy orders with their heads bowed in prayer, the remainder a noisy, chatting throng.

They arrived at the church, where it was William's turn to officiate, with Michael assisting. As William prided himself on the speed with which he could rattle through the sacred words, Mass was soon over, and Michael led the way home.

The rain had stopped and the sun was out, bathing the town in warm yellow rays. Everywhere were signs of advancing spring – blossom on the churchyard hedges, wildflowers along the sides of the road, and the sweet smell of fresh growth. Then a waft of something less pleasant wafted towards them, from the ditch that Tyled Hostel used as a sewer.

They reached Michaelhouse, where Agatha, the formidable laundress who ran the domestic side of the College, had breakfast ready. Women were forbidden to enter Colleges, lest they inflamed the passions of the residents, although exceptions were made for ladies who were old and ugly. Agatha was neither, although it would be a brave man who tried to force his attentions on her.

A few students peeled off to change or visit the latrines, but most went directly to the hall, where vats of meat-heavy pottage were waiting. There was also bread and honey for those who disliked rich fare first thing in the morning. Bartholomew opted for the lighter choice – he had already let his belt out once because of Michael's improved victuals, and did not want to waddle down the aisle to marry Matilde.

The meal was soon over, and Michael intoned a final Grace. Usually, Bartholomew went to the conclave to put the finishing touches to his lectures, but that day he went to his room to collect what he would need for examining bodies. Michael joined him there.

'I cannot stop thinking about yesterday,' said the monk, and shuddered. 'Those poor people were inside that burning shed for an age – we did not exactly hurry to the Spital, and even when we did arrive, it was some time before Eudo raised the alarm. Why did no one hear them sooner?'

Bartholomew had wondered that, too. 'Maybe the fire-fighters made too much noise.'

'But they did not, Matt. One of the first things I noticed was that they were labouring in almost complete silence, with none of the yelling and screeching that usually accompanies such incidents. If the victims had shouted, they would have been heard.'

Bartholomew regarded him unhappily – his reflections during the night had led him to much the same conclusion. 'So either their pleas were deliberately ignored or something happened to keep them quiet until it was too late.'

Michael raised his hands in a shrug. 'Yet everyone seemed genuinely shocked by the tragedy – I was watching very closely. Of course, the Spital's patients *are* insane . . .'

'The staff are not. They are all members of Tangmer's family.'

'Could it have been a suicide pact – the victims decided to die together, but one opted to spare the girl at the last minute?'

'Perhaps the bodies will give us answers. But the Spital is a curious place, do you not think? Its patients are like no lunatics that I have ever encountered.'

Michael agreed. 'There is an air of secrecy about it that is definitely suspicious. However, I think I know why. Not one madman spoke the whole time I was listening, and at one point, Prioress Joan shouted orders in French. I assumed no one would understand her, but most of them did.'

Bartholomew regarded him askance. 'You think they are French raiders, poised to attack us as they did in Winchelsea? That does not sound very likely!'

'I think they are French,' said Michael quietly, 'but not raiders. Most are women, children and old men, so I suspect they are folk who have been living peacefully in our country, but who suddenly find they are no longer welcome. The Spital is their refuge.'

Bartholomew considered. The monk's suggestion made sense, as it explained a lot: the peculiar silence, the inmates keeping their distance, the policy of discouraging visitors, and Tulyet, Leger and Norbert being asked to repel spectators.

'Amphelisa is French,' he said. 'Perhaps they are her kin. Moreover, she told me that the child we rescued is called Helene Girard . . . Hélène Girard.' He gave it two different pronunciations – the English one Amphelisa had used, followed by the French. Then he did the same for the other name he had heard: Delacroix.

'Then I am glad I have decided to investigate the matter,' said Michael, 'because if we are right, the chances are that the fire was set deliberately with the Girard family inside. Ergo, five people were murdered. It would have been six if you had not saved Hélène.'

Bartholomew frowned. 'That is a wild leap of logic, Brother! Moreover, the Spital is outside your jurisdiction – you have no authority to meddle.'

'The Senior Proctor will meddle where he likes,' declared Michael haughtily. 'And such a ruthless killer at large most certainly *is* my business, as I have an obligation to keep our scholars safe. Besides, I have not forgotten Paris the Plagiarist, even if you have.'

Bartholomew blinked. 'You think that whoever stabbed him also incinerated an entire family? But what evidence can you possibly—'

'Paris was French, and I am sure we shall shortly confirm that the Girards were French, too. So was Bonet the spicer. It cannot be coincidence, and as Paris was a scholar, it is my duty to find out what is happening. But I cannot sit here bandying words with you. I must visit the castle, and tell our Sheriff what we have reasoned.'

'What *you* have reasoned,' corrected Bartholomew, then

pointed out of the window. 'But you are spared a trek to the castle, because Dick is here to see you.'

The suite allocated to the Master of Michaelhouse was in the newer, less ramshackle south wing, and comprised a bedchamber, an office and a pantry for 'commons' – the edible treats scholars bought for their personal use. Needless to say, Michael kept this very well stocked, so Tulyet was not only furnished with a cup of breakfast ale, but a plate of spiced pastries as well. The Sheriff listened without interruption as Michael outlined his theory, although he gaped his astonishment at the claim that the Spital was a haven for displaced Frenchmen.

'I am right,' insisted Michael. 'The King issued his call to arms because of what the Dauphin did in Winchelsea, so, suddenly, the war is not something that is happening in some distant country, but is affecting people *here*. Even many of our scholars, who should be intelligent enough to know better, are full of anti-French fervour.'

'While the town is convinced that the Dauphin will appear at any moment to slaughter them all,' acknowledged Tulyet ruefully. 'A belief that Sir Leger and Sir Norbert exploit shamelessly to make folk practise at the butts.'

'Leger and Norbert,' said Michael in distaste. 'I have heard them in taverns, ranting that all Frenchmen should be wiped from the face of the Earth. It is a poisonous message to spread among the ignorant, who are incapable of telling the difference between enemy warriors and innocent strangers – as Paris the Plagiarist may have learned to his cost.'

'And Bonet,' sighed Tulyet. 'But Leger and Norbert have been moulded by the army, where they fought French warriors, massacred French peasants and destroyed French crops. I do not offer this as an excuse, but an explanation.'

71

'So you believe me?' asked Michael. 'About the Spital "lunatics" being French?'

Tulyet nodded slowly. 'On reflection, yes. I heard some of the children whisper in that language yesterday. Moreover, none of the adults seemed mad, which suggests they are there for some other reason.'

'So what will you do about it?' asked Bartholomew uneasily.

'Speak to them – determine whether they are hapless civilians caught in a strife that is none of their making, or spies intent on mischief.'

'They cannot be spies,' objected Bartholomew. 'Half of them are children.'

'It would not be the first time babes in arms were used as "cover" by unscrupulous adults,' said Tulyet soberly. 'However, I can tell you one thing for certain: something or someone prevented the Girards from escaping the fire, which means they were murdered.'

'Do you think they were killed because they were French?' asked Bartholomew.

'Perhaps, but we will find out for certain when you examine the bodies – or when Michael and I poke around the remains of the shed together.'

Michael smiled. 'You do not object to joining forces with the University, a foundation stuffed to the gills with enemy soldiers, if the town is to be believed?'

Tulyet raised his eyebrows. 'Can you blame them? Your scholars strut around whinnying in French, and flaunting the fact that few of them are local. It is deliberately provocative.'

'It is,' conceded Michael. 'And I shall speak to de Wetherset again later, to see if we can devise a way to make them desist.'

'Good,' said Tulyet. 'Because now is not the time to antagonise us – not when so many are being taught how to fight. More than a few itch to put their new skills into practice.'

Michael stood. 'Then we had better make a start. If our killer hates Frenchmen enough to burn women and children alive, we need to catch him fast.'

'I have just come from the Spital,' said Tulyet, not moving. 'The shed is still too hot for retrieving the victims, so I suggest meeting there at noon.'

'Then in the meantime, Matt and I will question the folk who live along the Trumpington road. Perhaps one of them will have noticed someone slinking along intent on murder and arson.' Michael raised a hand to quell Bartholomew's immediate objection. 'I know it will interfere with your teaching, but it cannot be helped. We must catch the culprit – or culprits – before any more blood is spilled.'

'I will speak to my informants,' said Tulyet. 'See if they have heard rumours about groups of Frenchmen living in the area. I hope they would have already told me if there were, but there is no harm in being sure.'

'None at all,' agreed Michael.

The three of them left the College, and walked to the high street, where Tulyet turned towards the castle, and Bartholomew and Michael aimed for St Mary the Great. It was Wednesday, the day when the market was dedicated to the buying and selling of livestock, so the town was busier than usual. Herds of cows, sheep and goats were being driven along the main roads, weaving around wagons loaded with crates of poultry. The noise was deafening, as none of the creatures appreciated what was happening and made their displeasure known with a cacophony of lows, bleats, honks, squawks and quacks.

It seemed normal, but Bartholomew knew the town well enough to detect undercurrents. Locals shot challenging glances at the students who trooped in and out of the churches, looks that were, more often than not, returned in full. Then he saw four King's Hall men backed into a corner by a gaggle of angry bakers. The scholars' hands hovered over the hilts of their swords, but it was the bakers who made a hasty departure when Michael bore down on them.

'They accused us of being French,' said one student defensively. His name was Foxlee, and it had been him and his three friends who had tried to pick a fight with Isnard the previous day. 'But I was born not ten miles from here, and I have lived in England all my life.'

'Whereas I hail from Bruges,' put in another, 'and while France may consider Flanders a vassal nation, my countrymen and I will *never* yield to their vile yoke.'

'At least they had heard of Bruges,' said a third. 'When I told them I was from Koln, they asked which part of France it was in. Do none of these peasants have brains, Brother?'

They spoke loudly enough to be heard by passers-by. These included Isnard and one of his more dubious associates – Verious the ditcher, a rogue who supplemented his meagre income with petty crime.

'If you are English, why do you wear them French clothes?' Verious demanded.

'What French clothes?' asked Bruges, startled, although Bartholomew could understand why Verious had put the question, as all four scholars wore elegant gipons, tied around the waist with belts made from gold thread. The skirts fell elegantly to their knees, and their feet were encased in calfskin boots. Around their heads were liripipes – scarves that could double as hoods. All were blue, which was King's Hall livery, although there was no sign of the academic tabards that should have covered their finery. But it was the dash of the exotic that rendered the ensemble distinctly un-English – mother-of-pearl buttons, lace cuffs and feathers.

'He cannot tell the difference between French fashions and those favoured by the Court,' scoffed Foxlee. 'If the

King were to ride past now, this oaf would probably accuse *him* of being French as well.'

'You seem to have forgotten your tabards,' said Michael coolly, preventing Verious from snarling a response by raising an imperious hand. 'Doubtless you will want to rectify the matter before the Senior Proctor fines you.'

'And any townsman who jeers at them will be reported to the Sheriff for breaking the King's peace,' put in Bartholomew hastily, as Verious and Isnard drew breath to cackle their amusement at the speed with which the King's Hall lads departed.

'We will be in flames within a week unless Dick and I impose some serious peacekeeping measures,' muttered Michael as he and Bartholomew went on their way. 'The only problem is that the triumvirate veto anything I suggest.'

Bartholomew frowned his mystification. 'Do they want the University to burn then?'

Michael scowled. 'This is what happens when our colleagues elect a man who thinks he knows better than me. When de Wetherset was last in charge, the town was a very different place. He does not understand that things have changed.'

'Then you had better educate him before he does any irreparable harm.'

They began their enquiries at the Hall of Valence Marie and then Peterhouse, although no one at either College could tell them anything useful. Opposite Peterhouse was a row of houses, some of which were rented to the University for use as hostels. Unfortunately, the residents had either been out or had noticed nothing unusual until they had seen the smoke, at which point the culprit would likely have been well away. The fourth house they visited was larger than the others, and had recently been renovated to a very high standard.

'It is a dormitory for Tyled Hostel,' explained Michael as they knocked on its beautiful new door. 'That place has more money than is decent.'

A student came to escort them to a pleasant refectory at the back of the house, where he and his friends were entertaining – the triumvirate were ensconced there, enjoying cake and honeyed wine. De Wetherset and Aynton were members of Tyled, but it was strange to see Heltisle – the Master of Bene't – in a hostel, as he usually deemed such places beneath him, even wealthy ones like Tyled, and was brazen in his belief that Colleges were far superior foundations. Then Bartholomew saw several metal pens displayed on the table, and realised that Heltisle was there in the hope of making a sale.

The triumvirate looked sleek and prosperous that day, and had donned clothes that were bound to aggravate the locals. De Wetherset's gold pilgrim badge glittered on a gorgeous velvet hat; Heltisle seemed to have done his utmost to emulate the Dauphin; and even the usually sober Aynton wore French silk hose. It was needlessly provocative, and Bartholomew was disgusted that they did not set a better example.

'We have already asked these lads if they saw anything suspicious yesterday,' said Aynton with one of his benign grins. 'None did, because they were all at a lecture.'

'But Theophilis told us that the dead lunatics were from a family called *Girard*,' said Heltisle, pronouncing the name in the English way. 'Is it true?'

'Yes,' replied Michael cautiously. 'Why? Did you know them?'

'They are the ones that de Wetherset and I hired as proxies in the call to arms,' replied Heltisle. 'At considerable expense.'

'What a pity,' said Bartholomew with uncharacteristic acerbity. 'Now you will have to go to the butts yourselves.'

'We are too important to waste our time there,' declared

Heltisle. 'Besides, *I* do not need to practise. I am already an excellent shot and very handy with a sword.'

'Not that we will ever have to put such talents to work, of course,' put in de Wetherset. 'If we are obliged to march to war, we shall be employed as clerks or scribes.'

'No – *generals*,' countered Heltisle. 'Directing battles from a safe distance.'

Bartholomew laughed, although he knew the Vice-Chancellor had not been joking.

'*I* did not hire a Girard,' put in Aynton. 'My proxy was Bruges the Fleming from King's Hall. But after you said such an arrangement smacked of cowardice, Brother, I released him from my service. I do not want to earn the contempt of townsfolk or of fellow scholars.'

'His name is Bruges, you say?' asked de Wetherset keenly.

'Yes, but you are too late to snag him for yourself,' said Aynton apologetically. 'Theophilis overheard me talking to him, and hired him on the spot. He told me the University would need to keep some of its officials back, if the Chancellor, the Vice-Chancellor, the Commissary *and* the Senior Proctor are obliged to go and fight the French.'

'You see, Brother?' murmured Bartholomew. 'You are reckless to trust Theophilis – he has ambitions to rule the University all on his own.'

Michael ignored him. 'How well did you know these Girard men?'

'We met them twice,' replied Heltisle. 'Once to discuss the matter, and once to hand over the money we agreed to pay.'

He named the sum, and Bartholomew felt his jaw drop. It was a fortune.

'We understand one of the children survived,' said de Wetherset. 'Perhaps you would see that the money stays with her, Brother. We had a contract with her kin, and it is hardly her fault that they are no longer in a position to honour it.'

'That is generous,' said Michael suspiciously.

'It is,' agreed Heltisle, and smiled craftily. 'Perhaps word of our largesse will spread, and another lunatic will offer us his sword.'

'No,' said de Wetherset sharply. 'It is *not* self-interest that guides us. The truth is that I feel sorry for the girl – parents, aunt, uncle and brother, all dead. It is a heavy burden to bear.'

Heltisle retorted that he was a sentimental fool, and an ill-tempered spat followed, with Aynton struggling to mediate. While they bickered, Bartholomew pulled Michael to one side and spoke in an undertone.

'Do you think someone heard what the Girards were paid and decided to steal it? There are plenty who would kill for a fraction of that amount.'

'We shall bear it in mind,' Michael whispered back. 'But why would the Girards offer to bear arms against their countrymen? Or did they take the money with no intention of honouring the arrangement? After all, it cannot be cheap to stay in hiding, so any means of gaining a quick fortune . . .'

'Perhaps we should include de Wetherset and Heltisle on our list of murder suspects – they realised the Girards aimed to cheat them and took revenge.'

'If they are capable of incinerating an entire family, they would not be hiring proxies to go to war on their behalf – they would be itching to join the slaughter in person.'

Bartholomew supposed that was true, although he decided to watch both scholars carefully until their innocence was proven. He was about to say so, when there was a knock on the door and two men were shown in bearing missives for the Chancellor's attention. Michael's jaw dropped when he saw the couriers' clothes.

'Those are *beadles'* uniforms!' he breathed, shocked. 'How dare you wear—'

'These are a couple of the new recruits Heltisle has hired,' explained de Wetherset. 'To protect us against the growing aggression of the town.'

Michael gaped at him. It was the Senior Proctor's prerogative to choose beadles, and he took the duty seriously. They were no longer a ragtag band of louts who could gain employment nowhere else, noted for drunkenness and a love of bribes, but professionals, who were paid a decent wage and were treated with respect. They were picked for their ability to use reason rather than force, although they were reliable fighters in a crisis. Heltisle's men were surly giants, who looked as though they would rather start a fight than stop one.

'If you thought we needed more men, you should have told me,' said Michael between gritted teeth. 'I would have been more than happy to—'

'I assumed you would not mind,' said Heltisle slyly. 'After all, you regularly relieve de Wetherset of the duties that go with *his* office, so I thought you would not object to me doing the same to you.'

'I hardly think—' began Michael indignantly.

'I took on a dozen,' interrupted Heltisle, enjoying the monk's growing outrage. 'All good fellows who will make townsmen think twice about crossing us.'

'And how will you pay for them?' demanded Michael curtly. 'Because it will not be out of the Senior Proctor's budget.'

'We shall use the Destitute Scholars' Fund,' replied Heltisle, and shrugged when Michael regarded him in disbelief. 'It is only penniless low-borns who need it, and I do not want them here anyway.'

'These "penniless low-borns" are often our best thinkers,' said Bartholomew quietly. 'Our University will be a poorer place without them.'

79

'Rubbish,' stated Heltisle contemptuously, and turned back to Michael, indicating the new beadles as he did so. 'My recruits are a cut above the weaklings you favour, and will be a credit to the University.'

'I hope you are right,' said Michael tightly. 'Because any inadequacies on their part will fall at your door, not mine.'

'No, all beadles are *your* responsibility,' said Heltisle sweetly. 'And there is another thing: a letter arrived from the Bishop this morning. It was addressed to you, but I assumed it was really meant for the Chancellor, so I opened it.'

Michael struggled not to give him the satisfaction of losing his temper. 'How very uncouth. I would *never* stoop to such uncivilised antics.'

This was a downright lie, as he stole missives addressed to the triumvirate on a daily basis. Grinning, Heltisle produced the document in question. It was thick with filth, so he had wrapped it in a rag to protect his hands.

'It fell in a cowpat,' he explained gloatingly. 'Are you not going to take it and see what it says?'

'I will tell you, Brother,' said Aynton, shooting the Vice-Chancellor an admonishing look for his childishness. 'It is about a field in Girton. The Bishop owns it, but he wants to transfer the title to St Andrew's Church.'

It was Michael's turn to grin. 'You are right, Heltisle – the Bishop *would* rather the Chancellor sorted it out. Unfortunately, the deeds pertaining to that piece of land are so complex that they will take weeks to unravel. I recommend he delegates the matter to a deputy. You, for example.'

He bowed and sailed out. As Bartholomew turned to follow, he heard de Wetherset remark that perhaps he *had* better do as the Senior Proctor suggested, as a Chancellor could not afford to waste time on trivialities. He did not catch Heltisle's reply, but he did hear Aynton rebuke him for foul language.

\*　\*　\*

Out on the street, Michael's temper broke, and he railed furiously about Heltisle's effrontery. Bartholomew let him rant, knowing he would feel better for it. The tirade might have gone on longer, but they bumped into Theophilis, who had been in the Gilbertine Priory, giving a lecture on his *Calendarium*. Michael was far too enraged for normal conversation, so Bartholomew took the opportunity to ask the Junior Proctor about the proxy he had snapped up when Aynton had decided against using one.

'Bruges the Fleming.' Theophilis spoke so silkily that Bartholomew's skin crawled. 'I hired him for you, Brother. The University will need strong leaders if lots of us are called to fight, and you are the only man I trust to watch our interests while I am away.'

'You are kind, Theophilis,' said Michael. 'But as a monk in major holy orders, I am exempt from the call to arms. I do not need a proxy.'

'I know that,' said Theophilis impatiently. 'But you will need a good man at your side, so Bruges will stand in for whoever you select to help you. Perhaps you will pick me, but perhaps you will decide on another – the choice will be yours to make.'

'You see, Matt?' said Michael, when the Junior Proctor had gone. 'His intentions *are* honourable. He was thinking of the University, not himself.'

Bartholomew did not believe it for an instant, but knew there was no point in arguing. He and Michael went to the house next to Tyled's dormitory, where they learned that the owners – a tailor and his wife – were 'far too busy to gaze out of windows all day like lazy scholars'.

When they emerged, Tulyet was waiting to report that none of his spies had heard the slightest whisper of groups of Frenchmen in the area – and they had all been alert for such rumours, given what had happened to Winchelsea.

'Perhaps the Gilbertines will have noticed something

useful,' said Michael, although his shoulders slumped; their lack of success was beginning to dishearten him.

They had not taken many steps towards the priory before they met Sir Leger and Sir Norbert, marching along with an enormous train of townsfolk at their heels, most from the nearby King's Head tavern. The two knights wore military surcoats, and their hands rested on the hilts of their broadswords. All their followers carried some kind of weapon – cudgels, pikes or knives.

'What are you doing?' demanded Tulyet, aghast. 'You cannot allow such a great horde to stamp about armed to the teeth! It is needlessly provocative.'

'Needlessly provocative?' echoed Leger with calculated insolence. 'We are preparing to repel a French invasion, as per the King's orders.'

'All true and loyal Englishmen will applaud our efforts,' put in the swarthy, hulking Norbert, 'which means that anyone who does not is a traitor. Besides, if there is any trouble, it will not be us who started it, but that University you love so much.'

'Quite,' said Leger smugly. 'Because all we and our recruits are doing is walking along a public highway, minding our own business.'

'Do not test me,' said Tulyet tightly. 'I know what you are trying to do and I will not have it. Either you behave in a manner commensurate with your rank, or I shall send you back to the King in disgrace. Do I make myself clear?'

Norbert looked as though he would argue, but the more intelligent Leger knew they had overstepped the mark. He nodded sullenly, jabbing his friend in the back to prevent him from saying something that would allow Tulyet to carry out his threat.

'Where were you going?' Bartholomew asked in the tense silence that followed.

'The butts,' replied Leger stiffly. 'For archery practice.'

'The butts are ours on Wednesdays,' said Michael. 'You cannot have them today.'

When the King had first issued his call to arms, a field near the Barnwell Gate had been hastily converted into a shooting range – 'the butts'. As it was the only suitable land available, both the town and the University had wanted it, so Tulyet and Michael had agreed on a time-table: the town had it on Tuesdays, Thursdays, Saturdays and Sundays, while scholars had it on Mondays, Wednesdays and Fridays. There had been no infringe-ments so far, but everyone knew it was only a question of time before one side defaulted, at which point there would be a fracas.

'Take them to the castle instead,' ordered Tulyet. 'It is time they learned something of hand-to-hand combat. I shall join you there later, to assess the progress you have made. I hope I will not be disappointed.'

There was a murmur of dismay in the ranks, as infantry training was far less popular than archery. Norbert opened his mouth to refuse, but Leger inclined his head.

'Good idea,' he said. 'We shall teach everyone how to use a blade. I have always found throat-slitting and stab-bing to be very useful skills. Men! Forward *march*!'

'There will be a battle before the week is out,' predicted Tulyet, watching them tramp away. 'They itch to spill your blood, and the University itches to spill ours. But I had better go and make sure they do as they are told. While I do, ask the Gilbertines if they saw our murderous arsonist slinking past, and we shall go to the Spital as soon as I get back.'

The Gilbertine Priory was a beautiful place, and Bartholomew knew it well, as he was often summoned to tend poorly canons. They had a more liberal attitude towards women than the other Orders, and had not minded at all when Michael had asked them to house a few nuns during the *conloquium*. They had offered them the use of their guesthouse, a building that stood apart from the main precinct, although still within its protective walls.

Its Prior was a quiet, decent man named John, who had one of the widest mouths Bartholomew had ever seen on a person. He appeared to have at least twice as many teeth as anyone else, and when he smiled, Bartholomew was always put in mind of a crocodile.

'We were having a meeting in our chapel, so the first we knew about the blaze was when our porter came to tell us that you were racing out to the Spital,' John said apologetically. 'But perhaps your nuns saw something – our guesthouse overlooks the road.'

He left them to make their own way there. As they went, Michael told Bartholomew that he had housed ten nuns there – nine from Swaffham Bulbeck and one from Ickleton Priory.

'Both foundations are wealthy,' he explained, 'and I thought they might become Michaelhouse benefactors if I put them somewhere nice. It was a serious mistake.'

'Why?'

'Because last year, Abbess Isabel of Swaffham Bulbeck visited Ickleton on behalf of the Bishop. She was so shocked by what she found that its Prioress – Alice – was deposed. And which nun should be sent to represent Ickleton at our *conloquium*? Alice!'

'That must be uncomfortable for both parties,' mused Bartholomew.

'It is more than uncomfortable,' averred Michael. 'It has resulted in open warfare! I offered to find one faction alternative accommodation, but neither will move, on the grounds that it will then appear as if the other is the victor.'

Bartholomew was intrigued. 'What did Abbess Isabel find at Ickleton, exactly?'

'Just the usual – corruption, indolence, licentiousness.'

'Those are usual in your Order, are they?'

Michael scowled. 'I meant those are the most common offences committed by the rare head of house who strays from the straight and narrow. Alice allowed her friends to live in the priory free of charge, and gave them alms that should have gone to the poor. She also let her nuns miss their holy offices, and too many men were regular visitors.'

'Then it is no surprise that the Bishop deposed her. But are you sure that Abbess Isabel did not exaggerate? I have met her, and she is very easily shocked.'

'She is,' acknowledged Michael. 'Probably because she is generally considered to be a saint in the making.'

Bartholomew was surprised to hear it. 'Is she?'

'She was to have married an earl, but when she expressed a desire to serve God instead, he chopped off her hands. That night, he was struck dead and her hands regrew.'

Bartholomew regarded him askance. 'Surely, you do not believe that?'

'The Pope did, and granted her special dispensation to wear a white habit instead of a black one, as an expression of her purity. But how did you meet her?'

'She is the one who found Paris the Plagiarist's body. She was so upset that she fainted, so I carried her into a tavern to recover – where she saw the landlady's low-cut bodice and swooned all over again. I wondered at the time why her habit was a different colour. I wanted to ask, but she did not seem like a lady for casual conversation.'

'No,' agreed Michael. 'Saints are not, generally speaking.'

Abbess Isabel was a slender, sallow woman whose bright white habit made her appear ghostly. She emerged from the Gilbertines' stable on a donkey, and Michael whispered that she was scheduled to speak on humility at the *conloquium* that day.

'Hence her arrival on a simple beast of burden,' he explained. 'A practical demonstration of self-effacement. Of course, the fact that she feels compelled to show us how humble she is does smack of pride . . .'

Suddenly, the Abbess raised her pale eyes heavenwards in a rapt expression. Her black-robed retinue immediately grabbed the donkey's bridle and formed a protective ring around her, to ensure that her communication with God was not interrupted.

'We could be here a while,' murmured Michael. 'She goes into trances.'

'Or perhaps it is a ruse to avoid *her*,' said Bartholomew, nodding to where another nun was coming from the opposite direction. 'The deposed Alice, I presume?'

Alice was short and thin, and her beady black eyes held an expression of such fierce hatred that Bartholomew was sure she should never have been allowed to take holy orders. The malevolent glower intensified when she saw Isabel being pious. Then she began to scratch so frantically at her scalp that he suspected some bothersome skin complaint – perhaps one that rendered the sufferer unusually bad-tempered.

'I was astonished when I learned that *she* was Ickleton's sole delegate,' whispered Michael. 'I assumed she was still in disgrace.'

'Perhaps her replacement wanted rid of her for a while,' suggested Bartholomew. 'Having a former superior under your command cannot be easy.'

'Especially one like Alice, who is bitter and quarrelsome. Of course, Swaffham Bulbeck is not the only convent Alice has taken against. She has also declared war on Lyminster, because the Bishop's sister lives there. Putting them in the Spital was another mistake on my part, as they invariably meet when they ride to St Radegund's each morning. There have been scenes.'

Alice marched towards Michael, bristling with anger. 'I have a complaint to make, Brother. That worldly Magistra Katherine spoke at the *conloquium* today, and she was so boring that I had to leave.'

'You call Katherine worldly?' blurted Michael. 'After you were dismissed for—'

'I made one or two small errors of judgement,' interrupted Alice sharply. 'And was then condemned by people who are far worse sinners than I could ever hope to be.'

'*Hope* to be?' echoed Bartholomew, amused.

Alice ignored him. 'Katherine is like her brother – a hypocrite. How dare he dismiss me when *he* fled the country to escape charges of murder, theft, kidnapping and extortion!'

She had a point: the Bishop had indeed been accused of those crimes, and rather than stay and face the consequences, he had run to Avignon, to claim sanctuary with the Pope. Everyone knew he was guilty, so Bartholomew understood why Alice objected to being judged by him. Michael opened his mouth to defend the man whose shoes he hoped to fill one day, but Alice was already turning her vitriol on someone else she did not like.

'And that Abbess Isabel is no saint,' she hissed. 'She is selfish and deceitful.'

Isabel was not about to hang around being holy while Alice denigrated her to the Bishop's favourite monk. She barked an order that saw her nuns drop the donkey's bridle and step aside. Then she rode forward to have her say.

'You are a disgrace, Alice,' she declared, her pale eyes cold and hard. 'It is wrong to make light of your own crimes by pointing out the errors of others. There is no excuse for what you did.'

'And you never make mistakes, of course,' jeered Alice.

'You are perfect in every way. How wonderful it must be to be you.'

'She *is* perfect,' declared one of Isabel's nuns angrily. 'Just ask the Pope. We are honoured to serve her, so keep your nasty remarks to yourself.'

'Yesterday's fire,' interposed Michael quickly. 'The arsonist almost certainly used the road outside to reach the Spital. Did any of you notice anything suspicious?'

'No,' replied Isabel shortly. 'If we had, we would have told you already.'

'I was not here,' said Alice haughtily. 'I was at the *conloquium*.'

'But I prayed for the Girard family all night,' Isabel went on, as if her enemy had not spoken, 'which was not easy with Alice lurking behind me – I could feel her eyes burning into the back of my head. She will be bound for Hell unless she learns to replace malice with love.'

Alice bristled. '*I* was praying for the Girards, but you were praying for yourself – that your so-called piety will win you a place among the saints.'

'While you are here, Brother,' said another of the nuns frostily, 'perhaps you will tell *Sister* Alice to keep her maggot-infested marchpanes to herself. She will deny sending them to the Abbess, but we all know the truth.'

'Liar!' snarled Alice. 'I have better things to do than buy you lot presents.'

'What time did you arrive at the *conloquium*, Alice?' asked Michael, speaking quickly a second time to nip the burgeoning spat in the bud.

'Not until the afternoon,' admitted Alice. 'Before that, I was in a town church, practising my own presentation, which is later this week.'

'So you cannot prove where you were at the salient time?' asked Isabel, raising her white eyebrows pointedly.

Alice bristled. 'I sincerely hope you are not accusing *me* of setting this fire. Why would I do such a thing?'

'To harm the ladies from Lyminster,' replied another of Isabel's retinue promptly. 'You hate them almost as much as you hate us, and your enmity knows no bounds.'

'And you, Isabel?' asked Michael before Alice could defend herself. 'Where were you?'

'Praying,' replied the Abbess serenely. 'In St Botolph's Church. All my sisters were with me, so none of us can help you identify your arsonist. Now I have a question for *you*, Brother: have you caught Paris the Plagiarist's killer yet? I cannot forget the sight of his dead white face, and it disturbs me to think that his murderer might pass us in the street.'

'He might,' acknowledged Michael. 'And our best – perhaps our only – chance of catching him now is if *you* remember anything new.'

'Then I shall tell God to jog my memory,' said Isabel, and smiled. 'So you will soon have the culprit under lock and key, because He always accedes to my demands.'

'That shows you are no saint,' spat Alice at once. 'No one makes *demands* of God.'

Isabel's entourage took exception to this remark. A furious quarrel ensued, and this time, not even Michael could quell it.

Bartholomew backed away, pulling the monk with him. 'You are brave to have anything to do with this *conloquium*, Brother,' he murmured, 'if these delegates are anything to go by.'

'Fortunately, they are not,' said Michael with a heartfelt sigh. 'Shall we see if Dick is ready for the Spital?'

Tulyet had trailed his knights and their followers to the castle, and was confident that they were all condemned to an unpleasant afternoon wrestling each other in the dusty bailey. He hurried back to the Trumpington road, where he found Bartholomew and Michael still busy with the nuns. While he waited for them to finish, he discussed the town's unsettled atmosphere with Prior John, who was worried that it might spread to infect his peaceful convent.

'It would not normally worry me,' confided John, 'but Michael's nuns are a querulous horde, who never stop squabbling. I would never have agreed to take them had I known what they were like. All I can say is thank God I am a Gilbertine, not a Benedictine!'

Tulyet laughed. Then Michael and Bartholomew appeared, so he bade John farewell and set off towards the Spital with them. They had covered about half the distance when they met big Prioress Joan riding a spirited stallion. He and Michael admired her skill as she directed it over the treacherous, rock-hard ruts, although Bartholomew's attention was fixed on the horse – it had an evil look in its eye and he did not want to end up on the wrong end of its teeth.

'Here is a handsome beast,' said Michael, approvingly. 'The horse, I mean, not you, Abbess. Does he belong to your convent?'

'Do you ask as the Bishop's spy or as a man who appreciates decent horseflesh?' said Joan, a twinkle in her eye. 'Because if it is the former, then of course Dusty belongs to the convent. You know as well as I do that Benedictines are forbidden expensive possessions.'

'Horses do not count,' averred Michael, although Bartholomew was sure St Benedict would have begged to differ. 'You call him Dusty? An unworthy name for such a fine creature.'

'A grand one would raise alarms when we submit our accounts,' explained Joan with a conspiratorial grin. 'But no one questions hay for a nag called Dusty. Would you like to take him for a canter later? I do not usually lend him out, but I sense you could manage him.'

'Are you sure he could bear the weight?' asked

Bartholomew, looking from the monk's substantial girth to the horse's slender legs.

'Ignore him, Brother,' said Joan, giving Bartholomew a haughty glare. 'People accuse me of being too large for a woman, but they do not know what they are talking about. The truth is that I am normal, while everyone else is excessively petite.'

'And I have unusually heavy bones, although few are intelligent enough to see it,' said Michael, pleased to meet someone who thought like him. He eyed Bartholomew coolly. 'Even my closest friend calls me plump, and has the effrontery to criticise my diet.'

'Then that is just plain rude,' said Joan, offended on his behalf. 'A man's victuals are his own affair, just as a woman's size is hers.'

'Quite right,' agreed Michael. 'Shall we ride out together and discuss this vexing matter in more detail? I shall borrow something from King's Hall – they have the best stables.'

Joan revealed her long teeth in a delighted smile. 'After the *conloquium*, when I am not obliged to listen to my sisters whine about the difficulties involved in running a convent. In my opinion, if you have a problem, you solve it. You do not sit about and grumble like men.'

'Problems like your priory's chapel,' mused Michael. 'Part of it collapsed, so you rebuilt it with your own hands. Magistra Katherine told me.'

Joan blushed modestly. 'She exaggerates – I had lots of help. Besides, I would much rather tile a roof than do the accounts. I thank God daily for His wisdom in sending Katherine to me, as she is an excellent administrator. I could not have asked for a better deputy.'

'We are on our way to the Spital, to find out what happened to the Girard family,' said Tulyet. 'You were there when the fire started, so what can you tell us about it?'

'Nothing, I am afraid. I was in the stables grooming Dusty at the time. Katherine was due to give a lecture in St Radegund's, but when I saw the shed alight, I sent a message asking for it to be postponed, as it seemed inappropriate to jaunt off while our hosts struggled to avert a crisis. I spent most of the time calming the horses.'

'Did you notice any visitors to the Spital yesterday?' Tulyet asked. 'I know Tangmer discourages them, but it is possible that someone sneaked in *un*invited.'

'Just Sister Alice, who will insist on paying court to us, even though we find her company tiresome. Moreover, I always want to scratch when she is around, because she claws constantly at herself. When she is with us, my nuns and I must look like dogs with fleas.'

'So you saw nothing to help?' Michael was beginning to be frustrated by the lack of reliable witnesses.

Joan grimaced. 'I am sorry, Brother. All my attention was on the horses. Try asking my nuns – I have left them in the Spital to pray for the dead. I am the only Lyminster delegate who will attend the *conloquium* today, but only because I am scheduled to talk about plumbing. If it were any other day, I would join my sisters on their knees.'

They were nearly at the Spital when they were hailed by Cynric. The book-bearer carried a sword, and had one long Welsh hunting knife in his belt and another strapped to his thigh. He had also donned a boiled leather jerkin and a metal helmet.

'These are what I wore at Poitiers,' he reminded Bartholomew, who was eyeing them disapprovingly. 'When you and me won that great victory.'

Four years before, he and Bartholomew had been in France, when bad timing had put them at the place where the Prince of Wales was about to challenge a much larger army. They had acquitted themselves adequately, but Cynric's account had grown with each telling, and had reached the point where he and the physician had defeated the enemy with no help from anyone else. Bartholomew still had nightmares about the carnage, although Cynric professed to have enjoyed every moment and claimed he was proud to have been there.

'Please take them off,' begged Bartholomew. 'They make you look as though you are spoiling for a fight.'

'I *have* to wear them – Master Heltisle put me in charge of training scholars at the butts,' argued Cynric. 'And if I do not look the part, no one will do what I say. But never mind that – me and Margery have something to tell you.'

They had not noticed the woman at the side of the road. Margery Starre was a lady of indeterminate years, who made no bones about the fact that she was a witch. Normally, this would have seen her burned at the stake, but she offered a valuable service with her cures and charms, many of which worked, so the authorities turned a blind eye. Bartholomew was wary of her, as she believed that the Devil – with whom she claimed to be on friendly terms – had helped him to become a successful physician. He dreaded to imagine what would happen if she shared this conviction with his colleagues. Heltisle, for one, would certainly use it to harm him.

'One of those Black Nuns came to me with a peculiar request,' she began without preamble. 'And I thought you should know about it.'

'Not that,' said Cynric impatiently. 'Tell them about the Spital ghost – about it being the spirit of some hapless soul sacrificed by pagans.'

'I saw it with my own eyes,' said Margery obligingly. 'A white spectre, which wobbled along the top of the wall, then disappeared into thin air.'

'Clippesby saw it, too,' put in Cynric. 'I overheard him telling the hens about it this morning.'

'It did not speak,' Margery went on, 'but I could tell it was a soul in torment.'

'Could you?' said Bartholomew curiously, although he knew he should not encourage her. 'How?'

'By its demeanour. And because it left trails of water on the wall – tears. The Spital should never have been built there, as it is the site of an ancient temple.'

'How can you tell?' demanded Bartholomew, sure she could not. The land on which the Spital was built was no different from its surroundings, and there was nothing to suggest it was special – no ditches, mounds, springs or unaccountable stones.

'Because Satan told me,' replied Margery grandly. 'He dropped in yesterday morning, and said he plans to take up residence there. I imagine it was him who started that fire – not deliberately, of course, but because his fiery hoofs touched dry wood.'

'You are right,' said Bartholomew sombrely. 'The Devil *was* involved in starting the blaze, because only a very evil being could want people roasted alive.'

Margery sniffed. 'Satan is not evil – just misunderstood. He—'

'You mentioned a nun,' interrupted Michael, unwilling to listen to such liberal views about the Prince of Darkness. He was a monk, after all. 'She came to you with "a peculiar request".'

'It was Alice, the short, spiteful one who was deposed from Ickleton,' replied Margery. 'She asked me to make her some candles that reek of manure.'

Michael frowned his bemusement. 'Why would she want something like that?'

'To send to folk she does not like. The recipients will light them in all innocence, then spend days trying to dislodge the stink from their clothes.'

'I see,' said Michael. 'And Alice told you all this willingly?'

Margery nodded. 'She was reluctant at first, but hate burns hot inside her, and once she started, she could not stop. One of her targets is that elegant, arrogant nun, who thinks she is better than everyone else because her brother is the Bishop . . .'

'Magistra Katherine,' supplied Bartholomew.

'Yes, so if *she* dies in suspicious circumstances, you will know who to question first. Another enemy is Prioress Joan, who called her a spiteful little harpy. And a third is Abbess Isabel, whose report to the Bishop saw her disgraced.'

'Did Alice buy spells that would kill or hurt them?' asked Bartholomew uneasily. He did not believe in the efficacy of such things, but if Alice was attempting to purchase some, then her intended victims should be warned to be on their guard.

'I do not deal in those,' replied Margery loftily, although his relief evaporated when she added, 'other than for very special customers.'

'I assume you refused to make these smelly candles, too,' said Bartholomew.

'Of course not! She paid me a fortune to invent them, and I like a challenge. If I succeed, I can sell them to others who want to annoy their foes. You may have one – free of charge – for that nasty old Heltisle if you like.'

Bartholomew laughed. 'It is tempting, but I do not think Matilde would approve.'

'She would! She cannot abide him either. Mind you, that villain Theophilis is worse. He sniffs around poor Master Clippesby like a dog on heat, and I do not like it.'

'We should go,' said Tulyet, tired of listening to her. 'Time is passing.'

He set a cracking pace, and no one spoke again until they reached the Spital. When they arrived, he glanced up at the towering walls.

'God's blood!' he blurted. 'What is *that?*'

Bartholomew and Michael looked to where he pointed,

95

and saw something pale rise from the ground and ascend the wall. There was an approximate head and body, with two trailing wisps that might have been legs. It floated upwards, then disappeared over the top.

'It is someone playing a trick,' determined Michael. 'Go and look in the undergrowth, Matt. You are better at these things than me.'

Bartholomew took a stick and thrashed around in the weeds at the foot of the wall, but there was nothing to see – no tell-tale footsteps or hidden pieces of twine.

'If it is a prank, then it is a very clever one,' he told Michael eventually. 'I have no idea how it was managed. Perhaps it really was a ghost.'

'Do not be ridiculous,' said Michael firmly. 'There is no such thing as ghosts. Well, other than the Holy Ghost, of course, but that is different.'

# CHAPTER 5

There was a bell rope outside the Spital's main entrance so that visitors could announce their arrival. Michael gave it a tug, and when nothing happened, pulled harder. Then he exchanged a look of astonishment with Bartholomew and Tulyet when, instead of the usual cheery jangle that characterised such arrangements, a bell of considerable size boomed out. It echoed mournfully around them, stilling the merry chatter of sparrows in the nearby bushes.

'Goodness!' murmured Bartholomew, when the deep hum had died away. 'How very sinister! It feels as though we are about to ask for admittance to the Devil's lair.'

'Do not jest about such matters,' admonished Tulyet uneasily. 'There is something distinctly odd about this place. Perhaps Margery is right about Satan making it his own – and the thing we just watched shimmer over the wall was one of his familiars.'

'It was a trick,' said Michael firmly, 'even if we did find no evidence to prove it. However, we shall use it to our advantage, because if folk believe this place is infested by evil sprites, they will keep their distance. Then if the lunatics do transpire to be French, they are less likely to be discovered.'

'Alternatively,' cautioned Bartholomew, 'local folk may object to such a place on their doorstep, and will raze it to the ground. Then we shall have dozens of victims, not five.'

They were still debating when the massive Eudo opened the gate. He peered out warily, standing so that his bulk prevented them from seeing inside.

'You cannot come in,' he stated in a tone designed to brook no argument.

'Oh, yes, we can,' countered Tulyet. 'People died here yesterday, and it is our duty to investigate. So either let us in now or we shall return with soldiers.'

His stern face convinced Eudo to do as he was told. The moment they were inside, the big man closed the gate and secured it with a thick bar.

'People do not like lunatics,' he explained. 'Ergo, we have to protect ours.'

'So I see,' remarked Tulyet, looking to where several men were stationed on the walls, clearly standing guard. They were not armed, but sack-covered mounds revealed where weapons were stashed.

The Spital was a very different place than it had been the previous day. The inmates no longer stood in a frightened cluster, but joined the staff in a variety of humdrum activities – sweeping, gardening, laundry. There was not a child in sight. Two inmates moved as though they were not in complete control of their limbs, while three others jabbered self-consciously.

'Not even madmen do dirty household chores without aprons to protect their clothes,' Michael murmured as they followed Eudo to the hall. 'That bell is not to announce visitors, but to warn the inmates to take up pre-agreed roles and positions. All this quiet industry is an act, although not a very convincing one.'

'I agree,' whispered Tulyet. 'But let us go along with the charade, and see what we can learn before we reveal that we know they are Frenchmen in disguise – wealthy Frenchmen, as hiring an entire hospital cannot be cheap.'

'I suspect they are middling folk – craftsmen and traders,' said Bartholomew. 'The one beating rugs has burns like a blacksmith, while the woman weaving baskets is so dexterous that it must be her profession.'

They turned at a shout, and saw the portly Warden Tangmer waddling towards them, red-faced and breathless in his haste. Eudo's tiny wife Goda was with him, wearing an elaborately embroidered kirtle that made her look like an exotic doll. Bartholomew wondered if her everyday one had been spoiled fighting the fire.

Tulyet opened his mouth to explain why they were there, but the Warden spoke first.

'We shall bury our dead behind the chapel,' he announced. 'We are digging their graves now, so please leave us to do it in peace.'

'Not until we have ascertained why a whole family was trapped inside a burning shed,' said Tulyet sharply.

Tangmer winced. 'It was an accident. We are bursting at the seams with lunatics, so every building is needed to accommodate them all, even ramshackle ones that go up in flames when candles are knocked over.'

Eudo glared at Michael. 'Which is your fault for foisting those nuns on us.'

Michael raised his eyebrows. 'I did it because *you* told me that all your patients are held in secure accommodation inside the hall, and that the guesthouse was never used for that purpose. If you had been honest with me, I would have billeted my sisters elsewhere.'

'I did not know you were fishing for beds at the time,' retorted Eudo sullenly. 'I thought you wanted assurances that your precious University is in no danger from escaped madmen.'

'So the nuns' arrival meant that some patients were moved to the shed?' asked Tulyet. He waited until Eudo and Tangmer nodded before continuing. 'You are lying again – yesterday, you told me that it was full of tools and building supplies.'

Tangmer gave a pained smile. 'It is. However, the Girards elected to use it anyway – like a family house.'

'There were no windows,' added Eudo, 'so you had to

use candles or a lamp inside. It was also full of dry timber, so if one of the youngsters knocked one over . . .'

'The door was open when the alarm was first raised,' said Tangmer, his heckling defiance replaced by anguish. 'I ordered it closed, thinking it was the best way to contain the blaze. There had been plenty of time for anyone inside to get out, so I do not understand how this terrible thing could have happened. Goda said the shed was empty.'

'I was sure it *was* empty,' put in Goda, shaking her head unhappily. 'I could not believe it when voices . . .'

'Did you search it?' asked Tulyet. 'Properly?'

Goda grimaced. 'I went in as far as I dared, but no one was there. All I can think is that they were hiding behind the logs at the very back.'

Tulyet frowned. 'Why would they hide?'

'Because we had a visitor, and they were terrified of those,' explained Goda. 'I see now that I should have looked harder, but it never occurred to me that they would be more frightened of strangers than a fire.'

'What visitor?'

'Sister Alice, who came to see the nuns. I do not know why, as they loathe each other.'

'Alice did not mention that to us just now,' muttered Bartholomew. 'Curious.'

'She came today as well,' Goda went on, 'even though it was early and we were not really ready for . . .'

She trailed off, chagrined, when she realised she had almost let slip something that was meant to be kept quiet. Eudo blundered to her rescue.

'Ready for the day's chores,' he blustered. 'Some patients were not even dressed, and we were afraid that Alice would go away thinking we are all as lazy as . . . as *Frenchmen*. That race is worthless, and we hate them.'

'We do,' agreed Tangmer with a sickly smile. 'After what happened at Winchelsea, I shall kill any Frenchman on sight. We all would – every last soul among us.'

100

'Does that include your wife?' asked Bartholomew archly. 'Or is she exempt?'

'Amphelisa?' gulped Tangmer, eyes wide in his panicky face. 'She is not French!'

Tulyet indicated Bartholomew. 'I have brought the University's Corpse Examiner to look at the bodies, because I find it very strange that an entire family would rather roast alive than meet a nun.'

'Do you?' Tangmer exchanged an agitated glance with Eudo. 'Well, I suppose there is no harm in it, but I have a condition – that none of you speak to our patients. They are in a very fragile state after yesterday, and we cannot have them distressed further.'

'Where are the bodies?' asked Tulyet briskly. 'Still in the shed?'

'We retrieved them and put them in the chapel,' replied Tangmer. 'Poor souls.'

The Spital's chapel was a pretty place adjoining the central hall. There were two ways in – a small priests' door in the north side and a larger entrance from the hall itself. Tangmer opted to use the former, clearly to prevent his visitors from seeing more of his domain than absolutely necessary. As soon as they were inside, he dismissed Eudo and Goda, obviously afraid one would inadvertently say something else to arouse suspicion.

Inside, the first thing that struck Bartholomew was the smell – not the scent of damp plaster, incense and dead flowers that characterised most places of worship, and not the stench of charred corpses either. Instead, there was a powerful aroma of herbs, so strong that he wondered if it was safe.

'Amphelisa distils plant oils in here,' explained Tangmer, seeing his reaction. 'Under the balcony at the back. Well, why not? It uses space that would be redundant otherwise. Come. Allow me to show you.'

The chapel comprised a nave and a chancel. The balcony was suspended over the back half of the nave, reached by a flight of steps with a lockable door at the top. A knee-high wall ran across the front of the balcony, topped by a wooden trellis screen that reached the roof.

'We installed that so lepers can watch the holy offices without infecting the priest,' explained Tangmer, as Bartholomew, Michael and Tulyet stopped to stare up at it.

'But lepers are rare these days,' Bartholomew pointed out. 'So why bother with something that is never likely to be used?'

Tangmer looked pained. 'We had no idea they *were* scarce here until after we opened our doors, because there are plenty of them in Fra—' He stopped abruptly, alarm in his eyes.

'In France?' finished Bartholomew. 'You may be right.'

'In *Framlingham*, where Amphelisa comes from,' blurted Tangmer unconvincingly, and hastened on before anyone could press him on the matter. 'So it was a shock to find our charitable efforts might be wasted. Then Amphelisa suggested taking lunatics instead, on the grounds that they are also shunned by society through no fault of their own.'

The area below the balcony was low and dark. The left side was stacked with unseasoned firewood, while the remainder served as Amphelisa's workshop – two long benches loaded with equipment, and shelves for her raw ingredients. She was there when they arrived, bent over a cauldron, wearing another burgundy-coloured robe. Bartholomew recalled the reek of powerful herbs around her the previous day, strong enough to mask the reek of burning shed.

'As we have no lepers, we use the balcony to store her finished oils,' gabbled Tangmer, obviously aiming to distract his visitors in the hope of preventing them from asking more awkward questions. 'It locks, which is helpful, as most are expensive to produce. And some are toxic. Would you like to see them?'

He indicated that Amphelisa was to lead the way before they could decline. She nodded briskly and hurried up the steps to unlock the door with a key she kept around her neck, calling for them to follow. Bartholomew was willing, although Michael and Tulyet were less enthusiastic, neither liking the aroma of the highly concentrated oils.

The balcony was a large, plain room, lit only by the light that filtered through the screen at the front. Peering through the trellis afforded a fine view down the nave and into the chancel beyond. Opposite the screen was a stack of crates. Amphelisa opened the nearest to reveal a mass of tiny pots, each one carefully labelled – Bartholomew read lavender, rosewood, pine and yarrow before she closed it again.

'We send them to London,' she said. 'And as we spent nearly all our money on building this Spital, every extra penny is welcome. Would you like a free pot of cedarwood oil, Doctor? There is nothing quite like it for killing fleas and other pestilential creatures.'

'I might try some on my students then,' drawled Michael, while Bartholomew wished she had offered him some pine oil instead, as it was useful for skin diseases.

'This is not the best place for a distillery,' he said, pocketing the phial before following her back down the stairs. 'It is poorly ventilated and the fumes may be toxic. Moreover, you work with naked flames and there is firewood nearby. It is asking for trouble.'

Amphelisa waved a hand in a gesture that was unmistakably Gallic. 'The wood is still damp – it will smoke, but will take an age to ignite. But you are not here to discuss oil with me – you want to see the dead. They are in the chancel. Follow me.'

'And then you can leave,' said Tangmer, although with more hope than conviction.

The bodies had been placed in front of the altar. Two men knelt beside them. One was the dark-featured 'lunatic' who had said his name was Delacroix. The other was an elderly man with a shock of white hair, who was praying aloud in Latin – Latin that had the distinctive inflection of northern France. Both men leapt up when they realised they were not alone.

'Go, go!' cried Tangmer in English, flapping his hands at them. 'This is no place for madmen. Amphelisa – take them out. They cannot be in here unsupervised.'

'No, wait,' countered Michael in French. The two men stopped dead in their tracks, causing Tangmer and Amphelisa to exchange an agitated glance. 'Are you priests?'

Tangmer frantically shook his head, warning them against engaging in conversation. The pair edged towards the door, clearly aiming to bolt, but Tulyet barred their way. The two inmates regarded each other uncertainly.

'I am Father Julien,' replied the old one eventually. He had a sallow, lined face, although wary grey eyes suggested that his mind was sharp. 'I am ill. I came here to recover.'

'We aim to find out what happened to your friends,' said Michael, aware that the clipped English sentences were designed to give nothing of the speaker's origins away. 'So Matt will look at their bodies, to see how they died.'

'Why bother?' snarled Delacroix in French. He was in shirtsleeves that day, which revealed his neck; a scar around it that suggested someone had once tried to hang him. 'No one wants us here, and now you have five less to worry about. But we are not—'

'Hush, Delacroix!' barked Tangmer, while Amphelisa

and Julien paled in horror. 'Do not use that heathen language in this holy place. You know what we agreed.'

'Enough of this charade,' said Tulyet, tiring of the game they were playing. 'We are not fools. We know there are no lunatics here – just Frenchmen in hiding.'

There was a brief, appalled silence. Then Amphelisa opened her mouth to deny it, but Tangmer forestalled her by slumping on a bench with a groan of defeat.

'How did you guess?' he asked in a strangled whisper.

Amphelisa stood next to him, one hand on his shoulder and her face as white as snow. Julien's expression was resigned, but Delacroix scowled in a way that suggested he was more angry than dismayed at being found out.

'Tell us your story,' ordered Tulyet. 'If your presence here is innocent, you will come to no harm.'

'No harm?' sneered Delacroix. 'I walked through your town yesterday, and I heard what was being said about France on the streets. You hate us all, regardless of whether or not we support the Dauphin and his army.'

'Yes,' acknowledged Michael, 'there *is* much anti-French sentiment, and had you been caught there, you might well have been lynched. But we are not all ignorant bigots. We will hear what you have to say before passing judgement.'

'I *had* to do it,' whispered Tangmer, head in his hands. 'They came to me – a host of bewildered, frightened people, including children. How could I turn them away?'

'We paid you,' spat Delacroix. 'That is what convinced you to hide us, not compassion.'

'The money was a consideration,' conceded Tangmer stiffly, 'but our chief motive was pity. These people are not soldiers, but families driven from their homes by war. We call them our *peregrini*, which is Latin for strangers.'

'Why choose here?' asked Tulyet, before Michael could say that he did not need Tangmer to teach him a language he used on a daily basis. 'Cambridge is hardly on the beaten track.'

'Because Julien is my uncle,' explained Amphelisa. Her French was perfect, and was the language used for the rest of the conversation.

'So he is your uncle and every member of the Spital's staff is a Tangmer,' said Tulyet drily. 'You are fortunate to boast such a large family.'

'My husband has a large family,' said Amphelisa with quiet dignity. 'I only have Julien, as all the rest were killed in France two years ago. After their deaths, Julien brought the surviving villagers to England, where they lived peacefully until the raid on Winchelsea . . .'

'Winchelsea was where we settled, you see,' explained Julien. 'But it was attacked twice, and each time, the Mayor accused us of instigating the carnage – that we told the Dauphin when best to come.'

'Why would the Mayor do that?' asked Tulyet sceptically.

'Because he should have defended his town,' replied Julien, 'but instead, he hid until it was safe to come out. He needed a way to deflect attention from his cowardice, so he found some scapegoats – us.'

'*We* fought for Winchelsea,' said Delacroix bitterly. 'My brothers and I tried to repel the raiders at the pier, and both of them died doing it. The town should have been grateful, but instead, they turned on us.'

'We had to abandon the lives we had built among folk we believed to be friends,' said Julien. 'Our situation looked hopeless, but then I remembered Amphelisa's new Spital . . .'

'But why stay in England?' pressed Tulyet. 'Why not go home?'

Bartholomew knew the answer to that, because the marks on Delacroix's neck were indicative of a failed lynching, plus there was the fact that these *peregrini* had fled France *two years ago* . . .

'You are Jacques,' he surmised. 'Men who rebelled against their aristocratic overlords, and who were outlawed when that rebellion failed.'

This particular revolt, known as the Jacquerie, had been watched with alarm in England, as there had been fears that it might spread – French peasants were not the only ones tired of being oppressed by a wealthy elite. The Jacques had voiced a number of grievances, but first and foremost was the fact that they were taxed so that nobles could repair their war-damaged castles, on the understanding that the nobles would then protect the peasants from marauding Englishmen. The nobles did not keep their end of the bargain, and village after village was looted and burned. Crops were destroyed, too, and the people starved.

The Jacquerie foundered when its leader was executed, after which the nobles retaliated with sickening brutality. Thousands of peasants were slaughtered, many of whom had had nothing to do with the uprising. Those who could run away had done so, although most of them had nowhere else to go.

'Only six men from our village dabbled in rebellion,' said Julien quietly. 'The remaining two hundred souls did not, but they were murdered anyway. Thirty of us escaped, mostly old men, women and children. I led them, along with the six Jacques, to Winchelsea, thinking it would be safe.'

'Were the Girards among the six?' asked Bartholomew.

'Only the two men,' replied Julien, then nodded at Delacroix. 'He is another, along with three of his friends.'

Delacroix went pale with fury. 'You damned fool! Now we will *have* to leave. We cannot stay here if the truth is out.'

'Where will you go?' asked Tulyet, obviously hoping it would be soon.

Bartholomew understood why the Sheriff wanted them

gone. First, he had his hands full keeping the peace between University and town, and did not have the time or the resources to protect strangers as well. But second and more importantly, there was a radical minority – Cynric among them – who thought the Jacquerie had been a very good idea, and who would love to hear what Delacroix had to say about social justice and insurrection.

'Delacroix is right,' said Michael gently, when there was no reply to Tulyet's question. 'You cannot stay here – it is too dangerous.'

'You have been dissuading folk from visiting this place with rumours of hauntings and pagan sacrifices,' put in Bartholomew, 'and the "ghostly manifestation" you staged for us was clever, too. But it will not work for much longer. Curiosity will win out over fear, and people will come to see these things for themselves.'

'Especially if Margery Starre sells them protective charms,' added Michael. 'And they feel themselves to be invulnerable.'

Meanwhile, Tulyet was regarding Delacroix appraisingly. 'The Girard men sold themselves as proxies when our King issued his call to arms. Why? It was a needless risk.'

Delacroix shrugged. 'We needed the money – we are running out, and we cannot expect Tangmer to feed us all for nothing.'

'No,' agreed Tangmer fervently; Amphelisa shot him a reproachful glance.

'But they would never have gone to the butts,' continued Delacroix. 'It would have been suicide. They were going to get Tangmer to declare them too mad to venture out.'

Michael drew Bartholomew aside while Tulyet continued to question the two *peregrini*. 'Perhaps you were right – de Wetherset and Heltisle *did* guess that the Girards aimed to cheat them, and killed them for revenge.'

But Bartholomew was no longer sure. 'I do not see the

Chancellor and his deputy scrambling over walls with a tinderbox. Also, de Wetherset told us to give the money to Hélène. If he had been angry enough to kill her kin, he would have demanded it back.'

'Maybe he was salving his guilty conscience,' shrugged Michael. 'He is not entirely without scruples, although I cannot say the same about Heltisle. I say we put them both on our list. Of course, Delacroix is an angry man, so perhaps these murders can be laid at his feet. Look at the bodies now, Matt, and see what they can tell you.'

Unwilling to perform in front of an audience, Bartholomew ordered everyone out. They went reluctantly and stood by the side door, where Tulyet demanded to know what had prompted Delacroix to join the Jacquerie, and Delacroix snarled answers that did nothing to secure his removal from a list of murder suspects.

Bartholomew took a deep breath and began. Four victims were burned beyond recognition, although one was relatively undamaged. He began with him, and immediately made a startling discovery. He considered calling Tulyet and Michael at once, but decided to spare them the sight of what needed to be done next. He worked quickly, and when he had finished, put everything back as he had found it.

He went outside to wash his hands. Even after a vigorous scrub, they still stank of charred flesh, so he splashed them with some of Amphelisa's cedarwood oil. Then he went to where Michael and Tulyet were waiting for him.

'The fire did not kill them,' he began. 'Or rather, it did not kill the adults – the lad died from inhaling smoke. The other four were stabbed.'

'Stabbed?' echoed Michael, startled.

'Death was caused by one or more wounds from a double-edged blade, inflicted from behind,' Bartholomew went on. 'A dagger. If you find the weapon, I may be able to match it to the wounds.'

'But the boy died from the smoke?' asked Tulyet. 'How do you know?' His expression was one of dismay and disgust. 'Please do not tell me that you looked inside him!'

'It was the only way to be sure,' said Bartholomew defensively.

He had long believed that dissection would be a godsend in cases such as this, where answers would otherwise remain elusive, and for years he had itched to put his skills to the test. But now he had formal permission from the University to do it, he found it made him acutely uncomfortable. He was nearly always assailed by the notion that the dead knew what he was doing in the name of justice and did not like it.

'So you found smoke in his innards,' surmised Michael, speaking quickly before Tulyet could further express his disquiet. He was not keen on the dark art of anatomy either, but he certainly appreciated the answers it provided.

Bartholomew nodded. 'There are no other marks on him, so I suspect he was dosed with a soporific – that he went to sleep and never woke up. The same must have happened to Hélène, who is also wound-free. There was smoke in the lungs of one of the women, too – almost certainly the one who passed Hélène to safety.'

'So her injury was superficial?' asked Tulyet.

'No, it was fatal – it punctured her lung. It just did not kill her instantly.'

'Probably Hélène's mother,' mused Tulyet, 'using her dying strength to save her child. It is a pity you failed to rescue her – she could have told us who did this terrible thing before she breathed her last.'

'Does Hélène know?' asked Bartholomew. 'Has anyone spoken to her?'

'I did, and so did Amphelisa, but with no success. I

have asked Amphelisa to persist, but do not expect answers – if you are right about the soporific, Hélène may have slept through the entire thing.'

'Matt's findings explain a good deal,' said Michael. 'Such as why the family did not leave when the shed began to burn. They were either dead, wounded or asleep. The killer must have left the bodies where they would not be spotted by the casual observer.'

At that point, the Spital folk began to edge towards them, keen to learn what had been discovered. Amphelisa was holding Hélène, who drowsed against her shoulder, making Bartholomew suspect that whatever she had been fed the previous day was still working. It meant the dose had been very powerful.

Delacroix's face darkened in anger when Tulyet told them what Bartholomew had found, while Father Julien's hands flew to his mouth in horror. Amphelisa held Hélène a little more tightly, and Tangmer closed his eyes, swaying, so that Eudo and Goda hastened to take his arms lest he swooned.

'Hélène refused to drink her milk today,' whispered Amphelisa, stroking the child's hair, 'because she said yesterday's was sour. So she was right – someone put something in it that changed the taste.'

'Did she say anything else?' asked Tulyet keenly.

'That she did not finish it, so her brother had it instead.' Amphelisa looked away. 'All I hope is that it rendered him unconscious before . . .'

'Does she remember who gave it to her?'

'She collected it from the kitchen, which is never locked, so anyone could have sneaked in to . . .' Tangmer was ashen-faced. 'How could anyone . . . to poison a child's milk!'

'Hélène had a daily routine,' said Julien wretchedly. 'After church, she fetched the milk from the kitchen for herself and her brother, which she took to the shed to drink. Her family liked that shed. They called it their house and treated it as such.'

'Who else knew all this?' asked Michael.

Amphelisa raised her hands in a Gallic shrug. 'Everyone here. However, none of us is responsible for this terrible deed. The staff are all Henry's kin, while the *peregrini* would never hurt each other.'

'There were visitors yesterday,' said Delacroix in a strained voice. His fists were clenched at his sides and he looked dangerous. 'Tell them, Tangmer.'

Tangmer took a deep breath to pull himself together. 'First, Verious the ditcher came to clear a blocked drain, after which the miller delivered flour. Then there were your two new knights, Sheriff, who arrived with tax invoices for me to sign.'

'Do not forget the nuns,' said Delacroix tightly. 'Twenty from Lyminster, plus the one who was deposed for whoring – Sister Alice.'

'I hardly think nuns poison children and burn the bodies,' said Michael coolly. 'Especially ones from my Order.'

Delacroix regarded him with open hatred. 'You would not say that if you had been in France two years ago. The Benedictines were as rabid as anyone in their desire for vengeance against those who baulked at paying crippling taxes to greedy landowners.'

'Do the nuns know your "lunatics" are Jacques, Tangmer?' asked Tulyet before Michael could respond.

'No, because we have taken care to keep them in the dark,' replied Amphelisa. 'Although it has not been easy. Fortunately, they spend most of their day at the *conloquium*, and only come here to sleep.'

'The soporific fed to Hélène must have been uncommonly strong,' mused Bartholomew, examining the child. 'She did not finish her milk, but she is still drowsy. Do you keep such compounds here?'

Amphelisa regarded him warily, knowing what was coming next. 'This is a hospital for people with serious diseases. Of course we have powerful medicines to hand.'

'How easy is it to steal them?'

'They are stored in the balcony, which you have already seen is secure. I keep the only key on a string around my neck.'

'Then can you tell if anything is missing?' asked Michael.

'I could try, although it would entail examining every pot in every crate, and there are dozens of them. It would take a long time.'

'Do not bother,' said Bartholomew. 'The culprit may not have taken a whole jar, just helped himself to what he needed, then disguised the fact by topping it up with water. I doubt you will find answers that way.'

He glanced at Michael and Tulyet, glad it was not *his* responsibility to solve the crime. He did not envy them their task one bit.

It was a grim procession that trudged from the chapel to the remains of the shed. Tangmer was sobbing brokenly, although it was impossible to know whether his distress was for the victims or because their deaths reflected badly on the place he had founded. Amphelisa walked at his side with the sleeping Hélène, her face like stone. Tiny Goda and massive Eudo followed, hand in hand, with the *peregrini* in a tight cluster behind them. Bartholomew, Michael and Tulyet brought up the rear, but hung well back, so they could talk without being overheard.

'I think the Girards were killed by a fellow *peregrinus*,' whispered Tulyet. 'None are strangers to bloodshed and some are Jacques – violent revolutionaries.'

But Bartholomew was uncertain. 'They are alone in the middle of a hostile country. I should think they know better than to fight among themselves.'

'There were thirty of them – now twenty-five – which makes for a sizeable party,' argued Tulyet. 'Differences of opinion will be inevitable. Moreover, living in constant fear of exposure will test even the mildest of tempers, as all will know that the wrong decision may cost the lives of their loved ones. *I* would certainly kill to protect my wife and son.'

'Would you?' asked Bartholomew, rather startled by the confidence.

Tulyet reflected. 'Well, to protect my wife. Dickon can look after himself these days.' He smiled fondly. 'He is in Huntingdon at the moment, delivering dispatches for me. Did I tell you that he is going to France soon? Lady Hereford wrote to say that her knights "can teach him no more". Those were her exact words.'

He swelled with pride, although Bartholomew struggled not to smirk. Lady Hereford had offered to help Dickon make something of himself, but the little hellion had defeated even that redoubtable personage, because Bartholomew was sure her carefully chosen phrase did not mean that Dickon had learned all there was to know. The lad was a lost cause, and Bartholomew was always astonished that Tulyet, usually so shrewd, was blind when it came to his horrible son.

'The strain on these people must be intolerable,' said Michael, prudently changing the subject. 'Delacroix is on a knife-edge, and it would take very little for him to snap.'

'Yet this does not feel like a crime where someone has snapped,' mused Bartholomew. 'It was carefully planned, almost certainly by someone who knew the Girards' liking for a flammable building.'

'I agree,' said Tulyet. 'We should also remember that four people were stabbed and none fought back, which suggests the culprit knew how to disable multiple victims at once. Delacroix and his cronies were active in the violence that was the Jacquerie . . .'

'They certainly top my list of suspects,' said Michael. 'But here we are at the shed, so we shall discuss it later. We do not want them to know what we are thinking quite yet.'

The shed was barely recognisable. It had collapsed in on itself, and comprised nothing but a heap of blackened timber and charred thatch. Amphelisa pointed out the spot where the bodies had been found.

'There were stacks of wood between them and the door,' she explained. 'So the only way Goda could have seen them was if she had gone to the very back of the building and peered behind the pile. That is beyond what could reasonably be expected of her.'

'The place was thick with smoke,' added Goda. 'It was hard to see anything at all.'

Tulyet, Michael and Bartholomew were meticulous, but there was nothing to explain why anyone should have stabbed four people and left them with their sleeping children to burn. Tulyet was thoughtful.

'This reminds me of the first Winchelsea raid,' he said, 'where other families were shut inside a burning building and left to die. It was in a church, and became known as the St Giles' Massacre.'

'But those victims were not stabbed and poisoned first,' Michael pointed out. 'At least here, no one was burned alive.'

'Hélène's mother was,' countered Bartholomew soberly.

Feeling they had done all they could at the Spital, they turned to leave, but as Bartholomew picked his way off the rubble, a charred timber cracked under his foot. He stumbled to one knee, and it was then that he saw something they had missed.

'Here is the weapon that killed the Girards,' he said. 'The blade is distinctive, because it is abnormally wide and thick. Shall we test it against the wounds, to be certain?'

'We believe you,' said Michael hastily, keen to be spared the ordeal.

Bartholomew hesitated. 'There is something else, although I cannot be sure . . .'

'Just tell us,' ordered Tulyet impatiently.

'Bonet the spicer,' said Bartholomew. 'His wounds were unusually wide, too.'

'You think *this* weapon killed him as well?' asked Tulyet sceptically.

'The only way to be sure is to measure his injury against the blade,' replied Bartholomew. 'I can do that, if you like.'

'Bonet was buried today, and we are *not* digging him up,' said Tulyet firmly. 'But what about the scholar who was stabbed – Paris? Could this blade have killed him as well?'

'No,' replied Michael, before Bartholomew could speak, 'because I have that in St Mary the Great. I shall show it to you tomorrow.'

Tulyet turned the dagger over in his hands. 'This is an unusual piece – I have never seen anything quite like it. However, I can tell you that it would have been costly to buy. The hilt is studded with semi-precious stones and the blade is tempered steel.'

He took it to where the Spital's people – staff and *peregrini* – were milling around restlessly. They all craned forward to look, then shook their heads to say none of them had seen it before.

'Ask in the town,' suggested Delacroix tightly. 'Or at the castle – your two new knights are rich enough to afford quality weapons, and they hate the French, too.'

'They do,' acknowledged Tulyet. 'But they are also blissfully ignorant about who is hiding here.'

'Are you sure?' asked Bartholomew in a low voice. 'Tangmer mentioned them coming to deliver tax documents. Perhaps they saw something to raise their suspicions then.'

'They will be questioned,' said Tulyet firmly. 'Along with the miller, Verious and the nuns. It seems our killer has claimed seven French victims, so we must do all in our power to stop him taking an eighth.'

# CHAPTER 6

Bartholomew did not want to investigate seven murders, especially as it was his last term as a scholar, so every day was precious. He tried to slip away, but Michael blocked his path and demanded to know where he thought he was going.

'You cannot need me when you have Dick,' objected Bartholomew. 'Besides, I have no jurisdiction here. It is not University property and no scholar has died.'

'Paris the Plagiarist was a scholar,' said Michael soberly. 'And as I am sure all seven deaths are connected, you *do* have jurisdiction here. Moreover, the Girards were hired as proxies by our Chancellor and his deputy, which is worrisome. You *must* help me find out what is going on.'

Tulyet agreed. 'I should tell you now that de Wetherset and Heltisle are on my list of suspects. It is possible that they found out the Girards had no intention of honouring the arrangement and killed them for it.'

'Much as I dislike Heltisle, I do not see him dispatching children,' said Bartholomew. 'And if de Wetherset cared about the money, he would not have given it all to Hélène.'

'We should not lump the two of them together in this,' said Michael. 'De Wetherset is unlikely to soil his hands with murder – he is an intelligent man, and would devise other ways to punish a deceitful proxy. Heltisle, however, is cold, hard and ambitious. I would not put any low deed past him.'

'I can see why he dispatched the plagiarist – a man who brought our University into disrepute – but why kill the spicer?' asked Bartholomew uncertainly.

'Bonet supplied the University with goods,' shrugged Michael. 'Perhaps there was a disagreement over prices. I know for a fact that Heltisle wants to renegotiate some of our trade deals when the current ones expire.'

'I shall leave de Wetherset and Heltisle to you,' said Tulyet. 'But first, we should speak to the people here – staff, Frenchmen *and* nuns.'

He marched away to organise it, while Bartholomew grumbled about losing valuable teaching time. The monk was unsympathetic.

'You may have no University to resign from unless we find our culprit. It is possible that these murders are a sly blow against us – Paris was a scholar; Bonet sold us spices; and now we have our Chancellor and his deputy's proxies murdered.'

Bartholomew was not sure what to think, but there was no time to argue, as Tulyet was waving for them to join him in the hall. Once inside, all three gazed around in admiration. It was a high-ceilinged room with enormous windows that allowed the sunlight to flood in. The tables and benches were crafted from pale wood, while the floor comprised creamy white flagstones, a combination that rendered it bright, airy and cheerful.

'This is wasted on lepers and lunatics,' muttered Michael. 'Indeed, I could live here myself. It is much nicer than Michaelhouse.'

Tulyet wanted to question the *peregrini* first. They shuffled forward uneasily. All hailed from the wealthier end of village life – craftsmen and merchants who earned comfortable livings, and who had been respected members of the community before war and rebellion had shattered their lives. There were nine children including Hélène, seven women of various ages, five very old men and the four Jacques.

Most questions were answered by Father Julien, with occasional help from a stout woman named Madame

Vipond – the weaver Bartholomew had seen outside. While the two of them spoke, Delacroix and his companions snarled and scowled, so it soon became apparent that the Jacques resented the priest's authority and itched to wrest it from him.

'We had no choice but to leave France,' Julien told Tulyet. 'The barons burned every house in our village, and as I have already said, they murdered all but thirty of our people. None of the dead were Jacques.'

'Because we were away when the barons came,' objected Delacroix, detecting censure. 'How could we defend our village when we were not there?'

'My point exactly,' murmured Julien acidly.

'We chose to resettle in Winchelsea because my husband and I had sold baskets there for years,' said Madame Vipond after a short, uncomfortable silence. 'I knew it well and thought we could rebuild our lives among good and kindly people. We gave money to charitable causes and adopted their ways. We tried to become part of the town.'

'And when the Dauphin's raiders came, my brothers died trying to defend it,' spat Delacroix. 'Then what did those *good and kindly people* do? Accuse us of being spies! So we ran a second time, abandoning all we had built there. We have virtually no money, so it will be difficult to leave here and settle somewhere else. Perhaps you will give us funds, Sheriff.'

'Why would I do that?' asked Tulyet, startled. 'I have my own poor to look after.'

'Because we could stir up trouble if you refuse,' flashed Delacroix. 'You want to stay on our good side, believe me. We—'

'Delacroix, stop!' cried Julien. 'We are not beggars, and we do not make threats.'

'Well, I suppose we have this,' said Delacroix, brandishing a fat purse. 'The money earned by the Girards for being proxies. It will keep the wolf from the door for a while.'

'How does it come to be in *your* possession?' demanded Michael immediately.

Delacroix regarded him evenly. 'I took it from their bodies when we removed them from the shed – for safe-keeping.'

'Give it to Michael,' ordered Julien. 'He will return it to its rightful owners.'

'It is Hélène's now,' said Michael, before Delacroix could refuse and there was more sparring for power. 'Chancellor de Wetherset wants her to have it.'

Unexpectedly, Delacroix's eyes filled with tears at the kindness, while a murmur of appreciation rippled through the others.

'Are you sure?' asked Julien warily. 'He will receive nothing in return except our gratitude.'

'He knows,' said Michael. 'However, the offer was made when he thought Hélène was the child of lunatics. He may reconsider if he learns the truth, so I recommend you stay well away from the town.' He looked hard at the Jacques. 'Especially you.'

'He is right,' agreed Tulyet. 'Tensions are running unusually high at the moment, so you must leave as soon as possible. How soon can it be arranged?'

'We will go today,' sniffed Delacroix. 'We know where we are not wanted.'

'It takes time to prepare twenty-five people for travel when most are either very old or very young,' countered Julien. 'We shall aim for Friday – the day after tomorrow.'

'Very well,' said Tulyet. 'Now tell us about the Girard family. Did you like them?'

'We did,' replied Madame Vipond, although she did not look at the Jacques. 'They were strong and wise, and our lives here will be harder without them.'

'Did you see anything that might help us catch their

killer?' asked Tulyet. 'Or did any of you visit them in the shed yesterday?'

'It was their private place,' explained Julien, 'where they went for time together as a family. They disliked being disturbed.'

'So what happened when the fire began? Who first noticed it?'

'Delacroix saw smoke when he went to the kitchen for bread,' replied Julien. 'He sent Goda to raise the alarm, while he went to see about putting it out. The rest of us stayed well back, so we would not get in the way.'

'Did it cross your minds that the Girards might still be inside?'

'Of course not!' snarled Delacroix. 'The door was open, so we naturally assumed they had left.'

'And Goda seemed certain that it was empty,' elaborated Julien. 'Then Tangmer ordered it shut to contain the blaze – at that point, he still thought we could put it out.'

'Goda,' mused Michael. 'Are you on good terms with her?'

'You think *she* is the killer?' Delacroix laughed derisively. 'The Girards knew how to look after themselves – they would never have been bested by a tiny little woman.'

'Besides, Goda has no reason to harm us,' added Julien, shooting him a glance that warned him to guard his tongue. 'No one here does.'

'What about the dagger?' asked Tulyet, laying it on the table. 'I have scrubbed the soot off it, so examine it again now it is clean. Do you recognise it?'

There was a moment when Bartholomew thought he was playing tricks – that Tulyet had substituted the murder weapon for another in the hope of catching the culprit out – but then he saw the wide blade and the jewelled hilt, both of which gleamed expensively. It was a world apart from the greasy black item he had plucked from the rubble.

'No,' said Julien, peering at it. 'But it is ugly – a thing specifically designed for the taking of life. You should throw it in a midden, Sheriff, where it belongs.'

'I think it is handsome,' stated Delacroix, a predictable response from a warlike man. 'But I have never seen its like before.'

One by one, the other *peregrini* approached to look, but all shook their heads.

'So none of you noticed anything unusual about the shed before the fire?' pressed Michael when they had finished. 'No strangers loitering? No visitors you did not know?'

'Just the ones we have already mentioned,' replied Julien. 'The miller, the ditcher and the two knights from the castle.'

'Plus all those Benedictine nuns,' put in Delacroix, glaring at Michael.

They interviewed the Spital staff next, beginning with Tangmer and Amphelisa, although Bartholomew quickly became distracted when Amphelisa described how she had mended a persistently festering cut on Delacroix's leg. He asked how she had come by such skills.

'From being near Rouen when the Jacquerie struck,' she replied. 'The slaughter was sickening. Delacroix will tell you that the barons were worse, but the truth is that both sides were as bad as each other.'

'Yet you agreed to house him here,' Bartholomew pointed out. 'Him and his five renegade friends.'

'Because Julien begged me to. Besides, the Girards said they wished they had never become involved with the Jacquerie, and I suspect Delacroix and his friends will feel the same way when they are older and wiser.'

Bartholomew was not so sure about that, but she changed the subject then, telling him her views on treating ailments of the mind with pungent herbs. He listened keenly, aware all the while of the scent of oils in her clothes. They made him wonder if he should distil some in Michaelhouse, as there were times when the presence of a lot of active young men, few of whom bothered to wash, drove him outdoors for fresh air. Then he remembered that it would not matter after July, because he would be living with Matilde.

Meanwhile, Michael and Tulyet questioned Tangmer, who seemed smaller and humbler than he had been before he had been caught harbouring Frenchmen.

'I founded this place to atone for my niece's crimes,' he said miserably, 'and to redeem the Tangmer name. But now foul murder is committed here. Will we never be free from sin?'

'Not as long as you shelter dangerous radicals and pass them off as lunatics,' said Tulyet baldly. 'So, what more can you tell us about yesterday?'

'Nothing I have not mentioned already. I *knew* I should have refused these people sanctuary, but Amphelisa . . . well, she is a compassionate woman. Of course, having those nuns here at the same time has been a nightmare. I live in constant fear that one will guess what we are doing and report us.'

He had no more to add, so Tulyet beckoned Eudo forward. The big man approached reluctantly, twisting his hat anxiously in his ham-like hands.

'Where were you when the fire started?' asked Tulyet, watching him fidget and twitch.

'Out,' replied Eudo, furtively enough to make the Sheriff's eyes narrow. 'I arrived home just as the alarm was being raised. I opened the gates then, so we could get water from the stream. We used buckets, you know. They were—'

'"Out" where exactly?' demanded Tulyet, overriding Eudo's clumsy attempt to divert the discussion to safer ground.

124

Eudo would not look at him. 'On private Spital business. I cannot say more.'

'Did you go alone?'

Eudo glanced at Tangmer, who nodded almost imperceptibly. 'Yes, but I cannot—'

'Who did you see on this mysterious excursion?' snapped Tulyet. 'And bear in mind that I am asking for your alibi. If you cannot provide one, I shall draw my own conclusions from all these brazen lies.'

'He is doing it for me,' interposed Tangmer, much to Eudo's obvious relief. 'I sent him to the town to buy some decent ale. You see, Amphelisa makes ours, but . . . well, she has a lot to learn about brewing. I am loath to hurt her feelings, so Eudo gets it for me on the sly.'

'I do,' nodded Eudo. 'But I cannot prove it, because I am careful never to be recognised there. Obviously, we cannot have word getting back to Amphelisa.'

It sounded a peculiar tale to Michael and Tulyet, who pressed Eudo relentlessly in an effort to catch him out. They failed.

'He has just put himself at the top of my list of suspects,' muttered Michael, when they had given up, leaving the big man to escape with relief. 'He is not even very good at prevarication – I have rarely heard such embarrassingly transparent falsehoods.'

'He is third on mine,' said Tulyet. 'After de Wetherset and Heltisle.'

Goda was next. She flounced towards them, resplendent in her handsome kirtle. Her shoes were new, too, and over her hair she wore a delicate net that was studded with beads. She was so tiny that when she sat on the bench, her feet did not touch the floor, so she swung them back and forth like a restless child.

'I was in the kitchen all morning, making bread,' she began. 'Delacroix came to beg some, then left. He was back moments later, jabbering about a fire. I ran outside, and saw smoke seeping through the shed roof.'

'Then what?' asked Michael.

'I yelled the alarm. All the staff dropped what they were doing and raced to put it out. However, I can tell you for a fact that none of them were near the shed when it started – I would have noticed.'

'Obviously, the fire was lit some time before the smoke became thick enough to attract your attention,' said Michael. 'Ergo, how do you know that a member of staff did not set the blaze and then slink away, ready to come running when the alarm was raised?'

'Because I was kneading dough, which is boring, so I spent the whole time gazing through the open door,' she replied promptly. 'I would have seen anyone go to the shed.'

'Yet someone did,' Michael pointed out. 'And we have five dead to prove it.'

'Oh, I saw the *Girards* popping in and out,' said Goda impatiently. 'But no one else. Perhaps they were weary of being persecuted, and decided to kill themselves.'

Michael felt he could come to dislike this arrogantly flippant woman. 'You think they stabbed themselves in the back? I am not even sure that is possible. And even if it is, why not choose an easier way to die?'

Goda shrugged. 'Unless you can find a way to quiz the dead, you may never know. However, I can assure you that no staff member had anything to do with it.'

'What about the *peregrini*?' asked Tulyet. 'There are tensions among them. Were any of them near the shed?'

'Not that I saw. And before you ask, the nuns were in the guesthouse, although they emerged to gawp when the shed began to burn in earnest.'

'Are you sure it was the Girards "popping in and out" of the shed?' asked Tulyet. 'Because someone committed a terrible crime there, and as you claim no one else was in the vicinity and we know the victims did not kill themselves . . .'

'Oh, I see,' she said, nodding. 'One time, it could have been the killer impersonating them. It is possible – the shed is some distance from the kitchen, and I was not watching particularly closely.'

'So, with hindsight, is there anything that struck you as odd?'

Goda shook her head. 'Obviously, this person took care *not* to be suspicious. What would be the point of donning a disguise, if you then go out and give yourself away with attention-catching behaviour?'

Michael fought down his growing antipathy towards her. 'The Spital had several visitors before the fire began. What can you tell us about those?'

'I only saw Sister Alice. She is always pestering our nuns, even though Magistra Katherine has told her that she is not welcome here. Prioress Joan is kinder, but even her patience is wearing thin. Magistra Katherine has the right of it, though: Alice is a thief, so the other nuns should have nothing to do with her.'

'A thief?' echoed Michael warily. 'How do you know?'

'Well, once, when all our nuns were at the *conloquium*, Alice visited the guesthouse while I happened to be cleaning under the bed. Rashly assuming she was alone, she began riffling through their things. I saw her slip a comb up her sleeve and walk off with it.'

Michael was not sure whether to believe her. 'Was it valuable?' he asked warily.

For the first time, Goda considered her answer with care, and he saw that the cost of things mattered to her.

'I would not have paid more than sixpence for it,' she replied eventually. 'I told our nuns when they got back, and it transpired that the comb belonged to Prioress Joan. I thought she would not care, given that she is not a vain woman, but she was very upset.'

'Could Alice have set the fire?' asked Tulyet, while Michael held his breath; he did not want a Benedictine to be the culprit.

'Possibly,' said Goda. 'But we have let no nun get anywhere near the *peregrini*, which would mean she killed five people she never met. That seems unlikely.'

'Look again at the murder weapon,' ordered Tulyet, laying it on the table in front of her. 'Have you seen it before?'

Goda spent far more time than necessary turning it over in her hands. When it became clear that she was more interested in assessing its worth than identifying its owner, Tulyet tried to take it back. There was a tussle when she declined to part with it.

'It is a nice piece,' she said watching covetously as Tulyet returned it to his scrip. 'What will you do with it once your enquiries are over? I doubt you will want to keep it, but I will give you a fair price.'

'I shall bear it in mind,' said Tulyet, taken aback and struggling not to let it show.

'That is a fine new kirtle,' said Michael, wondering if Alice was not the only one with sticky fingers. 'How did you pay for it?'

Goda regarded him coolly. 'By saving my wages. Unlike most people, I do not fritter them away on nothing. Not that my clothes are any of your affair. Now, is that all, or do you have more impertinent questions to put to me?'

'You may go,' said Tulyet coldly. 'For now.'

As time was passing, Tulyet suggested that he finished speaking to the staff on his own, while Bartholomew and Michael tackled the nuns.

'Prioress Joan has just returned from the *conloquium*,' he said, watching her dismount her handsome stallion while her ladies flowed from the guesthouse to welcome her back. Bartholomew recalled that she had left them to pray while she went to give a lecture on plumbing.

'And let us hope one of us has some luck,' sighed Michael, 'because I cannot believe that someone could stab four people, drug two children, set a building alight, and saunter away without being seen.'

The guesthouse was a charming building. Its walls were of honey-coloured stone, it had a red-tiled roof, and someone had planted roses around the door. Most of the windows were open, allowing sunlight to stream in, and the furniture was simple but new and spotlessly clean. All the nuns were there, except one.

'Our Prioress went to settle Dusty in the stables,' explained Magistra Katherine de Lisle. 'She spends more time with him than she does at her devotions.'

Bartholomew studied Katherine with interest. Like her prelate brother, she was tall, haughty, and had a beaky nose and hooded eyes. She was perhaps in her sixth decade, but her skin was smooth and unlined. A smirk played at the corners of her mouth, and he was under the impression that she considered herself superior to everyone else, and thought other people existed only for her to mock. He wondered if arrogance ran in the family, because her brother was also of the opinion that he was the most important thing in the universe.

'Caring for God's creatures is a form of worship,' said Michael, who was known to linger in stables at the expense of his divine offices himself. 'I will fetch her while the rest of you tell Matt about yesterday's tragedy.'

Bartholomew was happy with that, as he had no wish to visit a place where he would meet an animal that would almost certainly dislike him on sight – horses instinctively knew he was wary of them, and even the most docile of nags turned mean-spirited in his presence.

'There are a lot of you,' he remarked when the monk had gone.

'Twenty,' replied Katherine, a faint smile playing about her lips. 'We brought more delegates than any other convent.'

'Why?'

'Because Prioress Joan offered to bring any nun who wanted to travel. Some came for the adventure, others to meet fellow Benedictines, the rest to learn something useful. But *I* was invited personally by the organisers because I am a talented speaker who can preach on a variety of interesting subjects. I am not styled *Magistra* Katherine for nothing, you know.'

She began to list her areas of expertise, although as most pertained to theology, Bartholomew thought she was sadly mistaken to describe them as 'interesting'. Sensing she was losing his attention, she finished by saying that Joan's relaxed rule made for a contented little community of nuns at Lyminster.

While she spoke, the other sisters occupied themselves with strips of leather and pots of oil, filling the room with the sweet scent of linseed. Eschewing such menial work, Katherine picked up a book, clearly aiming to read it the moment Bartholomew left.

'To thank her for bringing us here, we are making new reins for Prioress Joan,' explained one nun, smiling. 'Or rather, for Dusty. He is strong, and is always snapping them.'

'They know the surest way to her heart,' said Katherine, then indicated the tome in her lap. 'Whereas I prefer to study Master Clippesby's treatise. He must be a remarkable man, because I have never encountered such elegant logic.'

'He is a remarkable man,' agreed Bartholomew, hoping they would never meet. The mad Dominican would not be what Katherine expected, and they would almost certainly disappoint each other. 'He has a unique way with animals.'

'Joan would like him then,' said Katherine with a smirk. 'Especially if he is good with horses. But his theories are astonishing. And what an imagination, to use chickens to speak his views.'

Clippesby would argue that the views were the birds' own, but Bartholomew decided not to tell her that. He changed the subject to Alice.

'Yes, the wretched woman did visit shortly before the fire started,' said Katherine. 'She will not leave us alone, despite our efforts to discourage her. You know why, of course.'

'Do I?'

'Because my brother was so shocked by the way she ran Ickleton Priory that he deposed her. Now she aims to avenge herself on him through me. But she will not succeed, because she is not clever enough.'

Unwilling to be dragged into that dispute, Bartholomew returned to the subject of the fire. 'Did you see Alice near the shed? Or talking to the . . . patients, particularly those who died?'

'Not yesterday or any other day,' replied Katherine. 'However, that is not to say she did not do it – just that we never saw her.'

All the nuns denied recognising the murder weapon, too, although Bartholomew had to be content with sketching it on a piece of parchment, as Tulyet had the original.

'We are unlikely to know anything to help you,' said Katherine, clearly impatient to get to her reading, 'because a condition of us staying here is that we keep away from the lunatics. We have obliged, because none of us want to exchange these nice, spacious quarters for a cramped corner in St Radegund's.'

'But you must look out of the windows,' pressed Bartholomew, loath to give up. 'And one faces the shed.'

'It does,' acknowledged Katherine. 'But it is nailed shut, and the glass is too thick to see through. The only ones that open overlook the road.'

Bartholomew saw she was right, and wondered if it was why Alice had rummaged through the nuns' belongings when they were out – no one from inside the Spital could have looked in and seen her, and she would have got away with it, if Goda had not been cleaning under the beds. Assuming Goda was telling the truth, of course.

'Is Joan missing a comb?' he asked.

'Yes,' replied Katherine. 'An ivory one. She was upset about it, as it was the one she used on Dusty's mane. Goda says Alice took it, which Alice denies, of course. If it is true, it will be part of some malicious plot against me or my brother. Her vindictiveness knows no bounds, so if you do arrest her for roasting lunatics, I should be very grateful.'

'Where were you when the blaze began?' asked Bartholomew, and when her eyebrows flew upwards in instant indignation, added quickly, 'Just for elimination purposes.'

Katherine indicated her sisters. 'We were all in here, except for the hour before the fire. At that point, I was in the garden behind the chapel and Joan was in the stables. We predicted that Alice would come, you see, and we aimed to avoid her.'

'Alice *did* come,' put in another nun. 'But she left when we told her that Magistra Katherine and Prioress Joan were unavailable. The rest of us were here until the alarm was raised, at which point Prioress Joan came to take us outside lest a stray spark set this building alight, too.'

Bartholomew regarded Katherine thoughtfully. 'You cannot see the shed from in here, but you can from behind the chapel . . .'

There was a flash of irritation in the hooded eyes. 'Very possibly, but I was engrossed in Clippesby's book and paid no attention to anything else.'

'But you heard the alarm raised,' pressed Bartholomew.

Katherine regarded him steadily. 'I was absorbed, not on another planet. Of course I stopped reading when everyone started shouting and I saw the smoke.'

'So you have no alibi,' said Bartholomew, hoping she would not transpire to be the killer, as the Bishop would be livid.

Katherine gave another of her enigmatic smiles. 'I am afraid not, other than my fervent assurance that high-ranking Benedictine nuns have better things to do than light fires in derelict outbuildings.'

Unfortunately, her fervent assurance was not enough, thought Bartholomew, watching her open the book to tell him that the interview was over.

He was about to leave when Michael walked in with Joan, deep in a conversation about hocks and withers. She was taller than Michael, who was not a small man, and her hands were the size of dinner plates.

'Have you answered all his questions?' she asked of her nuns, jerking a huge thumb in Bartholomew's direction. 'Nice and polite, like I taught you?'

'We have,' replied Katherine, resignedly closing her book again. 'Although he is disturbed by my inability to prove that I did not incinerate an entire family.'

'Katherine often disappears to read on her own,' said Joan. 'Of course, you will probably say that *I* cannot prove my whereabouts either, given that I was with Dusty. Or will you? I understand your Clippesby talks to animals – perhaps he will take Dusty's statement.'

'It is no laughing matter,' said Michael sternly. 'People died in that fire.'

'Yes,' acknowledged Joan, contrite. 'And we shall continue to pray for their souls. However, as it happens, I can do better than Dusty for an alibi. One of the servants – that ridiculously tiny lass – was in the kitchen the whole time. And if I could see her, she must have been able to see me.'

'Goda?' asked Michael. 'So you can vouch for her?'

'I suppose I can,' said Joan. 'I would not normally have

noticed her, but she was wearing yellow, a colour Dusty does not like, and he kept snickering in her direction. She was certainly in the kitchen when the blaze would have started.'

'So, Brother,' drawled Katherine, amused, 'I am your only Lyminster suspect. My brother will be horrified when he learns that you have me in your sights.'

'Then let us hope we find the real culprit before it becomes necessary to tell him,' said Michael, smiling back at her.

'That poor family,' said Joan, sitting heavily on a bed. 'What will happen to their friends now? There cannot be many places willing to hide Frenchmen.'

'You know?' breathed Michael, shocked, while Bartholomew gaped at her. 'But how?'

'We are not fools,' replied Joan softly. 'Tangmer nailed the window shut to prevent us from seeing them, but we have ears – we often hear the children chattering in French.'

'Joan took a few of us to Winchelsea when we heard about the raid,' said Katherine. 'We wanted to help, and the town is only sixty miles from our convent. We arrived five days later, and although we were spared the worst sights, what remained was terrible enough. We heard the rumours about the "spies" who told the Dauphin when best to come. It did not take a genius to put it all together. We know exactly who these folk are.'

'Have you told anyone else?' asked Michael uneasily.

She shot him a withering glare. 'Of course not! These people have a right to sanctuary, just like any Christian soul. I shall not even tell my brother.'

'I hope the murders do not panic them into flight again,' said Joan. 'It will be more dangerous still on the open road, as I imagine the sentiments spoken on Cambridge's streets will be just the same in other towns and villages.'

'We shall include them in our prayers, along with the victims of Winchelsea.' Katherine nodded to her Prioress. 'Joan has already started work on a chantry chapel for those who lost their lives there.'

Joan blushed self-effacingly. 'It is the least we can do,' she mumbled.

'God only knows what led the Dauphin's men to do such dreadful things,' Katherine went on. 'All I can think is that they were possessed by the Devil.'

'I rather think they decided to murder, loot and burn without any prompting from him,' said Joan grimly. 'I trust they will make their peace with God, because *I* cannot find it in my heart to forgive them.'

Katherine touched her arm in a brief gesture of sympathy, and the Prioress turned away quickly to hide her tears, embarrassed to show weakness in front of strangers. Two or three of the younger nuns began to sob.

'Yesterday brought it all back to us,' said Katherine, and for once, there was no smug amusement in her eyes. 'Burned bodies and wounds inflicted in anger . . .'

Joan took a deep breath and dabbed impatiently at her eyes. 'I am more sorry than I can say that we failed to save the family here.'

'You will move to St Radegund's today,' decided Michael. 'The killer may strike again, and the Bishop would never forgive me if anything happened to his sister. Or any nun.'

'I would rather stay here,' said Katherine at once. 'St Radegund's is too noisy.'

'Worse, there will be no decent stabling for Dusty,' put in Joan, clearly of the opinion that his comfort was far more important than that of her nuns.

'I will arrange something for him,' promised Michael. 'He will not suffer, I promise.'

'I cannot see that *we* are in danger,' argued Katherine stubbornly. 'We are not French.'

'We do not know for certain why the Girards were targeted,' said Michael. 'It may have nothing to do with their nationality.'

'Oh, come, Brother,' said Katherine irritably. 'Of course it does! Why else would their children have been dispatched, too? But please do not uproot us now. The *conloquium* will finish in a few days, after which we will be gone.'

'*Five* days,' said Michael promptly. 'Too many to justify the risk. Please do as I ask.'

'Then we shall stay in the Gilbertine Priory instead,' determined Katherine. 'It will put us in Alice's objectionable presence, but that is a small price to pay for a quiet place to read.'

'Alice and Abbess Isabel's flock will be moving to St Radegund's as well,' said Michael. 'So pack your belongings, and I shall arrange for an escort as soon as possible.'

Katherine rolled her eyes, although Joan nodded briskly and ordered her nuns to begin preparations. They did as they were told reluctantly, and it was clear that Katherine was not the only one who resented the loss of their comfort.

'Speaking of Alice,' said Michael, 'did Matt ask you about the comb she took?'

Joan scowled. 'It was Dusty's favourite, and I was vexed when I found it gone. Alice denies it, of course, although Goda has no reason to lie. Doubtless she aims to use it for mischief, so if it does appear in suspicious circumstances, please remember the malice she bears us.'

'The malice she bears *me*,' corrected Katherine. 'It was my brother who deposed her.'

'My head is spinning,' confessed Tulyet, as he, Bartholomew and Michael walked back to the town at the end of the day. 'I need to sit quietly and reflect on all we have been told – although I can confirm that Goda *did* see Joan in

136

the stables, so they have alibis in each other. We can cross them off our list of suspects.'

'Then who remains on it?' asked Michael. 'I would say—'

'Not tonight,' interrupted Tulyet wearily. 'I cannot think straight. We shall discuss it in the morning, by which time I will have questioned the ditcher, the miller and my two knights. Who knows? Perhaps one will confess, and we shall be spared the chore of pawing through all these facts, lies, claims and suppositions.'

'Then meet us in the Brazen George,' said Michael, naming his favourite tavern, a place where he was so regular a visitor that the landlord had set aside a chamber for his exclusive use. 'You are right: our minds will be fresher tomorrow.'

'I am not sure what to do about the *peregrini*,' sighed Tulyet. 'Instinct tells me to set guards, to prevent the surviving Jacques from spreading their poisonous message. But if I do, I may as well yell from the rooftops that the Spital holds a secret.'

Michael agreed. 'We should let Tangmer continue what he has been doing. It will only be for two more days, and then they will be gone. Do not worry about the rebels – Julien has promised to keep them under control.'

'I hope he can be trusted,' said Tulyet worriedly. 'We do not need a popular uprising to add to our troubles. What will you do now, Brother?'

'Matt and I will visit Sister Alice and demand to know why she neglected to mention visiting the Spital before the fire broke out. Then I must arrange for the nuns to move to St Radegund's. After that, there is a rehearsal of the Marian Singers.'

'I do not know them,' said Tulyet politely. 'Are they new?'

'You *do* know them,' countered Bartholomew wryly. 'They were formerly known as the Michaelhouse Choir.

137

However, as even speaking that name causes grown men to weep, Michael has decided to revamp their image.'

The monk's eyes narrowed. He was fiercely defensive of his talentless choristers, and hated any hint that they were less than perfect.

Tulyet laughed. 'You think naming them after the Blessed Virgin will make folk reconsider their opinions?'

'I named them after the church where we practise,' said the monk stiffly. 'St Mary the Great is the only place large enough to hold us all these days.'

Tulyet changed the subject, seeing it would be too easy to tread on sensitive toes. 'Then *you* can speak to the ditcher and the miller. They sing bass, do they not?'

Michael inclined his head. 'But here we are at the Gilbertine Priory, where Sister Alice is staying. She has filched combs, commissioned stinking candles, and foisted her company on people who do not want it, so perhaps the Spital murders are just a case of unbridled spite, and we shall have our killer under lock and key tonight.'

'I do not envy you the task of challenging her, Brother,' said Tulyet. 'I have met her twice: once when she informed me that Abbess Isabel aims to assassinate the King, and once when she claimed that Lyminster Priory cheats on its taxes. When I declined to act on either charge, she called me names I never expected to hear on the lips of a nun.'

The Gilbertine Priory looked pretty in the early evening sunlight, and Bartholomew and Michael arrived to find the hospitable canons fussing over their guests with cordials and plates of little cakes. Alice was not there, but the nuns from Ickleton were, including their saintly Abbess, whose habit was so white it glowed. Needless to say, none were pleased to learn they were to be moved to a place that was already bursting at the seams.

'But why should we go?' demanded Isabel, her voice rather petulant for someone with aspirations of sainthood. 'None of us are French and I like it here.'

'I cannot risk it,' said Michael firmly. 'Please do as I ask.'

'Very well,' sighed Isabel with very ill grace. 'Although it is foolish and unreasonable. However, you must find us a spot well away from Alice. We find her company irksome.'

'Did she mention the Spital fire to you?' asked Michael hopefully. 'I know she went there the morning it happened.'

'In the last forty-eight hours, she has uttered less than a dozen words to me,' replied Isabel tartly, 'none of which should have come from the mouth of a lady. She is so eaten up with bitterness that she is barely sane.'

Bartholomew and Michael went to Alice's room, and found her sitting at a table. She scrabbled to hide what she was doing when she saw them at the door, but Michael swooped forward and discovered that she had made a reasonable imitation of the Bishop's seal and was busily forging letters from him. She was more angry than chagrined at being caught, and began to scratch her shoulder.

'So tell the Bishop about it,' she challenged. 'He has already stripped me of my post and treated me with callous contempt. What more can he do?'

Michael read one of the counterfeit messages and started to laugh. 'Abbess Isabel is unlikely to believe that he wants her to walk naked from the castle to St Mary the Great. Or that she is then to stand in the market square and pray for the French.'

Alice scowled. 'It is not—'

'Just as the Sheriff did not believe that she wants to kill the King,' Michael went on. 'You make a fool of yourself with these ridiculous plots. It is time to stop.'

139

Alice regarded him sullenly. 'Why should I? I am the victim here and—'

'Speaking of victims, we have witnesses who say you were in the Spital when five people died. What do you have to say about that?'

'That I had nothing to do with it. I tried to pay my respects to Magistra Katherine and Prioress Joan, but they were too busy to receive me, so I left – *before* the blaze began. Next, I went to practise my lecture in an empty church, and I arrived at the *conloquium* later that afternoon. I told you all this yesterday.'

'No, you did not,' countered Michael. 'You failed to mention the Spital at all.'

Alice regarded him with dislike. 'It slipped my mind. So what?'

'Can you prove you left before the fire started?' asked Michael, keeping his temper with difficulty. 'Because you were seen arriving at the Spital, but no one mentioned you leaving.'

'Is it my fault that your so-called witnesses are unobservant asses? However, if you want a culprit, look to Magistra Katherine. I imagine she claims she was reading, and thus has no alibi. Am I right?'

'Yes,' acknowledged Michael. 'But—'

'I saw her sneaking around in a very furtive manner,' interrupted Alice. 'So was that hulking Joan, who is too stupid to be a prioress. She is more interested in horses than her convent, and delegates nearly all her own duties to her nuns.'

Bartholomew went to the window, well away from her, partly because her scratching was making him itch, but mostly because he was repelled by her malevolence. Moreover, one of Vice-Chancellor Heltisle's patented metal pens lay on the table, and it was very sharp – he felt Alice was deranged enough to snatch it up and stab him with it.

'Explain why you stole her comb.' Michael raised a hand when Alice started to deny it. 'You were seen.'

Alice struggled to look nonchalant. 'Perhaps I did pick it up, but only to look at – I never took it away. Joan is careless with her things, and probably mislaid it since.'

'Even if that is true, there is no excuse for poking about among other nuns' belongings.'

'I was looking for a nose-cloth, if you must know. Joan always keeps a good supply in her bag.' Alice smiled slyly. 'If you do not believe me about the comb, then search this room right now. You will not find it.'

The offer told them that she had hidden it somewhere they were unlikely to look, so they did not waste their time. Michael continued to bombard her with questions, but she stuck to her story: that she had visited the Spital the previous morning, but left when the nuns declined to receive her. She had seen or heard nothing suspicious near the shed, and was well away before the fire started.

'Your culprit will be Magistra Katherine, Prioress Joan, one of their sanctimonious nuns, or a lunatic,' she finished firmly. 'Not one of them can be trusted. I, however, am entirely innocent.'

They reached the Trumpington Gate, where Cynric was waiting to say that Bartholomew had a long list of patients waiting to see him. Bartholomew was pleased, as most lived some distance from the high street, so he would not be forced to listen to the Marian Singers massacre Michael's beautiful compositions. He visited a potter near the Small Bridges, and was amazed when he could still hear the racket emanating from St Mary the Great.

He took the long way around to his next patients – two elderly Breton scholars from Tyled Hostel, who were more interested in informing him that they had not voted for de Wetherset as Chancellor than explaining why they needed his services. Eventually, it transpired that they were suffering from a plethora of nervous complaints, all resulting from fear that they might be attacked for being French.

His next call took him past the butts. This was bordered by the Franciscan Priory to the north, the Barnwell Gate in the south, the main road to the west and the filthy King's Ditch to the east. It comprised a long, flat field with a mound, like an inverted ditch, at the far end. The mound was the height of a man and was topped with targets – circular boards with coloured rings. A line in the grass marked where the archers stood to shoot.

It was Wednesday, so it was the University's turn to use the ground, and as darkness had fallen, it was lit with torches. Night was not the best time for such an activity, but the daylight hours were too precious – to working men and University teachers – to lose to warfare, so practices had to be held each evening.

The University's sessions were meant to be supervised by the Junior Proctor, but Theophilis had left Beadle Meadowman to write the attendees' names in a ledger and ensure an orderly queue, while he joined the Michaelhouse men at the line. The students were trying to listen to Cynric, but Theophilis kept interrupting, and when they stepped up to the mark, most of their arrows flew wide. Cynric turned and stamped away in disgust.

'That stupid Theophilis!' he hissed as he passed Bartholomew. 'He keeps interfering, and now our boys are worse than when we started. He has undone all my good work.'

'Come and shoot, Matthew,' Theophilis called, his hissing voice distinctly unsettling in the gloom. 'Or you will be marked as absent.'

'I have patients,' Bartholomew called back, pleased to have an excuse.

'And I have documents to read, teaching to prepare, and lecture schedules to organise,' retorted Theophilis.

'But the King issued an edict, and *I* am not so arrogant as to ignore it.'

Inwardly fuming – both at the wasted time and the public rebuke – Bartholomew marched up to the line, grabbed a bow and sent ten arrows flying towards the targets. As he did not aim properly, most went wide, although four hit the mark, showing that he had not forgotten everything he had learned at Poitiers. He handed the weapon back without a word and went on his way, pausing only to ensure that his name was in the register.

He visited two customers near the castle, and was just crossing the Great Bridge on his way home when he met Tulyet hurrying in the opposite direction.

'I have been looking everywhere for you, Matt! Poor old Wyse is dead. Will you look at him? It seems he fell in a ditch and drowned. As it is a Wednesday, he was probably drunk.'

Will Wyse was a familiar figure in Cambridge. He eked a meagre living from selling firewood, and would have starved but for the generosity of the Franciscans, who gave him alms every Wednesday. He always celebrated his weekly windfall by spending exactly one quarter of it on ale in the Griffin tavern.

Tulyet led Bartholomew across the river, then a short way along the Chesterton road, to where the unfortunately named Pierre Sauvage stood guard over Wyse's body. Sauvage handed Bartholomew a lamp, and the physician saw that Wyse had apparently stumbled, so that his head had ended up in the ditch at the side of the road. The rest of the body was dry. Bartholomew knelt to examine it more closely.

'An accident?' asked Tulyet, watching him. 'A fall while he was in his cups?'

'He was murdered,' replied Bartholomew. 'You see that blood on the back of his head? It is where someone hit him from behind. The blow only stunned him, but his assailant dragged him here, dropped him so his face was in the water, and left him to drown.'

Tulyet gaped at him. 'Murdered? But who would want to kill Wyse?'

'Someone who wanted his money,' predicted Sauvage. 'Everyone knows he had some on a Wednesday, and that he always staggered home along this road after the Griffin.'

'But his purse is still on his belt,' countered Tulyet.

'Perhaps the culprit was also drunk,' shrugged Sauvage, 'but sobered up fast and ran away when he realised what he had done.'

Tulyet shook his head in disgust. 'Carry the body to St Giles's, then go to the Griffin and see what his friends can tell you. Perhaps there was a drunken spat. Take Sergeant Orwel – he is good at prising answers from reluctant witnesses.'

'He is at choir practice,' said Sauvage. 'But he should be finished by the time I have taken Wyse to the church. Of course, no townsman did this. We would never risk the wrath of the Franciscans – they were fond of Wyse and will be furious when they find out what has happened to him. It will be the work of a University man.'

Bartholomew blinked. 'What evidence do you have to say such a thing?'

'First, Wyse was old and frail, so posed no threat to a puny book-man,' began Sauvage, suggesting he had given the matter some serious thought while he had been guarding the body. 'Second, the culprit was clever, like all you lot, so he killed his victim in a place where no one would see. And third, scholars hate the sight of blood, which is why Wyse was drowned rather than stabbed.'

'That is not evidence,' said Bartholomew impatiently. 'It is conjecture. There is nothing to suggest that a scholar did this. Indeed, I would say the Sheriff has the right of it, and Wyse died as a result of a disagreement with his friends.'

'Well, you are wrong,' stated Sauvage resolutely. 'You wait and see.'

While Bartholomew visited patients, Michael organised an escort for the nuns, then went to St Mary the Great, his mind full of the music he would teach that evening. There was a *Jubilate* by Tunstede, followed by a *Gloria* he had composed himself, and finally some motets for the next matriculation ceremony. De Wetherset had vetoed the Marian Singers taking part in such an auspicious occasion, but Michael was not about to let a mere Chancellor interfere with his plans, and continued to rehearse so as to be ready for it.

He entered the nave and looked around in astonishment, sure half the town had turned out to sing. He experienced a stab of alarm that there would not be enough post-practice food. As it was, they were obliged to share cups – one between three.

Of course, it was his own fault that the choir had grown so huge. He had always known that some of its members were women, and had never been deceived by the horsehair beards and charcoal moustaches. However, he had recently been rash enough to say there was no reason why a choir should consist solely of men, at which point the disguises were abandoned and women arrived in droves. Feeding everyone was an ever-increasing challenge.

He looked fondly at the many familiar faces. There were a host of beadles, Isnard the bargeman and Verious the ditcher, although Michael was less pleased to see Sergeant Orwel among the throng. Orwel was a hard-bitten, vicious, bad-tempered veteran of Poitiers, who had been the cause of several spats between scholars and townsfolk. Michael had never understood why Tulyet continued to employ him, unless it was for his ability to intimidate.

However, the moment Orwel began to sing, Michael forgot his antipathy: the sergeant transpired to be an unexpectedly pure, clear alto. Outside, passers-by were astounded to hear a haunting quartet, sung by Michael, Orwel, Isnard and Verious.

Afterwards, over the free bread and ale, Michael cornered the witnesses he hoped would have insights into the fire. Unfortunately, the miller had been hurrying to unload his wares lest close proximity to lunatics turned him insane himself, so had noticed nothing useful. Disappointed, Michael went in search of Verious, who he found sitting with Isnard and Orwel.

'Terrible business about the Spital,' said Isnard conversationally. 'We heard forty lunatics were roasted alive.'

Michael marvelled at the power of rumour. 'There were not—'

'It was that dolphin and his rabble,' growled Verious. '*They* did it.'

'What do you mean?' asked Michael worriedly. Had the ditcher guessed the truth when he had been at the Spital and shared the secret with his dubious friends? If so, the *peregrini* would have to leave at once, before hotheads from the town *and* the University organised an assault.

'The dolphin came up the river from the coast,' explained the ditcher darkly. 'Looting and burning as he went. Our soldiers guard the gates, so he dared not invade the town, but the Spital is isolated. The Frenchies saw it and seized their chance. Poor lunatics!'

'I think the Sheriff would have noticed an enemy army rampaging about the countryside,' said Michael drily. 'However, someone burned a shed with six people inside it, and I intend to find the culprit. You were in the Spital yesterday, Verious – did *you* notice anything unusual?'

The ditcher swelled with importance as everyone

looked expectantly at him. 'I saw the lunatics doing what lunatics do – swaying and gibbering.'

'But did you see anyone near the shed?' pressed Michael. 'Or go near it yourself?'

Verious grimaced. 'No, because them Tangmer cousins would not leave me alone. Every time I tried to slip away to have a nose around, one would stop me. It meant I saw nothing very interesting.'

'I spotted two of Tangmer's madmen in the town the day before the fire,' put in Isnard helpfully. 'They were chatting to Sir Leger and Sir Norbert, who addressed one as Master Girard. Was he among the dead?'

Michael nodded, although he hated providing Isnard with information that would almost certainly be repeated in garbled form. There was no point in begging discretion, as this would only lead to even wilder flights of imagination.

'What were they saying?' he asked.

'I could not hear,' came the disappointing reply.

'I could,' growled Orwel. 'Because *I* saw them talking together, too. But I could not tell what lies the lunatics were spinning to our two good knights, because they were speaking French, and I have never befouled my brain by learning that vile tongue.'

'French?' asked Michael, alarmed.

It would be the knights' first language, given that they were part of the ruling elite, but he was appalled that the Girards should have used it with strangers. Had Leger and Norbert guessed the truth and acted on it? If so, it would put Tulyet in an invidious position – he could hardly hang the King's favourites, yet nor could he overlook their crime.

'Here comes Cynric,' said Isnard, glancing up. 'Driven away from the butts again by your interfering Junior Proctor, no doubt. That Theophilis cannot keep his opinions to himself, even though he knows less about archery than a snail.'

147

'I have something to tell you about the Spital, Brother,' announced Cynric grandly. 'We need not worry about the French attacking it again.'

'No?' asked Michael warily. 'Why not?'

'Because I have just been to see Margery Starre, and she says it is now Satan's domain,' explained Cynric. 'And he has put it under his *personal* protection. Anyone assaulting it can expect to be sucked straight down to Hell.'

'Well, then,' said Michael, hoping that would be enough to protect the *peregrini* until they could slip away. 'We had all better keep our distance.'

# CHAPTER 7

By the following morning, everyone knew that Satan had moved into the Spital, and would not welcome uninvited guests. However, while the news encouraged superstitious townsfolk to stay away, it had the opposite effect on those in holy orders.

'The Devil will not tell *me* what I can and cannot do in my own town,' declared Father William indignantly, as he and the other Fellows sat in the conclave after breakfast. 'Who does he think he is?'

'That tale is a lot of nonsense started by Cynric,' said Theophilis in the sinister whisper that Bartholomew was coming to detest. 'I shall be glad when you leave the University and take that heretic with you, Bartholomew. I dislike the fact that he – and you, for that matter – has befriended a witch.'

'Cynric is not a heretic,' objected Bartholomew, although he was aware that the book-bearer was not exactly a true son of the Church either. 'And I am no friend of Margery Starre.'

'Really?' asked Aungel guilelessly. 'Because she always speaks very highly of you. When I collect the cure she makes for my spots, she always says—'

He stopped abruptly, aware that he had not only dropped his former teacher in the mire, but had done himself no favours either. Theophilis was quick to pounce.

'You will not buy her wares again, Aungel,' he ordered sharply. 'And I shall put Bartholomew's association with that woman in my weekly report to the Chancellor.'

'Come to the Spital with me, Theophilis,' said William,

eyes blazing fanatically. 'You and I will send Lucifer packing together.'

'Good idea,' said Theophilis, and turned to Michael. 'And while we are there, I shall investigate the murdered lunatics. *I* am your Junior Proctor, so if anyone helps you solve the mystery, it should be *me*.' He glared pointedly at Bartholomew.

'It is kind of you to offer,' said Michael. 'But I need you to monitor the triumvirate. I say this not for my benefit, but for your own – you will never rise in the University hierarchy if the Chancellor regains too much power, as he will prevent me from promoting you.'

'Of course,' said Theophilis, paling at the awful prospect of political stagnation. 'I shall go to St Mary the Great at once. Meadowman told me that a letter arrived for de Wetherset at dawn, so I should find out who sent it.'

'You should,' agreed Michael. 'It is the time of year when nominations for lucrative sinecures arrive, and it would be a shame if you lose out to someone less deserving.'

Theophilis made for the door at such a lick that he startled the hens that Clippesby was feeding under the table. They scattered in alarm.

'Keep those things away from me,' he snarled, flapping his hands at them. 'They should not be in here anyway – unless they are roasted in butter.'

'You would eat Gertrude?' breathed Clippesby, shocked. 'The nominalist?'

Theophilis forced a smile. 'Of course I would not eat her, Clippesby. I am too fervent an admirer of her philosophy. Forgive me, Gertrude. I spoke out of turn.'

He bowed to the bird and left, leaving Clippesby to smooth ruffled feathers. William watched him go, then went to recruit Aungel for a holy assault on the Spital.

'I do not understand why you trust Theophilis,' said

Bartholomew, once he and Michael were alone. 'He is only interested in furthering his own career, and cares nothing for yours.'

'Almost certainly. However, he also knows that the only way he will succeed is with my support, so he will do anything to keep my approval.' Michael stood and stretched. 'We should go to meet Dick. We have a lot to do today.'

'Have we?' asked Bartholomew without enthusiasm.

Michael nodded. 'Once we have discussed our findings with him, we must speak to Leger and Norbert about their conversation with the Girards. I want to know why they kept an encounter with two murder victims to themselves.'

'It might be wiser to let Dick do that,' said Bartholomew, thinking that while the ruffianly pair might not assault a monk, the same could not be said about a physician. He was no coward, but there was no point in deliberately courting danger.

'You may be right. Next, we shall go to St Mary the Great, where I will show you the blade that killed Paris the Plagiarist. You never saw it, because it got kicked under a stone and Theophilis did not find it until the following day.'

'*Theophilis* found it? And it was missed during the initial search?'

'Yes, but when he showed me where it had fallen, I was not surprised that no one had spotted it sooner. I want you to compare it to the weapon that killed the Girards.'

'The wounds on them and Paris were not the same size,' said Bartholomew. 'I told you that yesterday. Theirs were more akin to Bonet's, but he is buried, so we will never know if he was killed with the weapon we found at the Spital. Incidentally, have you asked where Theophilis was when the fire started?'

Michael's eyes were round with disbelief. 'Lord, Matt!

151

What is it about my poor Junior Proctor that you so dislike? He never says anything nasty about you.'

'Spying is distasteful, but he happily rushed to do it, which says nothing good about him. He spends a lot of time with de Wetherset and Heltisle, and he is ambitious. If they offer him a better deal, he will take it – then it will be *you* who is the subject of his snooping.'

'I shall bear it in mind, although I am sure you are wrong.'

'So *did* you ask where he was when the fire started?'

Michael was growing exasperated. 'Why would Theophilis, a Fellow of Michaelhouse, renowned canon lawyer and possible future Chancellor, stab a few frightened Frenchmen? I have discussed the war with him in the past, and he is of the same opinion as you and me – that the leaders of both sides should bring about a truce before any more blood is spilled.'

'So you have not asked him,' surmised Bartholomew in disgust.

'You *know* where he was – here, in the hall, keeping the peace while William revealed his ignorance of the nominalism–realism dispute.'

Bartholomew raised a triumphant finger. 'No, he was not! Aungel said he left shortly after it started, and did not return for some time – which is why my students were able to savage William so ruthlessly. Theophilis was not here to keep them in line.'

'I forgot – he *did* mention going out,' said Michael. 'Heltisle had a meeting, and refused to reveal who with, so Theophilis followed him. Unfortunately, he lost him by King's Hall, so he returned to his duties here.'

'It is not a very convincing alibi, is it?' said Bartholomew, unimpressed. 'No one can really verify what he was doing.'

'I suspect that is true for half the town, which is why this case will not be easy to solve. But solve it we must, because we cannot rest until this killer is caught. So if you are ready . . .'

Bartholomew nodded to where William was still badgering Aungel to join him in a righteous assault on Satan. 'What about him? We cannot let *him* go anywhere near the Spital, because if he learns who is inside . . .'

'I shall ask him to visit his fellow Franciscans and find out what they know about Wyse. He will enjoy that, as he is always clamouring to be a proctor. By the time he has finished, he will have forgotten all about his holy mission against the Devil.'

Bartholomew hoped Michael was right.

Taverns were off limits to scholars, on the grounds that they tended to be full of ale-sodden townsfolk. In times of peace, Michael turned a blind eye to the occasional infraction, but Paris's murder meant the stricture had to be enforced much more rigidly. Unfortunately, several hostels had flouted the rule the previous night, and there had been drunken fights.

'We have seen trouble in the past,' muttered Michael as he and Bartholomew hurried to their meeting with Tulyet, 'but it is worse this time because everyone is armed.'

He and Bartholomew entered the Brazen George via the back door, where they were less likely to be spotted. The room the landlord always kept ready for him was a pleasant chamber overlooking a yard where hens scratched happily. They reminded Bartholomew of Clippesby's treatise.

'How many copies has Heltisle sold?' he asked. 'Do you know?'

'Enough to build the dogs a veritable palace *and* pay for the conclave windows to be glazed.' Michael shook his head admiringly. 'Clippesby has been stunningly clever – he also added a clause that obliges Heltisle to bear the cost of all these new copies himself. Unless he builds a kennel in the next few days, our Vice-Chancellor will be seriously out of pocket.'

'Then let us hope no one warns him,' said Bartholomew pointedly.

'Theophilis would never betray us. Stop worrying about him, Matt.'

There was no point in arguing. Landlord Lister arrived, so Bartholomew sat at the table and listened as Michael began to order himself some food.

'Bring lots of meat with bread. But no chicken. I am disinclined to eat those these days, lest one transpires to be a nominalist and thus a friend to my Order.'

'You cannot be hungry, Brother,' said Bartholomew disapprovingly. 'You have just devoured a huge meal at College—'

'Unfortunately, I did not,' interrupted Michael stiffly. 'You stuck that dish of peas next to me, which meant I could not reach anything decent. Besides, I was up half the night, and I need sustenance. After choir practice, there were the brawls to quell *and* I had to make sure the nuns from the Spital and the Gilbertine Priory were safely rehoused in St Radegund's.'

'Was there room for them all?'

'Not really, and the *conloquium* is a nuisance, getting in the way of preventing civil unrest, solving Paris's murder and controlling de Wetherset. Or rather, controlling Heltisle and Aynton, as they are where the real problem lies. They have never liked me, and de Wetherset is far too willing to listen to their advice.'

'Heltisle is a menace, but Aynton—'

'Did I tell you that most spats last night were about Wyse?' interrupted Michael, unwilling to hear yet again that the Commissary was harmless. 'You said he was murdered.'

'He *was* murdered. I hope Dick catches the culprit

soon, because he was an inoffensive old sot who would have put up no kind of defence. It was a cowardly attack.'

'The town cries that a scholar killed him, and the University responds with angry denials. Wyse's death may not come under my jurisdiction, but we shall have no peace until the suspect is caught, so I will have to look into the matter. And you will help. Do not look irked, Matt – your town and your University needs you.'

Tulyet arrived a few moments later, looking tired – keeping the King's peace in the rebellious little Fen-edge town was grinding him down, too. He immediately began to complain about de Wetherset, who was in the habit of obsessing over minute details in any agreements the town tried to make with him. Thus negotiations took far longer than when the Senior Proctor had been in charge.

'He never used to be this unreasonable,' he grumbled. 'What is wrong with the man?'

'He just needs a few weeks to assert himself, after which he will be much more amenable,' said Michael soothingly. 'The situation will ease even further once I persuade him to dismiss Heltisle and Aynton.'

Tulyet brightened. 'Will you? Good! I am sure Heltisle encourages de Wetherset to be awkward, although Aynton is a bumbling nonentity whom you should ignore. But you are sensible and accommodating, and I have grown complacent. This new regime is an unpleasant reminder that your University contains some very difficult men.'

'Here is Lister,' said Michael, more interested in what was on the landlord's tray. 'You two may discuss the murders while I eat.'

'I believe we have one killer and seven French victims,' began Bartholomew. 'We may know for certain once we have compared the dagger that killed Paris to the one used on the Girard family. It is a pity Bonet's was stolen, and that he is already buried.'

Tulyet helped himself to a piece of Michael's bread. 'So we have a French-hating killer *and* a rogue who drowns helpless old drunks. Two culprits, not one.'

'Did Sauvage learn anything useful in the Griffin last night?' asked Bartholomew.

'Yes, but only after Sergeant Orwel arrived to help him,' said Tulyet. 'Orwel knows how to get the truth from recalcitrant witnesses. Sauvage does not.'

'And?' asked Michael, his mouth full of cold beef.

'The other patrons *did* see someone watching Wyse with suspicious interest – someone who then followed him outside. Unfortunately, the bastard kept his face hidden. However, his cloak was of good quality, and his boots were better still.'

'Really?' asked Michael. 'The Griffin does not usually attract well-dressed patrons.'

'These witnesses also saw this man take a book out of his scrip, and they noticed his inky fingers,' Tulyet went on. 'Two things that "prove" the culprit is a scholar. It is what ignited the trouble between us and your students last night.'

'*Did* he read and have inky fingers?' asked Bartholomew. 'Or did these so-called witnesses make it up?'

'I suspect he did, as too many of them gave identical testimony for it to be fiction. Of course, some townsmen can read . . .'

'And are clever enough to know who will be blamed if books and inky hands are flashed around,' finished Michael. 'It could be a ruse to lead us astray. Now, what about the Spital deaths? Summarise what we know about those while I nibble at this pork.'

'The Girard family considered the shed to be theirs,' began Tulyet, 'which I suspect created friction, as petty things matter to folk under strain.'

'We saw for ourselves that there are two distinct factions among the *peregrini*,' added Bartholomew. 'The majority side with Father Julien, but the Jacques follow Delacroix.'

'The Jacques,' muttered Tulyet. 'Members of a violent uprising that destabilised an entire country. I am not happy with such men near my town.'

'No,' agreed Michael, dabbing his greasy lips with a piece of linen. 'But take comfort from the fact that there are only four of them – hopefully too few to be a problem.'

Tulyet looked as if he disagreed, but did not argue, and only returned to analysing the murders. 'Hélène collected milk from the kitchen, then joined her family in the shed. There, she found the milk had a peculiar taste and refused to drink most of it, which saved her life. Shortly afterwards, the adults had been stabbed and the fire started.'

'Has Hélène recalled anything new?' asked Bartholomew.

'Unfortunately not,' replied Tulyet. 'She just remembers feeling sleepy.'

Bartholomew thought about the milk. 'The soporific must have been added in the kitchen. Does that mean the culprit is a member of staff? No one else can get in there.'

Tulyet grimaced. 'If only that were true! Last night, I broke in with ease. Then I entered the kitchen, refectory and dormitory without being challenged once. I was obliged to teach the Tangmers how to implement some basic security measures.'

'But the Girards were killed in broad daylight,' argued Bartholomew. 'It is one thing to sneak in under cover of darkness, but another altogether to do it during the day.'

'Unfortunately, the layout of the Spital offers plenty of cover for a competent invader,' countered Tulyet. 'Ergo, the culprit might well hail from outside.'

'Suspects,' said Michael briskly. 'First, the *peregrini*.'

'They are high on my list, too,' said Tulyet. 'Especially as I have learned that they arrived in the area two days before Paris was stabbed. Now, the Girards were no angels – they were territorial over the shed, they took money with no intention of honouring agreements, and two were Jacques. Meanwhile, Delacroix is angry, bitter and violent – perhaps the Girards quarrelled with him.'

'Or Father Julien did,' said Michael. 'I like the man, but perhaps he decided that dispatching one awkward, divisive family was the best way to save the rest.'

'What about the Spital staff?' asked Bartholomew. 'Little Goda is in the clear, because Prioress Joan saw her in the kitchen when the fire was set. The two of them can have no more than a passing acquaintance, so there is no reason to think they are lying for each other.'

'My clerks cross-checked my notes about who was with whom when,' said Tulyet. 'And it transpires that every member of staff has at least two others to vouch for him except Tangmer, his wife and Eudo. Eudo and Tangmer *say* they were together, but their accounts are contradictory.'

'So they lied,' mused Michael. 'Interesting.'

'Very. Amphelisa was alone in her workshop, and I am inclined to believe her because of the way she cares for Hélène – you do not try to kill a child, then adopt her as your own. Moreover, she is the one who agreed to house the *peregrini* in the first place, very much against her husband's better judgement.'

'Then there is Magistra Katherine,' Bartholomew went on. 'She was reading behind the chapel, so she has no alibi either.'

'I cannot see the Bishop's sister dispatching a family of strangers,' said Michael.

'Why not?' asked Bartholomew. 'Her brother sanctions murder.'

'I hardly think it is something that runs in a family,' retorted Michael stiffly. 'A more likely suspect is that spiteful Sister Alice, who went a-visiting at the salient time.'

'Then we have an entire town that hates the French,' added Tulyet. 'I know no one is supposed to know that the Spital is full of them, but these secrets have a way of leaking out. What did the ditcher and the miller tell you, Brother? Could either of them be the killer?'

'No,' said Michael with conviction. 'Neither is clever enough to have devised such an audacious plan, and nor would they kill children with poisoned milk. Furthermore, they are not observant, and would never have identified the "lunatics" as French.'

'Sir Leger and Sir Norbert might have done, though,' mused Bartholomew. 'And Isnard and Sergeant Orwel did see them talking to the Girards.'

Tulyet grimaced. 'My new knights hate the French, and if the Girards gave themselves away . . . But let us not forget that de Wetherset and Heltisle hired the Girards as proxies.'

'I wonder if Theophilis was there when that happened,' said Bartholomew reflectively, 'perhaps spying on them for you, Brother.'

'If Theophilis had the slightest inkling that Frenchmen were posing as lunatics, he would have told me,' said Michael firmly. 'However, Aynton would not – *he* cannot be trusted at all.' He scowled when Bartholomew began to object. 'If you insist on including Theophilis, then I insist on including Aynton.'

Bartholomew raised his hands in surrender. 'Although neither of us really thinks de Wetherset and Heltisle are the kind of men to poison children.'

'*I* would not put it past them,' countered Tulyet. 'It would not be the first time seemingly respectable scholars resorted to abhorrent tactics to get their own way.'

'So where does that leave our list?' asked Michael. 'Summarise it for me.'

'The *peregrini*, specifically Julien and the Jacques,' began Tulyet. 'Amphelisa, Tangmer and Eudo from the Spital;

Magistra Katherine and Sister Alice from the Benedictine Order; Leger and Norbert from the castle; and de Wetherset, Heltisle, Aynton and Theophilis from the University.'

'And a lot of dim-witted townsfolk and students who think we are about to be invaded by the Dauphin,' added Michael. 'Although we all have reservations about Amphelisa being the culprit, while I sincerely doubt de Wetherset and Theophilis are involved, and Matt thinks Aynton is as pure as driven snow.'

'So how do we set about finding the culprit?' asked Bartholomew.

'You tackle the scholars and the nuns,' replied Tulyet, 'while I concentrate on the townsfolk. We shall share the suspects at the Spital.'

'And your knights?' asked Michael. 'Will you take them, too?'

'No – we shall do that together.' Tulyet winced. 'Their military service has turned them into French-hating fanatics. They also know how to break into buildings and set fires. It is entirely possible that one of them – Leger, most likely – guessed what the Spital is hiding.'

Michael stood abruptly. 'Come with us to look at the knife that killed Paris, Dick. You know weapons better than we do.'

On their way out of the Brazen George, a message arrived for Michael. It was from Heltisle, and ordered him to report to St Mary the Great immediately. The monk read it once, then again to be sure. When he had finished, he screwed it into a ball and flung it on the ground.

'How dare he summon me!' he fumed. 'I have enough to do, without being sent hither and thither at the whim of a man whose appointment I did not sanction.'

'You are on your way there anyway,' said Tulyet pragmatically. 'And he might have something important to tell you. If not, it can be your pretext for ignoring him next time.'

'There will not be a next time! And I am glad you two will be with me – it means that if I feel compelled to punch him, one can drag me off while the other sets his broken nose.'

Tulyet backed away. 'I rather think this is a confrontation that an outsider should not witness. Go and do your punching and meet me by the Great Bridge in an hour. Bring the knife that killed Paris. In the interim, I will start questioning townsfolk about the fire.'

He hurried away, and Bartholomew and Michael stepped on to the high street just as Aynton was passing. The Vice-Chancellor beamed amiably and fell into step beside them, so Michael used the opportunity for an impromptu interrogation.

'Where were you when the Spital fire started?' he asked, cutting into the Commissary's rambling account of a brawl he had witnessed the previous night.

Aynton blinked his surprise. 'Me? Why?'

'Because I should like to know,' replied Michael coolly.

Aynton gave a little laugh. 'I am afraid I cannot tell you *precisely*, because I do not know *precisely* when the fire began. However, I was probably in St Mary the Great with de Wetherset and Heltisle. Oh, and Theophilis, who was spying on us, as is his wont. Can you not find him anything more respectable to do, Brother?'

'You were there all morning?' asked Michael, irked to learn that his Junior Proctor was compromised, although Bartholomew wondered if Theophilis had done it on purpose, to let the triumvirate know whose side he was really on.

Aynton continued to grin amiably. 'Yes, other than the time I went out. I shall pontificate on the Chicken Debate later this month, so I take every opportunity to practise.

161

I go to the Barnwell Fields, where I can speak as loudly as I like without disturbing anyone.'

Michael stifled a sigh of exasperation. 'So you were alone for part of the time?'

Aynton raised his eyebrows. 'I was, although I hope you do not suspect *me* of the crime.' He chortled at the notion. 'Perhaps Clippesby will ask the sheep to give me an alibi. Would that suffice?'

'Not really,' said Michael coldly. 'Because it transpires that you knew two of the victims – they were the proxies hired by de Wetherset and Heltisle.'

'I did not *know* them,' argued Aynton pedantically. 'I met them twice. All I can tell you is that they had shifty eyes and looked around constantly, as if they feared an attack. So, now I have proved that my acquaintance with them was superficial, you can cross my name off your list of suspects. Eh?'

He gave a cheery wave and sailed away. Michael watched him go with narrowed eyes.

'If that was not the response of a guilty man, I do not know what is. How dare he claim he was in a field talking to sheep and expect me to believe it!'

'Perhaps it was the truth,' said Bartholomew. 'He has always been eccentric.'

They entered St Mary the Great, and headed for Michael's sumptuous office. Theophilis was in it, riffling through the documents on the desk.

'What are you doing?' demanded Bartholomew, indignant on Michael's behalf.

Theophilis regarded him with an expression that was difficult to read. 'Looking for next week's theology lecture schedule,' he replied smoothly. 'Father William assures me that he is on it. I hope he is not, because I refuse to listen to him again.'

Michael sighed. 'He has used this tactic to win a slot before, and it occasionally works. Tell him the programme is full. Or better yet, suggest he delivers his tirade to his fellow Franciscans. They are less likely to lynch him, and it will still satisfy his desire to be heard.'

Theophilis inclined his head and slithered away to do the monk's bidding.

Bartholomew picked up the document on the top of the pile. 'Here is the schedule. I wonder why he felt the need to rummage when what he wanted was in plain sight.'

'He could not see the wood for the trees, I suppose,' shrugged Michael. 'But do not worry about him prying. I keep nothing sensitive here – not as long as the likes of Aynton and Heltisle are at large. Now where did I put that dagger? Hah! Here it is.'

The weapon was a handsome thing, one its owner would surely be sorry to lose. It was also distinctive, with a jewelled handle of an unusual shape and a blade of tempered steel.

'It is not the same as the one that killed the Girards,' said Bartholomew, turning it over in his hands. 'The blade is longer and thinner. However, the design is almost identical, and it would not surprise me to learn that they came from the same place.'

'You mean the same forge?'

'No, I mean the same geographical region. Have you seen Cynric's knives? They look alike, because they were all made in Wales. But I am no expert – Dick will tell you more.'

Michael put the weapon in his scrip. 'We shall do it as soon as I find out why Heltisle feels the need to flex muscles he does not have. And while we are there, we shall ask him where *he* was when his proxy was stabbed and incinerated.'

De Wetherset was in his poky office, assessing applications from prospective students. Bartholomew was impressed to note that each was given meticulous attention before a decision was made – Suttone had delegated the entire process to his clerks, while the Chancellor before that had only read the first line. His iron-grey hair was perfectly groomed, and he exuded authority and efficiency.

Heltisle was behind him, leaning over his shoulder to whisper. His clothes would not have looked out of place at Court – he had abandoned his College livery in favour of a purple mantle that any baron would have envied, while his hat was trimmed with fur. He oozed a sense of wealth and entitlement – just the attitude that townsfolk found so aggravating.

His shifty blush when Michael and Bartholomew walked in made it clear that he had been talking about them. As he straightened, a strand of his hair snagged on the pilgrim badge in de Wetherset's hat. De Wetherset sighed and fidgeted impatiently while Heltisle struggled to free himself, and the process was complicated further still when the Chancellor jerked away suddenly and caught his hand on one of his deputy's metal pens. The resulting cut was insignificant, but de Wetherset made a terrible fuss, obliging Bartholomew to provide a salve.

'Why did you want me, Vice-Chancellor?' asked Michael, when the kerfuffle was finally over. 'Please state your case quickly. I am a busy man.'

Heltisle eyed him coldly. 'Why are you still involved in the Spital affair?'

'The Spital *murders*. And of course I am still involved. Why would I not be?'

'Because it is not University property and the victims were not scholars,' replied Heltisle. 'Ergo, it is not our concern. Moreover, the place is said to be under Lucifer's personal control, and we cannot be associated with that sort of thing.'

'Superstitious nonsense,' declared Michael. 'And the

164

murders *are* my concern, because they were almost certainly committed by the same rogue who killed Paris, who *was* a scholar. Moreover, you hired two of the victims to train at the butts on your behalf. Surely you want to know who deprived you of your proxies?'

'Not really,' sighed de Wetherset. 'It will not bring them back, poor souls. Did you arrange for our money to be given to the orphaned child, by the way? You must let us know if we can do anything else to help her.'

'There is, as a matter of fact,' said Michael. 'You can answer a question: where were you both on Wednesday morning?'

De Wetherset's eyes widened with shock. 'Surely you cannot think we had anything to do with these deaths?'

'He does,' growled Heltisle, tight-lipped with anger. 'And it is a gross slur on our character. You should dismiss him at once for his—'

'No, Heltisle,' interrupted de Wetherset, raising a hand to stop him. 'Michael is right – we had a connection to the victims, so of course we must account for our where-abouts.' He turned back to Michael. 'We were in here, working.'

'Just the two of you?' asked Bartholomew, enjoying the way that Heltisle bristled at the indignity of being inter-rogated like a criminal.

'Aynton was here for a while,' said de Wetherset. 'But then he went out, probably to practise a lecture he intends to give.'

'Can anyone confirm it?'

'No,' replied Heltisle, barely able to speak through his clenched teeth. 'The door was closed, because we were engaged in *confidential* University business, and it was necessary to thwart eavesdroppers.'

The look he gave Michael suggested that Theophilis's usefulness as a spy was well and truly over.

'But it does not matter, because Heltisle and I have

alibis in each other,' said de Wetherset. 'That is what alibis are, is it not – one person proving that another is entirely innocent?'

Michael nodded. 'Although we prefer independent witnesses, rather than friends who owe each other their loyalty. But if that is all you have, we shall have to make the best of it.'

'You were ensconced in here together all morning?' pressed Bartholomew, suspicious of Heltisle's aggressively defensive answers.

'Yes,' said Heltisle shortly.

'No,' said de Wetherset at the same time. He gave his Vice-Chancellor an exasperated glance. 'You know we were not – you went out to buy parchment and you were gone for quite a while.'

'Because there was a long queue in the shop,' said Heltisle, struggling to mask his annoyance at the revelation. 'Then I had an errand to run for my College.'

'But I stayed here, and I am sure some clerk or other will confirm it,' said de Wetherset rather carelessly. 'Just ask around.'

'Your theory is wrong anyway, Brother,' said Heltisle, launching an attack to mask his discomfiture. 'Paris and the others were *not* dispatched by the same hand. How could they be when there is no connection between them? No wonder you have failed to catch the killer – you cannot see the obvious.'

'I am afraid I agree, Brother,' said de Wetherset apologetically. 'Your premise is indeed flawed.' Then he grimaced. 'We were too lenient with Paris. Plagiarism is a terrible crime, and we should have made an example of him, to prevent others from following suit.'

'Quite right,' nodded Heltisle. 'The next culprit should be hanged.'

'Unfortunately, plagiarism is not a capital offence,' said de Wetherset ruefully. 'Much as we might wish it were

166

otherwise. There is nothing more vile than stealing an idea and passing it off as one's own.'

'But as it happens, you no longer need concern yourself with Paris,' Heltisle went on, smugness restored. 'As you have failed to catch his killer, Aynton will investigate instead.'

'Impossible!' snapped Michael. 'Only proctors have the authority to—'

'We have amended the statues to say that he can,' interrupted Heltisle, positively overflowing with spiteful glee. 'Aynton will succeed where you have let us down.'

'I am sorry, Brother,' said de Wetherset; he sounded sincere. 'But I feel the case requires fresh eyes. The unsolved murder of a scholar is causing friction with the town, and we need answers before it becomes even more problematic. I hope you understand.'

'Aynton mentioned nothing of this when we met him just now,' said Michael stiffly.

'Perhaps it slipped his mind,' said de Wetherset charitably, although Bartholomew suspected that the Commissary's courage had failed him and he had opted to let someone else break the news. 'But look on the bright side: it will leave you more time for your peacekeeping duties.'

'I have ideas about how to improve your performance there, too,' said Heltisle, before Michael could respond. 'For a start, you can order Tulyet to impose a curfew on all townsfolk. If they are indoors, our scholars can wander about where they please without fear of assault, and the town will be a much nicer place.'

'I hardly think—' began Bartholomew, shocked.

Heltisle cut across him. 'However, this curfew is the *only* matter on which you may converse with him. For all other business, you must refer him to us. The University has made far too many concessions over the last decade, and it is time to seize back the rights that you have allowed him to leech away.'

'Then thank you very much,' said Michael with a sudden, radiant smile. 'It will be a great relief to lose that particular burden. You are most kind.'

'Am I?' said Heltisle, smugness slipping. 'I thought you would object.'

'Oh, no,' replied Michael airily. 'I am delighted. After all, why should *I* be blamed when the town takes umbrage at all these harsh new policies, and takes revenge by placing the instigators' severed heads on a pike?'

Heltisle paled. 'Severed heads?'

'I have been walking a tightrope with the town for years,' said Michael, continuing to beam. 'So I am most grateful to pass the responsibility to someone else.'

Heltisle was so angry that Bartholomew edged towards the door, afraid the Vice-Chancellor might fly at them with one of his sharp metal pens. De Wetherset swallowed hard, and glared accusingly at his Vice-Chancellor.

'Perhaps this is not the best time to—'

Michael went on happily. 'But now the onus of dealing with the town lies with you, it should be *you* who informs the Sheriff about the curfew you want. Good luck with that! However, you might want to exempt bakers, or our scholars will have no bread to break their fast. And brewers who need to tend our ale. And dairymaids who—'

'We do not need you to tell us what to do,' snapped Heltisle, struggling to hide his dismay when he realised his solution would be impossible to implement.

'Yet the town *must* learn that we are not to be trifled with,' said de Wetherset thoughtfully. 'So we shall put on a good show at the butts tonight. Then they will see we are a force to be reckoned with, militarily speaking.'

'Not tonight, Chancellor,' Michael reminded him. 'It is the town's turn to practise.'

'I know that,' said de Wetherset. 'It is the point – they cannot witness our superior skills unless they see us in action, and the only way to do that is by joining them.'

'That would be a serious mistake,' warned Bartholomew. 'We cannot have armed scholars and armed townsfolk in the same place. It would be begging for trouble!'

'How dare you argue with the Chancellor!' snapped Heltisle, then glowered at Michael. 'Moreover, this would not be an issue if *you* had secured the University a good bargain at the butts. I shall summon Tulyet here later, with a view to renegotiating.'

'You can try,' said Michael, 'although I doubt he will respond to messages ordering him to report to you. Besides, the butts are town property, and he lets us use them out of the goodness of his heart. Be wary of unreasonable demands.'

'I know what I am doing,' retorted Heltisle tightly, not about to lose another battle to Michael's greater understanding of the situation. 'And I will prevail.'

'Incidentally, Heltisle has hired another half-dozen beadles for you, Brother,' said de Wetherset with a conciliatory smile. 'Do not worry about the cost, as we shall pay for them with the funds set aside for sick scholars.'

Bartholomew was shocked and angry in equal measure. 'And what happens to students who fall ill or suffer some debilitating accident? How will they survive until they are back on their feet again?'

'Their friends will have to bear the burden,' replied de Wetherset, and turned back to Michael before Bartholomew could remonstrate further. 'Increasing our little army will show the town that we are not to be bullied. You can teach them their trade, and Bartholomew can help you.'

'Me?' blurted Bartholomew. 'But I have classes to take.'

'If that were true, you would be lecturing now,' sneered Heltisle. 'But you are here, so they cannot be that important. Besides, you only teach medicine, which is a poor second to theology and law.'

'I am training physicians,' said Bartholomew indignantly.

'Who will be a lot more useful than theologians or lawyers when the plague returns.'

'They were not very useful last time,' retorted Heltisle. 'At least lawyers could make wills, while theologians knew how to pray. Besides, I do not believe the Death will return.'

'I do,' said de Wetherset, and crossed himself. 'So did Suttone, which is why he left us.'

'Is it?' asked Heltisle slyly. 'Or was there another reason?'

Bartholomew's eyes narrowed. 'What are you saying?'

Heltisle smirked. 'My lips are sealed. You must find another source of gossip.'

'Ignore him, Matt,' said Michael, once they were outside. 'It is not the first time Heltisle has hinted that Suttone resigned for unsavoury reasons of his own. But it is a lie – a shameful attempt to hurt someone who is not here to defend himself. He aims to besmirch Michaelhouse and unsettle us at the same time.'

'I wish de Wetherset had not appointed him,' said Bartholomew unhappily. 'The power seems to have driven him mad, and all he cares about is besting you. And to be frank, I am not sure de Wetherset is much better. How dare he raid the funds reserved for the sick and poor! It is an outrage! Moreover, it is sheer lunacy to alienate Dick.'

'It is, and de Wetherset knows it. However, he was elected on a promise to stand up to the town, so that is what he is doing. He will posture and strut to show the University gaining the upper hand, but once he has won a few battles, he will settle down.'

Bartholomew hoped he was right, and that irreparable harm was not done in the process. 'What will you do now?' he asked. 'Leave the murders to Aynton and concentrate on training these new beadles?'

Michael regarded him askance. 'Of course not! I shall

continue to do my duty as I see fit, and Meadowman can lick Heltisle's men into shape. We shall speak to Leger and Norbert with Dick, as planned, then make enquiries about the triumvirate, and find out what they were really doing on Wednesday.'

'You do not believe what they told you?'

'I do not believe anything without proof, and I am suspicious of their need to shut themselves up together. I suspect they were just plotting against me, but we should find out for certain.'

They reached the Great Bridge, where Tulyet was waiting, angry because Sergeant Orwel had reported that Leger and Norbert had taken themselves off hunting and were not expected back until the following day.

'It is our turn at the butts tonight, and they are supposed to supervise,' he said between gritted teeth. 'I suppose this is their revenge for me refusing to let them do it yesterday.'

'You think you have troubles,' sighed Michael, and told him about his confrontation with the Chancellor and his deputy.

Tulyet grimaced. 'Their antics are absurd, but I will not allow them to destroy all we have built. I shall find an excuse to avoid them until they no longer feel compelled to challenge me at every turn. Now, what about the knife that killed Paris? Do you have it?'

Michael handed it to him. 'Matt says there are similarities to the one that claimed the Girards' lives. What do you think?'

Tulyet examined it carefully. 'He is right. I would bet my life on the hilts being made in the same area, while the blades are crafted from steel of matching quality. However, I have never seen their like manufactured in this country.'

Bartholomew stared at him. 'Could they be French?'

Tulyet shrugged. 'It would be my guess, but I cannot

171

be certain. Perhaps Leger and Norbert will know. They were a-slaughtering there until recently.'

'Leger is not stupid enough to admit to anything incriminating,' predicted Bartholomew. 'Norbert, on the other hand . . .'

'Of course, my two knights are not the only ones with French connections,' said Tulyet. 'Do not forget that the *peregrini* hail from there.'

They agreed what each would do for the rest of the day: Tulyet to see what more could be learned about Wyse's killer, and Michael and Bartholomew to re-question everyone on their list of suspects. Tulyet would show the blade that had killed the Girards around, and Michael would do the same with the one found at the scene of Paris's murder.

'Good hunting,' said Tulyet, as he strode away.

The first thing Bartholomew and Michael did was return to St Mary the Great to ask if any clerks or secretaries could confirm the triumvirate's alibis. None could, but someone suggested they ask a Dominican friar who had been near de Wetherset's office at the time in question, repairing a wall painting. Bartholomew and Michael hurried to his priory at once, only to learn that the artist had been absorbed in his work and had not noticed the triumvirate's comings and goings at all.

As they passed back through the Barnwell Gate, they met a group of thirty or so nuns who had played truant from the *conloquium*, brazenly flouting Michael's order for them to stay at St Radegund's. The working sessions that day were aimed at sisters who struggled to balance the books, which was dull for those for whom arithmetic was not a problem. Ergo, a few of the more numerate delegates had organised a jaunt to the town – a foray to the market to shop for bargains, followed by a guided tour of the Round Church.

Leading the little cavalcade was Joan, wheeling Dusty around in a series of intricate manoeuvres that drew admiring glances from those who appreciated fine horsemanship. She looked more like a warrior than a nun, with her powerful legs clad in thick leather riding boots, and her monastic wimple covered by a functional hooded cloak. Her delight in the exercise was obvious from the glee on her long, horsey face.

Behind her was Magistra Katherine, clinging to the pommel of her saddle for dear life, although her mount was a steady beast with a dainty gait. Like its rider, it seemed to regard those around it as very inferior specimens, and it carried itself with a haughty dignity.

Abbess Isabel was astride her donkey, and Bartholomew nearly laughed when he saw that someone had dusted it with chalk to make it match its owner's snowy habit. She rode with her hands clasped in prayer, eyes lifted to the skies, and looked so saintly that people ran up to beg her blessing. Katherine smirked sardonically at the spectacle.

At the end of the procession was Sister Alice, although as her dubious accounting skills were what had led the Bishop to investigate her priory in the first place, she was someone who might have benefited from lessons in fiscal management. She was scowling at the other nuns, her expression so venomous that those who were asking for Abbess Isabel's prayers crossed themselves uneasily.

The ladies had evidently found much to please them at the market, as they had hired a cart to tote their purchases back to St Radegund's. It was driven by Isnard, while Orwel walked behind it to make sure nothing fell off. The boxes were perfectly stable, but the sergeant steadied them constantly, at the same time contriving to slip a hand inside them to assess whether they held anything worth stealing.

'The offer still stands, Brother,' called Joan. 'You may borrow Dusty here whenever you please. The roads make for excellent riding at the moment, as they are hard and dry.'

'It is tempting to gallop away, and let de Wetherset and Heltisle run the University for a week,' sighed Michael, 'by which time everyone will be frantic for me to return. But I know where my duty lies.'

'Are you still exploring the Spital murders?' asked Katherine, struggling to keep her seat as her proud horse decided it could do better than Dusty and began to prance.

'The Chancellor has asked Commissary Aynton to do it instead,' replied Michael, artfully avoiding the question.

'Then perhaps you will do us the honour of joining the *conloquium*,' said Katherine. 'Not today – you will learn nothing from watching Eve Wastenys struggle to teach the arithmetically challenged – but tomorrow, when we discuss the Chicken Debate. You will discover that female theologians have some very intelligent points to make.'

'Some of them do,' muttered Joan, and glared at Alice, who had baulked at exchanging pleasantries with the Senior Proctor and had ridden on ahead. 'But other nuns' tongues are so thick with poison that it is best not to listen to anything they say.'

Katherine hastened to elaborate. 'Last night, Sister Alice announced to the entire gathering that Lyminster reeks of horse manure and should be suppressed.'

'Her venom towards us springs purely from the fact that Magistra Katherine is the Bishop's sister,' said Joan in disgust. 'Even though Katherine had nothing to do with the decision to depose her. This malevolence is grossly and unjustly misplaced.'

'I will speak to her,' promised Michael. 'You are right to be vexed: her behaviour is hardly commensurate with a Benedictine. Incidentally, Goda has confirmed your alibi for the fire – she says she saw you in the stables.'

Joan smiled toothily, natural good humour bubbling

to the fore again. 'I am relieved to hear it! I should not like to be on anyone's list of suspects.'

Katherine grimaced. 'What about me? Or is it just God and His angels who can verify my whereabouts? Are you on speaking terms with them, Brother? If so, they will assure you that I was engrossed in Clippesby's treatise.'

'I tried to read that,' said Joan, 'but I only managed the first page. He should have had *horses* discussing these philosophies, as I could not imagine chickens doing it. Perhaps you will recommend that he uses something more sensible next time, Brother.'

'But he chose chickens for a reason,' explained Katherine earnestly, while Bartholomew smothered a smile that Joan could not envisage talking hens, but had no issue with talking nags. 'Namely to demonstrate that two small, simple creatures can grasp the essence of—'

'I have never been much of a philosopher,' interrupted Joan, making it sound more like a virtue than a failing. 'My steeds do not care about such matters, and if my nuns do . . . well, I can refer them to you.'

And with that, she began to show off Dusty's side-stepping skills, while Katherine fought to prevent her own mount from doing likewise. Between them, they hogged the whole road, although as they were nuns, no one swore or cursed at them. While they were occupied, Abbess Isabel abandoned her circle of admirers and came to talk.

'Have you caught the plagiarist's killer yet, Brother?' she asked, crossing herself with a thin, unnaturally white hand. 'I cannot get his dead face out of my mind, and I know his soul cries out for vengeance.'

'You will have to rely on Commissary Aynton to supply that,' said Michael, but then produced the dagger from his scrip. 'Here is the blade used to stab him. Is it familiar?'

The Abbess stared at it for a long time, but eventually shook her head. 'Will you be able to identify the killer from it?'

'Perhaps. It is distinctive, so someone may recognise the thing.'

'Then I shall pray for your success,' said Isabel. 'Right now, in fact. Goodbye.'

She jabbed her donkey into a trot, and was off without another word. A train of folk ran after her, still begging for her prayers, but she barely glanced at them, and seemed keen to put as much space between her and Michael as possible.

'That was peculiar,' remarked Bartholomew, watching her disappear. 'I wanted her to repeat exactly what she saw when she stumbled across Paris's body, but she was gone before I could ask.'

'She did leave rather abruptly,' acknowledged Michael, 'almost as if she had something to hide. Yet I do not see her stabbing anyone. You can see just by looking that she is holier than the rest of us.'

'And if you do not believe it, ask her,' said Bartholomew drily. 'However, I *can* see her killing Paris. She is a fanatic, and they tend to consider themselves bound by different rules than the rest of us.'

Michael scoffed at the notion of the pious nun being a murderer, but they were prevented from discussing it further by Joan, who had finished showing off with Dusty, and came to find out what they had said to disconcert Isabel. Michael showed her – and Katherine – the dagger. Joan leaned down to pluck it from the monk's hand, although Katherine fastidiously refused to touch it.

'It is an ugly thing,' Katherine declared with a shudder. 'No wonder Isabel fled! I do not like the look of it myself, and I am used to such things, as my brother collects them.'

'The Bishop collects murder weapons?' asked Bartholomew warily.

'When he can get them,' replied Katherine. 'And they—'

'Actually, this *is* familiar,' interrupted Joan, frowning. 'I am sure I have seen it before.'

'Seen it where?' demanded Michael urgently. 'Or, more importantly, carried by whom?'

Joan closed her eyes to struggle with her memory, but eventually opened them and shook her head apologetically. 'It will not come, Brother. And even if it did, you would have to treat it with caution, as one weapon looks much like another to me. However, I shall keep mulling it over. Perhaps something will pop into my head.'

'I doubt it will,' predicted Katherine. 'And you would do better to reflect on spiritual matters. Or, better yet, praying that the *conloquium* will be a success, even when women like Sister Alice stain it with spite.'

'Oh, I pray for that all the time,' said Joan, 'although it does not seem to be working.'

# CHAPTER 8

Although Bartholomew and Michael spent the rest of the day quizzing and re-questioning witnesses, they learned nothing new. As evening approached, Michael went to watch Heltisle's new beadles embark on their first patrol, while Bartholomew dismayed his students by informing them that they were going to study – it was rare that classes continued after the six o'clock meal, and they had been looking forward to relaxing.

They grumbled even more when it became clear that they were going to work in the orchard, as it was chilly there once the sun had set. But Bartholomew's room was too small to hold everyone, and Theophilis had bagged the hall for Clippesby, who had agreed to present a preview of his next treatise. This would feature the philosophising hens again, and was a more in-depth look at some of the issues raised in his first exposition.

The Dominican's lecture sparked a vigorous debate, and Theophilis in particular asked a great many questions. It ended late, although not as late as Bartholomew, who lost track of time entirely and only stopped when his lamp ran out of oil, plunging the orchard into darkness. As a result, there were yawns and heavy eyes aplenty when the bell rang for church the following morning.

After their devotions, Michael led everyone back to the College for breakfast. With the resilience of youth, the students quickly rallied, and the hall soon rang with lively conversation, most of it about Clippesby's latest hypotheses. Michael summarised them for Bartholomew and his medics, then made some astute observations of his own. Theophilis jotted everything down on a scrap of parchment.

'For Clippesby to incorporate in his final draft,' he explained as he scribbled. 'What was that last point again, Brother?'

'There is no need to make notes for me, Theophilis,' said Clippesby politely. 'I can remember all these suggestions without them.'

'What, *all* of them?' asked William, astonished and disbelieving in equal measure.

'I have help.' Clippesby indicated the two hens that he had brought with him, which hunted among the rushes for scraps of dropped food. 'Ma and Gertrude act as amanuenses.'

'Can they write, then?' asked Theophilis with a smirk to let everyone know he was having fun at the Dominican's expense.

'Of course not!' said Clippesby, regarding him askance. 'They are chickens.'

The students laughed harder and longer than the rejoinder really warranted, which told Bartholomew that he was not the only one who disliked the Junior Proctor. Or perhaps it was just that they were protective of Clippesby, who had always been a great favourite of theirs. Thus snubbed, Theophilis fell silent, although he continued to record all that was said about Ma's new and intriguing definition of hermeneutic nominalism.

Bored with theology, Aungel began to whisper to Bartholomew. 'I hope Brother Michael will not win a bishopric or an abbacy very soon, because if he leaves the University, Theophilis will become Senior Proctor, and he will not be very good at it. He is too deceitful. For a start, we do not even know his real name.'

Bartholomew frowned. 'What do you mean?'

Aungel shrugged. 'No one calls their child *Theophilis*, so he must have chosen it for himself. "Loved by God" indeed! He should let us be the judge of that. Incidentally, Chancellor de Wetherset has been going around saying that Michael is no longer allowed to investigate murders. I hope he is wrong, or Paris will never have justice.'

'Have you heard any rumours about who might have killed Paris?'

'Oh, plenty,' replied Aungel, 'including one that claims de Wetherset, Heltisle and Aynton did it, because his plagiarism brought disgrace to the University. Which it did, of course. They do not do that sort of thing at Oxford.'

'We do not do that sort of thing here,' averred Bartholomew. 'Paris was an aberration.'

'A dead aberration,' said Aungel, 'although even he deserves vengeance.'

A short while later, Bartholomew and Michael discussed their plans for the day, which did not include training Heltisle's new beadles, as Michael's time with them the previous evening led him to declare them a lost cause.

'They are useless,' he spat. 'Not worthy to be called beadles, so I shall refer to them as "Heltisle's Horde" from now on. Worse, monitoring them took my attention away from my real duties, and there was nearly a skirmish because of it.'

'What happened?'

'It was the town's turn to practise at the butts, but some of our scholars tried to join in. Dick managed to keep the peace, but only just. But to business. We shall go to the castle first, as he sent word that Leger and Norbert are home and available for questioning. Perhaps they will recognise the daggers.'

'I wish someone would,' said Bartholomew. 'I thought Joan might, and I was disappointed when her memory failed her.'

'Perhaps she will remember today. I hope so, as there will be serious trouble unless we can present some answers soon. Last night, the town again accused the University of killing Wyse. I managed to avert trouble, but it was not easy.'

'How are the *peregrini*?' asked Bartholomew. 'Still safe?'

'For now, although they must leave tomorrow, because there will be a bloodbath if they are caught here. Of course, if it transpires that the Jacques murdered Paris, Bonet and the Girards, we shall have to hunt them down and bring them back.'

'But only the Jacques,' said Bartholomew. 'Not the old men, women and children.'

'So perhaps we had better speak to them again before they go,' Michael went on. 'And tonight, we shall both have to make an appearance at the butts.'

'Not you – as a monk, you are exempt from wasting your time there.'

'Exempt from training, but not from supporting the efforts of my colleagues,' sighed Michael. 'If I stay away, the triumvirate will accuse me of being unpatriotic.'

'Not the triumvirate,' growled Bartholomew. 'Heltisle. He is the poisonous one, aided and abetted by the insidious Theophilis.'

'Aided and abetted by Aynton,' countered Michael. 'De Wetherset must be sorry he appointed them, because they are losing him support hand over fist.'

'They are losing you support, too,' warned Bartholomew. 'Their antics reflect badly on all the University's officers, not just the Chancellor.'

'Yes,' acknowledged Michael. 'But to win a war, you must make some sacrifices, so I shall let them continue for now. Do not look so worried! I know what I am doing.'

Bartholomew hoped he was right, and that overconfidence would not see the downfall of a man who really did have the University's best interests at heart.

The castle lay to the north of the town. It had started life as a simple motte and bailey, but had since grown into a formidable fortress. It stood atop Cambridge's only hill, and was enclosed by towering curtain walls. Its function was usually more administrative than military, but the King's call to arms had resulted in a flurry of repairs and improvements. The chains on the portcullis had been replaced, unstable battlements had been mended, and the dry moat was filled with sharpened spikes.

'Do you really think the French will raid this far inland, Dick?' asked Bartholomew.

Tulyet shrugged. 'We are not difficult to reach from the sea, and it is better to be safe than sorry. However, an invasion worries me a lot less than the presence of Jacques in the Spital. True, our local hotheads are more likely to kill them than listen to their seditious ideas, but they make me uneasy, even so.'

Michael was more concerned with his own troubles. 'I have been ordered to leave the Spital murders to Aynton.'

Tulyet eyed him keenly. 'Because he will never find answers, thus leaving the killer to go free? If de Wetherset and Heltisle are the guilty parties, that would suit them very nicely.'

Michael's expression was wry. 'I did wonder if one of them had his own reasons for wanting an unskilled investigator on the case.'

'I sincerely hope this is an order you intend to flout,' said Tulyet.

Michael smiled. 'Naturally, although I shall need some help from you. I do not want Aynton knowing about our findings, lest he impedes the course of justice, either by design or accident. When he comes to you for information, would you mind misdirecting him?'

'With pleasure. Now, did anyone recognise the dagger you showed around yesterday?'

'Prioress Joan thought it was familiar,' replied Michael. 'She could not recall why, but I suspect she has seen it – or one similar – on someone's belt.'

182

'And where has she been staying?' pounced Tulyet. 'In the Spital, with the Jacques!'

'She has promised to reflect on the matter,' said Michael, 'so perhaps she will surprise us and produce a name.'

'Leave Paris's blade with me when you go,' instructed Tulyet. 'I will show it and the one from the Girards to the garrison. However, my money is on the culprit being at the Spital. I went there again at dawn, just to keep the Tangmers and their guests on their toes.'

'Did you learn anything new?' asked Michael.

Tulyet nodded. 'The Jacques intended to slip away this morning, leaving the rest of the *peregrini* to fend for themselves, but Delacroix fell ill during the night. He accuses Father Julien of poisoning him, which is possible, as the priest will not want his flock to be without men who can protect them.'

'And is Delacroix poisoned?' asked Bartholomew. 'Or just unwell?'

'He cannot stray more than two steps from the latrines, so who knows? Are you ready for Leger and Norbert? We should tackle them before they decide to go hunting again.'

The two knights were in the hall, the vast room that served as a refectory for Tulyet's officers, staff and troops. They had taken seats near the hearth, where a fire blazed, even though the day was warm. They lounged comfortably, boots off, armour loosened, and weapons arranged on the bench next to them. Neither acknowledged Tulyet as he approached, which was a deliberate affront to his authority.

'I have questions for you,' said Tulyet, sweeping the arsenal on to the floor with one swipe of his hand before sitting down and indicating that Bartholomew and Michael were to perch next to him.

The faces of both knights darkened in anger as their precious swords and daggers clattered on the flagstones. Bartholomew hoped Tulyet knew what he was doing, feeling it was rash to antagonise such brutes. It was the first time he had studied them closely, and he could not help but notice the array of scars, thickened ears and callused hands, especially on Norbert. All were signs of lives spent fighting.

'What questions?' snarled Leger, retrieving his sword and inspecting it for damage.

'We can begin with what you discussed with the Girard men the morning they were murdered,' said Michael. 'Then you can tell us why you did not bother to mention it to us.'

The pair exchanged glances. Leger's expression was calculating, but there was a flash of panic in Norbert's eyes.

'Who told you—' the bigger knight began belligerently.

'That does not matter,' interrupted Tulyet. 'The point is that you were seen, and I demand an explanation.'

'You *demand*?' echoed Leger incredulously. 'We are representatives of His Majesty, personally appointed by him to oversee Cambridge's preparations for war.'

'And I am his Sheriff,' retorted Tulyet. 'So I outrank you. Now, answer our questions or I shall send you back to the King in disgrace.'

Norbert bristled, but Leger was intelligent enough to know that Tulyet meant it, and began to answer the question, albeit sullenly. 'We did not know they were Spital lunatics at the time. We just saw them walking along, and we could tell, just by looking, that they were warriors, so we asked why they had not been to the butts.'

'How did they respond?'

'We could barely understand them,' shrugged Leger. 'One was mute, while the other had a toothache that mangled his words. Our English was not equal to the

184

conversation, so we forced them to use French, which was better, but only marginally.'

It was impossible to tell if the two knights had fallen for the Jacques' ruse, although Bartholomew wondered why the Girards had gone out in the first place, as it was a reckless thing to have done.

'Did they tell you they were from the Spital?' he asked.

'No, they said they were fletchers, and thus exempt from the call to arms,' growled Norbert. 'It is only now that we learn they were lunatics – and lying lunatics into the bargain.'

'We are going to the Spital this afternoon, to assess the rest of them,' added Leger. 'If they seem as rational as the pair we met, I want them all at the butts.'

'I would not recommend putting weapons in the hands of madmen,' said Bartholomew hastily. 'They might run amok and turn on you. And that is my professional medical opinion.'

It was pure bluster, but the knights agreed to leave the Spital men in peace anyway.

'Now, let us discuss the fire,' said Tulyet. 'Where were you when it began?'

Norbert regarded him coolly. 'I hope you are not accusing us of setting it.'

'Just answer the question,' barked Tulyet.

Norbert came to his feet fast. Tulyet did not flinch, even though the other man towered over him. Prudently, Leger gestured that his friend was to sit back down.

'We cannot recall, Sheriff,' he said with a false smile. 'Our remit is to train troops, so we spend a lot of time trawling taverns for likely recruits. We were in the King's Head at one point on Wednesday morning, but I cannot tell you precisely when.'

'The King's Head is near the Spital,' remarked Bartholomew.

Leger ignored him and continued to address Tulyet.

'So you will just have to take our word that we were else-where at the salient time. That should not present too great a difficulty, given that we are fellow knights.'

'Why should he believe you?' asked Michael acidly. 'You failed to report meeting two of the victims not long before their murders, which hardly presents you in an honest light.'

'It slipped our minds,' shrugged Leger. 'It was a discussion about nothing, so why should we remember? Or do you think we should tell the Sheriff every time we exchange words with men of fighting age? If we did, none of us would get any work done.'

He regarded the monk with sly defiance, and it was clear that pressing the matter further would be a waste of time, so Tulyet showed them the weapons that had killed Paris and the Girards. Leger gave them no more than a passing glance, but Norbert took them and studied them carefully.

'Such fine craftsmanship,' he breathed appreciatively. 'Where did you find them?'

'One was planted in the back of an elderly priest,' replied Michael pointedly. 'The other was used to murder defenceless lunatics.'

Norbert handed them back to Tulyet. 'Then the killer is a fool for leaving them behind. And if he is a fool, even you should be able to catch him.'

There was no more to be said, so Bartholomew, Michael and Tulyet took their leave.

'Do you believe they "forgot" their encounter with the Girards?' asked the physician when they were out in the bailey again. 'Because I do not. Moreover, they cannot prove where they were, and I can certainly see them dispatching a family with ruthless efficiency.'

'So can I,' replied Michael. 'Leger's answers were too glib, and I sense there was more to the encounter than they were willing to confess.'

'I agree,' said Tulyet, 'although I am not sure it involves murder. They are not poisoners – they would have stabbed everyone, including the children.'

'So are they on your list of suspects or not?'

'They are,' said Tulyet. 'Just not right at the top. But I shall show both weapons to the garrison, and if Leger and Norbert ever owned them, I will find out – soldiers notice such things. And if that yields no answers, I shall flash them around the town. Someone will recognise them, I am sure of it.'

But Bartholomew had a bad feeling the Sheriff's confidence was misplaced.

Bartholomew and Michael headed for St Radegund's. To reach the convent, they had to pass through the Barnwell Gate, which was manned that day by some new and vigilant sentries, who had been given the choice of a week's military service or the equivalent time spent in gaol as punishment for brawling with scholars. Among them was Verious the ditcher. All were under the command of the sullen Sergeant Orwel and his helpmeet Pierre Sauvage. Orwel sported a new hat that was black and rather feminine, leading Bartholomew to suppose he had stolen it from the nuns the previous day.

'Stop,' Orwel ordered roughly, whisking the headpiece out of sight when he saw the physician staring at it. 'The Barnwell Gate is closed today.'

'Is it?' asked Michael coolly. 'Then why has that cart just driven through?'

'You cannot pass, Brother,' said Verious apologetically. 'Sir Leger thinks there are French spies in the area, and we are under orders to keep them out.'

'We are not French spies,' said Michael. 'Moreover, we want to leave, not come in.'

Verious became flustered, unwilling to annoy the man who provided his choir with free victuals *or* the physician who never charged him for medicine when he was ill. He turned to the others for help. 'Brother Michael makes a good point. He is—'

'*I* am in charge here,' snapped Orwel. 'And I say the gate is closed. Sir Leger told me that *anyone* might be a French spy, even folk we know.'

'For heaven's sake!' snapped Michael irritably. 'I am the University's Senior Proctor!'

'I do not care what you call yourself,' growled Orwel. 'Now bugger off.'

There was a murmur of consternation, as the others saw membership of the choir and complimentary medical care flash before their eyes. They backed away, aiming to put some distance between themselves and the gruff sergeant, but Orwel barked at them to stand fast.

'But Brother Michael and Doctor Bartholomew cannot be spies,' protested Verious, distraught. 'If they were, they would be slinking about on tiptoe.'

Bartholomew struggled not to laugh at this piece of logic.

'Sir Leger said to stop all scholars from leaving town,' Orwel persisted, although only after he had given Verious's remark serious consideration. 'Or have you forgotten that one of them murdered poor Wyse?'

'Of course not,' snapped Verious. 'But these two did not do it. The culprit will be some foreigner – a man from King's Hall or Bene't College, which are full of aliens.'

'Sir Leger gave us our orders,' stated Orwel stubbornly. 'So we must follow them.'

'Sir Leger this, Sir Leger that,' mocked Michael. 'Can no one here think for himself?'

'Sir Leger recommended that we stay away from doing that, so he can do it for us,' replied Verious, quite seriously. 'We are all relieved, as thinking for ourselves has led to a lot of trouble in the past.'

This time, Bartholomew did laugh, although Michael failed to see the funny side.

'Stand aside before you make me angry,' he snapped. 'Matt and I need to visit the nuns. And do not smirk like that, Verious. Our intentions are perfectly honourable.'

'Of course they are,' said Verious, and winked.

'When the King calls us to arms, I shall be first over the Channel,' confided Sauvage, somewhat out of the blue. 'Then I shall avenge Winchelsea by slaughtering entire villages.'

'"Entire villages" were not responsible for Winchelsea,' argued Michael impatiently. 'That was a small faction of the Dauphin's—'

'Every Frenchman applauds what was done,' interrupted Orwel fiercely. 'So they all deserve to die. Now are you two going to piss off, or must we arrest you?'

'Arrest Brother Michael and Doctor Bartholomew?' cried Sauvage, horrified. 'You cannot do that! They will tell the Sheriff and he will be furious with us – they are his friends.'

'Besides, you will die if you try to take Doctor Bartholomew somewhere he does not want to go,' added Verious. 'He fought at Poitiers, where Cynric said he dispatched more of the enemy than you can shake a stick at. And look at my nose. You see where it is broken? Well, he did that. I tell you, he is *lethal*!'

Verious and Bartholomew had once come to blows, although it had been more luck than skill that had seen the physician emerge the victor. He was about to say so, disliking the notion that he should own such a deadly reputation, when Orwel stepped aside.

'I did not realise you were a veteran of Poitiers,' he said obsequiously. 'You may pass.'

'Will I be allowed back in again?' asked Bartholomew warily.

Orwel nodded. 'And if this lot give you any trouble,

189

send for me. I was at Poitiers, too, so we are comrades-in-arms. Those always stick together, as you know.'

'He does know,' said Michael, sailing past. 'But he does not countenance insolence or stupidity, so you might want to watch yourself in future.'

St Radegund's Priory was a sizeable foundation, far larger than was necessary for the dozen or so nuns who lived there. However, even the spacious refectory, massive dormitory and substantial guest quarters were not large enough to accommodate all the *conloquium* delegates, especially now that the twenty from the Spital and the ten from the Gilbertine Priory had joined them. Most bore the discomfort with stoic good humour, although a few complained. Needless to say, Sister Alice was among the latter.

'I had to reprimand her,' said Prioress Joan, who was basking in the adulation of her colleagues for a thought-provoking presentation entitled *Latrine Waste and Management*. 'Her moaning was beginning to cause friction.'

She looked larger and more horse-like than ever that day, towering over her sisters like a giant, but there was a rosy glow about her, and she radiated vitality and robust good health.

'Joan was the only one brave enough to do it,' put in Magistra Katherine, the inevitable smirk playing around her lips. 'Everyone else is afraid of annoying Alice, lest the woman turns her malevolent attentions on them.'

'No one wants to suffer what I have endured at her hands since we arrived,' elaborated Abbess Isabel, whose white habit positively glowed among all the black ones. 'But Prioress Joan took the bull by the horns, and Alice has been quiet ever since.'

'Well, something had to be done,' shrugged Joan, clearly pleased by the praise. 'I told her to bathe, too, because if I have to watch her claw at herself like a horse with fleas for one more day . . .'

Even the thought of it made some nuns begin scratching, and Bartholomew watched in amusement as Michael did likewise. Others joined in, until there were upwards of twenty Benedictines busily plying their nails. Then the monk asked if there was anything he could do to make their stay more pleasant, and the scratching stopped as minds turned to less itchy matters.

'I will survive a few cramped nights, but poor Dusty may not,' declared Joan, fixing Michael with a reproachful eye. 'You said he could have the old bakery, but the moment I finished cleaning it out, the nuns from Cheshunt dashed in, claiming they would rather share with him than with Alice. But he prefers to sleep alone, so shall I oust them or will you?'

'Neither,' said the monk, thinking fast. 'I will take him to Michaelhouse. Cynric knows horses, so he will be well looked after there.'

Joan beamed and clapped him on the shoulder. 'I was right about you, Brother! You are a *good* man. May I visit him whenever I please?'

Michael hesitated, uneasy with women wandering unsupervised in his domain. Then he glanced at Joan, and decided that it would be a deranged scholar indeed who considered her to be the lady of his dreams. He nodded, then changed the subject by asking about the dagger that had killed Paris, which she had half-recognised earlier.

'I *know* it is familiar,' she said with a grimace. 'But the answer continues to elude me, even though I have been wracking my brain ever since. But I shall not give up. It will come to me eventually.'

'Then let us hope it is sooner rather than later,' said Michael, disappointed, and moved to another matter. 'How is the *conloquium* going?'

'Not well,' sighed Abbess Isabel, although Bartholomew

was sure that every other nun had been about to say the opposite. 'We have made no meaningful policy decisions, despite the fact that I have been praying for some ever since I arrived. This is unusual, as God usually does exactly what I want.'

'Oh, come, Isabel,' chided Joan. 'We have decided a great deal. For example, none of us will ever store onions in a damp place again, having heard Abbess Sibyl of Romsey wax lyrical on the subject.'

'So there you are,' drawled Katherine. 'A decision that will impact every nun in our Order, made by us, here at St Radegund's.'

Joan was oblivious to sarcasm. 'And it is an important one! I use an onion poultice on Dusty's hoofs, so it is imperative to ensure a year-round supply.' She beamed. 'And the *conloquium* has certainly made *me* count my blessings. I have listened to other prioresses list the problems they suffer with their flock, and mine are angels by comparison.'

Isabel sniffed. 'Anyone would be an angel compared to Alice. She was on the verge of turning Ickleton into a brothel before I came along. Your brother should have done more than depose her, Magistra Katherine – he should have ordered her defrocked.'

'Perhaps he did not want to be denounced as a hypocrite,' suggested Joan with a shrug of her mighty shoulders. 'We all know *he* enjoys a romp with—'

'He believes in second chances,' interrupted Katherine swiftly, and changed the subject. 'The *conloquium* has been worthwhile for me, because it brought Clippesby's thesis to my attention. Unfortunately, I still have not had the pleasure of meeting him.'

'No,' said Michael ambiguously. 'You have not.'

'I suppose the conference has been worthwhile,' conceded Isabel grudgingly. 'Magistra Katherine explained the nominalism–realism debate in a way we all understood. Then

Sister Florence of York showed us how to get an additional habit out of an ell of cloth, while Alice taught us something called "creative accounting".'

'I would not recommend you follow *that* advice,' said Katherine drily. 'Her intention was to land you all in deep water with your bishops.'

Isabel shrugged off her bemusement and turned to Michael. 'What of the murders? I have been praying for the victims' souls, even though the ones at the Spital were insane and thus outside God's grace.'

'The insane are not outside God's grace,' objected Bartholomew, startled. 'If anything, they are further *inside* it, as they cannot be held responsible for their sins. Unlike the rest of us.'

'I would not know,' retorted Isabel loftily. 'I do not have any sins.'

'Right,' said Michael, after a short, startled silence. 'We need to speak to Alice. Will someone fetch her? While we wait, I shall ensure your victuals are up to scratch. I am obliged to monitor *all* aspects of this *conloquium*, including the quality of the food.'

It was some time before Michael declared himself satisfied that the delegates were being properly fed. Then he and Bartholomew went to the church, where Alice had been ordered to sit until he was ready to see her.

The church was the convent's crowning glory, a large, peaceful place with a stout tower. Parts of it had suffered from the lack of funds that affected many monastic foundations, so there were patches of damp on the walls, while some of the stained glass had dropped out of its frames. It smelled of mould, old wood and the wildflowers that someone had placed on every available surface.

Most nuns waiting in a holy place would have used the time for quiet prayer, but such a rash thought had not crossed Alice's mind. She paced angrily, muttering under her breath about the indignities she was forced to endure. Abbess Isabel and Magistra Katherine were the names most frequently spat out, although some venom was reserved for the nuns who had opted to share their sleeping quarters with a horse rather than her. She scratched so vigorously as she cursed that Bartholomew asked if she needed the services of a physician.

'All I need is to know why I was dragged here,' she snarled. 'I was in a session on medicine, learning lots of useful things. You hauled me out, so I missed most of it.'

'Medicine?' asked Bartholomew with interest.

'Strong ones, used to cure serious ailments. I was enjoying myself.'

'Perhaps you were,' said Michael. 'But only qualified *medici* should administer such potions, and we do not want any more suspicious deaths to explore.'

'*I* am not a killer,' declared Alice indignantly. 'And if you are here to accuse me of stealing Joan's comb again, I shall complain to the Bishop about being hounded for an incident that I have already explained away.'

'We came to ask if you have remembered anything new since we last spoke,' said Michael. 'You will appreciate that we are eager to catch the rogue who murdered five Spital people, particularly as I suspect that he also stabbed a spicer and an elderly priest.'

'You mean an elderly *plagiarist*,' mused Alice. 'Perhaps you should look to your University for a suspect, Brother, rather than accusing innocent nuns.'

'I accuse no one,' said Michael. 'All I want from you is information. You were in the Spital when the killer struck, and I thought you might have noticed something to help us.'

Alice's face was full of spite. 'I can only repeat what I told you before – that I saw Katherine scurry off alone. She doubtless told you she was reading, but you cannot believe her. She is kin to the most evil, corrupt, dishonest man who ever lived – the Bishop of Ely!'

'Of course,' said Michael flatly. 'Anything else?'

Alice gave the matter serious consideration, and for a while no one spoke. A bell rang to announce the end of one set of lectures, followed by a genteel rumble of voices as the nuns discussed which talk they wanted to attend next. Then the bell chimed to mark the beginning of the next session, after which there was silence. A dog barked in the distance, and an irritable whinny suggested Dusty was eager for attention.

'I can tell you that it was easy to enter the Spital,' said Alice eventually. 'The Tangmers will claim they guard the gate assiduously, but I walked in unchallenged several times. Of course, I imagine they are more careful now.'

'I hope so,' muttered Bartholomew.

'So the killer may have come from outside?' asked Michael.

'Well, the staff *were* more interested in monitoring the billeted nuns than guarding their madmen, so it is possible. The Tangmers are an odd horde, and their chapel is an accident waiting to happen, as it is stupid to store firewood in a place where oils are heated with naked flames. Perhaps that is what happened to the shed: Amphelisa was experimenting in it.'

'Why would she do that when she has a well-equipped workshop?'

'Because the workshop is in the chapel,' explained Alice. 'And thus out of bounds during services. Perhaps she could not wait until Mass was finished, so found somewhere else to work in the interim – in which case, she did the killer a favour by incinerating his victims.'

Bartholomew pondered the suggestion. Perhaps Amphelisa did find it frustrating to be ousted every time the chapel was needed, especially if Julien was the kind of priest who kept all his sacred offices. It was entirely possible that she had opted to use the shed, which everyone said was tinder-dry and filled with wood. No one had seen her near it, but the staff were her kin by marriage, so unlikely to betray her.

Michael continued to press Alice for more information, but when it became clear that she had said as much as she was going to, they took their leave.

'I do not know what to think about this comb Alice is supposed to have stolen,' said Michael, when he and Bartholomew were heading back to the town. He was astride Dusty and the physician walked at his side, careful to stay well away from an animal that he sensed was keen to bite, kick or butt him. 'Is she guilty? Or is she falsely accused, as she claims?'

'Does it matter?' asked Bartholomew. 'It hardly compares to murder, and I do not know why we are even talking about it.'

'Because it is the key to the characters of some of our suspects and witnesses,' replied Michael. 'Whether they are thieves, liars or vindictive manipulators.'

'Alice stole it,' said Bartholomew impatiently. 'Unless you believe she really was riffling through someone else's bags in search of nose-cloths. There is something so distasteful about her that she is currently at the top of my list of suspects.'

'Above Theophilis?' asked Michael. 'The Devil incarnate, according to you?'

'Perhaps not above him,' acknowledged Bartholomew. 'He is deceitful, as illustrated by the fact that he spied on the triumvirate for you – betraying men who trust him.'

'But he did not betray them,' Michael pointed out. 'Not when they seem to know exactly what he was doing. And the last time we discussed this, you said he had failed me deliberately, because he was actually on their side. You cannot have it both ways.'

'Then what about the way he behaves towards Clippesby? Pretending to befriend him, but then mocking him behind his back?'

'That is distasteful, but hardly evidence of a criminal mind. But here is where you and I part company. I shall spend the rest of the day at the Spital and St Mary the Great, trying to tease more information from everyone we have already interviewed.'

'You do not want me with you?' asked Bartholomew, brightening.

'I do, but a message arrived when we were with the nuns. You are needed by patients, one of whom is Commissary Aynton. Go to him, and while you ply your healing hands, see if you can find out exactly what *he* was doing on the morning of the fire.'

'He has already told us – he was either with de Wetherset and Heltisle in St Mary the Great, or practising his lecture on the sheep.'

'Then press him to elaborate, and see if you can catch him in an inconsistency.'

# CHAPTER 9

Cynric was waiting for Bartholomew by the Barnwell Gate, because the town was growing increasingly restive and he was protective of the physician. Together they walked past the butts, where one or two archers were already honing their skills, taking advantage of the fact that most folk would arrive later, once the day's work was done.

'There will be trouble tonight, boy,' predicted Cynric. 'It is the town's turn to practise, but de Wetherset plans to turn up as well. He wants everyone to think he is brave for not buying another proxy, although the truth is that there is no one left for him to hire.'

'Warn Michael and Theophilis,' instructed Bartholomew. 'One of them *must* convince him to wait until tomorrow before flaunting his courage.'

'I am not speaking to Theophilis,' said Cynric, pursing his lips. 'I cannot abide him. He spent all morning humouring Clippesby by the henhouse, then told Father William that Clippesby is a lunatic who should be locked away.'

'What do you mean by "humouring" him?'

'Making a show of asking the chickens their opinions, then pretending to appreciate their replies. I tried to draw Clippesby away, but Theophilis sent me to de Wetherset with a letter, which he said was urgent. But it was not.'

'How do you know?'

'Because I read it,' replied Cynric unrepentantly. 'All it said was that Brother Michael had gone to St Radegund's to talk to the nuns. It was a ruse to get me out of the way.'

Bartholomew had taught Cynric to read, although he

198

had since wondered if it had been a wise thing to do. He pondered the question afresh on hearing that the book-bearer had invaded the Chancellor's private correspon-dence, and yet it was interesting to learn that Theophilis reported Michael's movements to de Wetherset. It confirmed his suspicion that the Junior Proctor was not to be trusted.

'You can tell Michael that as well,' he said. 'Although you should make sure Theophilis never finds out what you did.'

Cynric turned to what he considered a much more interesting subject. 'Margery says the Devil is already very comfortably settled in the Spital.'

'Stay away from that place,' warned Bartholomew, afraid Cynric would go to see the sight for himself – he did not want his militant book-bearer to encounter like-minded Jacques.

'I shall,' promised Cynric fervently. 'I have no desire to meet the Lord of Darkness, although Margery tells me that he is not as bad as everyone thinks. But even before Satan moved in, the Spital had a sinister aura. I want nothing to do with it.'

'Good,' said Bartholomew. 'But advise Margery to keep her heretical opinions to herself. The University's priests will not turn a blind eye to those sorts of remarks for ever, and we shall have a riot for certain if they execute a popular witch.'

Bartholomew found Aynton at his home in Tyled Hostel. The Commissary was in bed, one arm resting on a pile of cushions. His face was white with pain.

'It happened at the Spital this morning,' he explained tearfully, 'and if I had a suspicious mind, I might say it was deliberate.'

'What was deliberate?' asked Bartholomew, sitting next to him and beginning to examine the afflicted limb.

'I assume you know that de Wetherset wants me to solve the Spital murders,' whispered Aynton. 'Well, I was interrogating Warden Tangmer, when his cousin – that great brute Eudo – pushed me head over heels. My wrist hurts abominably, but worse, look at my boots! He has ruined them completely!'

Bartholomew glanced at them. They were calf-height, flimsy and so garishly ugly that he thought the scuffs caused by the fall had improved rather than disfigured them.

'Pity,' he said, aware that the Commissary was expecting sympathy. 'But I am sure a good cobbler can fix them.'

'He says the marks are too deep,' sniffed Aynton. 'I shall continue to wear them, as they cost a fortune, but they will never be right again. And my arm is broken into the bargain!'

'Sprained,' corrected Bartholomew, applying a poultice to reduce the swelling. 'Eudo must have given you quite a shove to make you fall over.'

'The man does not know his own strength. I suspect he did it because I was berating Tangmer for allowing his lunatics to play with swords. Some were engaged in a mock fight when I arrived, you see, which is hardly an activity to soothe tormented minds.'

'No,' agreed Bartholomew, supposing the Jacques had been practising the skills they might need to defend themselves, and that their imminent departure meant they were less concerned about being seen by visitors.

'Between you and me, there is something odd about that Spital,' Aynton went on. 'I think it harbours nasty secrets.'

Bartholomew kept his eyes on the poultice lest Aynton should read the truth in them. 'Well, its patients *are* insane, so what do you expect? I wish I could help them, but ailments of the mind have always been a mystery to me.'

The last part was true, at least.

'I would have thought you had enormous experience

with lunatics,' said Aynton caustically. 'Given that most of our colleagues are around the bend.'

Bartholomew laughed. 'A few, perhaps.'

'It is more than a few,' averred Aynton. 'It would take until midnight to recite a list of all those who are as mad as bats. Shall I start with Michaelhouse? Clippesby, Father William, Theophilis and Michael. And you, given your peculiar theories about hand-washing. Then, in King's Hall, there is—'

'Michael is not mad,' objected Bartholomew. 'Nor is Theophilis.'

He did not bother defending Clippesby for obvious reasons, while anyone who had met William would know that he was barely rational. And as for himself, he did not care what people thought about his devotion to hygiene, because the results spoke for themselves – he lost far fewer patients than other *medici*, and if the price was being considered insane, then so be it.

'Theophilis spends far too much time with Clippesby,' said Aynton disapprovingly. 'They are always together, talking and whispering. He should be careful – lunacy is contagious, you know.'

Bartholomew declined to take issue with such a ridiculous assertion. 'And Michael? What has he done to win a place on your list?'

Aynton lowered his voice. 'He does not like me. I cannot imagine why, as I have given him no cause for animosity. Indeed, I have done my utmost to be nice to him, but he rejects my overtures of friendship.'

'So anyone who does not like you is mad?'

'It demonstrates a warped mind, which means he should not hold a position of such power in the University. De Wetherset is right to clip Michael's wings.'

Bartholomew regarded him in surprise, aware that Aynton's eyes had lost their customary dreaminess, and were hard and cold. 'I hardly think—'

'Michael's influence is waning, and unless he wants to be ousted completely, he must learn to accept it. Yes, he has made the University strong, but it is inappropriate for the Senior Proctor to wield more power than the Chancellor, and it is time to put an end to it.'

Bartholomew felt treacherous even listening to such sentiments, and turned his attention back to medicine, eager to end the discussion.

'Does this hurt when I bend it?'

'*Ow!* Be gentle, Matthew! I am not one of your dumb beggars, impervious to pain.'

Bartholomew opened his mouth to retort that his paupers most certainly did feel pain, but decided it was another topic on which he and Aynton were unlikely to agree. He remembered what Michael had asked him to do.

'You say you were practising a lecture on the morning of the Spital fire,' he began.

'I was,' replied Aynton curtly. 'But I have said all I am going to on the subject, so do not press me again. If you do, I shall lodge a complaint for harassment.'

Bartholomew took his leave, disturbed to have witnessed a side of the amiable academic that he had not known existed. Perhaps Michael was right to be wary of him.

But once outside, breathing air that was full of the clean scents of spring – new grass, wild flowers and sun-warmed earth – he wondered if he had overreacted. After all, what Aynton said was true: Michael did wield a disproportionate amount of power. Moreover, lots of patients were snappish when they were in pain, so why should Aynton be any different? Bartholomew pushed the matter from his mind and went to his next customer.

He was just passing King's Hall when he spotted two figures, one abnormally large, the other abnormally small. Eudo had tried to disguise himself by pulling a hood over his head, although his great size made him distinctive and several people hailed him by name. By contrast, his minuscule wife was clearly delighted with the way she looked and made no effort at all to conceal her identity. She wore a light summer cloak pinned with a jewelled brooch, and the gold hints in her hair were accentuated by a pretty fillet.

'We wanted to stay at home and protect the . . . patients,' blurted Eudo when Bartholomew stopped to exchange pleasantries. 'But Hélène is having nightmares, so Amphelisa sent us to buy ingredients for a sleeping potion.'

He indicated the basket he carried. Bartholomew glanced in it once, then looked again.

'Mandrake, poppy juice, henbane,' he breathed, alarmed. 'These are powerful herbs – too powerful for a child. It is not—'

'Amphelisa knows what she is doing,' interrupted Goda shortly. 'And if we want your opinion, we will ask for it.'

'Has she made sleeping potions for Hélène before?' asked Bartholomew. 'One strong enough to make her drowse through a fire, perhaps?'

Rage ignited in Eudo's eyes. He moved fast, grabbing Bartholomew by the front of his tabard and shoving him against a wall. Bartholomew tried to struggle free, but it was hopeless – Eudo's fingers were like bands of iron.

'Eudo, stop!' hissed Goda, glancing around to make sure no one was watching. 'You will make him think Amphelisa *did* poison the children. But she did not, so she does not need you to defend her. Let him go.'

Bartholomew was surprised when Eudo did as he was told.

'Is this what happened to Commissary Aynton?' he asked curtly, brushing himself down. 'He put questions that frightened you, so you pushed him? I know it was no accident.'

'Oh, yes, it was,' countered Goda fiercely. 'Aynton *claimed* that some of our patients were playing with swords. We told him he was mistaken, so he began prancing around to demonstrate what he thought he had seen. He bounced into Eudo and lost his balance.'

'Which would never have happened if he had not been jigging about like an ape,' growled Eudo. 'It was his own fault.'

Bartholomew suspected the truth lay somewhere in between – that Eudo had shoved Aynton in an effort to shut him up, but that Aynton had been off balance, so had taken an unintended tumble. Even so, it was unacceptable behaviour on Eudo's part, and Bartholomew dreaded to imagine what he might do without Goda to keep him in line.

'Does Amphelisa distil oils anywhere other than the chapel?' he asked, switching to another line of enquiry.

'That is none of your—' began Eudo in a snarl, although he stopped when Goda raised a tiny hand. There were two silver rings on her fingers that Bartholomew was sure had not been there the last time he had seen her.

'We could tell you,' she said sweetly. 'But our tongues will loosen far more readily if you have a coin to spare.'

Bartholomew raised his eyebrows. 'You want to be paid for helping me catch the person who murdered five people in your home?'

Goda shrugged. 'Why not? You earn three pennies for every corpse you assess, so why should you be the only one to turn a profit from death?'

Bartholomew had never considered himself as one who 'turned a profit from death' before, and the notion made him feel faintly grubby. He floundered around for a response, but Eudo spoke first.

'Your question is stupid! Of course Amphelisa does not work anywhere else. How can she, when all her distilling equipment is in the chapel? It cannot be toted back and forth on a whim, you know. Or do you imagine she produces oils out of thin air?'

Goda glared at him for providing information that could have been sold, but then her attention was caught by someone who was approaching from the left.

'Smile, husband,' she said between clenched teeth. 'Here comes Isnard the bargeman, and if he thinks we are squabbling with his favourite *medicus* . . .'

Eudo's smile was more of a grimace, but it satisfied Isnard, who proceeded to regale them with the latest gossip.

'You need not worry about your Spital being haunted any longer,' he began importantly. 'Because Margery Starre just told me she was mistaken about it standing on the site of an ancient pagan temple.'

Eudo was alarmed. 'But I have seen ghosts with my own—'

'Tricks,' interrupted Isnard with authority. 'Margery went to visit Satan last night, as she and him are on friendly terms, but he was nowhere to be found. What she *did* find, however, was a piece of fine gauze on twine, which could be jerked to make an illusion.'

'Oh,' said Eudo uncomfortably. 'But—'

'Moreover, Margery was *paid* to tell us that the Devil was taking up residence there,' Isnard went on, 'which she did, because she thought it was Satan himself begging the favour.'

Bartholomew frowned. 'Why would she think that?'

'Because she was visited by someone huge in a black cloak with horns poking from under his hood. Naturally, she made assumptions. But when she went to see him at the Spital and found evidence of trickery . . . well, she realised the whole thing was a hoax.'

Bartholomew was secretly gratified to learn that the self-important witch had been so easily duped. Perhaps it would shake her followers' faith in her, which would be no bad thing, especially where Cynric was concerned.

'You say she was tricked by someone huge?' he asked, looking hard at Eudo.

'Yes – someone *pretending* to be Satan,' said Isnard, lest his listeners had not deduced this for themselves. 'Well, two someones actually, as the deceiver had a minion with him, who did all the talking.'

'Is that so?' said Bartholomew, aware that neither Goda nor Eudo would meet his eyes.

'Margery is none too pleased about it,' said Isnard, 'so you Spital folk might want to stay out of her way for a while. She says it is heresy to take the Devil's name in vain.'

The warning delivered, Isnard went on his way, swinging along on his crutches as he looked for someone else to gossip with. Bartholomew watched him go, aware of a rising sense of unease as it occurred to him that there would now be repercussions.

'Go home and inform Tangmer that his ruse has failed,' he told Goda and Eudo. 'And that some folk may resent being deceived and might want revenge.'

'Let them try,' snarled Eudo. 'We will teach them to mind their own business.'

'The Lyminster nuns saw through the *peregrini*'s disguises,' Bartholomew went on, 'which means that others will, too. They must leave at once.'

Goda softened. 'They plan to go at dusk.'

'I hope they find somewhere safe,' said Bartholomew sincerely. 'But when did you pretend to be Satan, exactly, Eudo? I was under the impression from Margery that it was on Wednesday morning, more or less at the time when the fire started.'

Eudo opened his mouth to deny it, but then shrugged. 'It was. So what?'

'It means you have an alibi,' explained Bartholomew.

'Who was the minion? It was not Goda – she was baking all morning, in full view of Prioress Joan. Was it Tangmer?'

Eudo sagged in defeat. 'He is better at that sort of thing than me, so we decided to do it together. But we could hardly tell you, the Sheriff and Brother Michael that we were off bribing witches when the Girards were murdered, could we? So he invented the tale about Amphelisa not being very good at brewing . . .'

Which explained why Tangmer and Eudo had been so furtive when asked to give an account of their where-abouts, thought Bartholomew. But they were definitely in the clear for the murders, as it would have taken time to dress appropriately and then convince Margery to do what 'Satan' wanted. The list of suspects was now two people shorter.

Bartholomew returned to College, where he dashed off messages telling Michael and Tulyet what he had learned. He sent Cynric to deliver them, then went to the hall and interrogated his students on the work he had set them to do. Unimpressed with their progress, he lectured them on what would be expected of the medical profession if the plague returned, aiming to frighten them into working harder. Islaye, the gentle one, looked as though he might be sick; the callous, self-interested Mallett was dismissive.

'It will not return, sir,' he declared confidently. 'God has made His point, and He has no reason to punish us a second time.'

'Actually, He does,' said Theophilis, who had been listening. His soft voice sent an involuntary shiver down Bartholomew's spine. 'It has only been ten years, but we are already slipping back into evil ways. For example, there is a rumour that someone has been dressing up as Satan. That is heresy, and if I catch the culprit, I will burn him in the market square.'

Unwilling to discuss that, Bartholomew returned to his

original theme. 'There are reports of plague around the Mediterranean, and local physicians predict that it will spread north within a year. Ergo, you must work hard now, to be ready for it.'

'Just like physicians were ready last time,' scoffed Theophilis. 'No wonder poor Suttone upped and left in the middle of term – he did not trust you lot to save him.'

At that point, Theophilis's students, deprived of supervision, grew rowdy enough to disturb Father William. Irritably, the Franciscan ordered him back to work, and there was an unseemly spat as one took exception to being bossed around by the other.

'Master Suttone *was* terrified of the plague,' said Mallett to Bartholomew, while everyone else watched the spectacle of two Fellows bickering. 'But that is not why he left.'

Heltisle had claimed much the same, and Bartholomew hoped the malicious Vice-Chancellor had not been spreading nasty untruths.

'Then what was?' he asked coolly, a warning in his voice.

Mallett was uncharacteristically tentative. 'I happened to be passing St Mary the Great one night, when I overheard a conversation between Suttone and Heltisle . . .'

'And?' demanded Bartholomew, when the student trailed off uncomfortably.

'And I did not catch the whole thing, but I did hear Heltisle tell Suttone that there would be repercussions unless he did as he was told. The next day, Suttone resigned. You will not repeat this to Heltisle, will you, sir? I do not want to make an enemy of him – he has connections at Court, and I want a post with a noble family when I graduate.'

Bartholomew frowned. 'Are you saying that Suttone was *coerced* into leaving? How? Did he have some dark secret that he wanted kept quiet?'

'I got the impression that he did,' replied Mallett. 'But I have no idea what it was.'

Bartholomew was exasperated. 'Why have you waited so long before mentioning it? If your tale is true, then it means Heltisle may have the means to hurt Michaelhouse. You must know how much he hates us.'

Mallett shrugged. 'I do, but I have to think of myself first. I was going to tell you at the end of term, once my future is settled, but . . . well, I suppose I owe this place some loyalty.'

'You do,' said Bartholomew angrily, and indicated the other students, whose attention had snapped away from William and Theophilis at the sound of their teacher's sharp voice. 'And to your friends, who will still be here after you leave.'

'Yes,' acknowledged Mallett sheepishly. 'But there is another reason why I was reluctant to speak out. You see, I overheard this discussion very late at night . . .'

'After the curfew bell had sounded and you should have been at home,' surmised Bartholomew, unimpressed.

'What were you doing?' asked Islaye coolly. 'Visiting that sister you have been seeing – the one who was billeted at the Spital, and who you insist on meeting at the witching hour?'

Mallett shook his head. 'She only arrived a couple of weeks ago. The confrontation between Heltisle and Suttone was back in March, when Suttone was still here.'

'Just tell me what was said,' ordered Bartholomew tersely. 'I do not want to know about your dalliances with nuns.'

Mallett gaped at him. 'Dalliances? No, you misunderstand! I went to the Spital to meet my *sister*. She is one of the Benedictines who lodged there before Brother Michael moved them to St Radegund's. I had to visit her on the sly, because Tangmer refused to let me in. He said I might upset his lunatics.'

'Well, you might,' muttered Islaye sourly. 'You are not very nice.'

'I even offered to cure his madmen free of charge,' Mallett went on, ignoring him, 'but Tangmer remained adamant. He is an ass – my sister says that founding the Spital broke him and he has no money left. Ergo, he should have accepted my generous offer.'

'How does she know about his finances?' asked Bartholomew, although he was aware that they were ranging away from what Heltisle had said to Suttone.

'She overheard him telling his cousins. Everyone thinks he is rich, but his fortune is gone, and he will only win it back when he has some rich lunatics to look after. She says the current batch – who are not as mad as you think – only pay a fraction of what they should. Amphelisa does not mind, but Tangmer does.'

'I see,' said Bartholomew, wondering if he had been precipitous to declare Tangmer and Eudo innocent of murder. Perhaps killing the Girards had been a way to oust guests who prevented them from recouping their losses. 'But never mind the Spital. Tell me about the quarrel between Heltisle and Suttone.'

'There is no more to tell,' said Mallett apologetically. 'Other than that Suttone was on the verge of tears, while Heltisle was gloatingly triumphant. It should not surprise you: Heltisle has been dabbling in University politics for years, and is as crafty as they come, whereas Suttone was an innocent in that respect.'

'He was,' agreed Islaye. 'However, if Heltisle did harm him, he will answer to Brother Michael. *He* will not let that slippery rogue get away with anything untoward.'

Bartholomew was sure Islaye was right.

Mallett's story had infuriated Bartholomew, because he was sure that Heltisle *had* done something unkind to Suttone, especially since it had happened when Michael was away and thus not in a position to intervene. As a consequence, he did not want to spend his evening at the butts, where he was likely to run into the Vice-Chancellor, afraid his antipathy towards the man would lead to an unseemly confrontation.

Unfortunately, he knew his absence would be noted, and he was loath to provide Heltisle with an opportunity to fine him. Faced with two unattractive choices, he asked Aungel to go with him, hoping the younger Fellow's company would take his mind off Heltisle's unsavoury antics. They chanced upon Theophilis in the yard, and the three of them began to walk there together. Theophilis held forth conversationally as they went.

'There was nearly a fight at the butts last night. De Wetherset and Heltisle took their students there, but it was the town's turn, and insults were exchanged.'

Bartholomew was disgusted. 'They went anyway, even after Michael told them not to? What were they thinking?'

'Apparently, Heltisle had informed de Wetherset that the Sheriff had invited them to share the targets. It was only when they were at the butts that Heltisle admitted to lying.'

'So what happened?' asked Aungel, agog.

'Tulyet threatened to hang the first person who drew a weapon in anger,' replied Theophilis. 'You could see he meant it, so our lot went home.'

Bartholomew shook his head in disbelief. Did Heltisle *want* the University to be held responsible for igniting a riot? Then he stopped walking suddenly, and peered into the shadows surrounding All Saints' churchyard.

Sister Alice was slinking along in a way that was distinctly furtive, pausing every so often to check she was not being watched. Curious, Bartholomew began to follow her, and as Theophilis and Aungel were also intrigued by her peculiar antics, they fell in at his heels. None of them were very good at stealth, so it was a miracle she did not spot them.

Eventually, they reached Shoemaker Row, where Alice peered around yet again. The three scholars hastily crammed themselves into a doorway, where Bartholomew struggled to stifle his laughter, aware of what a ridiculous sight they must make. Irked, Theophilus elbowed him sharply in the ribs.

Alice stood for a moment, listening to the sounds of the night – a dog barking in the distance, the rumble of conversation from a nearby tavern, the mewl of a baby. Then she scuttled towards a smart cottage in the middle of the lane and knocked on the door.

'That is where Margery Starre lives,' whispered Aungel, as the door opened and Alice slithered inside. 'Visiting witches is hardly something a nun should be doing. No wonder she did not want to be seen!'

Bartholomew crept towards the window. The shutter was closed, but by putting his ear to the wood he could hear Margery's voice.

'Of course I can cast cursing spells,' she was informing her guest. 'But are you sure that is what you want? Once you start down such a path, there is no turning back.'

'I started down it ages ago,' Alice retorted harshly, 'after I was ousted from my post for no good reason. They started this war, but I shall finish it.'

The voices faded, leading Bartholomew to suppose they had gone to a different room. He was disinclined to hunt out another window, because he was suddenly assailed by the conviction that Margery knew he was out there – she had other uncanny abilities, so why not seeing through wood? He slipped away, and told the others that he had been unable to hear. He would happily have confided in Aungel, but he could not bring himself to trust Theophilis.

'I thought Alice was trouble the first time I set eyes on her,' the Junior Proctor declared as they resumed their journey to the butts. 'I have an instinct for these things, which is why Brother Michael appointed me as his deputy, of course.'

'You mean his inferior,' corrected Aungel. 'He does not have a deputy.'

Theophilis shot him a venomous look. 'I shall be Chancellor in the not-too-distant future, so watch who you insult, Aungel. You will not rise far in the University without influential friends.'

'Is that why you are always pestering Clippesby?' asked Aungel, regarding him with dislike. 'Because he is a great theologian, and you aim to bask in his reflected glory? His next thesis is almost ready and—'

'On the contrary,' interrupted Theophilis haughtily. 'All the time I have spent with him has been for one end: to assess whether he should be locked in a place where he can do no harm.'

Aungel bristled. 'Clippesby would never hurt anyone – he is the gentlest man alive. Besides, it was *you* who insisted on sitting in the henhouse all afternoon, not him. He wanted to read in the hall.'

'The way I choose to evaluate another scholar's mental competence is none of your business,' snapped Theophilis, nettled. 'So keep your nose out of it.'

'It *is* his business,' countered Bartholomew. 'And mine, too. We look out for each other at Michaelhouse.'

'I *am* looking out for Clippesby,' said Theophilis crossly. 'I am trying to determine whether he should be allowed to wander about unsupervised in his fragile state. He may come to grief at the hands of those who do not under-stand him. I have his welfare at heart.'

Bartholomew was far from sure he did, but the Junior Proctor's claims flew from his mind when they arrived at the butts. The town had not forgiven the University for disrupting its turn the previous evening, and had turned out in force to retaliate in kind.

As ordering one side home would have caused a riot for certain, Michael and Tulyet had divided the targets in half, so that the University had the four on the left part of the mound, and the town had the four on the right. Neither faction was happy with the arrangement, and Michael's beadles and Tulyet's soldiers were struggling to keep the peace.

'Lord!' breathed Aungel, looking around with wide eyes. '*Everyone* is here – the whole University and every man in the town. We will never get a chance to shoot.'

'No,' agreed Bartholomew, 'so round up everyone from Michaelhouse and take them home. There is no point in risking them here needlessly. No, not you, Theophilis. You must stay and help Michael.'

'But it might be dangerous,' objected Theophilis. 'Or do you mean to place me in harm's way because I believe Clippesby is mad?'

'I place you there because you are the Junior Proctor,' retorted Bartholomew tartly. 'It is your job.'

Aungel was wrong to say that the whole University and every man in the town was at the butts, because more were arriving with every passing moment, adding to what was becoming a substantial crush. The beadles and soldiers had joined forces to keep the two apart, but Bartholomew could tell it was only a matter of time before their thin barrier was breached.

He looked around in despair. There were far more townsmen than scholars, but many students were trained warriors who could kill stick-wielding peasants with ease. If the evening did end in a fight, he would not like to bet on which side would win.

'Why not send them *all* home?' he asked Tulyet.

The Sheriff was watching Leger and Norbert try to instruct a gaggle of men from the Griffin, all of whom were much more interested in exchanging insults with the Carmelite novices than anything the knights could tell them about improving their stance and grip.

'Because as long as they are here, we can monitor them,' explained Tulyet tersely. 'If we let them go, they will sneak around in packs and any control we have will be lost.'

'How long do you think you can keep them from each other's throats?' asked Bartholomew uneasily.

'Hopefully, for as long as is necessary. Unfortunately, your new beadles are useless. Half are cowering behind the Franciscan Friary, while the rest itch to start a fight.'

He darted away when a Carmelite novice 'accidentally' hit Leger with a bow. Then Bartholomew heard Sauvage calling to him, urging him to abandon 'them French-loving University traitors' and stand with loyal Englishmen instead. Bartholomew pretended he had not heard, and retreated behind a cart, where he watched the unfolding crisis with growing consternation.

Most of King's Hall had turned out. They included the four friends who had nearly come to blows with Isnard on the way to the Spital fire. They strutted around like peacocks, and other foundations were quick to follow their example, causing townsmen to bristle with indignation. The name Wyse could be heard, as townsfolk reminded each other that one such arrogant scholar had slaughtered a defenceless old man.

The King's Hall men considered themselves far too important to wait for their turn to shoot, so they strode to the front of the queue and stepped in front of the Carmelites. Bartholomew held his breath, hoping the University would not start fighting among itself. If it did, the town would pitch in and that would be that. But Michael saved the day by promising the friars a barrel of ale if they allowed King's Hall to go ahead of them.

First at the line was the scholar who had declared himself to be a Fleming – Bruges. He took a bow from

Cynric without a word of thanks, and to prove that he was an accomplished warrior, he carried on a desultory conversation with his friends while he sent ten missiles thudding into the target. There was silence as everyone watched in begrudging admiration.

'King's Hall will never allow the French to invade,' he bragged, thrusting the bow so carelessly at Cynric that the book-bearer dropped it. 'It does not matter if these ignorant peasants can shoot, because Cambridge has *us* to defend it.'

'We are not ignorant, you pompous arse,' bellowed Sauvage, a 'witticism' that won a roar of approval from the town. 'And *we* will defend the town, not you.'

'You?' drawled Bruges with a provocative sneer. 'I hit the target ten times. What was your score, peasant?'

'It was only four,' scoffed the student from Koln. 'And not one hit the middle.'

'You two are *foreign*,' yelled Sauvage, red with mortification as Koln's cronies hooted with derisive laughter. 'You are here to spy and report to your masters in Paris.'

'And we cannot allow that,' shouted Isnard, although what a man with one leg was doing at the butts, Bartholomew could not imagine. Archery required two hands, and the bargeman needed at least one for his crutches. 'We should trounce them.'

'Come and try, cripple!' goaded Bruges. 'We will show you what we do to cowardly rogues who stab elderly plagiarists.'

'We did not kill Paris!' declared Isnard, outraged. '*You* did. He—'

'Enough!' came Michael's irate voice, as he and Tulyet hurried forward to intervene. 'Koln, if you are going to shoot, get on with it. If not, stand back and let someone else have a turn.'

'And do not even think of jeering at him, Sauvage,' warned Tulyet, 'unless you fancy a night in gaol. Now, take your bow again, and this time mark your target *before* you draw. Isnard, if you must be here, do something useful and sort these arrows into bundles of ten.'

'Can he count that high?' called Bruges, although he blanched and looked away when Michael swung towards him with fury in his eyes.

Tulyet began to instruct Sauvage, who was delighted to be singled out by so august a warrior, and called his friends to watch, drawing their attention away from the scholars. Unsettled by the Senior Proctor's looming presence, there was no more trouble from King's Hall either. Bartholomew heaved a sigh of relief. Trouble had been averted – for now, at least.

For an hour or more, the two sides concentrated on the business at hand, each studiously ignoring the efforts of the other. Bartholomew began to hope that the evening would pass off without further incident after all, but then it was Bene't College's turn to shoot. Heltisle and his students shoved their way forward, full of haughty pride.

'Allow me to demonstrate,' Heltisle began in a self-important bray and, to everyone's astonishment, proceeded to send an arrow straight into the centre of the target.

It was the best shot of the evening, and raised a cheer from the University, although the townsfolk remained silent. His second missile split the first, and he placed the remaining eight in a neat circle around them. Then he shoved Cynric aside, and began to instruct his students himself. He took so long that a number of hostel men grew impatient with waiting.

'Take your lads home,' ordered Michael, easing the Vice-Chancellor away from the line so that Ely Hall could step up. 'There is no need to keep them here.'

'I would rather they stayed, Brother,' came a familiar voice. 'There is much to be learned from watching the efforts of others.'

It was de Wetherset. Bartholomew had not recognised him, because it was now completely dark, and while torches illuminated the targets and the line, it was difficult to make out anything else. Moreover, the Chancellor had dressed for battle – a boiled leather jerkin, a metal helmet, and a short fighting cloak on which was pinned his pilgrim badge. Unfortunately, rather than lending him a warlike mien, they made him look ridiculous, and a number of townsfolk were laughing. So far, he had not noticed.

'There will be a scuffle if too many men crowd the line,' argued Michael tightly, 'so, I repeat – Heltisle, go home.'

'If he does, it will leave us in a vulnerable minority,' countered de Wetherset. 'Besides, this is *our* night – if we concede the butts today, what is to stop the town from taking advantage of us in other ways tomorrow?'

'And you are here, Brother,' said Heltisle silkily. 'Or are you unequal to keeping us safe from revolting townsmen?'

'Oh, we need have no fears on that score, Heltisle,' said de Wetherset pleasantly. 'I trust Michael to protect us. If I did not, I would have stayed at home.'

'Then do what I tell you,' hissed Michael, exasperated. 'I cannot keep the peace if you overrule my decisions.'

'Very well,' conceded de Wetherset with an irritable sigh. 'We shall leave the moment we have seen what Ely Hall can do.'

'Did Suttone ever see you shoot, Heltisle?' asked Bartholomew casually, although he knew it was hardly the time to quiz the Vice-Chancellor about what Mallett claimed to have overheard. 'He often mentions you in his letters.'

'Does he?' asked Heltisle, instantly uneasy. 'What does he say?'

'That he wishes he had not resigned,' bluffed Bartholomew, glad it was dark, so Heltisle could not see the lie in his face. 'He is thinking of coming back and standing for re-election.'

'He cannot,' declared Heltisle in alarm. 'No one would vote for him – not now our scholars have had a taste of de Wetherset.'

'You are too kind, Heltisle,' said the Chancellor smoothly, and turned to smile at Bartholomew. 'I am glad to see *you* here – a veteran of Poitiers is just the example our students need. Perhaps you would give us a demonstration of your superior skills.'

'My skills lie not in shooting arrows, but in sewing up the wounds they make,' retorted Bartholomew. 'I can demonstrate *that*, if you like.'

De Wetherset laughed, although Bartholomew had not meant to be amusing. 'Regardless, I hope you are stockpiling bandages and salves. We shall need them when the Dauphin's army attacks our town.'

Bartholomew raised his eyebrows. 'I doubt he will bother with us – not when there are easier targets on the coast.'

But de Wetherset shook his head. 'He will know about our rich Colleges, wealthy merchants, and opulent parish churches. Of course he will come here, and anyone who thinks otherwise is a fool.'

Again, there was relative peace, as all attention was on the archers and their targets, although Heltisle did not take his scholars home and his example encouraged other Colleges and hostels to linger as well. For a while, the only sounds were the orders yelled by Cynric and Tulyet.

'Ready your bows!'

'Nock!'

'Mark!'

'Draw!'

'Loose!'

Then the twang and hiss as the missiles sped towards their targets, followed by a volley of thuds as they hit or jeers from onlookers if they went wide. Even as the arrows flew, Cynric and Tulyet were repeating the commands – the power of the English army lay in the ability of its archers to shoot an entire quiver in less than a minute, and it was not unknown for a good bowman to have two or more arrows in the air at the same time.

'Heltisle is the best shot so far,' said Cynric, when it was the physician's turn to step up to the mark. There was a short delay while White Hostel, which had just finished, went to retrieve the arrows so they could be reused. 'Although Valence Marie was almost as good. Gonville is rubbish, though.'

Bartholomew peered into the gloom. 'The Carmelite novices were here earlier – no surprise, as they have always been a bellicose horde – but do I see the Franciscans, too?'

'Yes – friars and monks are exempt, but not novices, so youngsters from all the Orders are here. Normally, our overseas students would stand in for them, but most of those are lying low, lest they are accused of being French.'

'*I* would not want to be an overseas scholar at the moment,' came a voice from the shadows. It was Aynton, the bandage gleaming white around his wrist. He walked carefully, so as not to soil his ugly boots. 'I hope we can protect them, should it become necessary.'

So did Bartholomew. 'How is your arm? You should be resting it at home.'

'Heltisle said there might be trouble tonight, so I felt obliged to put in an appearance,' explained Aynton. 'Hah! It is your go. Show us what a hero of Poitiers can do, eh?'

Bartholomew was horrified when scholars and towns-folk alike stopped what they were doing to watch him, and heartily wished Cynric had kept his tall tales to himself. Feeling he should at least try to put on a good show, he was more careful than he had been the last time, and listened to the advice Cynric murmured in his ear. His first shot went wide, but the next nine hit the target. None struck the centre, but he was satisfied with his performance even so.

'I thought you would be a lot better than that,' said Sergeant Orwel, disappointed.

'If you really were at Poitiers, you should know that accuracy was not an issue there,' said Cynric loftily. 'The enemy was so closely packed that it was impossible *not* to hit them, no matter where you pointed your bow.'

'Bartholomew never fought at Poitiers,' sneered Bruges. 'What rubbish you believe! Next you will claim that *Sauvage* is English, when it is obvious that he is a filthy French—'

'*You* dare question the origin of another man's name?' demanded Norbert, his face hot with indignation. 'You, who has one that the King of France would be proud to bear?'

'I am Flemish,' declared Bruges, offended. 'Only imbeciles cannot tell the difference.'

'How about a wager, Frenchie?' called Orwel. 'A groat says that four of us can beat any four of you.'

'A whole groat,' drawled Bruges caustically, while on the University side, a frantic search was made for Heltisle. 'I am dizzy with the excitement of winning such a heady sum. How shall we give our best when the stakes are so staggeringly high?'

'So you can pay then?' called Orwel, not a man to appreciate sarcasm. 'Good.'

Unfortunately for the scholars, Heltisle was nowhere to be found, so four King's Hall men – Bruges, Koln and two local students named Foxlee and Smith – stepped up to the line. They ignored the anxious clamour from the other scholars, who pointed out that while Bruges was a decent shot, the other three were only average, so room should be made for a trio from Valence Marie. Meanwhile, four townsmen were chosen and stood waiting.

'Ready your bows,' shouted Cynric quickly, when King's Hall refused to yield and tempers on the University side looked set to fray. 'Nock! Mark!'

There was a flurry of activity as all eight participants scrambled to obey.

'Draw! *Loose!*'

Thuds followed hisses, and everyone peered down the field. All the targets bristled with arrows, and it was clear that the result would be very close. The eight archers trotted off to inspect them more closely. Meanwhile, someone yelled that one round was not enough, so two more teams were assembling, ready to shoot the moment the targets were clear.

'Which of you will pay the groat?' demanded Leger triumphantly. 'Because *we* won.'

'You cannot know that!' objected Cynric. 'Not yet.'

'I can see all our arrows clustered together,' argued Leger. 'Whereas your bowmen are hunting in the grass for theirs. We *did* win!'

'Lying scum!' yelled someone from White Hostel. '*We* won and I will punch anyone who claims otherwise.'

'Come here and say that,' roared Leger. 'Now give us the groat or—'

'Ready your bows!'

Bartholomew was not sure who had called the next archers to order, because the speaker was deep in the shadows. However, it came from the town side, and mischief was in the air, as the first teams were still down at the targets.

'Wait!' he shouted urgently. 'Not yet.'

'Nock! Mark! Draw! *Loose!*'

The commands came in a rapid rattle, so authoritatively that eight arrows immediately flew from eight bows. A good part of butts training was conditioning men to follow orders immediately and unquestioningly, so it was no surprise that the second teams had reacted without hesitation. There was a collective hiss, followed by several thuds and a scream.

'Down bows! Down bows!' howled Cynric frantically, snatching the weapons away before anyone could reload. 'No one shoot! *Down* bows!'

Bartholomew did not wait to hear if it was safe to go. He set off towards the mound at a run, aware of others sprinting at his heels. He aimed for the shrieks.

He arrived to see that Foxlee had been shot in the leg, while Koln – mercifully unhurt – lay on the ground with his hands over his head, crying for a ceasefire. Others had not been so fortunate. Bruges and Smith from King's Hall were dead, as was one townsman.

De Wetherset was among those who had hurried after Bartholomew. He scrambled up the mound, breathing hard, his face a mask of horror. Then Tulyet arrived.

'Christ God!' the Sheriff swore when he saw the bodies. 'Who gave the order to shoot?'

'A townsman,' replied de Wetherset shakily. 'But I cannot believe he intended anyone to die, as his own side was down here, too. Clearly, it is a prank gone badly wrong.'

Bartholomew was not so sure. Nor was Koln, now on his feet and shaking with fury.

'Of course the culprit meant there to be bloodshed!' he yelled. 'It was brazen murder! Someone will pay for this!'

'Just stop and think,' snapped de Wetherset. 'The town would never hurt one of—'

'I want revenge,' howled Koln. 'Well, lads? What are you waiting for? Will you allow town scum to dispatch our friends?'

There was a short silence, then all hell broke loose.

\* \* \*

There were moments during the ensuing mêlée when Bartholomew wondered if he was dreaming about Poitiers. He still had nightmares about the battle, and the screams and clash of arms that resounded across the butts were much the same. He yelled himself hoarse calling for a ceasefire, but few heard, and those who did were disinclined to listen.

'Stay with me, boy,' gasped Cynric, whose face was spattered with someone else's blood. 'Back to back, defending each other. You were wise to take the high ground – it will be easier to fight them off from here.'

Bartholomew knew there was no point in explaining he had not chosen the mound for strategic reasons but because it was where the first victims lay.

'No killing, Cynric,' he begged. 'Try to disarm them instead.'

'Right,' grunted Cynric, as he swung his cutlass at a stave-wielding townsman with all his might. 'After all, they mean us no harm.'

'Norbert!' gulped Bartholomew, watching in shock as a lucky thrust by a baying Bene't student passed clean through the knight's lower body. 'I must help—'

Cynric grabbed his arm before he could start towards the stricken man. 'You will stick with me if you value your life. And the lives of others – your skills will be needed later.'

'Goodness!' cried Aynton, stumbling up to them. He carried a bow in his uninjured hand, which he was waving wildly enough to deter anyone from coming too close. His face was white with terror. 'What do we do? How can we stop it?'

'You cannot,' gasped Cynric. 'Now stay behind us. You will be safe there.'

Bartholomew watched in despair as a phalanx of flailing swords from King's Hall, led by the enraged Koln, cut a bloody swathe through a contingent of apprentices.

Then his attention was caught by a seething mass of townsfolk, all of whom were howling for French blood, and seemed to think it could be found on the mound. None of them believed Aynton's frightened bleat that he had none to offer, and they surged upwards with murder in their eyes.

Just when Bartholomew thought his life was over, there came a thunder of hoofs. It was Tulyet on a massive warhorse, next to Michael on Dusty and several mounted knights from the castle. None slowed when they reached the skirmishers, so that anyone who did not want to be trampled was forced to scramble away fast. The riders wheeled their destriers around and drove them through the teeming mass a second time, after which most combatants broke off the fight to concentrate on which way they would have to leap to avoid the deadly hoofs. Tulyet reined in and stood in his stirrups, towering over those around him.

'How dare you break the peace!' he thundered, his voice surprisingly loud for so slight a man. 'Is this how you serve your country? By fighting each other? Disarm at once!'

'But we were fighting *French* scholars,' shouted a potter, too full of bloodlust to know he should hold his tongue. 'They are the enemy. We were—'

'Arrest that man,' bellowed Tulyet, pointing furiously at him.

Two of his soldiers hurried forward to oblige, much to the potter's dismay.

'*We* did not start this,' shouted Koln, whose face was white with rage in the flickering torchlight. '*They* did – the town scum.'

'You are under arrest, too,' snarled Michael. 'See to it, Meadowman.'

The beadle bundled the startled King's Hall man away before he could draw breath to object. Then de Wetherset spoke, begging his scholars to disperse. Most did, although the livid faces of Michael and Tulyet did more to shift them than any of the Chancellor's nervous entreaties. Soon, all that were left were the dead and wounded.

'Casualties?' demanded Tulyet in a tight, clipped voice.

'Eight dead,' replied Bartholomew, not looking up from the miller he was struggling to save. 'Three scholars and five townsmen. There will be others before morning.'

'Eight,' breathed Michael, shaking his head in disgust. 'All lost for nothing.'

'Take the wounded to the Franciscan Friary,' ordered Tulyet. 'And spread word that if anyone, other than soldiers or beadles, is out on the streets tonight, he will hang at dawn.'

'Not scholars,' said de Wetherset hoarsely. 'You do not have the authority to impose that sort of sanction on us. Tell him, Brother.'

'Then *I* will impose it,' said Michael shortly. 'Because he is right – *anyone* out tonight will be presumed guilty of affray and punished accordingly.'

Tulyet nodded curt thanks, then hurried away to organise stretchers and bearers, while Michael went to give what comfort he could to the dying – he was not a priest, but had been granted dispensation to give last rites during the plague and had continued the practice since. Bartholomew turned to Cynric, knowing he needed the help of other *medici*.

'Fetch Rougham and Meryfeld. Then go to Michaelhouse and tell my students to bring bandages, salves, needles and thread.'

Fleetingly, it occurred to him that when de Wetherset recommended that he stockpile medical supplies, he had not imagined that he would be needing them that very night.

Cynric nodded briskly. 'Anything else?'

'Yes – go to the Spital and ask Amphelisa for a supply

of the strong herbs that she uses for pain. I do not have nearly enough to do what will be necessary this evening.'

'Then thank God Margery found out that the Devil does not live there,' muttered the book-bearer, crossing himself before kissing a grubby amulet. 'I would not have been able to go otherwise, as I have no wish to encounter Satan.'

'You already have,' said Bartholomew soberly. 'I am sure he was here tonight.'

# CHAPTER 10

The bells were chiming for the night office by the time Bartholomew and his helpers had carried all the wounded to the Franciscan Priory. Despite their best efforts, another three men died, bringing the death toll to eleven – four scholars and seven townsfolk. Their bodies were taken to the chapel, where the friars recited prayers for their souls.

Rougham and Meryfeld, physicians who only ever tended paying customers, quickly bagged the wealthy victims, leaving Bartholomew with the rest. This did not bother him, as he had always been more interested in saving lives than making money. However, he was pleasantly surprised to learn that Amphelisa felt the same way – she not only donated her pain-dulling herbs for free, but stayed to help him saw and stitch. She was a constant presence at his side, always ready with what was required and enveloping him in the sweet scent of the distilled oils that had soaked into her burgundy work-robe.

'It is a good thing I sent Eudo and Goda to replenish my stocks today,' she murmured, helping Foxlee to sip a poppy juice cordial. 'Or we would have run out by now.'

'For Hélène.' Bartholomew spoke absently, because he was removing the arrowhead from Foxlee's leg, and it was perilously close to an artery. 'To help her sleep.'

Amphelisa shot him a startled look. 'Hélène will have camomile and honey. I am not in the habit of dosing small children with henbane and mandrake.'

Bartholomew glanced up at her. 'Then why did Eudo and Goda tell me—'

'I cannot control what they say when I am not there to correct them,' she interrupted shortly. 'Goda is a fey soul who probably misheard, while Eudo is slow in the wits.'

'He is not too stupid to convince the town's favourite witch that he was Satan.'

Amphelisa scowled. 'That was *your* fault! Until then, we had kept the curious away by jigging bits of gauze around on twine. But did you run away screaming? Oh, no! You had to poke about in the bushes for evidence of trickery. We had to devise another ruse, and claiming that Satan had moved in was the best we could manage in a hurry.'

'What will you do now that Margery is telling everyone the truth? Ask for your money back? I understand that "Satan" paid a handsome fee to ensure her cooperation.'

'It no longer matters, because the *peregrini* have gone,' said Amphelisa. 'Someone started a rumour about French spies, so they decided to leave at once.'

'All of them? Delacroix was ill the last I heard.'

'I gave him nettle root to stop his bowels, and he was first through the gate.' She gave a wan smile. 'Then I started a tale of my own – that our patients went to London for specialist treatment. London is south, but the *peregrini* went north, so if anyone gives chase . . .'

'So the Spital no longer has "inmates"?'

'None, and anyone may come to check our hall. Indeed, I hope they do. Then they will see it is a good place, and will give us some real lunatics to look after.'

'And you need fee-paying patients,' said Bartholomew, dropping the arrowhead into a basin, and pressing a clean cloth to the wound.

'How do you . . .' She trailed off, then shook her head in disgust. 'Mallett! I thought I saw him sneaking about with one of the nuns, and he is your pupil. *He* told you!'

Bartholomew glanced to where Mallett was arguing with two tailors over payment for services rendered. He had no doubt that the student would win. He turned back to his own patient. Foxlee barely flinched as he began to sew, which was testament to Amphelisa's skill – she had administered enough medicine to blunt the pain, but not enough to send their patient into too deep a sleep.

'If Eudo and your husband were pretending to be denizens of Hell when the Girards were murdered, we can cross them off our list of suspects,' said Bartholomew, his eyes on his stitching. 'While the rest of the staff have alibis in each other . . .'

'But I was alone,' finished Amphelisa, guessing exactly where he was heading. 'I am not your culprit, though. I was the one who offered them sanctuary.'

Tulyet had said the same, Bartholomew recalled, and had claimed that she would not have taken such loving care of Hélène if she had murdered the girl's family. He said nothing, and Amphelisa grabbed his arm, forcing him to look at her.

'Henry and I founded the Spital – a place of comfort and healing – because we wanted to do some good, as well as to make amends for the wrongs of the past. Do you really think we would undo all that by committing murder?'

It was a good point, but hardly the time to discuss it. Bartholomew left her to bandage Foxlee's leg and moved to his next patient, who had suffered a serious gash across the chest. After that there were more wounds to clean and sew shut, so many that he began to wonder if anyone had escaped the mêlée unscathed. He finished eventually and slumped on a bench, flexing shoulders that were cramped from bending. By then, all his helpmeets had gone except two of his senior students.

'Go home now,' he told them tiredly. 'You did well tonight.'

'No, *you* go home sir,' said Mallett, whose purse looked a lot fuller than it had been before the skirmish. 'It will be light in a couple of hours, at which point you will have to examine this lot again. So snatch a bit of sleep, while Islaye and I mind things here.'

'Everyone is resting peacefully now anyway,' put in Islaye, who had wept every time a patient had died, and had been unable to look at some of the wounds Bartholomew had been obliged to repair. 'Except Norbert, who is in too much pain.'

'Serves him right,' muttered Mallett, who had not uttered a word of comfort to anyone. 'He called me a Frenchman yesterday.'

Bartholomew was too exhausted to point out that such an 'insult' hardly warranted being fatally stabbed through the bowels. He went to tend Norbert himself, thinking that neither student was suitable company for a man on the verge of death. The knight opened pain-filled eyes as Bartholomew knelt next to his pallet.

'Give me medicine to ease the agony,' he whispered. 'And stay with me awhile.'

Bartholomew set about preparing a potion so strong that Norbert would be unlikely to wake once he had swallowed it. It would not kill him – the wound would – but Norbert would sleep until he breathed his last. He cradled the dark, greasy head in his arm, and helped him drink until every drop was gone. Norbert lay back, his face sheened in sweat.

'And now I shall confess my crimes.'

'Not to me,' said Bartholomew, beginning to rise. 'You need a priest.'

Norbert gripped his arm. 'I said *crimes*, not sins. The Franciscans have already given me absolution, so I do not fear for my soul. But I want to tell you what happened tonight, because it was me who called the order to ready bows. However, I did *not* call the order to shoot.'

Bartholomew reflected on what he could remember of the sequence of events. 'Yes – the voice of whoever shouted the first order *was* different from whoever bellowed the second. But both came from the town's side of the butts.'

'It was someone behind me. I looked around, but it was too dark to see, and there were so many people . . . It was some fool mouthing off without considering the consequences.'

'Even fools know that if you shoot at people you might hit them.'

Norbert winced. 'I wanted to give those arrogant King's Hall bastards a fright by making them *think* they were about to be shot. I never meant for it to actually happen.'

'Close your eyes,' said Bartholomew, not sure what to think. 'Sleep is not far off now.'

'I have not finished. You should also be aware that the Spital's secret is out. By morning, everyone will know the place is full of Frenchmen. A nun told me last Monday.'

Bartholomew frowned. 'Which nun?'

'She spoke through a half-closed door, so I never saw her face. She said it was an abomination that French scum were hiding in our town, and she wanted me to kill them.'

Bartholomew struggled to understand the implications of what he was being told. 'If this nun spoke to you on Monday, it means that you knew there were Frenchmen in the Spital when the fire broke out on Wednesday.'

'Yes, I did. Leger and I were pleased that some were roasted, but *we* did not do it. I swear on my immortal soul that neither of us went anywhere near the Spital that morning.'

'Why did you not tell Dick all this?'

'Because Leger wants to be Sheriff, so it is in our interests to see Tulyet's investigation fail. But now my end is near . . . well, his ambitions are less important than my conscience.'

Bartholomew was still grappling to understand what Norbert had done. 'But some of the Spital's fugitives were

Jacques – rebels. You should not have kept that to your-selves.'

'We didn't – we have been spreading the word slowly and carefully through the town. Leger says that instant rumours can be dismissed as falsehoods, but measured hints and whispers are far less easy to ignore. We watched the tale take hold more strongly tonight, and by morning, everyone will know who is in the Spital.'

Bartholomew was glad the *peregrini* had gone, although he hoped the generous souls who had taken pity on them would not suffer in their stead. 'Where did you meet this nun?'

'At St Radegund's, when I was delivering messages from the King to various abbesses.'

'What else can you tell me about her?'

'Just that I could hear her scratching as she spoke. It is not a nice habit in a woman.'

Alice, thought Bartholomew. The Lyminster nuns had guessed the truth about the Spital's lunatics, so it was no surprise that Alice had done so, too. Yet confiding in Norbert was akin to arranging a massacre. Was she so twisted by hatred that she would bring about the deaths of harmless women and children?

Norbert seemed to sense his thoughts. 'Yes,' he whis-pered. 'She *is* evil. I could hear the malevolence in her voice as she spoke to me.'

Bartholomew hurried straight home to tell Michael what Norbert had confessed, only to find the Master's quarters empty. He scribbled a note detailing his findings, and left it on the desk. Then he returned to his own room and fell into an exhausted sleep. Not long after, the bell rang to call everyone to morning prayer. He rose and shuffled wearily into the yard, where Cynric was waiting to talk to him – the book-bearer had visited the Franciscans' chapel during the night, and had made an alarming discovery among the dead. Bartholomew listened to his tale in horror.

Michael did not appear for the service, so Bartholomew fretted all through it, unsettled by Cynric's news. The monk was missing for breakfast, too, and Bartholomew only picked at the meaty pottage that was served. William took Michael's place at the high table, booming the pre- and post-prandial Graces with great relish and many grammatical mistakes.

When the meal was over, Bartholomew told Aungel which texts to teach that day, oblivious to the young Fellow's dismay at what he considered to be unrealistic goals, then hurried to his room, where he gathered fresh supplies for the wounded at the friary. Michael arrived just as the physician was about to leave, his face grey with fatigue and his habit bearing signs of the previous night's skirmish.

'We declared a total curfew in the end,' he said. 'But that did not stop some feisty souls from sneaking out. Dick, Theophilis and I raced about like hares all night, quelling one spat only for another to break out. Dick hanged three of the worst offenders this morning.'

'They were executed for affray?' asked Bartholomew uneasily.

'For murder – they were caught red-handed and there is no doubting their guilt. However, he is keen for everyone to think it was for rioting – he made the threat, and must be seen to carry it out, or no one will believe him the next time he is compelled to do it.'

'What is happening on the streets now?'

'Nothing – the mischief-makers have gone home at last.' Michael grimaced. 'We should be hunting the rogue who stabbed Paris, Bonet and the Girards – and whoever dispatched poor old Wyse – but instead all we do is struggle to keep a lid on this brewing war.'

'What did the triumvirate do to help last night?'

234

'They disappeared into St Mary the Great, where they stayed until dawn. No doubt they were plotting against me while I risked life and limb outside. What was the final death toll?'

'It will be fourteen by now, although only four were scholars.'

'Eighteen, then,' said Michael softly, 'if we include the three who were hanged and their victim. Eighteen dead for nothing!'

'Do you want official causes of death?' asked Bartholomew, and gave his report without waiting for an answer. 'Nine townsmen died of knife wounds, while the tenth was shot. Of the scholars, two were bludgeoned, one was shot, and Bruges was stabbed.'

'Stabbed?' asked Michael. 'You mean shot – he and the other King's Hall lad were caught by the first volley of arrows. You said he was dead when you reached the mound.'

'He *was* dead, which is why I did not examine him very carefully – I was more concerned with the living at that point. But Cynric went to the Franciscans' chapel and saw the dagger still in Bruges's back. He pulled it out and brought it home. It is on the table.'

Michael went to look at it, then gaped his shock. 'But it is almost identical to the ones that were used on Paris and the Girard family! Are you telling me that the killer struck again – *while we were watching?*'

Bartholomew raised his hands in a shrug. 'He must have done, because Bruges was dead when I arrived at the targets. Cynric asked the surviving archers if they saw anyone else lurking around, but none of them did. The fact that it was dark did not help – the targets were illuminated, but the area around them was not.'

'Lord!' breathed Michael. 'Do you think one of them did it – that there were sour words between the opposing teams while they were deciding who won the contest?'

'Cynric said they watched each other very carefully, as everyone knew their rivals would try to cheat. Bruges was alive when the arrows were loosed, which means the killer struck *after* they landed, but *before* we all reached the targets to see who had been hit.'

'There goes our theory that Paris, Bonet and the Girards were killed for being French,' sighed Michael. 'Bruges is from Flanders.'

'I am not sure everyone appreciates the difference,' said Bartholomew soberly. 'I wager anything you please that the killer is sitting in his lair at this very moment, congratulating himself on ridding the town of another enemy.'

'Do you think *he* gave the order to shoot? The killer?'

Bartholomew rubbed his eyes tiredly. 'I explained all this in the message I left in your room. Did you not read it?'

'What message? My desk was empty.'

Bartholomew outlined what he had written, at the same time wondering who had taken the note. The obvious suspect was Theophilis, who had then carried it to his real masters in St Mary the Great. Or perhaps he was the killer, and was even now working out how to avoid being caught while simultaneously continuing his evil work.

'So Norbert yelled the order for the archers to prepare, to give King's Hall a fright, but someone else hollered the command to shoot,' summarised Michael when Bartholomew had finished. 'And all the while, our killer loitered boldly, awaiting his next victim.'

Bartholomew nodded. 'Norbert thought the second command came from a townsman who acted without considering the consequences. The killer just took advantage of it.'

'So we can discount Norbert and Leger for the Spital murders, because you believe what Norbert told you regarding their whereabouts?'

236

'Yes, and we can discount Tangmer and Eudo, too, which means we are left with the *peregrini*, Amphelisa, Sister Alice, Magistra Katherine, the triumvirate, Theophilis—'

'Not Theophilis or de Wetherset,' interrupted Michael. 'And not Heltisle either, much as it pains me to admit it. They are more likely to wound with plots than daggers.'

'But you see Aynton as a stabber?'

'I do. I told you: there is something about him that I do not trust at all.' Michael returned to the list. 'I cannot see nuns committing murder either.'

'Not even Sister Alice, who betrayed the *peregrini* to Norbert, along with the injunction to kill them all? Moreover, far from narrowing our list of suspects down, her gossip means that we now have to expand it to anyone who might have heard the rumour about Tangmer sheltering French spies.'

'Are you sure Norbert was telling the truth? I would not put it past him to lie on his deathbed, just to confound us.'

'He seemed sincere. Will you confront Alice today?'

'Of course, although you should not forget that Norbert did not see her face, and it is not difficult to don a habit, stand in the shadows and impersonate a nun. But first, I must sleep. There is no point in challenging anyone when my wits are muddy from fatigue. Will you come with me to St Radegund's later?'

'If I must,' replied Bartholomew without enthusiasm.

The Franciscans occupied a large swathe of land in the east of the town. It was bordered by the main road at the front and the King's Ditch at the back. Inside, it was pretty, dominated by its church, refectory and dormitory. It also had a substantial guesthouse, which had been converted into a makeshift hospital. Bartholomew walked in and satisfied himself that the surviving wounded were doing as well as could be expected.

'Norbert died,' reported Mallett. 'In his sleep, which was a pity, as I could have charged him for another dose of poppy juice if he had woken.'

'You will go far,' muttered Bartholomew in distaste. 'You already think like most successful *medici*.'

'Thank you, sir,' said Mallett, flattered. 'But Islaye and I can manage here for a bit longer, if you have other things to do. It will be no trouble.'

Bartholomew was sure it would not, especially if fees were pocketed in the process. He replaced them with two of their classmates, and went in search of Prior Pechem, a dour, humourless man who had just completed his morning devotions and was on his way to the refectory to break his fast.

'Your tyranny in the classroom has paid off,' Pechem remarked. 'Your lads are much better than Rougham and Meryfeld, who have fifty years' medical experience between them.'

As Bartholomew had scant regard for his colleagues' abilities, this compliment fell on stony ground. 'I saw you and some of your novices at the butts last night,' he began.

Pechem nodded. 'The ones who are not exempt from this wretched call to arms. I accompanied them, lest there was trouble.'

'Were you there when the fight erupted?'

'Yes, but I whisked them all home the moment the knives came out. I know they were there to learn how to kill, but I am unwilling to let them put theory into practice just yet.'

'So what did you see?'

'Not much, because it was dark. I heard a yell to ready bows, followed by another – a different voice, from further away – to shoot. Then all was chaos, blood and confusion.'

'Did you recognise either of the voices?'

'Unfortunately not. However, both came from the townsfolk's side – the first from near the front, and the second from the back. Indeed, it was so far to the rear that the culprit may not have been part of the town faction at all.'

'What are you saying? That he may have been one of us?'

Pechem shrugged. 'I would hope not, but who knows? You do not need me to tell you that some of our students are eager to test their newly acquired skills on living flesh.'

'I hope you are wrong,' said Bartholomew unhappily.

'So do I, but I fear I am not. The first order was from some ass who aimed to give everyone a scare, but the second was from someone who wanted to see blood. He knew exactly what he was doing, suggesting a cold and calculating mind. I doubt he will be caught.'

'Do not underestimate Michael. He has snared cunning criminals before.'

'Yes, but that was when he had power. Now he must dance to de Wetherset's tune, and de Wetherset listens too much to Heltisle and Aynton.'

'You do not like them?'

'Let us just say that I have reservations. Of course, if there are any more incidents like last night, some of us will demand their resignation.'

'Please do not,' begged Bartholomew. 'They will shift the blame to Michael, because keeping the peace is the Senior Proctor's responsibility.'

'They can try, but we are not stupid – we know who is better for the University, and it is not de Wetherset and his power-hungry cronies.' Then Pechem gave one of his rare smiles and changed the subject. 'How is Clippesby? That man is a treasure.'

Bartholomew regarded him in surprise. 'We think so, but have you forgotten that he is a Dominican? A member of a rival Order?'

'His treatise means we are more kindly disposed towards those now. Before, we deplored their reckless adherence to nominalism, but Clippesby's hens demonstrated how we can accept their arguments while still remaining true to our own. He is a genius.'

'Yes,' agreed Bartholomew. 'We have known it for years.'

The wounded kept Bartholomew in the Franciscan Priory until mid-morning, after which he left Dr Rougham in charge and walked home. When he arrived, Michael's window shutters were open and voices emanated from his quarters. He climbed the stairs, and found the Master and his Fellows discussing the previous night's skirmish.

Michael reclined in his favourite chair, the colour back in his cheeks after a nap and a snack from his private pantry. Theophilis was on a bench next to him, while William sat on the windowsill. Aungel perched on a stool, straight-backed and formal, not yet ready to relax in the presence of men who had so recently been his teachers. Clippesby lay on the floor with two hedgehogs.

'You made friends of the Franciscans with your treatise,' Bartholomew told the eccentric Dominican.

'Not *all* Franciscans,' growled William, eyeing Clippesby with a combination of resentment and envy. 'Some of us still think your arguments are seriously flawed.'

'Are they?' asked Clippesby with a sweet smile. 'Please tell me how, so I can amend them. My next thesis is almost finished, and I should not like to repeat any mistakes.'

'I am not telling you,' blustered William. 'You must work them out for yourself.'

The others exchanged amused glances. William noticed and went on the offensive, aiming for Clippesby, because he knew the Dominican would not fight back.

'I suppose *they* are philosophers, too,' he scoffed, jabbing a filthy finger at the hedgehogs. 'And will tell you what to pen in your next "seminal" work.'

'Oh, no,' said Clippesby, all wide-eyed innocence. 'Hedgehogs have no time for logical reasoning – they prefer to spend their time exploring the town. It is *hens* who are the theologians, as you would know if you had read their discourse.'

'Exploring?' queried Theophilis, and when Clippesby's attention returned to the animals, he grinned at the others. 'Exploring what? Libraries, in search of tomes that will lead them to a greater understanding of theology?'

'Exploring the *town*,' repeated Clippesby patiently. 'For example, Olive and Henrietta here went to the Chesterton road on Thursday, where the scholar killed that old man.'

'So they did not analyse the naturalism of—' began Theophilis.

'Wait a moment,' interrupted Michael sharply. 'You witnessed Wyse's murder?'

'*I* did not,' replied Clippesby. 'Nor did Olive and Henrietta. However, they saw the culprit running away. They did not know he was a killer at the time, of course – they only realised it later, after the body was discovered.'

'And you only mention this now?' cried Michael. 'After Dick and I have been running ourselves ragged in a hunt for clues?'

'I have been busy,' shrugged Clippesby. 'Heltisle keeps lying about how many copies of my treatise have been sold, while Theophilis insists on entangling me in theological dis—'

'The killer,' snapped Michael in exasperation. 'His name, please.'

'Olive and Henrietta did not see his face,' said Clippesby. 'But his cloak fell open as he passed, revealing his scholar's tabard. There was also an academic hat tucked in his belt.'

'Did you recognise the livery?' pressed Michael.

'No, because it was too dark.'

'So how do you know it was the killer you saw?' interrupted Bartholomew.

'Because he held a bloodied rock, which he tossed into

241

the copse where Olive and Henrietta were sleeping. It is what caught their attention, you see, otherwise they might have dozed through the entire incident.'

'*Were* they asleep?' asked Theophilis with a sly smile. 'Or philosophising?'

Even Clippesby was beginning to tire of Theophilis's persistence. 'I just told you – hedgehogs do not engage in academic pursuits. Olive and Henrietta wanted a rest, away from the fuss generated by the chickens' theories.'

'In other words, stop asking stupid questions,' translated William. 'The hens have already written all they know about nominalism and realism, so if you want to delve any deeper into the matter, you will have to consult with me.'

Theophilis laughed and the others joined in. Their mirth was short-lived, though, as William glanced out of the window to see Commissary Aynton walking across the yard. As he could think of no clever riposte to put his colleagues in their place, he vented his spleen on the visitor instead.

'Here comes one of the Chancellor's dogs,' he sneered. 'Do you want me to send him packing, Brother? I will do it if your Junior Proctor is unequal to the task.'

Michael made a warning sound in the back of his throat as Theophilis started to reply. No foundation liked outsiders to know its members quarrelled, so by the time Aynton was shown in, he might have been forgiven for thinking that all Michaelhouse Fellows loved each other like brothers.

'Good morning, Commissary,' said Michael pleasantly. 'How may we help you?'

'I am here to help *you*, Brother,' said Aynton, beaming. 'With a report. De Wetherset, Heltisle and I questioned witnesses while you lay around in bed this morning. Not that there is anything wrong with sleeping, of course. I am sure you needed the rest.'

'I did,' said Michael stiffly. 'I was up all night.'

'So were we,' said Aynton. 'Working for the University's greater good. We discussed the riot *ad nauseam*, although we reached no firm conclusions.'

'I imagine not,' said Michael haughtily. 'There are none to reach with the information currently available. If there were, I would have drawn them myself and acted on them.'

'Of course you would,' said Aynton, so condescendingly that Bartholomew glanced uneasily at Michael, knowing that umbrage would be taken. 'I would never suggest otherwise.'

'Good,' said Michael, controlling himself with difficulty. 'So make your report. What did these witnesses tell you?'

'Well, we started by asking all those scholars who attended the butts if they knew who gave the order to shoot. They did – it was a townsman.'

'Any particular one?'

'They did not see, as he skulked behind his cronies. However, we know his motive – to avenge that old rogue Wyse by taking the lives of innocent scholars. Every University man we interviewed said the same thing, so it must be true.'

Michael gave a tight smile. 'But every townsman who was there claims the culprit is a scholar. So who should we believe, when everyone is convinced of his own rectitude?'

'Why, scholars, of course,' replied Aynton, astonished he should ask. 'Townsmen are given to lying. Besides, the command came from *their* side of the butts. I heard it myself.'

'So did I,' put in Theophilis. 'I agree with Aynton – a townsman *is* responsible. But we will catch him, Brother. You and me together.'

'Let us hope so,' said Michael. 'Is there anything else, Commissary, or are you ready to resume your enquiries into the murders of Paris and the others? Unless you have solved the mystery already, of course?'

Aynton chuckled. 'Not yet, Brother, not yet. But before I set off, I must pass you a message from the Chancellor: he would like to see you in his office at your earliest convenience. He asks if Bartholomew would attend, too, as he has more griping in the guts.'

'Probably from listening to you and Heltisle spout nonsense all night,' muttered William, and for once, Bartholomew thought the friar might be right.

Michael did not go to St Mary the Great immediately, aiming to make the point that the Senior Proctor could not be summoned like a minion. And as de Wetherset's medical complaint was not urgent, Bartholomew went to replenish his medical bag first.

Eventually, both were ready and they walked across the yard towards the gate. Before they could open it, Tulyet arrived with Sir Leger and Sergeant Orwel. Orwel was a bristling bundle of hostility, and looked around the College with calculated disdain. Leger was pale, and seethed with anger and grief for Norbert.

'I did all I could for him,' Bartholomew said gently, 'but his wound was too severe.'

'I know,' replied Leger, softening a little. 'The Spital woman – Amphelisa – told me.'

'He confessed things before he slipped into his final sleep,' said Bartholomew. 'About being cornered in St Radegund's on Monday, probably by Sister Alice, who urged him to kill the French spies hiding in the Spital.'

There was a moment when he thought Leger would deny it, but then the knight inclined his head. 'It surprised us – we are not used to nuns encouraging slaughter.'

'I hope it was not you two who started the rumour about the Spital,' said Tulyet coolly. 'The one that is all over the town this morning.'

Leger regarded him levelly. 'The nun confided in Norbert on Monday, but, as you have just remarked, the tale was not "all over the town" until today. If we were responsible, it would have been common knowledge on Tuesday or Wednesday, would it not?'

Bartholomew felt like reporting what Norbert had told him about the delay, but then decided against challenging a knight who was loaded with weapons. Besides, the spreaders of the tale were far less important than its originator.

'Why did you not mention this at once?' demanded Tulyet crossly. 'Surely, you must see it has a bearing on the murders we have been struggling to solve?'

Leger shrugged. 'We did not believe it could be true, so we dismissed it as malicious nonsense. Moreover, Norbert did not see this nun's face, and she certainly did not tell him her name. If it was Sister Alice, this is the first I know about it.'

'I will go to St Radegund's this morning,' determined Michael. 'If she hates the French enough to want them lynched by an ignorant mob, then she might well have stabbed Paris, Bonet, the Girards and now Bruges. After all, she did visit the Spital on the day of the fire.'

Bartholomew was suddenly aware that Orwel was listening rather gleefully, as if he was pleased by the route their suspicions had taken.

'Where were you when the order was given to shoot last night?' Bartholomew asked him sharply.

Leger spoke before the sergeant could reply for himself. 'He was with me – at the *front* of the crowd, and in the plain sight and hearing of many witnesses. But I am sure you were not about to accuse him of being the culprit, just as I am sure you would not accuse me. Why would you? You have no evidence to suggest that either of us was responsible.'

Bartholomew was not sure what to think about Orwel,

although he knew Leger was innocent, as he himself had seen the knight arguing with scholars at the salient time. He let the matter drop.

'Unfortunately, the rumour is not just that the Spital sheltered French spies,' said Tulyet to Michael. 'It is also that the University knew about it but chose to look the other way.'

'I *did* look the other way,' said Michael. 'Out of compassion and decency. So did you.'

'Yes, but our Sheriff is not a traitor,' said Orwel smugly, as if the same could not be said of the Senior Proctor. 'How can he be? He is kin to the King.'

'I am?' asked Tulyet, startled to hear it.

Orwel nodded. 'Your son Dickon told me before you sent him to Huntingdon. Ergo, *you* never ignored the fact that a nest of spies was on our doorstep. However, most scholars are French and proud of it. Take King's Hall, for example – it has members named Bruges, Koln, Largo, Perugia, San Severino—'

'None of those are French,' interrupted Bartholomew. 'And Bruges was from Flanders.'

'They are foreign and thus suspect,' said Orwel with finality, and glared at the physician. 'We probably fought some of them at Poitiers, so I do not understand how you can bear to be in their company.'

'Take a dozen soldiers and go to the Spital,' ordered Tulyet, before Bartholomew could reply. 'I am making you personally responsible for its safety, which means that if it suffers so much as a scratch, I shall blame you. And you do not want that, Orwel, believe me.'

Orwel opened his mouth to refuse the assignment, but a glance at Tulyet's angry face made him think better of it. He nodded curtly and stamped away.

'No one will bother with the Spital now,' said Leger when Orwel had gone. 'Amphelisa told me last night that the spies – or lunatics, if you prefer – have fled.'

'That is irrelevant,' said Tulyet wearily. 'The Spital took them in, and there are many hotheads who will see that alone as an excuse to attack it.'

'There is more likely to be an assault on King's Hall than the Spital,' argued Leger. 'Orwel may not have put his case very eloquently, but he is right – it *does* possess the lion's share of the University's foreign scholars, so it is where any trouble will start.'

'You had better hope not,' said Michael coolly. 'It is full of influential nobles and favourites of the King, and if any more of them are killed by townsmen—'

'*Norbert* was a favourite of the King,' interrupted Leger tightly, 'and *he* was murdered by a scholar. The University must pay for his death.'

'He died because he was fighting when he should have been keeping the peace,' countered Tulyet shortly. 'He would still be alive if he had done his duty.'

'You take their side in this?' breathed Leger, shocked. 'When they killed innocent townsfolk last night and Wyse before that?'

'No one who died last night was innocent,' said Tulyet shortly. 'They chose to take up arms and they paid the price. However, I will not tolerate lawlessness in my town, so I *will* find who yelled the order to shoot and I *will* catch whoever killed Wyse, Paris and the others. The culprits will be brought to justice, no matter who they transpire to be.'

'Good,' said Leger. 'I will help. It will be a scholar and I shall see him swing.'

'Will you arrange for Norbert to be buried?' asked Tulyet, tired of arguing with him. 'I am sure he would rather you did it than anyone else.'

'So now we have another mystery to solve,' sighed Michael when Leger had gone. 'Because you are right: we should hunt down the rogue who gave the order to shoot. It is ultimately *his* fault that we have eighteen dead.'

'Yes,' agreed Tulyet tautly. 'And I meant what I told Leger: the culprit will suffer the full extent of the law regardless of who he is – townsman or scholar. I hope you will support me in this.'

'Of course,' Michael assured him. 'He will answer for his actions, and so will three other criminals: the killer with the fancy blades; the coward who dispatched poor old Wyse; and the poisonous nun who spread the rumour about the *peregrini*.'

'Perhaps Alice will confess to everything,' said Tulyet. 'Then there will be no reason for the town and the University to fight. It will reflect badly on your Order, though . . .'

'Alice did not give the order to shoot,' said Bartholomew. 'It was a man's voice.'

'Interrogate her,' instructed Tulyet. 'I will try to keep the peace here. And when you come back, would you mind telling Heltisle that the Mayor did *not* order the archers to massacre scholars last night – he was nowhere near the butts and has a dozen witnesses to prove it.'

'I had better do that first,' said Michael wearily. 'It will take very little to spark another riot, and that sort of accusation might well be enough.'

'Perhaps that is what Heltisle hopes,' said Tulyet soberly. 'So that you and de Wetherset will be held responsible, leaving the way open for him to step into your shoes.'

'With Theophilis as his loyal deputy,' added Bartholomew.

# CHAPTER 11

Bartholomew and Michael hurried towards St Mary the Great, both aware that the atmosphere on the streets had deteriorated badly since they had last been out. Townsmen blamed the University for the riot, while scholars accused the town. The situation was exacerbated by wild and unfounded rumours – that King's Hall had installed French spies in the Spital, that the Dauphin was poised to march on Cambridge at any day, and that the Mayor intended to poison the University's water supply.

'I know hindsight is a wonderful thing,' said Bartholomew, 'but you should never have let the triumvirate take so much power. The next time someone tells me that the Senior Proctor has too much authority, I shall say that I wish you had more of it.'

'Quite right, too,' said Michael. 'I admit I hoped that Heltisle and Aynton would make a mess of things so de Wetherset would have to dismiss them, but I did not anticipate that they would create this much havoc in so short a space of time.'

They arrived at the church, where scholars had gathered to mutter and plot against the town. Most were armed, even the priests. Bartholomew paused to gaze around in alarm, but Michael pulled him on, whispering that time was too short for gawping.

They reached de Wetherset's poky office, although it was Heltisle, not the Chancellor, who sat behind its desk. The floor was covered with Michael's personal possessions, which had been unceremoniously dumped there. The monk's eyes narrowed.

'What is going on?' he demanded dangerously. 'And why are you reading my private correspondence with the Bishop? Those letters were locked in a chest.'

Heltisle was unable to prevent a triumphant grin. 'I know – we had to smash it to get inside. De Wetherset did not want your rubbish cluttering up his new quarters, and as we had no key, we had to resort to other means of clearing the decks. Where have you been?'

'Tending to urgent University business,' replied Michael tightly. 'Such as the scholars who died in last night's brawl, along with Paris the—'

'Paris!' spat Heltisle. 'The town did us a favour when they dispatched him. He should have been hanged the moment his crime was discovered.'

Michael eyed him coolly. 'Should he, indeed? Perhaps I have been looking in the wrong place for his killer. I doubt townsmen feel strongly about plagiarism, whereas scholars . . .'

Heltisle sneered. 'Do not accuse me of fouling my hands with his filthy blood. And before you ask, I did not kill the spicer or that drunken nobody on the Chesterton road either.'

'Wyse was not a nobody,' said Bartholomew, amazed to discover that he was capable of disliking the arrogant Master of Bene't even more than he did already. 'The Franciscans were fond of him, he was one of my patients, and he was a member of the Michaelhouse Choir.'

'The Marian Singers,' corrected Michael.

'Clippesby's treatise is selling very well, by the way,' said Heltisle, moving to another matter in which he felt victorious. 'What a pity your College will not reap the profits.'

Michael thought it best to stay off that subject, lest he or Bartholomew inadvertently said something to make Heltisle smell a rat. 'You have not answered my first question. Why are you so busily nosing through my private correspondence?'

'And what is it doing in here anyway?' put in Bartholomew.

Heltisle leaned back in the chair, his expression so gloating that Bartholomew did not know how Michael refrained from punching him.

'Forgive me, Brother,' he drawled. 'I was just passing the time until you deigned to appear. This is now your office. It was inappropriate for the Senior Proctor to have a grander realm than the Chancellor, so I told de Wetherset to put matters right.'

'So that is why lights burned in the church all night,' mused Michael. 'While I was busy preventing our University from going up in flames, you two were playing power games.'

Heltisle's smirk slipped. 'We were setting all to rights after your farce of a reign.'

'If the room was so important, why did you not just ask for it?' Michael was all bemused innocence. 'I would have moved. There was no need for you to demean yourselves with this sort of pettiness.'

'You would have refused,' said Heltisle, wrong-footed by the monk's response.

'I assure you, Heltisle, I have far more important matters to occupy my mind than offices. But you *still* have not explained why you see fit to paw through my correspondence.'

Heltisle glared at him. 'It is not *your* correspondence – it is the University's. And of course the Chancellor's deputy should know what it contains.'

Michael stepped forward and swept all the documents into a box. 'Then take it. I am glad to be rid of it, to be frank. It represents a lot of very tedious work, which I now willingly hand to you, Vice-Chancellor.'

'Now wait a moment,' objected Heltisle. 'I cannot waste my time with—'

'No, no,' said Michael, pulling him to his feet, shoving

the box into his hands and propelling him towards the door. 'You wanted it, so it is yours. I shall tell the Bishop to correspond with you about these matters in future. However, a word of warning – he does not tolerate incompetence, so learn fast. It would be a pity to see a promising career in ruins.'

'But none of these missives make sense to me,' snapped Heltisle, peering angrily over the top of the teetering pile. 'You will need to explain the background behind—'

'I am sure you can work it out.' Michael smiled serenely. 'A clever man like you.'

'No! I am too busy for this sort of nonsense. I am—'

'I suggest you make a start immediately. Some of it is urgent, and you do not want the Bishop vexed with you for tardiness. Perhaps you can do it instead of spreading silly lies about the Mayor. Oh, yes, I know where those tales originated, and I am shocked that you should stoop so low.'

Heltisle's face was a combination of dismay, anger and chagrin. 'You cannot berate *me* like an errant schoolboy. I am—'

'Go, go,' said Michael, pushing him through the door. 'I am needed to save the University from the crisis your puerile capers has triggered. I cannot stand here bandying words with you all day.'

'You might dismiss me, but you had better make time for de Wetherset,' said Heltisle in a final attempt to save face. 'He wants to see you at once.'

'Of course,' said Michael. 'I would have been there already, but I trod in something nasty on my way. I shall attend him as soon as I have scraped the ordure from my boot.'

When Heltisle had gone, Michael looked thoughtfully around the tiny space that was now his, while Bartholomew waited in silence, waiting for the explosion. It did not come.

Michael saw what he was thinking and laughed. 'Do not look dismayed on my account, Matt. I shall be back in my own quarters within a week.'

'Then what about the documents? Do you really not mind him nosing through them?'

Michael laughed again. 'I would have been vexed if he had not, given all the time I spent picking out the ones that would cause him the greatest problems.'

Bartholomew blinked. 'So you predicted this would happen and prepared for it?'

Michael raised his eyebrows in mock astonishment. 'Whatever gave you that idea?'

De Wetherset looked supremely uncomfortable in Michael's chair, behind Michael's desk and with Michael's rugs under his plump feet. Aynton was behind him, beaming as usual. The Commissary was immaculately dressed, right down to a fresh white bandage on his wrist – not one of Bartholomew's, which meant he had gone to a different physician for his follow-up appointment. His boots gleamed, although not even the herculean efforts of his servant could disguise their ugliness or the marks caused by his fall at the Spital.

'I knew you would understand,' said de Wetherset in relief, when the monk wished him well in his new domain, although Heltisle, who had followed, glowered furiously. 'A Chancellor cannot expect to be taken seriously if he operates from a cupboard at the back of the church while his Senior Proctor sits in splendour at the front.'

Michael grinned wolfishly. 'It does not matter to me who works where. Now, why did you want to see me, Chancellor? Or would you rather have your consultation with Matt first?'

'My stomach, Bartholomew,' said de Wetherset piteously. 'It roils again, and I need more of the remedy you gave me last time.'

'Nerves,' Bartholomew said, pulling some from his bag and handing it over. 'Arising from fear of how the Senior Proctor might react at being displaced.'

'Almost certainly,' agreed de Wetherset with a wry smile. 'But to business. How are the wounded in the friary? Should we expect more deaths?'

Bartholomew kept his reply brief when he saw that neither the Chancellor nor his deputy were very interested. Only Aynton was concerned, and announced his intention to visit the injured in their sickbeds, where he would caution them against future bad behaviour.

'Of course, none of it would have happened if the town had stayed away from the butts,' said de Wetherset, when the Commissary had finished babbling. 'It was our turn to use them, and they should have respected that.'

'They did it because you invaded their practice the night before,' said Bartholomew tartly.

'I hope you do not suggest that the skirmish was *our* fault,' said Heltisle indignantly. 'We are innocent victims in this unseemly affair.'

'We are,' agreed de Wetherset. 'However, I am sure Michael and I can work together to ensure it does not happen again. We want no more trouble with the town.'

'The best way to achieve that is to present culprits for some of the crimes that have been committed against us,' said Heltisle curtly. 'Unfortunately, the Senior Proctor is incapable of catching them.'

'Because I was ordered to leave it to Aynton,' Michael reminded him. 'Ergo, the failure cannot be laid at my feet. However, I have continued to mull the matter over in my mind, and I was on my way to confront one culprit when you dragged me here.'

'Really?' asked Aynton keenly. 'Who is it?'

'You will be the first to know when an arrest is made,' lied Michael. 'However, as I am here, perhaps you will tell me what *you* saw and heard at the butts last night.'

De Wetherset raised his hands apologetically. 'It was dark, and I was more concerned with staying away from jostling townies. I knew the contestants had gone to assess the targets, but I assumed they were all back when the order came to send off the next volley. I did not see who called it.'

'Nor did I,' said Heltisle. 'But I heard it, and I can tell you with confidence that it was a townsman. For a start, it was in English, and what scholar demeans himself by using the common tongue?'

'You were there?' asked Bartholomew suspiciously. 'You are our best archer, but neither you nor your students could be found when the town issued the challenge. Ergo, you were not at the butts at that point.'

Heltisle regarded him with dislike. 'We were on our way home, but raced back when we heard about the contest. So I *am* able to say with total conviction that the order to shoot came from the town.'

'I am not so sure,' demurred Aynton. 'The yell *was* in the vernacular, but I thought it had a French inflection.'

'I hope you are mistaken, Commissary,' gulped de Wetherset. 'Because if not, your testimony might lead some folk to think that the culprit is a scholar.'

'We are not the only ones who speak French,' said Aynton. 'Have you not heard about the spies in the Spital? It seems you two did not hire lunatics to act as your proxies in the call to arms, but members of the Dauphin's army!'

Heltisle gaped his horror. 'If that is true, I want my money back! I do not mind giving charity to a lunatic's orphan, but I will not have it used to coddle some French brat.'

De Wetherset was equally appalled, but not about the money. 'Are you saying that one of these French spies came to the butts with the express purpose of making us and the town turn on each other?' he asked in a hoarse, shocked voice. 'And we obliged him with a riot?'

Aynton nodded. 'Perhaps in revenge for his five countrymen being stabbed and burned.'

Bartholomew and Michael took their leave as the triumvirate began to debate the matter among themselves.

'Personally, I think Aynton yelled the order to shoot,'
said Michael, once he and Bartholomew were out of
earshot, 'and he accuses the *peregrini* to throw us off his
scent. But his claim is outrageous, because not even
Delacroix would take such a risk.'

'Are you sure?' asked Bartholomew soberly. 'It was dark
and crowded, so none of us would have recognised him.
Moreover, Aynton was right about one thing – setting us
at each other's throats would be an excellent way to avenge
his murdered friends.'

'I suppose it would,' conceded Michael unhappily.

Outside in the street, they met Warden Shropham from
King's Hall, who had come to discuss funeral arrangements for his two dead scholars. He was a shy, diffident
man, who was not really capable of controlling the
arrogant young men under his command, which explained why his College was nearly always involved
when trouble erupted. Feeling he should be there when
the Warden spoke to de Wetherset, Michael accompanied him back inside the church. Bartholomew went,
too.

'De Wetherset is in *there*?' whispered Shropham when
Michael indicated which door he should open. 'But that
is your office, Brother!'

'Heltisle decided to make some changes,' said Michael,
speaking without inflection.

Shropham made an exasperated sound. 'It was a bad
day for the University when he was appointed. Do not let
him best you, Brother – we shall all be the losers if you
do.'

He opened the office door and walked inside, leaving

Michael smugly gratified at the expression of support from the head of a powerful College.

'We have been discussing your deceased students, Shropham,' de Wetherset told the Warden kindly. 'And we have agreed that the University will pay for their tombs – two very grand ones.'

Shropham looked pained. 'I would rather not draw attention to the fact that they died fighting, if you do not mind – their families would be mortified.' His grimace deepened. 'I still cannot believe that you kept everyone at the butts once the townsfolk began to show up. If you had sent us home, Bruges and Smith would still be alive.'

'You blame *us* for last night?' demanded Heltisle indignantly. 'How dare you!'

De Wetherset sighed. 'But he is right, Heltisle – it *was* a poor decision. I assumed the beadles would keep the peace, but I was wrong to place my trust in a body of men who are townsmen at heart.'

Michael's jaw dropped. 'My beadles did their best – and they are loyal to a man.'

'Although the same cannot be said of the ones Heltisle hired,' put in Bartholomew, who had tended enough injured beadles to know who had done his duty and who had not. 'Most fled at the first sign of violence, and the ones who stayed were more interested in exacerbating the problem than ending it.'

'I am glad you are leaving at the end of term,' said Heltisle coldly. 'It will spare me the inconvenience of asking you to resign. I will not tolerate insolence from inferiors.'

'Even though he speaks the truth?' asked Shropham. 'Because I saw these men myself – they *were* useless.'

Heltisle indicated Michael. 'Then *he* should have trained them properly.'

Michael shot him a contemptuous look before turning back to Shropham. 'Do you know who called for the archers to shoot? Could you see him from where you stood?'

Shropham shook his head. 'I wish I had, because I should like to see him face justice. It is ultimately his fault that Bruges and Smith died.'

'Bruges was stabbed with this,' said Michael, producing the dagger. 'Is it familiar?'

'We scholars do not demean ourselves with weapons,' declared Heltisle before Shropham could reply. 'Of course, if it were a pen—' He picked up a metal one from the table, and turned it over lovingly in his fingers. 'Well, we can identify those at once.'

Bartholomew was not about to let him get away with so brazen a lie. 'You had the only perfect score at the butts last night *and* you once told us that you are handy with a sword. Ergo, you *do* demean yourself with weapons.'

Heltisle regarded him with dislike. 'Skills I acquired *before* I devoted my life to scholarship, not that it is any of your business.'

Meanwhile, Shropham had taken the dagger from Michael and was studying it carefully. He had been a soldier before turning to academia, although Bartholomew found it difficult to believe that such a meek, sensitive man had once been a warrior of some repute.

'It is French,' he said, handing it back. 'From around Rouen, to be precise. I had one myself once, but most are sold to local men. You should find out who hails from that region and ask them about it.'

'So there you are, Brother,' said Heltisle. 'Run along and do as you are told, while the rest of us decide how best to honour King's Hall's martyred scholars.'

Michael bowed and took his leave, while Bartholomew marvelled at his self-control – *he* would not have allowed himself to be dismissed so insultingly by the likes of Heltisle.

'The *peregrini* hail from near Rouen,' the physician said, once they were outside. 'And the Jacquerie was strong in that region . . .'

'So the daggers may belong to them,' surmised Michael. 'Aynton was right to suggest they might have ignited last night's trouble with an order to shoot. And we were right to consider the possibility of a falling-out among them that saw the Girards murdered.'

'If so, we can never interrogate them about it, because they have gone. Will you still speak to Alice? I doubt she has connections to Rouen.'

'Even if she is not the killer, we cannot have nuns from my Order waylaying knights and urging them to kill people. We shall speak to her first, then see what Amphelisa can tell us about daggers made near Rouen.'

'We have already shown her the one that killed the Girards. She did not recognise it.'

Michael's expression was sober. 'That was before Shropham told us where it was made. Perhaps she will recognise it when confronted with the truth. After all, it would not be the first time she has lied to us.'

In the event, Bartholomew and Michael were spared a trek to St Radegund's, because Sister Alice was walking along the high street. She was with Prioress Joan and Magistra Katherine, talking animatedly, although neither was listening to what she was saying. Katherine's distant expression suggested her thoughts were on some lofty theological matter, while Joan was more interested in the fine horse that Shropham had left tethered outside the church.

'Good,' said Michael, homing in on them. 'I want a word with you.'

'Me?' asked Joan, alarm suffusing her homely features. 'Why? Not because of Dusty? What has happened to him? Tell me, Brother!'

'He is quite well,' Michael assured her, raising his hands to quell her rising agitation, while Katherine smirked, amused that her Prioress's first concern should be for an animal. 'And perfectly content with Cynric.'

Joan sagged in relief. 'Is it about that dagger then? I have been mulling the matter over, and it occurs to me that I did not see it here, but at home. Obviously, we do not have that sort of thing in the convent, so now I wonder whether I spotted it in Winchelsea . . .'

'We went there after it was attacked, if you recall,' said Katherine. 'To offer comfort to the survivors and to help them bury their dead.'

'But I cannot be *certain*,' finished Joan unhappily. 'I am sorry to be such a worthless lump, but my brain refuses to yield its secrets.'

'Keep trying, if you please,' said Michael, disappointed. 'It is important. However, it was not you we wanted to corner – it is Alice.'

'Me?' asked Alice, scratching her elbow. 'Why? I have nothing to say to you. Besides, we are busy. The Carmelite Prior was so impressed by Magistra Katherine's grasp of nominalism that he offered to show us his collection of books on the subject.'

'To show *me* his books,' corrected Katherine crisply, 'while Joan is to be given a tour of his stables. You are invited to neither.'

Alice sniffed huffily. 'I do not want to see smelly old books and horses anyway.'

'No?' asked Katherine archly. 'Then why have you foisted yourself on us?'

'Because the streets are uneasy after last night's chaos,' retorted Alice, 'and there is safety in numbers. If anyone else had been available, I would have chosen them instead.'

'Of course you would,' said Katherine, before glancing around with a shudder. 'My brother always said this town is like a pustule, waiting to burst. He is right! I heard there are more than a dozen dead and countless injured.'

'But no horses harmed, thank God,' said Joan, crossing herself before glaring at Michael. 'Although I understand Dusty was ridden into the thick of it.'

'He behaved impeccably,' Michael informed her, unabashed. 'You would have been proud. Indeed, it is largely due to him that the death toll was not higher.'

Joan was unappeased. 'If there is so much as a scratch on him . . .'

'There is not, and he enjoyed every moment – he is far more destrier than palfrey. Did I tell you that Bruges the Fleming declared him the finest warhorse that ever lived? Coming from King's Hall, that was a compliment indeed.'

'Bruges is from Flanders?' asked Joan, surprised. 'I assumed he was French. He spoke to me in that tongue – loudly and arrogantly – the other day, when he told me that he wanted to buy Dusty. It made passers-by glare at us, which was an uncomfortable experience.'

'He will not do it again,' said Bartholomew soberly. 'He was among last night's dead.'

Joan gaped at him, but then recovered herself and murmured a prayer for his soul. 'Yet I am astonished to learn he was rioting. I assumed he was more genteel, given that he had such good taste in horses.'

'I do not know what you see in that ugly nag, Prioress,' put in Alice unpleasantly. 'Sometimes, I think you love him more than us, your Benedictine sisters.'

'I do,' said Joan baldly. 'Especially after this *conloquium*, where I have learned that most are either blithering idiots, greedy opportunists or unrepentant whores.' She regarded Alice in distaste. 'And *some* are all three.'

'I am none of those things,' declared Alice angrily. 'I am the victim of a witch-hunt by Abbess Isabel and the Bishop. I did nothing wrong.'

'You made bad choices and you were caught,' said Joan sternly. 'Now you must either accept your fate with good grace or renounce your vows and follow some other vocation.'

'As a warlock, perhaps,' suggested Katherine. 'Given that you know rather too much about maggoty march-panes, stinking candles and cursing spells.'

'You malign me with these vile accusations,' scowled Alice, although the truth was in her eyes. 'I am innocent of—'

'Speaking of vile accusations,' interrupted Michael, 'perhaps you will explain why you have been gossiping about spies in the Spital. And do not deny it, because Sir Norbert identified you by your constant scratching.'

Alice had been about to claw her arm again; Michael's words made her drop her hand hastily. 'But everyone is talking about the spies in the Spital. Why single me out for censure?'

'Because you are the originator of the tale,' said Michael harshly. 'You discovered the "lunatics" were French – oldsters, women and children fleeing persecution from those they considered to be friends – and you urged Norbert to kill them.'

'Did you?' asked Katherine, regarding her in distaste. 'And what would have happened to us during this slaughter? Or would our deaths have been an added bonus?'

'I had no idea you were living with French spies until I heard it from Margery Starre last night,' declared Alice. 'Those rumours did *not* start with me.'

'Look at this dagger,' ordered Michael, holding it out to her. 'It was used to kill Bruges. Others like it were employed on Paris, Bonet and the Girard family.'

'But not by me,' said Alice, barely glancing at it. 'Do you really think that I, a weak woman, could plunge blades into the backs of strong and healthy men?'

'How do you know they were stabbed in the back?' pounced Bartholomew.

Alice's eyes glittered. 'Because someone told me. I forget who.'

'Margery, probably,' muttered Katherine. 'A witch, who is hardly suitable company for nuns. And it takes no great strength to drive a blade into someone from behind anyway, which I know, because the survivors at Winchelsea told me.'

Alice sighed to show she was bored of the conversation. 'Shall we talk about something more interesting, such as getting me reinstalled as Prioress at Ickleton?'

Suddenly, Michael had had enough of her. 'You are under arrest for the murders of Paris, Bonet, the Girards and Bruges,' he said briskly. 'And for spreading malicious rumours.'

'Oh, yes,' sneered Alice. 'Pick on the innocent nun *again*. Well, I have killed no one, although that might change if you persist with these ridiculous charges.'

'Stop your whining – it is tedious beyond belief,' snapped Joan, then turned to Michael, tapping the dagger with a thick forefinger. 'This is similar to the other one you showed me, and the more I think about it, the more I suspect I *did* see its like in Winchelsea—'

'Which proves I am innocent, as I have never been there,' put in Alice triumphantly.

'Oh, yes, you have,' countered Katherine. 'You visited us in Lyminster a few months ago, delivering letters from your own convent.'

'Lyminster is not Winchelsea,' argued Alice. 'They are more than sixty miles apart. I went to one, but not the other, and you cannot prove otherwise.'

'Actually, I can.' Katherine gestured to Alice's clothes. 'There is Winchelsea-made lace at your wrists and Winchelsea-made buttons on your habit. Moreover, your Prioress told me that you took far longer to complete the return journey than you should have done, which is indicative that you treated yourself to a major diversion.'

Alice glared malevolently at her. 'There were floods and other perils, so I had to make my way along the coast instead of plunging straight back inland. It means nothing.'

Katherine regarded her with contempt. 'I knew you were a liar, a cheat and a whore, but I am shocked to learn you are a killer as well.'

'I am *not*!' cried Alice furiously. 'So what if I stopped briefly at the port where Joan saw those particular weapons? It does not mean—'

'Where will you keep her, Brother?' interrupted Joan. 'Not near Dusty, I hope.'

Michael hesitated. The proctors' cells were full of angry young men from the riot, and he could hardly put a nun among those, not even one as unlikeable as Alice.

'Leave her to us,' said Katherine, guessing his dilemma. 'St Radegund's has cellars.'

Bartholomew was relieved when Alice was marched away, although Michael fretted over what a public announcement of her crimes might do to his Order.

'*Is* she the killer?' the monk asked worriedly. 'She is vicious and deranged, but only against those she thinks have wronged her. What could she possibly have had against Bruges? Or any of the victims, for that matter?'

'Question her again later,' suggested Bartholomew. 'Once she is confined, she may be more willing to cooperate. And even if she is innocent of the murders, she still has the rumours to answer for – rumours that may yet spark more trouble.'

'True,' acknowledged Michael. 'But before we do anything else, we should see what Amphelisa has to say about these weapons being made near Rouen.'

They set off towards the Spital, both acutely aware of

the atmosphere of rage and resentment that continued to simmer after the previous night's skirmish. Townsmen knew they had suffered more casualties than the University, and were keen to redress the balance, while scholars itched to avenge the deaths of four students with promising futures.

The Trumpington road was busy, and Bartholomew noted with alarm that most people were going to or from the Spital – Tulyet was right to predict that it might suffer from the decision to shelter the *peregrini*. They arrived to find the gates closed and Tangmer's family standing an uneasy guard atop the walls. Outside was a knot of protestors, who were vocal but not yet physically violent. They were being monitored by Orwel and a gaggle of soldiers from the castle, all of whom bitterly resented being there.

Michael knocked on the gate, which was opened with obvious reluctance by the huge Eudo. He and Bartholomew were pulled inside quickly before it was slammed shut again. This provoked a chorus of accusations from those outside, who jeered that the Senior Proctor and his Corpse Examiner had gone to confer with fellow French-lovers. Inside, any staff not guarding the walls had clustered at the gate, ready to repel anyone who tried to enter by force.

'My wife is not here,' said Tangmer, who was pale with worry. 'She went to tend the wounded in the Franciscan Friary again. I hoped her compassion to the injured would make everyone think more kindly of us, but you all still howl for our blood.'

'The claim is that we sheltered spies,' put in Eudo, clenching his ham-sized fists in impotent anger. 'But all we did was take pity on frightened women and children.'

'And eleven men,' his little wife Goda reminded them. She was wearing a new fret in her hair, which had been sewn with silver thread and looked expensive. 'Six of whom were Jacques. We should not have done it, as it made us enemies in the University *and* the town.'

'Look at this dagger,' said Michael, presenting it. 'It and the ones that killed Paris, Bonet and the Girard family were made in or near Rouen.'

'Amphelisa hails from there,' said Goda at once. 'So do the *peregrini.*'

'Yes,' said Michael, watching Tangmer shoot her an agonised glance, while Eudo delivered a warning jab to the ribs that almost knocked her over. 'I know.'

'It is not Amphelisa's,' said Tangmer quickly. 'She does not own weapons. She is a gentle soul, dedicated to helping those in need, regardless of their colour or creed.'

'Then what about you?' asked Michael. 'Is this a gift from those grateful "lunatics"? We have reason to believe that daggers like these were seen in Winchelsea, which is where your *peregrini* settled after fleeing France.'

'They gave us a little money,' said Tangmer. 'They had to – we could not have fed them otherwise. But they never offered us gifts.'

'Delacroix and his friends carried plenty of knives,' said Eudo, 'but I paid them no heed. If you want to know if this blade is theirs, you will have to ask them. Unfortunately, they left us last night, as I am sure you have heard.'

'Without leaving the money for the food they ate last week,' put in Goda sourly. 'So if you go after them, perhaps you will collect it for us.'

Bartholomew and Michael stayed a while longer, quizzing every member of staff about the dagger, but no one admitted to recognising it. Eventually, they took their leave.

'Well?' asked Bartholomew, once they had run the gauntlet of the taunting, jeering throng outside and were heading back towards the town. 'What do you think? I have no idea whether any of them were telling the truth.'

'Nor do I,' admitted Michael. 'I doubt we will have it from Amphelisa either, but you had better go to the friary and try. Take the dagger with you. I will find Dick, and tell him we have arrested Alice. I imagine he will want to be there when I question her again.'

Bartholomew was glad to reach the Franciscans' domain, which was an oasis of peace after the uneasy streets. Yet not even it was immune to the festering atmosphere outside, and Prior Pechem had made arrangements similar to those at the Spital – guards on the gate and archers on the walls.

Bartholomew arrived at the guesthouse to find all his students there, ranging from the boys who had only recently started their studies, to Islaye and Mallett who would graduate at the end of term. There were so many that the wounded had been allocated two apiece. The reason soon became clear: tending the sick was a lot easier than the punishing schedule he expected them to follow at Michaelhouse, and they were eager for a respite. He was tempted to send them all home, but then decided that there was nothing wrong with some practical experience. Moreover, it would keep them too busy to join in any brawls.

Amphelisa was there, too, moving between the beds and talking softly to patients and students alike. She wore a very old burgundy cloak that day, because changing soiled dressings was messy work. It was one she used while distilling oils, so the scent of lavender and pine pervaded the room. Bartholomew waited until she was free, then cornered her by a sink, where he was pleased to see her washing her hands before tending the next customer.

'I would not know if Rouen produced beautiful weapons or not,' she informed him when he showed her the one that had killed Bruges. 'I have no interest in things that

267

harm – only in things that heal. I have told you this before.'

'Then perhaps you noticed if Delacroix or one of his friends had one,' he pressed.

'I did not – I was more concerned about their well-being than their belongings.'

Bartholomew opened his mouth to ask more, but there was a minor crisis with a patient, and by the time it was over, Amphelisa was nowhere to be seen. He was instantly suspicious, but Mallett informed him that she had been helping out for hours, and had expressed a perfectly understandable wish to go home and change her clothes.

'Although I like the smell of the cloak she was wearing,' he confided. 'So do our clients – it calms them. It must be the soporific oils that have soaked into it.'

Bartholomew remained in the friary for the rest of the day, taking the opportunity to do some impromptu teaching. He did not notice his students' exasperated glances when they saw their plan to escape him had misfired – he was working them harder than ever. He might have gone on all evening, but at dusk he was summoned by Isnard, who was complaining of a sore throat. The relief when he left was palpable.

He arrived at the bargeman's cosy riverside cottage to find him in despair. It was difficult to fight on crutches, so his contribution to the brawl had been to howl abuse at the enemy. He had done it with such gusto that he was now hoarse.

'And tomorrow is Sunday,' he croaked, 'when the Marian Singers will perform at High Mass. It would break my heart to miss it.'

Bartholomew prescribed a cordial of honey and black-currant, and told him to rest his voice. Unfortunately, Isnard had things to say, so there followed an exasperating interlude in which the bargeman mouthed the words and Bartholomew struggled to understand them.

'You arrested a nun,' Isnard began. 'But she did not kill Wyse. That was a scholar. We all saw him sitting in the Griffin, watching us with crafty eyes.'

'*You* saw him?' demanded Bartholomew. 'What did he look like?'

'We never saw his face, as he was careful to keep in the shadow. But I can tell you that he was fat.'

As a great many scholars were portly, this description was not very helpful. Bartholomew ordered Isnard to stay indoors and keep warm – it would make no difference to his voice, but would stop him from fighting scholars – and trudged back to Michaelhouse. As he was passing St Mary the Great, a door opened and Orwel slipped out. The sergeant looked around furtively before slinking away. Bartholomew frowned. Why was he in the church when he was supposed to be guarding the Spital?

He started to follow, aiming to ask, but lost him in the shadows of the graveyard.

Back in Michaelhouse, Bartholomew had done no more than drop his bag and look to see if his students had left any food lying around when Michael appeared. The monk turned his nose up at the slice of stale cake that Bartholomew offered to share, and invited him to the Master's suite for something better instead.

'Did you interview Alice?' asked Bartholomew, aware that his slice of beef pie was considerably smaller than the lump the monk had cut for himself.

'Dick and I decided to leave it until tomorrow, to give her time to reflect on the situation and hopefully come to her senses. Did you speak to Amphelisa?'

'Yes, but she had nothing to say. I did see Orwel sneaking out of St Mary the Great just now, though. I thought he was supposed to be guarding the Spital.'

'Perhaps Dick relieved him,' shrugged Michael. 'However, he may have been looking for me. He claims to have information about Wyse's murder, so I agreed to meet him behind the Brazen George at midnight. It is possible that he wanted to make sure I would be there – along with the money I agreed to pay.'

'Midnight?' asked Bartholomew uneasily. 'That is an odd time. Will it be safe? His intention may be to coax you to a dark place where you can be dispatched.'

'It might, which is why Dick will be there, too. However, I am fairly sure Orwel's motives are purely pecuniary.'

'What else did you do after we parted company?'

'I went to King's Hall and ordered them to stay indoors tonight. Unfortunately, Warden Shropham had already told them that the weapon used to dispatch Bruges was French, so now they think the town is sheltering a lot of enemy soldiers.'

'I have been thinking about these daggers,' said Bartholomew, handing back the one he had shown Amphelisa. 'They are well-made and expensive, yet the killer is happy to leave them in or near his victims. One of the reasons Alice was deposed was greed – she lined her own pockets at her priory's expense . . .'

'So you believe she is unlikely to be the culprit, because she is too mean to abandon a costly item,' surmised Michael. 'She would have taken it with her.'

Bartholomew nodded. 'The same is true of most towns-folk and scholars. Ergo, the culprit is wealthy – someone who can afford to lose them.'

'A rich scholar or a rich townsman,' mused Michael.

'Or a Jacques – a man who looted the houses of aristocrats in France and who may think he can do the same here when he runs low on funds. Of course, we must not forget de Wetherset, Heltisle and Theophilis – none of them are poor.'

'Nor is Aynton,' added Michael, and grimaced. 'The culprit is using these daggers to taunt us – daring us to link them to him.'

Bartholomew agreed, and wished he knew how to prompt Joan's memory, as he was sure the mystery would be solved once she remembered where – and with whom – she had seen the weapon before. 'Regardless, I do not think Alice stabbed anyone.'

'I am inclined to agree, although we shall keep her under lock and key anyway. She still started vicious rumours, and she is a divisive force at the *conloquium*. It is best she stays where she can do no more harm.'

'Is there any news about who gave the order to shoot last night?' asked Bartholomew hopefully. 'Or about Wyse's murder?'

Michael shook his head. 'Although every townsman blames us, and every scholar accuses the town. Dick and I have imposed another curfew until dawn, although a lot of hotheads have elected to ignore it. I fear for our foreign scholars, Matt – all of them, not just the French ones. I hope they have the sense to stay indoors.'

'So we know nothing new,' surmised Bartholomew despondently.

'Dick heard a rumour that the *peregrini* have taken up residence near the Austin Priory,' said Michael, referring to the foundation located a mile or so outside the town. 'So we rode out there to investigate.'

'I assume you did not find them.'

'Of course not. I decided to take Dusty, and as Prioress Joan was visiting him when I went to saddle up, she came, too, for the sheer joy of a canter along an empty road. She let me have Dusty, while she rode Theophilis's mean old brute. You should have seen how she handled him – he was a different horse.'

'Was he?' asked Bartholomew without much interest.

'The excursion allowed me to quiz her in depth about Alice. Apparently, Alice visited the Spital seven or eight times before the murders, so she probably did guess the "lunatics" were nothing of the kind. Ergo, I am sure it

271

*was* her who told Norbert, no matter how vigorously she denies it.'

'Probably.'

'She also sent Magistra Katherine some very dangerous gifts – candles that leaked poisonous fumes, a lamp that burst into flames, a book impregnated with a potion to burn the reader's fingers, blankets infested with fleas . . .'

'Fleas?'

Michael grinned. 'And in a twist of irony, she is the one who crawls with them. We should not forget the comb she stole from Joan either. That is still missing, and I am sure she intends it to be a part of some mischief yet to unfold. Shall we go to meet Orwel now?'

'Now?' asked Bartholomew, startled by the abrupt change of subject. 'It is too early.'

'I know, but Lister makes a lovely roasted pork on a Saturday night and I am ravenous.'

'You cannot be! You have just devoured most of a pie.'

'To line my stomach, Matt – to prepare it for the proper meal to come.'

It was not only Michael who liked Lister's roasted pork, and the tavern was full of muttering townsmen when they arrived. Bartholomew was glad of the private room at the back. Tulyet appeared much later, footsore and weary from asking questions of witnesses.

'The town is now certain that scholars killed Wyse, hid French spies in the Spital *and* engineered last night's riot,' he reported. 'A riot in which four of you died, but ten of us. I have done my best to quell the gossip, but folk believe what they want to believe.'

'Then let us hope Orwel knows who killed Wyse,' said Michael. 'They may be appeased if that culprit is brought to justice. I imagine he will name Aynton – the gently smiling spider in the web.'

'Or Theophilis,' countered Bartholomew.

'Theophilis would never betray me,' said Michael. 'Why would he, when I gave him his Fellowship, his post as Junior Proctor, a lucrative benefice—'

'No man likes to be beholden to another,' interrupted Tulyet. 'However, Theophilis does not have the courage for murder, so my money is on de Wetherset or Heltisle. It was a bad day for the University *and* the town when they took power.'

Bartholomew told him that he and Michael now thought the dagger belonged to someone wealthy. Tulyet scrubbed his face with his hands.

'Then I will interview burgesses tomorrow. You can do the same with rich scholars. However, the culprit cannot be a Jacques – they fled *before* Bruges was killed.'

'*If* they left,' said Bartholomew. 'Perhaps one lingered long enough to avenge himself on the place that killed his friends and forced him out of his cosy refuge.'

'Twenty-six dead,' sighed Michael. 'Paris, Bonet, five members of the Girard family, Wyse, the fourteen from the riot, plus the three who were hanged for murder and their victim. And more will follow unless we stop the contagion.'

Lister arrived at that point to collect the empty platters, and Bartholomew noticed that the landlord was careful to keep the door closed – he did not want his other customers to know that he welcomed scholars in his fine establishment.

'Did I tell you that the Chancellor came here earlier, Brother?' Lister asked. 'He and his henchman Heltisle. They wanted to hire this room for *their* sole use, so that you would have to find somewhere else.'

Michael gaped at him in disbelief. 'They did *what?*'

'I had to lie – tell them that it is out of commission due to a smoking chimney. Yet it is rash for me to make enemies of such powerful men – they could break me by deciding to drink here, as my other regulars would leave.'

'Do not worry, Lister,' said Michael between gritted teeth. 'They will never harm you or your business. I promise.'

Lister smiled wanly. 'Thank you, Brother. Of course, it will be irrelevant if the town erupts into violence again. The streets felt more dangerous today than they have ever done.'

The moment Lister had gone, Michael embarked on a furious tirade. 'How *dare* they! This is *my* refuge. I do not care about my office in St Mary the Great, but to invade a man's tavern . . . I will *not* share it with de Wetherset and Heltisle!'

'They do not want to share it,' Bartholomew pointed out. 'They want it all for themselves. It is another attempt to weaken you.'

'Well, they will never interfere with the important business of victuals,' vowed Michael. 'I will not permit it. But there is the linkman calling the hour. It is time to meet Orwel.'

They trooped outside. Tulyet took up station near the back gate, which he said was the one Orwel would use, while Bartholomew was allocated the door at the side. Michael went to stand in the middle of the yard. It was very dark, and Bartholomew was just wondering how he would be able to help should there be trouble, when Michael gave a sharp cry.

'What the— Help! There is a body!'

Bartholomew darted forward, but collided heavily with someone coming the other way. At first he thought it was Tulyet, but something caught him a glancing blow – aimed at his head but hitting his shoulder. He lunged blindly and grabbed a wrist, yelling for Tulyet. The arm was ripped free and he heard the side door open and slam shut again. Tulyet blundered past, fumbling for the latch in the dark. Then he was gone, too.

The commotion alerted Lister, who arrived with a lamp.

It illuminated Michael crouching next to someone on the ground. Bartholomew hurried towards them.

'It is Orwel,' said Michael, rolling the body over to look at its face. 'Is he dead?'

Bartholomew nodded. 'Struck on the head – just like Wyse. Only this time the blow was powerful enough to kill him outright.'

They looked up as Tulyet arrived empty-handed, his face a mask of anger and frustration.

'Who was it?' he demanded. 'Did you see?'

'It was too dark,' replied Bartholomew, and grimaced. 'But I think we have just let Wyse's killer slip through our fingers.'

'I would keep that quiet, if I were you,' advised Lister. 'Or the town will lynch you.'

# CHAPTER 12

The next day was Sunday, when bells all over the town rang to advertise their morning services. Scholars in academic or priestly robes hurried to and from their Colleges and hostels, while townsfolk donned their best clothes – if they had any – and stood in naves to listen to the sacred words that were sang, mumbled or bellowed, depending on the preference of the presiding priest.

Bartholomew had been summoned before dawn to tend one of the wounded at the Franciscan Priory. When he had finished, he went to St Edward's, where Orwel's body had been taken. This church celebrated Mass later than everyone else, so was empty, other than its ancient vicar, who was fast asleep on a tomb.

Bartholomew examined Orwel carefully, this time without the distraction of Michael and Tulyet clamouring questions at him. But there was no more to be learned in the cold light of day than there had been the previous night: Orwel had been struck, very hard, with a stone. Assailed by the uncomfortable sense that he was being watched – something he often experienced when he examined corpses on his own – Bartholomew put all back as he had found it, and hurried out into the warm spring sunshine with relief.

As he walked along the high street, he saw the Marian Singers assembling outside St Mary the Great, ready to bawl the *Jubilate* they had been practising. As Michael was late, Isnard assumed command, assisted by Sauvage. At first, the still-hoarse bargeman tried to impose order by whispering, and when that did not work, told Sauvage to relay his orders in a bellow. When he was satisfied with the way they looked, Isnard began to lead the choir inside – only to find his way barred by Aynton and some of Heltisle's Horde.

'Not today, Isnard,' said Aynton apologetically. 'Vice-Chancellor Heltisle is conducting the service, and he has opted for a spoken Mass – one without musical interludes.'

'There is no music involved with the Michaelhouse Choir,' quipped one of the Horde, a rough, gap-toothed individual whose name was Perkyn. 'Just a lot of tuneless hollering. Master Heltisle plans to disband them soon, on the grounds that they bring the University into disrepute.'

'The Michaelhouse Choir no longer exists,' croaked Isnard loftily. 'We are the *Marian Singers*. Moreover, we have nothing to do with the University, for which we thank God, because we would not want to belong to an organisation that is full of Frenchmen.'

'And none of *us* is foreign,' declared Pierre Sauvage. 'Unlike you lot – we know you turned a blind eye when all them French spies escaped from the Spital.'

'What are you saying, *Sauvage*?' sneered Perkyn, giving the name a distinctly foreign inflection. 'That we should have made war on women and children?'

'The French do,' stated Isnard. 'They slaughtered them by the hundred in Winchelsea. Besides, unless you hate the whole race, it means you love them all, and you are therefore a traitor. Chancellor Suttone said so in a sermon.'

Bartholomew was sure Suttone had said nothing of the kind – the ex-Chancellor had had his flaws, but making that sort of remark was certainly not among them.

'Suttone!' spat Perkyn. 'A rogue from Michaelhouse, who left Cambridge not because he was afraid of the plague, but because he wanted to get married.'

There was a startled silence.

'You are mistaken, Perkyn,' said Aynton, the first to find his voice. 'Suttone is a Carmelite, a priest who has sworn vows of celibacy.'

'He ran off with a woman,' repeated Perkyn firmly. 'I was there when de Wetherset and Heltisle discussed it.'

'They would never have held such a conversation in front of you,' said Aynton sternly. 'Not that Suttone is guilty of such a charge, of course.'

Perkyn glared at him. 'I was listening from behind a pillar, if you must know. They tried to keep their voices low, but I have good ears. And I am happy to spread the tale around, because I hate Michaelhouse – it is full of lunatics, lechers and fanatics.'

'Not lechers,' objected Isnard, which Bartholomew supposed was loyalty of sorts.

'You cannot keep us out, Perkyn,' said Sauvage, aware that he might not get his free victuals if the choir failed to fulfil its obligations. 'St Mary the Great belongs to everyone.'

'It is the *University* Church,' argued Perkyn. 'Not yours. Now piss off.'

'It will not be the University's for much longer,' rasped Isnard. 'It was ours before you lot came along and stole it, and the only reason we have not kicked you out before is because Brother Michael works here. However, now de Wetherset has ousted him, we are free to eject your scrawny arses any time we please.'

'De Wetherset did not *oust* Michael,' squawked Aynton, cowering as the choir surged forward threateningly. 'They agreed to exchange rooms.'

Bartholomew could bear it no longer, so went to intervene. He was too late. Isnard shoved past the Commissary, and entered the church with the rest of the Marian Singers streaming at his heels. Aynton followed like a demented sheepdog, frantically struggling to herd them in the opposite direction.

Inside, Heltisle had already started the office, confidently assuming that Aynton was equal to excluding those he had decided to bar. He faltered when he heard the patter of many feet on the stone floor.

Moments later, a terrific noise filled the building – the Marian Singers had decided to perform anyway, regardless of the fact that they had no conductor. They plunged into the *Jubilate*, gaining confidence and volume with every note. Bartholomew put his hands over his ears, and imagined Heltisle was doing the same. Certainly, the Mass could not continue, because the president would be unable to make himself heard.

The music reached a crescendo, after which there was a sudden, blessed silence. Delighted by their achievement, Isnard indicated that the singers were to go for an encore. After three more turns, he declared that they had done their duty, and led the way outside. When they had gone, Michael stepped out of the shadows by the door.

'Do not tell me you were there all along,' said Bartholomew.

Michael grinned. 'Just long enough to know that my choristers did themselves proud today, and annoyed Heltisle into the bargain.'

As it was Sunday, teaching was forbidden, but few masters were so reckless as to leave a lot of lively young men with nothing to do, so it was a Michaelhouse tradition that the Fellows took it in turns to organise some entertainment. Bartholomew usually opted for a light-hearted disputation, followed by games in the orchard or riddle-solving in the hall. Clippesby invariably contrived an activity that would benefit his animal friends – painting the henhouse or playing with dogs – while William always chose something of a religious nature.

That week, it was Theophilis's turn, and his idea of fun was a debate on the nominalism–realism controversy, followed by him intoning excerpts from his *Calendarium* – the list of texts that were to be read out at specific times over the Church year.

'Goodness!' breathed Michael, unimpressed. 'He will set them at each other's throats in the first half, and send them to sleep in the second.'

'Perhaps he *wants* them to quarrel, so he can tell everyone that we have a Master who cannot keep order in his own house,' suggested Bartholomew.

Michael made a moue of irritation. 'Hardly! He is in charge today, so if there are any unseemly incidents, the blame will be laid at his door, not mine.'

But Bartholomew looked at the Junior Proctor's artful, self-satisfied face, and knew he had chosen to air a contentious subject for devious reasons of his own. He realised he would have to stay vigilant if he wanted to nip any trouble in the bud. Unfortunately, Michael had other ideas.

'I need you with me today, Matt. I feel responsible for Orwel's death, given that he was trying to talk to me when he was murdered. It seems likely that a scholar killed Wyse, and as Wyse and Orwel were both brained with a stone . . . well, we must catch the culprit as quickly as possible to appease the town. Then there is the killer of Paris and the others . . .'

'Who is almost certainly not Alice, although she is arrested for it.'

'If we can identify the real killer, it may ease the brewing trouble,' Michael went on. 'Although I fear it is already too late, and we shall only have peace once we have torn each other asunder. And to top it all, I am obliged to waste my time fending off petty assaults on my authority from the triumvirate.'

Bartholomew was unhappy about leaving his College in hands he did not trust. He warned Aungel and William to be on their guard, but Aungel was too inexperienced to read the warning signs, while the Franciscan would be too easily distracted by the theology.

'Our lads may misbehave because they are angry,' said Aungel worriedly. 'Offended by the town braying that we harbour French soldiers, who will slaughter them all.'

'Whereas they are the ones whose patriotism should be questioned,' added William venomously. '*They* looked the other way while Frenchmen lurked in the Spital. I wish I had known they were there – I would have driven them out.'

'You would have ejected frightened women, old men and small children, whose only "crime" was to flee persecution?' asked Bartholomew in distaste.

'Why not?' shrugged William. 'We did it when I was with the Inquisition. And evil takes many different forms, Matthew, so do not be too readily fooled by "harmless" oldsters or "innocent" brats.'

'I am offended by this nasty gossip about Master Suttone,' said Aungel, before Bartholomew could inform William that he was not with the Inquisition now, and such vile opinions were hardly commensurate with a man in holy orders. 'I know he enjoyed ladies on occasion, but he would never have run off to marry one.'

At that moment, the gate opened and Cynric cantered in on Dusty, having just given the horse a morning gallop along the Trumpington road.

'Come quick,' he gasped. 'There is trouble at the Spital. When Orwel was killed, Sauvage was given the job of keeping it safe, but he abandoned it to sing in St Mary the Great. Now the Spital is surrounded by hostile scholars and townsfolk.'

'They have united against a common enemy?' asked William.

'Not united, no,' replied Cynric. 'They each have their own ideas about what should be done, and spats are set to break out. The Sheriff has the town element under control, but he begs you to come and deal with the scholars. He said to hurry.'

The monk was not about to run to the Spital – it was too far, and he did not want to arrive winded and sweaty. He rode Dusty, shouting for Bartholomew to follow. It was not difficult for the physician to keep up with him at first, as no one could ride very fast along Cambridge's narrow, crowded streets, but it was a different matter once they were through the town gate. Then all Bartholomew could see was dust as Michael thundered ahead.

By the time Bartholomew arrived, the crisis had been averted, largely due to the fact that the troublemakers remembered Dusty from the riot – some were still nursing crushed toes and bruised ribs from when the horse had bulled through their ranks, and they were unwilling to risk it again. Many scholars began to slink home, and townsmen followed suit when Leger galloped up in full battle gear. Eventually, only two clots of people remained: a motley collection of students who always preferred brawling to studying; and some patrons from the King's Head, who were never happy unless they had something to protest about.

'I can manage now, Sheriff,' said Sauvage. He was pale – the near loss of control had given him a serious fright. 'These few will be no problem, especially if Brother Michael leaves me some beadles to keep the scholars in line.'

Unfortunately, the only beadles available were Heltisle's Horde, who had no more idea about controlling crowds than Sauvage. Michael gave them instructions, but was far from certain they could be trusted to carry them out. Tulyet finished briefing Sauvage and came to stand with Michael and Bartholomew. So did Sir Leger, whose sour expression showed he was disappointed that a skirmish had been averted.

'The situation will not stay calm for long,' he predicted with more hope than was appropriate for a man who was supposed to be dedicated to keeping the King's peace. 'Tangmer was stupid to take the enemy under his roof. He brought this on himself.'

'The *peregrini* were not "the enemy",' said Bartholomew sharply. 'They were civilians, who left France to avoid being slaughtered.'

'They were Jacques,' growled Leger. 'And spies, who told the Dauphin when to attack Winchelsea. It was a pity they escaped that town before its Mayor could hang them.'

'The Mayor lied,' argued Bartholomew, more inclined to believe Julien's version of events than the one given by a politician who was alleged to be a coward.

'He did not,' countered Leger. 'But we will have our revenge, because the truth is that they have not vanished, but are still in the area. Sauvage spotted Delacroix behind Peterhouse last night, while I saw that priest near St Bene't's Church.'

'Are you sure it was Julien?' asked Bartholomew, wondering what reason the group could possibly have for lingering somewhere so dangerous.

'No,' admitted Leger. 'I gave chase, but lost him in the undergrowth – my armour is too bulky for slithering through bushes like a snake. However, I *am* sure that he and his friends mean us harm.' He gestured to the Spital. 'It would not surprise me if they were still in there.'

'Then let us go and see,' said Tulyet. 'If they are, we shall take them to the castle – for their own protection as much as ours. If they are not, we will make sure that everyone knows the Spital is empty. Agreed?'

The moment Bartholomew, Michael, Tulyet and Leger stepped into the Spital, it was clear that something was wrong. As before, the staff guarded the gates and patrolled the walls, but there was no sign of Tangmer, Eudo or their wives. Moreover, there was a sense of distress among them that seemed to have nothing to do with the situation outside.

The cousin who had opened the gate led the visitors to the chapel without a word, where all four recoiled at the stench emanating from Amphelisa's workshop. It was far more pungent than the last time they had been, and they saw that one workbench had been knocked over, spilling oils all across the floor. Amphelisa was mopping up the mess with a cloth, and her old burgundy cloak was soaked in it.

'The fumes may be toxic in so confined an area,' warned Bartholomew, covering his nose with his sleeve. 'Open the windows and both doors.'

'Come upstairs first,' rasped Amphelisa; her eyes were bloodshot. 'The balcony.'

She led the way to the room above, with its curious wooden screen. Tangmer was there with Eudo, who was sobbing uncontrollably. Goda lay on the floor like a discarded doll.

Bartholomew glanced at Amphelisa. 'Is she . . .'

'Dead,' whispered Amphelisa. 'She was supposed to be baking today, and when she failed to appear, Eudo went to look for her. He found her here.'

Bartholomew crouched next to the little woman. She had been stabbed, and the weapon was still in her chest. He could not bring himself to yank it out while her distraught husband was watching, but Leger had no such qualms. He grabbed it and hauled until it came free.

'Not French,' he said. 'Just a kitchen knife. What happened?'

As Eudo was incapable of speech – he retreated to a corner, where he rocked back and forth, weeping all the while – Tangmer replied. The Warden's face was ashen.

'She must have come to the chapel to pray, but encoun-tered the killer instead. There was a struggle – I assume you saw the mess downstairs? At some point, she managed to escape up here, but he got her anyway.'

The floor was covered in oily footprints, which suggested that Goda and her assailant had done a lot of running about before the fatal blow was struck. There were two distinctive sets: the tiny ones made by the victim, and the much larger ones of her attacker.

'I thought you kept this room locked,' said Bartholomew, bending to inspect them. 'Amphelisa told us that she carries the only key around her neck. So how did they get in?'

Amphelisa glanced uncomfortably at her husband.

'Tell them the truth,' said Tangmer wearily. 'Lies will help no one now.'

'I sometimes gave Goda my key when I needed something fetching from here,' replied Amphelisa unhappily. 'Unbeknownst to me, she made herself a copy. It is in her hand.'

The dead woman's fingers were indeed curled around a piece of metal. Bartholomew removed it and knew at once that it had been cut illicitly, as it was suspiciously plain and had no proper head. Then he looked at Goda's fine new kirtle, and answers came thick and fast.

'Was she stealing your oils and selling them on her own account?'

Amphelisa nodded slowly. 'We think so, although she must have negotiated a very canny deal with an apothecary to explain all the handsome clothes she has acquired recently. She has not worn the same outfit twice in days . . .'

'So who killed her?' demanded Tulyet. 'A member of staff? You have already said that these oils represent a vital source of income, so her thievery will impact on everyone here.'

'None of us hurt her,' said Tangmer firmly. 'She was family. Besides, we knew she was light-fingered when she married Eudo, but she made him happy, so we overlooked it.'

'Then have you had any visitors today?' asked Tulyet.

'No – we thought it best to dissuade them,' replied the Warden. 'For obvious reasons.'

'Then how do you explain her murder, if you are innocent and no one else came in?'

'A townsman or a scholar must have climbed over the wall,' said Tangmer helplessly. 'Like they did when the Girard family died. We try to be vigilant, but our Spital is huge, and it is not difficult to sneak in undetected. You know this, Sheriff – you did it yourself, to prove that our defences are less stalwart than we believed.'

'So you had a mysterious invader,' said Tulyet flatly. 'How convenient!'

Before he could ask more, Leger made an urgent sound. He was standing near the screen, and had been peering through it into the nave below.

'Someone is down there,' he whispered tightly. 'Eavesdropping.'

Tulyet was down the stairs in a flash, and Bartholomew ran to the screen just in time to see him lay hold of someone by the scruff of his neck.

'Hah!' exclaimed Leger triumphantly. 'It is that French priest. I said those bastards were still in the area, but I was wrong. The truth is that they never left!'

It did not take long to determine that Leger was right. The old men, women and children – but not the Jacques, who were conspicuous by their absence – were huddled in the guesthouse recently vacated by the nuns. They looked frightened and exhausted, and Bartholomew's heart went out to them. Before any questions could be asked, there was a commotion outside the gate. Tulyet told Leger to make sure the Spital was not about to be invaded.

'What if it is?' shrugged Leger insolently. 'Or would you have me defend French scum from loyal Englishmen?'

'I would have you defend a charitable foundation from a mindless mob,' retorted Tulyet sharply. 'This is a hospital, built to shelter people in need, and the King will not want it in flames. Now go and restore the peace – and not a word about what you have seen here, or you will answer to me. Is that clear?'

With ill grace, Leger stamped away. Once he had gone, the *peregrini* relaxed a little, and one or two of the smaller children even began to play. The Sheriff had been wise to dispense with Leger's menacing presence before starting to question them.

'Where are the Jacques?' he began.

'We do not know,' replied Julien tiredly. 'They left during the night. I did my best to find them and persuade them to come back, but to no avail. Sir Leger saw me in a churchyard, and I was lucky to escape from him.'

'Their flight is a bitter blow,' said the weaver – Madame Vipond – worriedly. 'Who will protect us now? Even Delacroix has gone, despite the rhubarb decoction I slipped into his ale to make sure he stayed put.'

Julien gaped at her. 'So he was right to claim he was poisoned?'

'It was not poison,' she sniffed. 'It was a tonic. He just happened to swallow rather a lot of it. Goda got it for me, although it cost me the last of my savings. Do not look at me like that, Father – I did what I thought was best for the rest of us.'

Julien turned back to Tulyet. 'Well, all I hope is that they have the sense to get as far away from here as possible. I am beginning to realise that we should have done the same.'

'So why did you stay?' asked Tulyet, making it clear that he wished they had not.

'Because Michael moved the nuns, and suddenly there

was an empty guesthouse available,' explained Julien. 'It seemed as if God was telling us to hide here for a while longer – to make proper plans, rather than just traipsing off and hoping for the best.'

Bartholomew looked at the children's bewildered faces, and the dull resignation in the eyes of the adults, and was filled with compassion. Could he take them to Michaelhouse? Unfortunately, word was sure to leak out if he did, and then there would be a massacre for certain – of his colleagues as well as the refugees. He wracked his brain for another solution, but nothing came to mind.

'We could not bring ourselves to oust them,' said Amphelisa. 'So we agreed to tell people that they had gone to London instead. After all, who would ever know the truth?'

'Everyone you invited here to search the place,' replied Bartholomew, shocked by the reckless audacity of the plan. 'You said you hoped they would see it is a good place, and would bring their lunatics here.'

'The offer was for folk to look around our hall, not the guesthouse,' argued Amphelisa pedantically. 'No one would have seen the *peregrini*.'

'If you had declared one building off-limits, even the most dull-witted visitor would have smelled a rat,' said Tulyet, disgusted. 'Your decision was irresponsible, especially as Delacroix *and* Julien were seen after they were supposed to have left. I appreciate your motives, Amphelisa, but this was a foolish thing to have done. Now none of you are safe.'

'Dick is right,' said Michael. 'You must leave today. All of you – staff and *peregrini*.'

'And go where?' asked Madame Vipond helplessly. 'The open road, where we will be easy prey for anyone? Another town or village, where we will be persecuted as we were in Winchelsea? At least here we have food and a roof over our heads.'

'Not food,' put in Tangmer. 'I have no money to buy more, and nor do you.'

'You mentioned the castle,' said Bartholomew to Tulyet. 'They would be safe there, under your protection.'

'That was before Goda was murdered,' said Tulyet. 'Once it becomes known that a local lass was stabbed in a place where Frenchmen were staying . . . well, you do not need me to tell you what conclusions will be drawn. None of us can guarantee their safety now, and the only thing these *peregrini* can do is get as far away as possible.'

'Goda,' said Michael, looking around at the fugitives. 'Do *you* know who killed her?'

'She brought us bread at dawn,' replied Julien. 'But since then, we have been huddled in here, trying to keep the children quiet. The windows are either nailed shut or they open on to the road rather than the Spital, which means we have no idea what is happening in the Tangmers' domain.'

'We had better pack,' said Madame Vipond exhaustedly to the others. 'And trust that God will protect us, given that people will not.'

'We cannot send them off to fend for themselves,' protested Bartholomew to Michael and Tulyet. 'It would be inhuman. We must find another way.'

Michael pondered for a moment. 'The *conloquium* will finish the day after tomorrow, and nuns will disperse in all directions to go home. Most are good women, and many hail from very remote convents. Let me see if one will accept some travelling companions.'

'Two days is too long,' argued Tulyet. 'We cannot trust Leger to keep his mouth shut for ever, and these folk will die for certain if they are discovered here.'

'Then we will just have to protect them,' said Bartholomew doggedly. 'Detail more soldiers to stand guard.'

'I cannot spare men to mind the Spital when I am

struggling to prevent my town from going up in flames,' said Tulyet irritably.

'Please, Dick,' said Michael quietly. 'I seriously doubt these people can move quickly enough to escape the bigots mustering outside, so they will be caught and murdered. I do not want that on my conscience and nor do you.'

Tulyet sighed in resignation. 'Very well – you have until dawn the day after tomorrow to organise an escape. But the agreement is conditional on the *peregrini* staying out of sight. If one is so much as glimpsed through a window or a gate, the deal is off. Do you understand?'

'Thank you, Sheriff,' said Julien with quiet dignity. 'We accept your terms. But what about Delacroix and his friends?'

'You had better hope they are well away,' said Tulyet sourly, 'because if they are lurking here, they are dead already.'

'Do you think Goda tried to stop them from leaving?' asked Bartholomew. 'And they stabbed her for it?'

Julien and Madame Vipond exchanged a glance that suggested it would not surprise them. Amphelisa was the only one who protested their innocence, although not for long.

Outside, Leger listened in mounting anger to what had been agreed. His face darkened and his fists clenched at his side.

'You place the comfort of foreigners above the safety of your town,' he snarled. 'How long do you think it will take before the truth seeps out? After that, anyone trying to defend this place will die, and for what? To protect *Frenchmen?*' He spat the last word.

'We four are the only ones outside the Spital who know the secret,' said Tulyet curtly. 'Michael, Matt and I will say nothing, so unless you cannot keep quiet . . .'

290

'I can,' said Leger sullenly. 'Although this is a stupid decision, and I will tell the King so when he demands to know why good men died for nothing.'

'No one will die, because you will prevent it,' said Tulyet briskly. 'I am assigning *you* the task of ensuring the Spital comes to no harm.'

'I refuse,' said Leger immediately. 'You cannot make me act against my principles.'

'Your principles preclude you from defending a charitable foundation?' asked Tulyet archly. 'Because that is all I require you to do – to keep the *building* safe.'

'A building with Frenchmen inside it,' retorted Leger. 'The enemy.'

'Oh, come, man,' snapped Tulyet. 'We are talking about a gaggle of women, old men and terrified children. Do you really think such folk represent a danger to you? However, if the challenge of defending this place from a ragtag mob is beyond your abilities, I can easily pick someone else to do it.'

'Then do,' flashed Leger. 'Because I am not—'

'Although if the Spital is damaged because you refuse to do your duty, you will answer to the King,' Tulyet went on. 'He has taken a personal interest in this place, and wants it to thrive. I seriously doubt you will keep his favour once he learns that you let it burn down because a few displaced villagers from Rouen were within.'

'Very well,' snarled Leger, throwing up his hands in defeat. 'But I want my objections noted, and I shall be making my own report to His Majesty.'

He stamped away without another word, his expression murderous. Tulyet watched him begin his preparations, then started to walk back to the town with Bartholomew and Michael.

'Are you sure he can be trusted?' asked Bartholomew uneasily. 'Because if not, it will cost the lives of everyone inside – *peregrini* and staff.'

'I am sure,' replied Tulyet. 'A massacre will reflect badly on his military abilities, and he will not want that on his record. Besides, now that Orwel and Norbert are dead, he is the only man with the skills and experience to mount a workable defence – other than my knights, and I cannot spare them. However, it is not Leger who concerns me, but the Jacques.'

'Why?' asked Bartholomew. 'They will be miles away by now. They would have gone after the Girards were killed, but Julien stopped them. They never wanted to linger here.'

'There is a rage in them that I have seen before,' explained Tulyet soberly. 'Their time in the Jacquerie and then in Winchelsea has turned them angry, bitter, violent and unforgiving. They will not overlook the Girard murders, no matter how much they and the victims might have quarrelled. They will want vengeance.'

'Unless they are the ones who killed them,' Bartholomew pointed out. 'They are on our list of suspects.'

'Regardless, I fear they have *not* disappeared into the Fens to escape the tedious business of protecting Julien's flock, but are here, in Cambridge, biding their time until they can avenge themselves on the country that took them in and then turned against them.'

'Perhaps,' said Michael. 'Yet I cannot believe that one of them stabbed Bruges at the butts. It would have been a shocking risk, and none of them are fools.'

'But it would be a good solution to the murders, would it not?' asked Tulyet. 'The culprit being neither a townsman nor a scholar?'

'Yes,' acknowledged Michael. 'But only if it is true.'

As the mood of the town felt more dangerous than ever, Tulyet decided it would be safer for Bartholomew and Michael to remain with him while they hunted killers. Michael objected, on the grounds that no one would dare assault the Senior Proctor, but Bartholomew was glad of Tulyet's protection. They went to the castle first, where Tulyet organised a hunt for the Jacques, promising a shilling to the soldiers who brought them back.

'Alive,' cautioned Bartholomew, visions of corpses galore delivered to the Sheriff's doorstep, the triumphant bearers safe in the knowledge that the dead could not say there had been a terrible mistake.

When the patrols had gone, Tulyet, Bartholomew and Michael went to the Griffin, to question its patrons about Wyse's killer, after which they interviewed rioters about the person who had yelled the order to shoot. They spent an age in King's Hall asking about its murdered scholars, and then went to St Radegund's, where Sister Alice informed them that all the evidence against her was fabricated. Finally, they spoke to the staff at the Brazen George, to see if they had noticed anything untoward around the time when Orwel had died.

But they learned nothing to take them forward. Afternoon faded to evening, and then night approached, dark and full of whispering shadows. Tulyet scrubbed vigorously at his face to wake himself up as the church bells rang to announce the evening services.

'We have done all we can with the murders today,' he said. 'Now I must go and keep the peace on our streets.'

'I have already briefed my beadles,' said Michael, 'although I told Meadowman not to trust Heltisle's Horde. I shall offer them to Leger soon – a gift of two dozen "prime fighting men" for the King's army.'

He and Bartholomew trudged back to Michaelhouse, where they sat on a bench in the yard and ate a quick meal of bread and cheese before Michael went to join his beadles. The yard used to be dark once the sun went down, but he had ordered it lit with lanterns after he had taken an embarrassing tumble. In the hope that logical analysis would present the answers that had eluded them all day, Bartholomew began to list his remaining suspects.

'The Jacques or Theophilis,' he said. 'I would like to include Heltisle, too, as he keeps trying to drag your attention away from the investigations by playing petty power games, but the truth is that I cannot see him stabbing anyone.'

'The Jacques are on my list, too,' said Michael, 'but with Aynton above them, rather than Theophilis. You are right about Heltisle – he is objectionable, but no killer. We can exclude de Wetherset for the same reason.'

'The only other people left are nuns – Sister Alice and Magistra Katherine, who cannot prove their whereabouts when the Girards were murdered.'

'But Katherine is the Bishop's sister, and too busy being intelligent and superior at the *conloquium* to stab people. I do not see Alice braving the butts either, much as I dislike her.' Michael stood and brushed crumbs from his habit. 'That meagre dinner will not see me through the night. I need something else. Come and have a couple of Lombard slices.'

He marched to his quarters and flung open the door. Theophilis was inside, going through the documents on the desk. The Junior Proctor jerked his hand back guiltily, but managed an easy smile.

'There you are, Brother. I am looking for the beadles' work schedules for the coming week. They are not in St Mary the Great, so I assumed they were here.'

'I gave them to Heltisle,' said Michael. 'Why did you want them?'

'Because Perkyn is ill, and must be removed from the rosters until he is well again. He complains of ringing ears after listening to the Marian Singers.'

Michael's expression hardened. 'Then tell him his services are no longer required. I heard the choir, and *my* ears are not ringing.'

294

Theophilis inclined his head and left, while Bartholomew wondered what lie the Junior Proctor would tell Perkyn to explain why he no longer had a job.

'He did not want the rotas,' he said, looking through the window to watch Theophilis cross the yard. 'The truth is that Heltisle uncovered nothing to hurt you in your office last night, so he sent him here to find something instead.'

'Well, if he did, Theophilis would not be looking for it on my desk, lying out for all to see. He knows anything important will be locked away. You are wrong about him, Matt.'

Bartholomew failed to understand why the monk refused to accept what was so patently obvious. He looked out of the window again while Michael riffled about in his pantry for treats, and saw Clippesby with a drowsing chicken – he was going to the henhouse to put her to roost. Theophilis changed course to intercept him, and asked a question to which the Dominican shook his head. Theophilis persisted, and Clippesby became agitated. So did the bird, which flew at Theophilis with her claws extended.

The Junior Proctor jerked away with a yelp. He looked angry, so Bartholomew hurried down to the yard to intervene – the hen was Gertrude, and it would be unfortunate if Theophilis hurt her, as the nominalists in the University were likely to see it as an act of war. The last thing they needed was another excuse for strife.

'This lunatic knows something about the murders,' spat Theophilis, jabbing his finger accusingly at Clippesby. 'He saw something last night, but declines to tell me what.'

'What did you see, John?' asked Bartholomew, while Clippesby retrieved the hen and stroked her feathers. She relaxed, although her sharp orange eyes remained fixed on Theophilis.

'You will not get a sensible answer,' hissed Theophilis.

'Just some rubbish about a mouse. He ought to be locked away where he can do no harm. All this nonsense about philosophising fowls! He is an embarrassment, and as soon as I have a spare moment, I am taking him to the Spital. They know how to deal with madmen.'

Clippesby regarded him reproachfully. 'But you have been fascinated by the birds' theories for weeks, so why—'

'You are a fool,' interrupted Theophilis, so vehemently that Clippesby flinched and the hen's hackles rose again. 'I thought you were more clever than the rest of us combined, but I was wrong. I should never have befriended you.'

'Not befriended,' said Bartholomew, suddenly understanding exactly why Theophilis had spent so much time in the Dominican's company. 'Milked for ideas.'

Theophilis regarded him contemptuously. 'You are as addle-witted as he is if you think I am interested in any theory *he* can devise.'

'But you *are* interested,' argued Bartholomew. 'Because Clippesby *is* cleverer than the rest of us combined. The whole University is talking about the Chicken Debate, and his arguments are respected by people on both sides of the schism. He has single-handedly achieved what others have been striving to do for decades.'

He saw that Michael had followed him outside and was listening. William had sidled up, too, although Theophilis was too intent on arguing with Bartholomew to notice either.

'Clippesby is a one-idea man,' the Junior Proctor said contemptuously. 'He has shot his bow and now his quiver is empty.'

'On the contrary, he has been working on his next treatise all term, and it promises to be every bit as brilliant as the first. It is almost ready, so you aim to steal it and pass it off as your own. *That* is why you have quizzed him so relentlessly.'

'Lies!' cried Theophilis outraged. 'I would never—'

'But first, you must get rid of him,' Bartholomew forged on. 'You began calling him a lunatic a few days ago, rolling your eyes and smirking behind his back. Now you aim to have him locked him away, so that no one will hear when he says "your" treatise is really his.'

'But he *is* insane! He *should* be shut in a place where he cannot embarrass us. And I resent your accusations extremely. Why would *I* claim credit for a discussion between hens?'

'Oh, I am sure you can adapt it to a more conventional format. And that is why you were in Michael's room just now – not spying for Heltisle, but looking for something that will allow you to discredit Clippesby.'

'What if I was?' flared Theophilis, capitulating so abruptly that Bartholomew blinked his surprise. 'I will make sure that this new treatise honours Michaelhouse, whereas Clippesby will just draw attention to the fact that we enrol madmen. It is better for the College if I publish the work under my name. Surely, you can see that I am right?'

Bartholomew was so disgusted that he could think of no reply, although the same was not true of William, who stepped forward to give Theophilis an angry shove.

'You are despicable,' he declared, as Theophilis's eyes widened in horror that his admission had been heard by others. 'There is no room in Michaelhouse for plagiarists.'

'There is not,' agreed Michael, regarding his Junior Proctor with hurt disappointment. 'Consider your Fellowship here terminated.'

'Do not expel him on my account,' begged Clippesby, distressed as always by strife. The hen clucked, so he put his ear to her beak. 'Gertrude says that—'

'You see?' snarled Theophilis, all righteous indignation. 'He is stark raving mad!'

'He is,' agreed William. 'Because *I* would not speak in

your defence if you had been trying to poach *my* ideas. It takes a very special lunatic to be that magnanimous.'

'You cannot eject me, because I resign,' said Theophilis defiantly. 'From Michaelhouse *and* the Junior Proctorship. I want nothing more to do with any of you.'

'Good,' said William. 'I will help you pack. Is *now* convenient?'

When Theophilis had been marched away by a vengeful William, Michael invited Bartholomew and Clippesby to his rooms for a restorative cup of wine. Bartholomew supposed he should feel triumphant that his doubts about the Junior Proctor's integrity should be correct, but instead he felt soiled. He glanced at Clippesby, who perched on a stool with the hen drowsing on his lap.

'What will poor Theophilis do now?' asked the Dominican unhappily. 'No other College will take him once they learn what he did. His academic career is over.'

'You are too good for this world,' said Michael. 'If he had tried to steal my ideas, I would have driven him from the country, not just the College.'

Clippesby kissed the chicken's comb. 'There was never any danger of him taking my ideas. Gertrude and Ma warned me weeks ago that his interest in them was not quite honourable, so they have been having a bit of fun with him.'

Michael regarded him warily. 'What kind of fun?'

A rare spark of mischief gleamed in the friar's blue eyes. 'Theophilis *will* publish a thesis soon, but as Gertrude and Ma have been largely responsible for its contents, it will have some serious logical flaws. Then they will help William prepare a counterclaim.'

Bartholomew shook his head wonderingly. 'Which will have the dual purpose of bringing more academic glory to Michaelhouse – William's refutation is sure to be flawless if your hens are involved – and embarrassing Theophilis by having his errors exposed by the least able scholar in the University. My word, John! That is sly.'

Clippesby kissed the bird again. 'Gertrude has a very wicked sense of humour.'

Michael eyed him with a new appreciation. 'It is a scheme worthy of the most slippery of University politicians. Perhaps I should appoint you as my new Junior Proctor.'

'No, thank you,' said Clippesby vehemently, then turned to Bartholomew. 'When you confronted Theophilis, did I hear you accuse him of spying for Heltisle?'

Bartholomew nodded. 'Why? Do you know something to prove it?'

'I know something to *disprove* it. Hulda the church mouse often listens to Heltisle and de Wetherset talking. She says they *did* ask Theophilis to monitor you, but he refused.'

'Did he say why?' asked Michael. 'And more to the point, why did this mouse feel compelled to eavesdrop on high-ranking University officials in the first place?'

'Because she was afraid they would conspire against you – which they did, by trying to buy your Junior Proctor. But Theophilis was loyal. He refused to betray you, even for the promise of your job.'

'Then what a pity he transpired to be an idea-thief,' spat Michael in disgust. 'Faithful deputies do not grow on trees. I do not suppose he was pumping you for ideas when any of these murders was committed, was he? Matt has him at the top of his list of suspects.'

'He was with Gertrude, Ma and me when Paris was stabbed,' replied Clippesby promptly. 'Does that help?'

Bartholomew was not sure whether to be disappointed or relieved. He had wanted Theophilis to be the culprit, especially in the light of what the man had tried to do to Clippesby, but it would be better for Michaelhouse if the killer was someone else. Then he recalled another thing that Theophilis had said.

'He mentioned you knowing something about the murders. Do you?'

'Just another snippet from Hulda the mouse – that she saw a nun running away from the Brazen George last night. It was not long after Orwel was bludgeoned, although Hulda did not know this at the time, of course.'

Michael gaped at him. 'A *nun* killed Orwel? Which one?'

'Hulda did not say this nun killed Orwel,' cautioned Clippesby. 'She said the nun was running away from the Brazen George shortly after Orwel died. She does not know her name, but the lady was thin, pale, and wore a pure white habit.'

Michael blinked. 'Abbess Isabel? She would never leave St Radegund's at that time of night! She knows the town is dangerous, because she is the one who found Paris's body.'

'How was she running?' asked Bartholomew of Clippesby. 'In terror? In triumph?'

The Dominican shrugged. 'She was just running.'

'Abbess Isabel is *not* the killer,' said Michael firmly. 'She would never risk her place among the saints by committing mortal sins.' He turned back to Clippesby. 'Was this mysterious white figure alone?'

Clippesby nodded. 'And not long before, Hulda saw her calling on Margery Starre.'

'Then it cannot have been Isabel,' said Michael at once. 'She would never visit a witch. I imagine someone stole her distinctive habit and used it as a disguise.'

'So ask Margery who it was,' suggested Clippesby. He bent his head when the hen on his lap clucked. 'But not tonight. Gertrude says she is busy casting spells to prevent another riot.'

'Then we shall see her tomorrow,' determined Bartholomew, although he could see that Michael itched to have answers immediately. 'We cannot disrupt Margery's

300

efforts to keep the peace, Brother. If we do, and trouble breaks out again, everyone will say it is our fault for getting in her way.'

'They will,' agreed Clippesby. 'And if more people die fighting, it will be even harder to restore relations between us and the town.'

Reluctantly, Michael conceded that they were right.

# CHAPTER 13

The next day saw a change in the weather. Blue skies were replaced by flat grey ones, and a biting north wind scythed in from the Fens. Bartholomew rose while it was still dark, woke Aungel with instructions for the day's teaching, then joined Michael for a hurried breakfast in the kitchen with Agatha the laundress, who had a great many things to say about the fact that the town and the University were teetering on the brink of yet another major confrontation.

'And it is not just each other they hate,' she declared, pursing her lips. 'There are divisions in both that mean the strife will be all but impossible to quell. I would not be in your shoes for a kingdom, Brother. Or the Sheriff's, for that matter.'

'She is right,' muttered Michael, as he and Bartholomew hurried to Margery's home in Shoemaker Row. 'Dick managed to stamp out some trouble last night, but all it did was give the would-be rioters more cause to resent him – and us.'

'Have you arranged an escape for the *peregrini* yet?' asked Bartholomew.

Michael grimaced. 'I need to be careful, because if I confide in the wrong nun . . . well, I do not need to explain to you that the matter is delicate.'

Although it was only just growing light, the streets were busy as folk took advantage of the curfew's end to see what was happening outside. They included both townsmen and scholars, the latter making no effort to pretend they were going to church. On the high street, some of Heltisle's Horde were engaged in a fracas with

302

students from King's Hall, while there was a quarrel in the market square between those who wanted to fight the French spies at the Spital and those who thought it was better to lynch them.

'Vengeance is for God to dispense, not you,' declared Prior Pechem of the Franciscans as he passed – a remark that meant there were then three factions yelling at each other.

An angry bellow from Michael was enough to make them disperse, although Bartholomew sensed it was only a matter of time before they were at it again. He suspected most cared nothing about the issues they supported, and their real objective was just a brawl.

He and Michael reached Shoemaker Row, where Margery's cottage looked pretty in the daylight – painted a cheerful yellow, with an array of potted plants on the doorstep. It was not how most folk would picture the lair of a witch.

'You will have to go in alone,' said Michael, who had been walking ever more slowly towards it. 'I cannot be seen dropping in on her – our students might interpret it as licence to do the same, and enough of them beat a track to her door as it is. Besides, I have my reputation to think of.'

'What about my reputation?' demanded Bartholomew indignantly.

'Already compromised – it is common knowledge that she likes you. Now hurry up! We cannot afford to waste time. If Margery confirms that Abbess Isabel was indeed out and about when Orwel was murdered, we will have to go to St Radegund's and demand an explanation.'

Bartholomew entered Margery's home with the same fear that always assailed him when he stepped across her threshold – that he would find her having a cosy chat with her good friend Lucifer. Or worse, brewing some concoction that contained human body parts. Instead, it

303

was to discover Cynric there, the two of them sitting companionably at the hearth, drinking cups of her dangerously strong ale.

'I am here for Dusty,' explained the book-bearer, not at all sheepish at being caught in such a place. 'He has a sore hoof, and Margery makes an excellent onion poultice for those.'

'She probably got the recipe from Satan,' muttered Bartholomew to himself, 'who uses it on his cloven feet.'

'No, it is my own formula,' said Margery pleasantly, startling him with her unusually acute hearing. 'So what brings you here, Doctor? And openly, too! The last time you came, you skulked outside with your ear to my window shutter.'

Bartholomew felt himself blush. 'I was following Sister Alice. She was walking along so furtively that I thought I should see what she was up to.'

'She wanted a cursing spell,' recalled Margery. 'But I did not give her one. I decided she was unworthy, so I fobbed her off with a pot of coloured water.'

'Oh,' said Bartholomew, wondering how 'unworthy' one had to be not to pass muster with one of the Devil's disciples. 'Did she say what she intended to do with it?'

'Wreak revenge on her enemies, who seem to include everyone she meets. I did not take to her at all, which is why I do not mind disclosing her secrets. I am more discreet with folk I like, such as yourself.'

'How about Abbess Isabel?' asked Bartholomew, speaking quickly to mask his discomfiture. 'Do you like her?'

Margery nodded. 'She is a little over-passionate about Christianity, but that happens when you spend all your life in a convent, and she cannot help it, poor soul. However, my fondness for her means I will not break her confidence.'

'No?' asked Bartholomew, wondering how to convince

her that it was important she did. Fortunately, he did not have to ponder for long.

'Unless you make it worth my while,' Margery went on. 'Do I detect the scent of cedarwood oil about you? Amphelisa's perhaps? That is excellent stuff – always useful.'

Bartholomew fished it from his bag and handed it over, marvelling that her sense of smell should be as sensitive as her hearing. 'She said it kills fleas.'

'I imagine it does, but it is also good for dissolving unwanted flesh.'

Bartholomew regarded her uneasily. 'Unwanted by whom?' But then he decided he did not want to know the answer, so changed the subject. 'Tell me about the Abbess.'

'She came to me on Saturday evening, shortly after you and Brother Michael went to the Brazen George – I saw you slip through its back door while I was walking home.'

'How did she seem to you?'

'You mean did she race out afterwards and brain Orwel?' asked Margery shrewdly. 'If she did, it had nothing to do with her discussion with me – which was all about a nun she aims to defrock. She is too tactful to mention names, but I knew she meant Alice.'

'How?'

'By her description of a discontented lady with a penchant for stinking candles. She wanted a list of all those Alice intends to hurt, so she could warn them to be on their guard. I obliged her, and in return she gave me a lock of her hair, which she says will be worth a lot of money after she is canonised.'

Bartholomew decided not to tell Margery that it took years for such matters to be decided, and that those arrogant enough to believe they were in the running would probably be rejected on principle.

'Is Isabel herself on Alice's list?' he asked.

'Oh, yes, along with the Bishop and a hundred others. I told her to watch herself, because while I am the best wise-woman in Cambridge, I am not the only one, and others are not as scrupulous as me. When Alice realises my coloured water is not having the desired effect, she will take her custom elsewhere.'

'Did Isabel heed the warning?'

'She promised she would. However, she said one thing that bemused me. She said that finding Paris the Plagiarist's body still haunts her dreams. But why would it? He cannot have been her first corpse, and I am told that his stabbing was not particularly bloody.'

'No more than any other,' said Bartholomew. 'And less than some.'

'There is more to her distress about him than she lets on,' finished Margery. 'It puzzles me, and if you aim to solve his murder, it should puzzle you, too.'

To reach St Radegund's, Bartholomew and Michael had to cross the market square, where there was no sign of the people who had been quarrelling there earlier. There were others, though, using the stalls as an excuse to loiter. The traders were becoming irked by all the looking but no buying, and it would not be long before it caused a spat.

Scholars prowled in packs, armed to the teeth. Some clustered around the baker's stall, a business owned by generations of Mortimers. Bartholomew was not sure which Mortimer ran it now, as they all looked alike, but the present incumbent's face was red with fury.

'They have no right,' he bellowed. 'It is illegal and immoral!'

His angry voice attracted an audience. It included Isnard the bargeman and Verious the ditcher, the latter excused sentry duty at the town gates on the grounds that he was not very good at it.

'What is illegal and immoral?' asked Michael.

'Cutting the price of bread,' snarled Mortimer, so enraged that Bartholomew was afraid he would give himself a seizure. 'We had a deal, and the University cannot suddenly decide only to pay half of it. That will barely cover the cost of the ingredients!'

Michael was bemused. 'Our contract fixes the price of bread until next year. Neither of us can change anything until then.'

'So you say, but Heltisle has declared all the agreements you negotiated null and void. He has a new list of prices – ones that favour scholars at *our* expense.'

'Refuse to sell him anything, then,' shrugged Isnard. 'He and his cronies will starve without bread, and he will soon come back with his tail between his legs.'

'No – he will buy it in Ely and I will be ruined,' said Mortimer bitterly. 'The bastard! He has me over a barrel.'

'You should not trade with scholars anyway,' put in Verious. 'Not when they hid French spies in the Spital – spies who then crept out and murdered Sauvage.'

'*Murdered* Sauvage?' echoed Bartholomew uneasily. 'He is dead?'

'Did you not hear?' asked Isnard. 'We found him this morning, not ten paces from here. He was stabbed, and his killer left the dagger sticking out of his back – a challenge for us to identify it and catch him.'

'*What?*' cried Michael, shocked. 'Why did no one tell me?'

'Because it is none of your business,' spat Mortimer. 'Sauvage was a townsman and he was murdered by the French. His death has nothing to do with the University, so you can keep your long noses out of it.'

'Poor Sauvage,' sighed Isnard. 'He should have told them his name – then they might have thought he was one of them and left him alone.'

'He would not have wanted that,' averred Verious. 'He would rather be dead than be thought of as French.'

'Where is his body?' demanded Michael. 'Holy Trinity?'

'Yes,' replied Isnard. 'Although we kept the dagger. Show him, Verious. Brother Michael is good at catching criminals – maybe he will win justice for poor Sauvage.'

'Do not bother, Verious,' sneered Mortimer contemptuously. 'Michael will do nothing about Sauvage, because all townsmen are dirt to the University.'

'We are not dirt to Brother Michael,' declared Isnard stoutly. 'He would not let us join his choir if we were.'

Verious produced the dagger from about his grimy person. There was no need to study it closely: it was of an ilk with the ones used on the other victims. Michael took it and slipped it in his scrip, much to Verious's obvious dismay.

'What makes you think French spies killed Sauvage?' asked Bartholomew of Verious, although it was Isnard who answered.

'First, because that dagger is the same as the ones used on their other victims, and we know those blades were French, because the Sheriff said so when he showed them to us. And second, because it is an expensive thing, but the killer left it behind. Only spies can afford that sort of extravagance.'

'Because they are paid directly by the dolphin,' elaborated Verious confidently, 'who is fabulously rich after plundering Winchelsea.'

Bartholomew opened his mouth to argue, then closed it again. There was no point when Verious and Isnard had already made up their minds. Michael continued to question them, but when it became clear they had no more to tell, he turned back to the enraged baker.

'I will see you receive a fair price for your bread, Mortimer. You have my word.'

Mortimer scowled at him. 'Unfortunately, your word is

308

worthless. Heltisle told us that the new Chancellor wants to rule for himself, so you are now irrelevant. You have dealt justly with us in the past, but a new order has arrived, and you are not part of it.'

Michael's face went so dark with anger that Bartholomew was alarmed for him.

'Take a deep breath, Brother,' he advised hastily. 'It is not worth—'

'What is de Wetherset *thinking*?' exploded Michael. 'Not just to antagonise tradesmen when we are on the verge of serious civil unrest, but to undermine my authority when I most need it? Does he *want* the University burned to the ground?'

'It was not him – it was Heltisle,' said Isnard, frightened by the sight of the Senior Proctor trembling with fury. 'Perhaps de Wetherset knows nothing about it.'

Michael closed his eyes and took the recommended deep breath, so that when he next spoke, his voice was calmer.

'It will not matter to Heltisle if we are attacked, because his College is surrounded by high walls, but what about the hostels? They have no such means to defend themselves.'

'He does not care about those,' said Bartholomew. 'He has always been an elitist.'

Michael stormed towards St Mary the Great, aiming to have strong words with Heltisle, but before he and Bartholomew could reach it, they saw him walking along the high street with de Wetherset and Aynton. The triumvirate had been to visit the Mayor, and carried documents bearing his seal. Two dozen beadles – the real ones, not the Horde – formed a protective phalanx around them, which was a necessary precaution as they were attracting a lot of hostile attention.

'Why are these men guarding you?' demanded Michael

between gritted teeth. 'They are supposed to be patrolling the streets to prevent brawls.'

Heltisle's eyes narrowed at the disrespectful tone, although de Wetherset had the grace to look sheepish. Meanwhile, Aynton beamed at everyone who glanced in his direction, clearly under the illusion that a friendly smile was all that was needed to heal the rifts that he and his two cronies were opening.

'Would you have us lynched by a mob?' asked Heltisle archly. 'An assault on us is an assault on the University, so it is imperative that we do not allow it to happen.'

'You would not need protection if you had an ounce of sense,' snarled Michael. 'I negotiated fair trade agreements with the town, and you are fools to meddle with them.'

'They were skewed in the town's favour,' argued de Wetherset, although his voice lacked conviction, as if he already doubted the wisdom of what he had done. 'And I *do* have the authority to broker new ones. It says so in the statutes.'

'It does,' put in Aynton timidly. 'But I am not sure that we went about it in the most diplomatic manner, Chancellor. Peace is—'

'To hell with peace,' growled Heltisle. 'The town attacked us at the butts and killed four of our most promising scholars. Such behaviour cannot be tolerated, and harsher trade deals are its reward.'

'The contracts you signed *were* to our detriment, Brother,' said de Wetherset, simultaneously uncomfortable and defensive. 'So we felt obliged to offer the town a choice: sell at more attractive prices, or have us buy supplies in Ely.'

Michael regarded him furiously. 'Yes, I agreed to higher premiums, but it bought us much goodwill, which will save us a fortune in the long run, as you should know from the last time you were Chancellor. But did you have to start all this nonsense now, when relations are so strained?'

'Relations are always strained,' said de Wetherset, not unreasonably. 'Ergo, there will never be a good time to initiate reform.'

'And if you cannot quell the resulting rumpus, you should resign,' finished Heltisle, his face a mask of triumph. 'Theophilis has already offered to take your place.'

'It is tempting,' said Michael icily, 'just for the pleasure of watching *you* destroyed. But I love the University too much to see it harmed, so I shall stay at my post. However, you have created an ugly mood, so I suggest you go home and stay there. Then my beadles can return to their real duties.'

'No, they will continue to guard us,' countered Heltisle challengingly. 'Oh, and Meadowman is under arrest, by the way. He refused to obey my orders, so I had to make an example of him. The others fell into line when they saw which way the wind was blowing.'

Bartholomew glanced at the beadles who guarded the triumvirate. None were happy with the situation in which they found themselves, and he was sure that if Michael asked, they would abandon the triumvirate and follow him in a heartbeat. But the monk had too much affection for his men to put them in such an invidious position.

'I understand you have continued to investigate the murders,' said de Wetherset, turning to another matter, 'even though we told you to leave them to Aynton.' He raised a hand when Michael opened his mouth to reply. 'I do not aim to scold you, Brother, but to ask if you have made any progress.'

'Because I have not,' said Aynton ruefully. 'I tried, but then I gave up, lest I inadvertently made matters worse.'

'You are wise, Commissary,' said Michael tightly. 'If only others had the intelligence to follow your example.' He did not look at Heltisle. 'And to answer your question, Chancellor, we shall have answers after we have been to St Radegund's.'

'St Radegund's?' echoed de Wetherset, puzzled. 'Why there?'

'Abbess Isabel was in the vicinity when Orwel was brained, and can identify the culprit,' replied Michael with rather more confidence than was warranted, especially given that Isabel might be the killer herself.

'Orwel?' asked Heltisle. 'Who is he?'

'A man who had information about Wyse's murder,' said Michael, continuing to address de Wetherset. 'Unfortunately, he was killed before he could share it.'

'I have never liked the Benedictines,' said Heltisle with a moue of distaste. 'Perhaps this abbess dispatched Paris and the others. I would not put such wickedness past a member of that unsavoury Order.'

'Then you have to admire her courage,' mused Aynton. 'The plagiarist was weak and old, but her other victims cannot have been easy meat.'

'Go, then, Brother,' said de Wetherset with an amiable smile. 'But visit the Jewry first, because a spat was brewing there when we walked past, and you should stamp it out before it erupts. Meanwhile, I shall heed your advice and return to St Mary the Great, where I will remain until all the fuss dies down. What about you, Aynton?'

'Oh, I shall be here and there,' replied the Commissary airily, 'healing rifts and urging everyone to be nice to each other. Or would you rather I stayed with you, Chancellor?'

'No, keeping the peace is more important,' replied de Wetherset. 'Heltisle?'

'I shall go home,' said Heltisle grimly. 'If there is to be a battle, I want Bene't ready to defend its rights and privileges.'

'Preparing for a skirmish is hardly the example our

Vice-Chancellor should be setting,' began Michael sharply. 'It is not—'

'Oh, yes, it is!' interrupted Heltisle. 'And if Michaelhouse does not do the same, it will reveal you to be cowards and traitors.'

'Michaelhouse will do what is right,' countered Michael. 'And that does *not* include indulging in unseemly acts of violence against the town.'

Although Bartholomew itched to race to St Radegund's at once, events conspired against him. First, there was the quarrel in the Jewry to defuse, then Michael insisted on freeing Meadowman. Bartholomew fretted at the lost time, feeling the crisis loom closer with every lost moment.

When they arrived at the gaol, Michael was appalled to discover that all the rioters he had arrested had been released without charge. Their places had been taken not just by Meadowman, but by half a dozen other beadles who had also refused to obey Heltisle.

'He wanted us to guard his College rather than patrol the streets,' said Meadowman indignantly as Michael let him out. 'He thinks it will be targeted in the event of trouble, because it houses one of the University's top officials. I pointed out that Bene't has high walls, stout gates and warrior-students, so can look after itself.'

'Whereas the hostels have no protection at all,' growled another man. 'Other than us.'

'He should not have released the prisoners either,' Meadowman went on angrily, 'although half were Bene't lads, so what do you expect? Now they will hare off to foment more unrest, while Heltisle's Horde looks on like the useless rabble they are.'

'You cannot return to normal duties now,' said Michael. 'Heltisle will just rearrest you. So don everyday clothes, monitor what is happening, and report back to me.'

'We can report to you now,' said Meadowman grimly.

'The town believes the University aims to crush it into penury; the University thinks the town intends to destroy it once and for all; and everyone is convinced the Dauphin is poised to do to us what he did to Winchelsea – with the connivance of either the town or the University, depending on which side you are on.'

'Then identify the ringleaders and shut them up,' ordered Michael. 'You may lock them in their cellars, hand them to the Sheriff, or threaten them in any way you please. Perhaps the trouble will fizzle out if they are muzzled.'

The beadles did not look hopeful, but sped away to do his bidding. Their disquiet and Michael's grim expression combined to make Bartholomew's stomach churn more than ever.

'Dusk,' predicted the monk hoarsely. 'That is when the crisis will come. Tempers will fester all day, and as soon as darkness cloaks everyone with anonymity, we will go to war.'

'There must be a way to stop it. We have averted catastrophes before.'

'But that was when *I* was in charge,' Michael pointed out bitterly. 'Now we have the triumvirate, who undermine all my efforts to restore calm. Heltisle accuses me of wielding too much power, but what about him? He seems to have gone mad with it.'

They resumed their journey to St Radegund's, but met Tulyet by the Barnwell Gate. The Sheriff was astride his massive warhorse, and had donned full armour. The men who rode with him were similarly attired.

'I have done my best to quash the rumours about French spies in the Spital,' he said, reining in. 'But it is only a matter of time before the whispers start again and folk march out there to besiege it. I have ordered Leger to spirit the Tangmers and their guests away the moment it is dark.'

314

'Perhaps he should do it now,' said Bartholomew worriedly.

Tulyet shot him a scornful glance. 'Then there will be a massacre for certain, because they will be seen by the mob already outside. He needs the cover of night to succeed.'

'Can you trust him to do it?' asked Bartholomew. 'He agreed to protect the buildings, not the people inside.'

'He will do it or answer to the King,' replied Tulyet savagely. 'Besides, once the Spital folk are safe, I hope our warring factions *will* converge on the place, as I would sooner that bore the brunt of their destructive fury than the town.'

'You seem to think a clash is inevitable, but we still hope to avert one. Michael and I are going to see Abbess Isabel, who may have killed Orwel and perhaps the others, too. An arrest may appease—'

'It is far too late for that,' interrupted Tulyet harshly. 'Any hope of a peaceful resolution disappeared when the University chose to renege on its trade deals. So, yes, there will be a clash, and *you* brought it about.'

'Not us,' objected Bartholomew. 'The triumvirate.'

Tulyet shook his head in disgust. 'I thought we had cast aside our differences and were moving towards a lasting peace, but it was all based on the sense and good-will of one man. Now others are in charge . . .'

One of his knights – a rough, hard-bitten warrior who had never approved of Tulyet's efforts to befriend the University – spat. 'We will never have peace with scholars, and unless we take a firm stand against them today, they will crush us for ever.'

'He is right,' said Tulyet sourly, watching him wheel away to bear down on a group of tanners who were preparing to lob stones at someone's windows. 'I *have* signed away rights in exchange for amity, and so have you, Brother. Perhaps we should not have done.'

'Of course you should,' said Bartholomew. 'Neither of us is going anywhere, so we have no choice but to work together, and if that means making compromises, then so be it.'

'What about the Jacques?' asked Michael. 'Have they been found yet?'

Tulyet shook his head. 'But if they are here, whispering poisonous messages in susceptible ears, I will hang them. Now, go to St Radegund's if you must, but do not be long. You will be more useful here than chasing killers who no longer matter.'

Bartholomew glanced up at the sky as they hurried on, wishing it would rain. No one liked getting wet, and inclement weather would drive most would-be rioters indoors. Unfortunately, the clouds were breaking up and it promised to be another fine day.

'It is about noon,' said Michael, wrongly thinking he was estimating the time. 'Which means we have just a few hours before the trouble begins in earnest. We must hurry.'

They passed through the Barnwell Gate unchallenged, as the sentries were patrolling the streets instead. This allowed folk to pour in from the outlying villages. Few carried goods to sell, and Bartholomew realised that word had spread about the brewing unrest, so they were coming to stand with the townsfolk. Tulyet was right: a clash was now inevitable.

They arrived at the convent to find the nuns just finishing a session on the burning issue of whether peas were better served with fish or meat.

'We spent four times longer on that than on apostolic poverty – a debate that has tied the Church in knots for years,' smirked Magistra Katherine. 'We resolved *that* inconsequential problem in less than an hour!'

'Fortunately, the *conloquium* is over tomorrow,' said

Prioress Joan. 'And we shall waste no more time indoors when we should be riding out in God's good clean air. How is Dusty?'

'Quite content,' replied Michael shortly. 'Now where is—'

'Is it true that your town is on the verge of a major battle?' interrupted Katherine. 'And if so, should we make arrangements to leave early?'

'Please do,' begged Michael. 'I cannot see the disorder spreading out here, but there is no point in courting trouble. Tell your sisters to start their journeys as soon as possible.'

Katherine inclined her head. 'Is it because of the *peregrini*? The town and the University are accusing each other of harbouring French spies?'

'Yes,' said Michael. 'But we need to speak to—'

'I hope no one remembers that *we* lodged in the Spital,' said Joan anxiously. 'They might accuse us of being French-lovers, and I do not want my nuns subjected to any unpleasantness.'

'Where is Abbess Isabel?' Michael managed to interject. 'We need to see her urgently.'

'So do I,' said Katherine with a grimace. 'She borrowed my copy of the Chicken Debate and I want it back. But she went out on Saturday, and no one has seen her since.'

'She has been missing for *two days*?' cried Michael. 'Why did no one tell me?'

'Her retinue assure us that she often disappears for extended periods when she wants to pray,' shrugged Katherine. 'They were not concerned, so neither were we.'

'Did she say where she was going to do it?' asked Bartholomew.

'No, but she was last seen aiming for the town,' replied Joan. 'I was going to look for her myself as soon as the pea issue was resolved – her own nuns may not be worried, but she has been a little odd of late, and I would like to make sure she is safe and well.'

'Odd in what way?' demanded Michael.

'Fearful and unsettled. Probably because she stumbled across that corpse – Paris's.'

'Have you searched the priory?' asked Bartholomew, wondering if the Abbess's timely disappearance meant a killer had escaped justice.

'We have, but we will do it again.' With calm efficiency, Joan issued instructions to the women who had come to listen. Obediently, they hastened to do as they were told.

'May we see her quarters?' asked Bartholomew. 'If her belongings have gone, it means she . . . might have decided to make her own way home.'

He dared not say what he was really thinking, because he was unwilling to waste time on explanations that could come later.

'You may not!' objected Katherine, shocked. 'We do not allow men into our sleeping quarters. It would be unseemly!'

Most of the remaining sisters agreed, but Joan sensed the urgency of the situation and overrode them. She led the way to the tiny cell-like room that Isabel had chosen for herself – an austere, chilly place that showed the Abbess placed scant store in physical comfort. Her only belongings were a spare white habit and a few religious books. In the interests of thoroughness, Bartholomew peered under the bed. Something was there, tucked at the very back, obliging him to lie on the floor to fish it out. It was an ivory comb.

'That is mine!' cried Joan, snatching it from him. 'Or rather Dusty's. What is it doing in here? I thought Alice had stolen it.'

'Goda said she had,' mused Michael, 'although Alice denied it. Perhaps Alice placed it here in the spiteful hope that Isabel would be accused of its theft.'

'If she did, she is a fool,' said Joan in disgust. 'No one will believe that an abbess – and Isabel in particular – would steal a comb.'

'There is only one way to find out,' said Michael. 'Speak to Alice again. And this time, there will be no games. She will tell us the truth or suffer the consequences.'

He did not say what these might be, and Bartholomew gritted his teeth in agitation. How could they be wasting time on combs when the town was set to explode? Or *was* Isabel the killer, and the peculiar travels of the comb would throw light on why a saintly nun had turned murderer? Stomach churning, he followed Michael to the cellar, where the errant Alice had spent her last two nights.

Captivity had done nothing to blunt Alice's haughty defiance. She reclined comfortably on a bed in a room that was considerably larger and better appointed than Isabel's, and the only thing missing, as far as Bartholomew could tell, was a window. Clearly, nuns had a different view of what should constitute prison than anyone else.

'I will answer your questions,' she conceded loftily. 'But in return, all charges against me will be dropped and I will be reinstated as Prioress of Ickleton.'

Michael ignored the demand. 'We found the comb you hid in Abbess Isabel's room. However, your plot to see her accused of theft has failed. The comb was stolen from the Spital, but she has never been there. *You* have, though.'

Alice was unfazed. 'I have already told you: I did not take it. You will have to devise another explanation for how it ended up where it did.'

Bartholomew pushed his anxieties about the deteriorating situation in the town to the back of his mind, because a solution was beginning to reveal itself to him at last. He was sure Alice *had* stolen the comb, but was less certain that she had put it in Isabel's room to incriminate her, because Joan was right: no one would believe the Abbess would steal, and Alice would know it. The only other explanation was that Alice had *given* it to Isabel, and the Abbess had secreted it there herself.

'I believe you,' he said, speaking slowly to give his thoughts time to settle. 'You would have chosen a far more imaginative hiding place than under a bed.'

'Is that where she put it?' scoffed Alice. 'What a fool! She should be demoted, so that someone more intelligent can be installed in her place. Someone like me.'

'So you did give it to her,' pounced Bartholomew. 'Why?'

Alice folded her arms. 'I refuse to say more until you promise me something in return.'

'Very well,' said Michael. 'I promise to recommend clemency when you are sentenced to burn at the stake.'

Alice gaped at him. 'Burn at the stake? What for?'

'Buying cursing spells from a witch. Do not deny it, because we have witnesses. So what will it be? Cooperation or incineration?'

Alice's hubris began to dissolve. 'You misunderstand, Brother. The spell was only a harmless bit of fun – nothing malicious.'

'No one will believe you. Now, the comb: why did you steal it?'

Alice looked at Michael's stern, angry face, and the remaining fight went out of her. 'Because Isabel charged me to visit the Spital, find the comb and bring it to her. In return, she promised to get me reinstated.'

'You believed her?' asked Michael, sure Isabel would have done nothing of the kind.

'Not at first,' admitted Alice. 'But I was desperate, so I decided to take a chance.'

'Did she say why she wanted it?' asked Bartholomew.

'She refused to tell me. And then, when I was accused of theft and needed her to prove my innocence, she denied all knowledge of our arrangement. She betrayed me!'

'So you bought a cursing spell to teach her a lesson,' surmised Bartholomew.

'To make her confess to what she had commissioned me to do. I am *not* a thief – just the agent of one.'

Michael regarded her in disgust. 'You lie! If Isabel *had* told you to steal, you would have trumpeted it from the rooftops when you were accused. But you never did.'

Alice shrugged and looked away. 'I wanted to, but I am not stupid – I know who folk would have believed, and challenging Isabel would have done me more harm than good. But I am telling the truth now: she is the dishonest one, not me.'

'Then how unfortunate for you that she has disappeared,' said Bartholomew, feeling vaguely tainted by the whole affair, 'and can never corroborate your tale.'

'Disappeared?' asked Alice uneasily. 'Do you mean she has slunk off to pray in some quiet church? Or that she has run away?'

Michael glanced at Bartholomew. 'Perhaps Isabel *is* the killer. She brained Orwel, realised that Clippesby might have witnessed her crime, and rather than claim yet another victim – one who is a *real* saint in the making – she elected to vanish.'

'Leaving her possessions behind?' asked Bartholomew doubtfully, assailed by the sudden sense that their reasoning was flawed, and that pursuing Isabel as a suspect would lead them astray at a time when they could not afford to make mistakes.

'Leaving her spare habit and a few books behind,' corrected Michael. 'None of which are essential to a woman fleeing the law.' He glared at Alice. 'Regardless, she is not in a position to help you, so tell us more about your dealings with her.'

'But I have told you everything already,' whispered

Alice, her plans for vengeance and a triumphant return to power in tatters around her, 'other than that she was writing a report which she said would cause a stir.'

'What report?' demanded Michael. 'It was not in her room.'

'I think she left it with the Gilbertines. But do not ask me what it contains, because she refused to let me read it.' Alice's small faced turned hard again. 'However, if it is more evidence of my so-called wrongdoings, it will be a pack of lies.'

'Of course it will,' said Michael, regarding her with distaste.

Out in the yard, Joan was waiting to tell them that St Radegund's had been scoured from top to bottom, but Abbess Isabel was not in it. Michael nodded brisk thanks for her help, declined her offer to look for Isabel in the town, and left the convent at a run. When he and Bartholomew reached the Barnwell Causeway, they saw a smudge of smoke, grey against the blue sky. Was it someone burning old leaves? Or had trouble erupted already?

'Isabel's report will be about Alice,' predicted Bartholomew as they trotted along, 'because Alice continues to claim that she was unfairly dismissed – that Isabel exaggerated or invented the charges against her. No would-be saint likes being accused of dishonesty, so I suspect Isabel aims to expose Alice's unsavoury character once and for all.'

'Alice was asked to steal and lie, and she did,' mused Michael, 'proving how easily she can be corrupted. It is possible, I suppose.'

'Although if Isabel *is* the killer, why not just dispatch Alice, like she has her other victims? It would have been a lot simpler.'

'She would have headed our list of murder suspects if

she had,' shrugged Michael, 'and that sort of allegation is a lot more serious than defaming a nun whom no one likes. Unfortunately, her disappearance has convinced me that she *is* the culprit. I am sorry for it, as her crime will reflect badly on my Order.'

'But *why* would she dispatch Orwel? Or any of the victims, for that matter? It makes no sense.'

'I had high hopes of answers at St Radegund's,' sighed Michael wearily, 'but we should have stayed home and worked on quelling the trouble instead.'

Bartholomew was inclined to agree, and looked at the plume of smoke again. He tried to determine where it originated, stepping off the road to see if he could identify a church to give him his bearings. It was then that he saw a flash of white deep in the undergrowth. His stomach lurched.

'Oh, Lord!' he gulped. 'It is the Abbess!'

As he and Michael fought their way through the thicket towards the body, Bartholomew noted twin tracks where feet had been dragged backwards along the ground. There were also splashes of blood, suggesting that Isabel had been attacked on the Causeway, then hauled off it, out of sight. She was well hidden, and he would have missed her if he had not left the road to look at the smoke. He crouched next to her and was startled when her eyes flickered open – he had assumed she was dead. Michael dropped to his knees and took her hand in his.

'Abbess?' he called. 'Can you hear me?'

Isabel did not move.

'Head wound,' said Bartholomew tersely, wondering how long she been there. Since she had visited Margery two nights before? But no – she could not have survived her injury that long. Moreover, the blood was wet, suggesting a recent assault.

'And there is the weapon,' said Michael, nodding at the bloodstained stone that lay next to her. 'The same as Wyse and Orwel.'

'So we were wrong about her,' whispered Bartholomew. 'She is not their killer.'

'She is trying to speak! You listen – your ears are sharper. What is she saying?'

Bartholomew did his best, but still only heard half the softly murmured words.

'She does not know who attacked her,' he relayed. 'She heard footsteps behind her, but was hit before she could turn around. The first blow caught her shoulder, so she tried to fight back, but the second knocked her down. Her assailant kept his face hidden the whole time.'

He strained to decipher more, aware that Isabel's voice was growing fainter as the effort drained her strength. Eventually, he sat back.

'She wants a priest now. She says she refused to die until God sent her one, as it will help her case . . . her beatification.'

He moved away so Michael could perform last rites. Isabel's eyes shone with an inner joy when the monk pronounced the final absolution, then it faded and she stopped breathing.

'Such faith,' said Michael softly in the silence that followed. 'I wish I . . . But never mind. What else did she tell you?'

'That we should go to the Gilbertines, where she has left a full report, and that the comb holds the key to all we need to know about Paris and the others.'

'What did she mean?'

'I could not hear that part. She also said that Alice is irredeemably wicked, because even when she was pretending to be her – Isabel's – friend by "acquiring" the comb, she was still sending her deadly gifts. Her dying wish is for Alice to be excommunicated.'

324

Michael winced. 'But she charged Alice to steal, declined to tell the truth when the theft became public knowledge, *and* was plotting to see Alice ousted from our Order. That is hardly an example of good fellowship.'

'She did witness Orwel's murder,' Bartholomew went on. 'It frightened her so much that she fled to St Edward's, where she has been hiding ever since.'

'Orwel's body was taken there,' mused Michael. 'Its vicar is almost blind, and no one ever attends his services, because he tends to fall asleep in them. By luck, she went to the only church where she *could* lurk for days without being noticed.'

Bartholomew groaned suddenly. 'The next morning, I went there to re-examine Orwel, to make sure there was nothing I had missed. I thought I sensed someone watching me.'

'And you did not go to investigate?' demanded Michael, unimpressed.

'No, because I often feel I am not alone when I examine corpses. I assumed it was my imagination or . . . It never occurred to me that it would be a *living* person.'

Michael shook his head in disgust. 'We might have had answers days ago if you had bothered to search the place. So what caused Isabel to leave in the end?'

'Peas,' said Bartholomew helplessly. 'She wanted to know if they are better eaten with meat or fish. She was considering her own contribution to the question as she hurried along the Causeway, which is why she failed to notice her attacker until it was too late.'

'That means he struck not long before we passed this way ourselves,' said Michael uneasily. 'I do not suppose she noticed anything to help us catch him?'

'She claimed it was Satan, wearing handsome boots over his cloven hoofs and a fine brooch on his hat. She says she snatched it from him, although I think her mind was wandering at that point.'

'Are you sure? Because there is something shiny by her hand.'

Bartholomew peered into the grass and saw Michael was right. It was a pilgrim badge, like the one de Wetherset wore. The monk gazed at it in alarm.

'I hope she is not suggesting that the Chancellor attacked her!' He flailed around for a better explanation. 'She mentioned handsome boots. De Wetherset's are not noticeably fine, but Aynton's are.'

Bartholomew regarded him soberly. 'Aynton's are as ugly as sin – he is not the attacker. It *is* de Wetherset – he always wears this badge in his hat.'

'Then someone stole it to incriminate him,' argued Michael. 'The killer is trying to lead us astray – and he is succeeding if you think the Chancellor would kill a nun.'

'*Think*, Brother! We told de Wetherset that Isabel had witnessed Orwel's murder and could identify the culprit. But we delayed coming here, because *he* told you to go to the Jewry first, after which you wanted to release Meadowman. He must have dashed straight to St Radegund's to prevent Isabel from—'

'No! The other nuns would have mentioned a visit from the University's Chancellor.'

'They did not mention it because he never got that far – he saw Isabel trotting along this road first. He dispatched her in exactly the same way that he killed Orwel and Wyse, with a stone.'

'You are wrong! De Wetherset would not—'

'We know a scholar sat in the Griffin and waited for Wyse to leave, because witnesses described a portly man with a good cloak, inky fingers and decent boots. It is de Wetherset!'

'But why? *Why* would de Wetherset dispatch a harmless ancient like Wyse?'

'To stir up trouble between us and the town.'

Michael was becoming exasperated. 'That is the most ridiculous claim I have ever heard! No Chancellor wants his University in flames. What would be the benefit in that?'

'Because he cannot rule properly as long as *you* are Senior Proctor – you are too strong and hold too much influence. But you are responsible for law and order, so what better way to discredit you than to create a situation that you cannot handle? He wants everyone to clamour for your dismissal so he can reign alone.'

Michael regarded him askance. 'There are easier ways to remove a man from office than destroying the University and its peaceful relations with the town.'

'Yes – like ransacking your office in the dead of night, undermining your trade agreements, and appointing a lot of useless beadles in your name.'

'Hah! De Wetherset was not the driving force behind all that – Heltisle was. You are wrong about de Wetherset, Matt. He probably would like me gone, but he would never harm the University to achieve it. Heltisle, on the other hand, is ruthless, and exactly the kind of man to frame a friend to benefit himself.'

Bartholomew considered. Heltisle as the culprit made more sense than de Wetherset, who had always been the more reasonable of the pair. 'So you think Heltisle disguised himself as de Wetherset and came to kill Isabel?'

'I think it is easy to remove a badge from a hat, and Heltisle was also present when we claimed that Isabel could identify Orwel's killer. And while the Chancellor would *never* provoke a war between the University and the town to oust me, Heltisle might. Although this is a dreadful accusation to make . . .'

'And Heltisle is a dreadful man.'

# CHAPTER 14

Michael paid a passing carter to take Abbess Isabel to St Radegund's, where she was received with grief, shock and dismay. Important heads of houses came to demand an explanation, so it was some time before he and Bartholomew managed to extricate themselves – although it would have been longer still if Prioress Joan had not intervened. Sensing their rising agitation at the delay, she ordered her colleagues to silence.

'They will tell us when there is more news,' she informed them briskly. 'Until then, I would rather they hunted Isabel's killer than stood around here chatting to us.' She turned to the scholars. 'So go – do your duty while we pray for this saintly lady's soul.'

Michael gave her a grateful nod, and he and Bartholomew hurried back to the town. Both were appalled by how many troublemakers from the villages were flooding in, eager to fight a foundation they had always resented, and the monk began to drag his heels.

'You do realise that someone may be manipulating us,' he said. 'That the killer *wants* me to accuse the Vice-Chancellor of a serious crime, so that we will be weak and divided when the crisis comes?'

'Then do not accuse him,' suggested Bartholomew. 'Just ask what he did after we said we were going to talk to Isabel. If he is innocent, he has nothing to fear.'

'It is not his fear that worries me,' muttered Michael. 'It is his indignation.'

They avoided the market square, which was almost certain to be thronged with angry tradesmen, and threaded through the maze of alleys opposite the butts instead. They were just walking up Shoemaker Row when they were hailed by Clippesby.

'There you are!' he cried in relief. 'Ethel told me that I would find you if I looked long enough, but I was beginning to think she was wrong.'

'What is the matter?' asked Bartholomew anxiously. He had seen that wild-eyed, frantic expression before, and it meant Clippesby was in possession of some troubling fact.

'Last week, Ethel – the College's top hen – heard Heltisle claim that Suttone had run off to get married. In other words, it was not fear of the plague that made him resign, but lust. Ethel did not believe it, so she wrote to Suttone, begging the truth. His reply arrived an hour ago. It is—'

'Not now!' snapped Michael, trying to push past him.

'Wait, Brother! *Listen!* Suttone explains everything. It was not the plague *or* a woman that made him go. He went because Heltisle *forced* him to. Here. See for yourself.'

Michael snatched the letter and read it, his face turning angrier with every word. Clippesby summarised it for Bartholomew.

'Heltisle threatened to destroy our College with lies unless Suttone did as he was told, and as Michael was away, Suttone had nowhere to turn for help. He bowed to the pressure, because he felt it was the best way to protect the rest of us.'

'Mallett overheard Suttone and Heltisle arguing the night before Suttone resigned,' said Bartholomew, recalling what the student had told him while they had tended the riot-wounded together. 'He thought Suttone was close to tears . . .'

'What in God's name did Heltisle threaten to do?' breathed Michael, staring at the letter. 'Suttone does not say.'

329

'Something very nasty,' said Clippesby, 'or he would have held his ground. But he crumbled, and Heltisle arranged for de Wetherset to be elected in his place.'

'So there we are,' said Bartholomew. 'Yet more evidence that Heltisle is less than scrupulous. We must stop him before he does anything else to further his ambitions.'

'He is at St Mary the Great,' supplied Clippesby. 'He *was* in his College, but a pigeon heard him tell a student that he wanted to keep an eye on de Wetherset.'

'We shall corner him there,' said Michael grimly, 'but let me do the talking, Matt. If you charge in and accuse him of murder, and it transpires that we are mistaken—'

'We are not mistaken,' said Bartholomew soberly.

Michael and Bartholomew hurried along the high street, acutely aware that everyone they passed was armed to the teeth. There was a good deal of vicious muttering, mostly directed against the French, who, it was rumoured, were poised to invade at any moment.

Bartholomew glanced up at the sky to gauge the time. They had spent much longer at St Radegund's than they should have done, and it would be dark in a couple of hours. Tradesmen were carting their wares to safer places, while homeowners nailed boards across windows and doors. Everywhere was a sense that now the day was nearly over, trouble was at hand.

'I fear Dick has given Leger an impossible task,' he said unhappily. 'Even under cover of darkness it will be difficult to spirit slow-moving ancients and children away from the Spital with no one noticing.'

'It will,' agreed Michael. 'But he *must* succeed. Failure is too awful to contemplate.'

'Perhaps we should help. They—' Bartholomew stopped walking suddenly and frowned his puzzlement. 'Look over there – Gonville theologians talking to candle-makers.'

'Yes, there will be a spat in a few moments. I could

330

intervene, but they will only pick a quarrel with someone else. It is not worth the time it would take.'

'No, *look* at them. They are not about to fight: they are having an amiable discussion.'

Michael narrowed his eyes. 'So what does that mean? That we are all friends again? Why, when only a few hours ago we were itching to kill each other?'

'I do not know, but it makes me more uneasy than ever.'

They reached St Mary the Great, where a number of Michael's beadles stood guard.

'The Vice-Chancellor *was* here,' said one. 'But then he and de Wetherset went out, taking a dozen of our lads to protect them. He promised to come back soon, though, and if you would like to wait inside, you can have a bit of our ale.'

'Thank you, Silas,' said Michael, heartened by the show of affection, as it meant the beadles would follow him when the crunch came. 'But we need to find him now.'

'Maybe Isnard knows where he went,' suggested Silas, eager to be helpful. 'Hey! Isnard! Have you seen Master Heltisle?'

'He was in the market square a few moments ago,' said Isnard, swinging towards them on crutches that were spotted with someone else's blood. 'But he left when I threw a stone at him. I wish it had hit the bastard! What he is doing to the trade agreements is—'

'Did you see where he went?' interrupted Michael urgently.

'Towards Tyled Hostel,' replied Isnard. 'But you two should go home and stay there, because there will be trouble tonight. We are going to find every Frenchman we can lay our hands on and hang them.'

'No, Isnard!' cried Bartholomew, shocked. 'You cannot—'

'We do not care if it is a townsman or a scholar,' interrupted Isnard, his usually good-natured face turned ugly with hatred. 'They will all die. Your own Heltisle just reminded us of the Winchelsea massacre, and it must be avenged.'

'So now we know the next stage of Heltisle's plan,' said Michael breathlessly, as he and Bartholomew ran towards Tyled Hostel. 'Uniting town and scholars in a purge against hapless foreigners. I will try to stop it, but I will fail in the face of such impassioned bigotry, and then he will demand my resignation.'

'There will be a bloodbath of innocents,' said Bartholomew, equally appalled. 'Look what happened to Bruges and Sauvage – I am sure they died just because of their names.'

'Heltisle has deployed the most insidious weapons of all,' panted Michael. 'Ignorance and intolerance. God help us all!'

Bartholomew was alarmed to note that it was not only the candle-makers and Gonville who had agreed to a truce for the purposes of fighting a common enemy. Trinity Hall's ranks were swelled with merchants, while several hostels had united with tradesmen from the market square. However, not everyone could bring themselves to do it, and King's Hall was engaged in a furious spat with a band of arrogant young burgesses. Heltisle had been fiendishly clever, thought Bartholomew, as when trouble did come, it would be impossible to know who was on whose side, thus exacerbating and prolonging the crisis.

They reached Tyled Hostel, where more of Michael's beadles had been allocated guard duty, although none were very happy about it. Their resentment intensified when some of Heltisle's Horde swaggered past, making the point that Michael's men were mere sentries while *they* could roam where they pleased. Michael homed in on the Horde's leader.

'You have no right to wear that uniform, Perkyn – not when I dismissed you for malingering. Moreover, why are you lurking down here? When the trouble starts, it will be on the high street or in the market square, so that is where you need to be.'

'Not according to Master Heltisle,' countered Perkyn, making no pretence of being under the Senior Proctor's command. 'He reminded us that Michaelhouse houses more Frenchmen than any other foundation in the University, so we are waiting to trounce them when they come out. They will not get past us to murder our women and children.'

Bartholomew suspected that Heltisle had given them tacit permission to assault anyone from the College, regardless of his origins. The Vice-Chancellor was attacking Michael on all fronts.

'We have exactly the same number of overseas students as Tyled Hostel,' Michael informed him curtly, 'and three fewer than Bene't. Now, enough nonsense. You will go—'

'Master Heltisle said you would try to order us away from your lair,' interrupted Perkyn insolently. 'And he told us to ignore you. So piss off!'

There was a collective intake of breath from the real beadles, which made Perkyn suddenly doubt the wisdom of taking on the Senior Proctor. Michael eyed the man coldly for a moment, then turned to his loyal followers.

'Arrest these fools. Heltisle is no longer in charge. *I* am.'

The real beadles cheered, then quickly rounded up the startled Horde and marched them towards the proctors' gaol. When they had gone, Michael hammered on Tyled Hostel's door, but no one was home except two elderly Breton scholars – the pair who Bartholomew had treated for a series of fear-induced nervous complaints a few days before. They tugged the visitors inside and closed the door quickly, both pale with terror.

'Heltisle came to collect de Wetherset's armour,' said one. 'And our students have gone to join the trouble outside. We tried to stop them, but they called us foreign traitors . . . They intend to fight when the trouble starts.'

'Where is Heltisle now?' demanded Michael.

'Gone to make sure Bene't is safe,' replied the second, close to tears. 'If you see Aynton, please ask him to come home. We are frightened here all alone.'

Bartholomew took them to Michaelhouse, where William, Aungel and Clippesby had already taken steps to defend the College from attack. Armed students patrolled the perimeter, and the gates could be barred at a moment's notice. One of the Bretons grasped Bartholomew's hand as he ushered the pair safely inside.

'I shall pray for you,' he whispered. 'You will need all the help you can get if you are to defeat the evil that has arisen among us.'

It was an uncomfortable journey to Bene't, as more than one person pointed out Bartholomew and Michael as men who hailed from a foundation housing foreigners. One was a patient, so Bartholomew stopped to reason with her, but Michael pulled him on. She had been drinking, which meant she was unlikely to listen.

Bene't was like a fortress, with students in armour stationed along the top of its walls and archers guarding its gates. Bartholomew was dismayed to note that several held weapons that shone with fresh blood. If they were willing to fight in broad daylight, what would the town be like when it was dark?

'Master Heltisle was here,' called a student, shouting down from the wall because he refused to open the gate. 'But then he went out again.'

'Where did he go?' demanded Michael, making no effort to disguise his exasperation.

'To rid the University of French infiltrators,' came the

belligerent reply. 'And to make sure that the town scum know their place – which is under our heel.'

'Now what?' asked Bartholomew, aware that last remark had been heard by several passing apprentices, so was sure to bring Bene't reprisals later.

'Back to St Mary the Great. Perhaps he went there while we have been chasing our tails out here.'

Heart pounding with tension, Bartholomew turned to run back along the high street. They passed Tulyet on the way, who reported tersely that Heltisle had refused to support another curfew on the grounds that scholars had a right to go where they pleased.

'But we would have a riot for certain if there was one rule for you and another for us,' finished Tulyet, his voice tight with anger. 'So now everyone has licence to be out tonight.'

'Have you heard from Leger?' asked Bartholomew anxiously.

'He sent a message to say that he will try to whisk his charges away as soon as darkness falls,' replied Tulyet. 'Pray God he succeeds, because I cannot help him.'

They went their separate ways, although Bartholomew paused for a moment to listen to Verious howling for all loyal Englishmen to destroy the enemy spies. The ditcher's face was bloated with drink, and Bartholomew doubted he was capable of distinguishing between an 'enemy spy' and folk he had known all his life. This was borne out when Isnard approached, and he would have been punched if the bargeman had not swiped irritably at him with a crutch.

Bartholomew felt as though he was in a nightmare, where every step took longer than it should, and St Mary the Great never seemed to be getting any closer. But they reached it eventually, and Michael aimed for the door.

'Heltisle *has* been here since we left,' said Bartholomew, suddenly hesitating.

'How do you know?' asked Michael uneasily.

'Because your beadles are no longer in place. I suspect he sent them away in the hope that this church will be attacked. It will be seen as a direct assault on the University, and will allow him to claim that you are incapable of defending us.'

'If you are right, then this is the last place he will be,' said Michael. 'He will not want to be inside when a mob marches in.'

'He knows nothing serious will happen until nightfall,' said Bartholomew. 'Until then, he will be busily gathering the documents he thinks he will need for when you have gone.'

The door was open, so they slipped inside. The church was empty, and not so much as a single clerk laboured over his ledgers.

'Good,' breathed Michael. 'They all have had the sense to hide.'

'Or gone to join the fighting,' Bartholomew whispered back. 'Now follow me quietly. I want to see what Heltisle is doing before we challenge him.'

He crept through the shadowy building to the grand room that had so recently been Michael's, and peered around the door. Then it was all he could do not to gasp in shock at what he saw. De Wetherset stood there with a stone in his hand, looming over someone who lay prostrate on the floor. The victim was Vice-Chancellor Heltisle.

# CHAPTER 15

Bartholomew's insistence on stealth meant that he and Michael had several moments when they could see de Wetherset, but the Chancellor was unaware of them. He was muttering to himself, and the savage expression on his portly features told them all they needed to know about the identity of the killer. He had donned his armour, suggesting that he aimed to be in the thick of whatever happened that night, making sure it did not fizzle out before it had achieved what he intended.

'I cannot believe it,' breathed Michael. He was ashen, partly from shock that de Wetherset should be guilty, but mostly from knowledge of the harm it would do the University when the truth emerged. 'How *could* he?'

De Wetherset crouched next to Heltisle, peered at the wound he had inflicted, and raised the rock for a final, skull-crushing blow.

'Stop!' howled Bartholomew, not about to stand by while it happened, even if the victim was the detestable Heltisle. 'No more, de Wetherset. It is over.'

The Chancellor whipped around in alarm. 'Thank God you are here!' he cried in feigned relief. 'It transpires that Heltisle is a false friend. I asked why he had sent all the beadles away from our church, and his response was to race forward and stab me.'

Bartholomew was amazed that de Wetherset should expect them to believe it. 'The wound is to the back of his head, which means he cannot have been rushing at you. I suspect he was sitting at the desk when you hit him. Besides, you have no injury.'

'He missed,' said de Wetherset, eyeing him with dislike.

337

'Although not from want of trying – his metal pen was aimed right at my heart. Of course I defended myself.'

'With a stone that just happened to be to hand?'

'One I brought here to prevent documents from blowing around,' replied de Wetherset. He smiled at Michael. 'I forgot how draughty this chamber is. You may have it back, Brother, because I prefer the smaller one. I wish Heltisle had not insisted on uprooting you.'

'Do you,' said Michael expressionlessly.

De Wetherset shrugged. 'I made a mistake in appointing him Vice-Chancellor – his judgement is very poor. But I am sure you and I can work together to rectify all the harm he has done with his ambition and greed.'

Michael glanced at Bartholomew. 'You had better see if you can help Heltisle.'

Bartholomew stepped forward, but de Wetherset blocked his path.

'Stay back for your own safety,' he urged. 'He is a very dangerous man.'

'Let me see him,' ordered Bartholomew, trying to peer around de Wetherset's bulk. 'He may still be alive, and you do not want another death on your conscience.'

'I have nothing on my conscience,' objected de Wetherset indignantly. 'I cannot be condemned for defending myself against a lethal attack, especially from Heltisle. No one likes him, and it is common knowledge that his policies have done much damage.'

Bartholomew was disgusted that the Chancellor aimed to blame a friend for his own misdeeds, but supposed he should not be surprised. De Wetherset had always been ruthless.

'Then how do you explain *your* pilgrim badge clutched in the hand of a murdered abbess?' he demanded, and brandished the brooch aloft.

'You found it?' cried de Wetherset. 'Thanks be to God! It was stolen last night, and I thought it had gone for

338

ever. Heltisle was the thief, of course, and you have just told me why – to see me accused of a crime I did not commit.'

He had an answer for everything, thought Bartholomew angrily, wishing Michael would just arrest the man so they could leave. He did not want to be in St Mary the Great when the inevitable mob marched in. Seeing Bartholomew did not believe him, the Chancellor turned to Michael.

'*You* know I am telling the truth, Brother. I heard a letter arrived from Suttone today. I imagine it revealed Heltisle as a bully who forced him to resign against his will. Yes?'

'Yes,' acknowledged Michael. 'Heltisle is no innocent. However, nor is he the mastermind behind the scheme to oust me and take control of the University. *You* are.'

'Can you prove it?' asked de Wetherset earnestly. 'No? Then I suggest you desist with these accusations and—'

'Why did you turn against Heltisle?' interrupted Michael. 'Were you afraid he would tire of being your henchman and claim the throne for himself?'

'I have already told you what happened,' snapped de Wetherset, growing exasperated. 'But we cannot stay in here quarrelling while the town seethes with unrest. We should leave. Then we shall say that Heltisle was killed by the rabble that will descend on this church at any moment—'

'Which is what you intended from the start,' said Bartholomew accusingly. 'That is why you sent the beadles away – so no one could ever testify that you were in here alone with him. But your accusation will ignite a brawl that—'

'Better a brawl than exposing our Vice-Chancellor as a criminal,' snapped de Wetherset. He addressed Michael again. 'You *know* I am right, Brother. Do not let

Bartholomew's asinine obsession with the truth destroy the University that you have nurtured so lovingly these last few—'

'There is blood on your boots,' interrupted Bartholomew.

'Of course there is – I have just been obliged to hit Heltisle in self-defence. There is blood on my tabard, too. See?'

'No – that is fresh. The spots on your boots are brown and dry. It is Orwel's blood. Or Wyse's. Not Isabel's – she is too recent as well. Now, let me examine Heltisle. He may be—'

'Stay where you are,' came a sharp voice from behind him.

Bartholomew whipped around and felt his jaw drop in dismay. It was Aynton and he carried a loaded crossbow.

Within moments, Aynton had propelled Bartholomew and Michael into the office and closed the door. Bartholomew was disgusted with himself. How could he not have predicted that the last member of the triumvirate would be to hand, and that he would side with the man who had given him his position of power? Aynton and de Wetherset were both members of Tyled Hostel, so of course they would be loyal to each other. Michael had been right to suspect the Commissary of unscrupulous dealings.

'They are mad, Aynton,' said de Wetherset. 'You should hear the nonsense they have been spouting about me. And then they killed Heltisle.'

Bartholomew blinked, hope rising. Did de Wetherset's words mean that Aynton was not part of the plot after all? His mind worked fast. How could he convince the Commissary that he was backing the wrong side? He glanced at Michael, whose face was full of grim resolve.

'Why did you embark on such a deadly path, de Wetherset?' the monk demanded. 'We could have governed the University side by side, as we did in the past.'

'There was no deadly path,' said de Wetherset, flicking a nervous glance at Aynton. 'And we could never have worked together, because you would have turned me into another Suttone. Everyone agrees that you are too strong.'

'It is true, Brother,' said Aynton quietly. 'It is not healthy for one man to wield so much power, and nor is it right that the Chancellor is just a figurehead.'

De Wetherset smiled so gloatingly that Bartholomew felt his hopes fade. Aynton might not have been part of the plan to remove Michael, but he was clearly in favour of it. Meanwhile, Michael regarded the Commissary in stunned disbelief.

'So you are happy that de Wetherset's intrigues have set us against the town?' he demanded accusingly. 'And destroyed all the goodwill that I have built over the last decade?'

'The town does not want our friendship,' snapped de Wetherset. 'They cheat us at every turn, and it is time we put an end to it. Is that not so, Commissary?'

Michael was disgusted. 'So you aim to replace all the fair agreements I made with ones of your own – ones that will benefit us, but that will cause hardship in the town.'

'I make no apology for putting the University first,' flashed de Wetherset.

'Then you are a fool! You might win us a few weeks of cheap bread and ale, but resentment will fester, and we will lose in the end.'

'How?' asked Aynton curiously.

'Because no foundation can prosper in a place where it is hated. Our scholars will be murdered by those you have wronged, and new students will opt to study elsewhere. Gradually, we will wither and die.'

'I know why de Wetherset killed Wyse,' said Bartholomew,

more interested in their current problems than future ones. 'Because the trouble between us and the town was taking too long to blossom. He chose a helpless, frail old drunkard, then made sure everyone knew that a scholar had killed him.'

Was that a flicker of surprise in Aynton's eyes or had Bartholomew imagined it?

'He sat in the Griffin, making a great show of reading and flaunting his inky fingers,' said Michael, taking up the tale. 'Then he trailed Wyse to a deserted road and hit him. Wyse was only stunned, so de Wetherset callously shoved his head in the ditch and left him to drown.'

Bartholomew expected him to deny it, but the Chancellor glanced at Aynton, decided he had an ally, and shrugged his indifference.

'Something had to be done. We were stuck in a stale-mate that benefited no one.'

Outside, there was a crash, followed by a cheer and a bellow of rage. The trouble was starting early. Bartholomew looked desperately at Aynton, hoping to see some sign that he wanted no part of de Wetherset's monstrous schemes, but the crossbow was still aimed at him and Michael, and it did not waver. He clenched his fists in impotent fury; it was hard to stand helpless while his town ripped itself apart.

'Then there was Orwel,' Michael went on. 'The Sheriff sent him to the Griffin to question witnesses, and what they confided allowed him to identify de Wetherset as Wyse's murderer.'

'I saw Orwel leaving this church once,' said Bartholomew, anxiety intensifying when he glanced out of the window to see dusk was not far off. 'I imagine he came to black-mail you.'

'He did,' said de Wetherset indignantly. 'And when I refused to pay, he arranged to meet the Senior Proctor and reveal all, although only in exchange for money, I imagine. So I realised I had to shut him up permanently – for the good of the University.'

'But Abbess Isabel saw you,' said Bartholomew. 'Although she assumed you were the Devil, and was so frightened that she hid in a church for two days.'

'You said she could identify me, so I had to silence her, too. I had no idea how to do it, but then a miracle occurred – I spotted her walking through the Barnwell Gate. I caught up with her on the Causeway and . . .'

'Three innocent lives,' said Michael harshly. 'All ended with a heavy stone. Are you happy with that price, Aynton, or do you consider it too high?'

'It is more than three,' said Bartholomew when Aynton made no reply. 'It was de Wetherset who yelled the order to shoot at the butts. He planned all along for there to be trouble that evening, which is why he arrived wearing his armour – armour he has donned again tonight, which should tell you all you need to know about his intentions.'

Aynton's crossbow wavered for the first time. 'You provoked that brawl on purpose?'

'I regret the loss of life, but it was necessary,' said de Wetherset shortly. 'It proved that Michael cannot protect us from the town. And if he is unable to control a few spade-wielding peasants, how will he fare against the Dauphin?'

'So you hate the French, too,' said Bartholomew in distaste, watching Aynton regard the Chancellor uncertainly. '*You* stabbed Paris, the Girards and—'

'I did not,' interrupted de Wetherset. 'I imagine that was Heltisle's doing. I thought he was strong and able, but he proved to be a petty despot with no redeeming features.'

At that point, Heltisle astonished everyone by sitting up with a bellow of rage, and stabbing the Chancellor in the foot with one of his metal pens.

\* \* \*

343

Outside in the street, it was growing dark. Some folk retreated inside their houses, praying the trouble would pass them by, but far more poured out to join in whatever was about to happen. In St Mary the Great, Heltisle's pen sliced through de Wetherset's foot and pinned it to the floor beneath. The Chancellor shrieked in pain and shock, and flailed at Heltisle with a knife. One swipe scored a deep gash across Heltisle's wrist, which began to bleed copiously.

'Stop!' roared Aynton, aiming his crossbow at them. 'You two did not act to strengthen the University against the town, but to benefit yourselves. You disgust me!'

'Thank God!' breathed Michael fervently. 'Now perhaps we can—'

'Of course we did it for the University,' snarled de Wetherset, his face a mask of agony. 'Or *I* did. Heltisle acted for himself.'

'Lies!' cried Heltisle. 'There is no blood on *my* hands. Everything I did was on his orders – hiring incompetent beadles, adjusting the trade agreements, antagonising the town—'

'And how willingly you did it,' sneered de Wetherset. 'You enjoyed every moment, and would have done more if I had not curbed your excesses.'

Heltisle gave him a look of disgust before addressing Aynton. 'Arrest these three idiots. None are fit to govern, so *I* shall assume command. Well? What are you waiting for?'

'Do you still have the key to this office, Brother?' asked Aynton. 'Good! We shall lock this pair inside, then set about mending the harm they have done.'

'No, you will obey *me*,' shrieked Heltisle, cradling his injured arm. '*I* am in charge. You heard what they said – Michael is so inept that he did not notice blood on a pair of boots, while de Wetherset is a murderer. You should have shot them the moment you arrived.'

'I am glad I did not,' said Aynton fervently. 'It took me a while to separate truth from lies, but my eyes are open now. Step away from the prisoners, Matthew. Do not even think of tending their wounds.'

'We cannot leave de Wetherset impaled,' said Bartholomew tiredly. 'And Heltisle will bleed to death unless I sew him up.'

'It is more important to tell Tulyet that we have identified the authors of all this mayhem,' said Aynton. 'Then peace will reign once more.'

'It is too late,' said Michael bitterly. 'The wheels of unrest have been set in motion, and nothing will stop us and the town from turning on each other now.'

'Good!' crowed de Wetherset. 'And when it is over, and you need a *strong* leader to crush what remains of the town, I shall lead the University to victory.'

'Actually, there will be no harm to us or the town,' countered Aynton, and looked pleased with himself. 'Because we have a common enemy – the French. I have spent the whole day telling everyone that the Dauphin is poised to invade, so we must stand together to defeat him. *That* is how we shall restore the harmony between us.'

'You have done *what?*' breathed Michael, aghast. 'Is that why some foundations have joined forces with townsfolk, making the situation more complicated than ever?'

'Yes, and it is a good thing,' Aynton assured him, beaming happily. 'It means no one will attack anyone else lest he hurts a friend. There is no French army waiting in the fens, of course. I just expanded on a false rumour that was circulating earlier in the week.'

'What false rumour?' asked Bartholomew uneasily.

'That the Spital is full of the Dauphin's spies. Do not look so worried, Matthew. It is not true. I met Warden Tangmer yesterday, and he assured me that no foreigner has ever set foot inside his gates.'

345

Bartholomew regarded him in horror. 'He was lying! There are women and children there – folk who are supposed to leave at nightfall.' He glanced at the window. 'About now, in fact.'

Aynton swallowed hard. 'But they cannot – they will be seen. Angry folk have been gathering there all afternoon, and the Spital is now surrounded by a sizeable mob. I assumed it would not matter – and better damage to a remote foundation than us or the town.'

'It looks as though I shall have my bloodbath after all,' said de Wetherset, and laughed.

Bartholomew refused to leave the Chancellor pinioned to the floor, so valuable moments were lost releasing him. Unfortunately, Heltisle had rammed the pen home with such force that it had shattered, and Bartholomew was far from sure he had removed all the fragments. Meanwhile, Heltisle stubbornly refused to let him tend his bleeding arm.

'I would sooner die,' he snarled defiantly.

'Send him home, Brother,' said Bartholomew, tired of trying to convince him. 'Tell his students to summon a *medicus* urgently or they will be looking for a new Master tomorrow.'

'Very well,' said Michael. 'But I am not doing the same for de Wetherset. He can sit in the proctors' gaol until I decide what to do with him.'

He had fetched beadles and stretchers while Bartholomew had been busy. Without further ado, Heltisle and de Wetherset were loaded up and toted away. The beadles made no effort to be gentle, and the faces of both men were grey with pain. When they had gone, Aynton turned to Bartholomew and Michael.

'Go to the Spital,' he ordered. 'I will stay here and help the Sheriff.'

'It should be me who stays,' objected Michael, sure Aynton would be of scant use to Tulyet.

346

'Please,' said Aynton quietly. 'I was an unwitting help-meet, but my conscience pricks and I must make amends. Besides, now de Wetherset and Heltisle are arrested, it means I am Acting Chancellor – a role I shall fill until you can arrange an election. Ergo, I outrank you. Now go – you have innocents to save.'

'Do you trust him?' asked Bartholomew, as he and Michael hurried through the now-dark church towards the door. 'He took a long time to choose a side – it should have been obvious that de Wetherset was guilty long before Aynton made his decision.'

'I have never trusted him. You are the one who thought he was harmless. But I sent Meadowman to Dick with a full account of what happened, and Dick is someone I *do* trust. He will keep Aynton in line.'

'Did you believe de Wetherset when he denied stabbing Paris and the others?' asked Bartholomew. 'I did – he confessed to the rest, so why baulk at those?'

Michael nodded tersely. 'The culprit is not Heltisle, either. He is a vile individual, but not one to poison children. Do we have any suspects left?'

'Aynton,' replied Bartholomew unhappily. 'But there is nothing we can do about him now. We must wait until we have rescued the *peregrini*, whose only crime was hoping to find a place where they could live free of fear and persecution.'

Night had fallen at last, and the high street and the alleys off it were full of whispers and bobbing torches. They added a tension to the atmosphere that did nothing to aid the cause of peace. Michael's beadles were everywhere, ordering scholars and townsfolk alike back to their homes, although with scant success.

'It is hopeless,' reported one in despair. 'The only good thing is the rumour about French spies at the Spital, as it has drawn many would-be rioters away. Even so, there are hundreds left, and if we avert a battle, it will be a miracle.'

'Here is Dick,' said Michael, as there was a rattle of hoofs on cobbles and the Sheriff cantered up. Both he and his horse showed signs of being in skirmishes, and the knights who rode with him were grim-faced and anxious.

'For God's sake, tell no one else about de Wetherset,' he said curtly. 'If word gets out that a scholar orchestrated all this mayhem . . .'

'We have many bridges to repair,' acknowledged Michael. 'But it can be done.'

'I hope you are right. But do you really want Aynton to "help" me while you jaunt off to the Spital?'

'Not really, so keep him close, and do not turn your back on him for any reason.'

Tulyet regarded him askance. 'Do not tell me that *he* is the killer!'

'I do not know what to think,' said Michael tiredly. 'Just be careful. And do not forget that the Jacques might take advantage of the unrest to harm the town that killed their friends. They will be used to this sort of turmoil, given their penchant for insurrection.'

Tulyet nodded. 'And you be careful at the Spital. The *peregrini* will still be there, because Leger cannot have led them to safety with so many indignant "patriots" milling about outside. I wish I could help you, but my duty lies here.'

'So does mine,' said Michael wretchedly. 'Perhaps I should stay and let Matt—'

'Go,' interrupted Tulyet. 'But please come back soon. It will take every good man we can muster if we aim to prevent University and town from wiping each other out permanently.'

Michael dared not take beadles to the Spital, knowing he would be deposed for certain if it emerged that he had left the University vulnerable in order to rescue foreigners. He hurried to the proctors' cells and gave Heltisle's Horde a choice: to prove themselves worthy of the uniform they wore or to be charged with affray. Most sneered their contempt for the offer, obviously expecting Heltisle or de Wetherset to pardon them, but half a dozen accepted, one of whom was Perkyn.

'How do you know they will not turn on us?' asked Bartholomew, uneasy with such a pack trotting at his heels. 'Or refuse to obey your orders?'

'I do not,' replied the monk. 'But the sight of an angry Senior Proctor with six "trusty" beadles may make some scholars see sense. It is a forlorn hope, but it is better than nothing.'

They hurried through the Trumpington Gate, Michael wheezing like a winded nag. Then a familiar figure materialised out of the darkness: Cynric. Bartholomew was glad to see him, because Heltisle's Horde was growing increasingly agitated as they began to understand the dangers that lay ahead of them. Cynric was more likely to prevent them from bolting than him or Michael.

'You cannot stop what will happen there,' the book-bearer said, nodding to where the Spital was a pale gold smear in the distance, illuminated eerily by the torches of the besieging force. 'It will only end with a spillage of French blood.'

'I am not giving up,' rasped Michael. 'Not yet.'

They set off along the Trumpington road, cursing as they stumbled and lurched on its rutted surface. At the Gilbertine Priory, lights blazed from every window and the canons gathered at their gate, distressed by the tumult in a part of the town that was usually peaceful.

'Brother!' called Prior John urgently, his huge mouth set in an anxious grimace. 'I have some things you should see.'

'Not now,' gasped Michael. 'There is trouble at the Spital.'

349

'I know,' said John drily. 'At least two hundred scholars have stormed past, and we lost count of the number of townsfolk. All were howling about killing Frenchmen.'

'Please,' begged Michael, trying to jig around him. 'We do not have time to—'

'It concerns Abbess Isabel,' persisted John, grabbing his arm and shoving a letter at him. 'She compiled a report for the Bishop, and left it with me two days ago. She told me to read it if anything happened to her. Well, I heard she was dead, so . . .'

Michael looked from the missive to the Spital, then back again, agonising over what to do. His eyesight was poor in dim light, and it would take him an age to decipher what was written. Seeing his dilemma, Bartholomew took the letter and scanned it quickly.

'The first part is about Alice,' he summarised briskly, 'and contains hard evidence that will see her on trial for theft and witchery. The second half is about the killer.'

'Which killer?' demanded Michael. 'De Wetherset or the one who stabbed Paris and the others?' He lowered his voice. 'Who may be Aynton.'

'Isabel says the key to the mystery is a comb, which was lying next to Paris's body when she happened across it.'

'There was no comb at the scene of the crime,' said Michael. 'I would have seen it.'

Bartholomew read on. 'It was familiar, and when she realised where she had seen it before, she fainted in horror. When she came to, the comb had gone. She wanted proof before making accusations, so she charged Alice to steal it so she could look at it more closely. In return, she promised to get Alice reinstated as Prioress of Ickleton.'

'A promise she had no intention of keeping,' noted Michael, 'given the first half of her letter.'

'Which she justifies with the claim that Alice broke the terms of the agreement by sending her tainted gifts. But that is irrelevant. What matters now is that she says the killer is the owner of the comb.' Bartholomew looked up. 'She accuses Prioress Joan.'

'Then she is wrong,' said Michael firmly. 'Perhaps the comb *was* at the scene of Paris's murder, and someone did retrieve it while Isabel swooned. However, there is nothing to suggest that Joan is the culprit. It is more likely that someone left it there to incriminate her – someone like Alice, in fact.'

'That is what Isabel thought at first,' said Prior John, waving a second letter. 'Especially when she heard you say that Joan had an alibi for the Spital murders and has promptly promised to identify the murder weapon for you. So Isabel spent two days praying and reflecting in a church, and sent this addendum to her report today.'

Bartholomew read it quickly. 'She begs the Bishop's forgiveness for not speaking out at once, but she is now certain that Joan killed Paris and the others. She claims that Joan's alibi will not stand up to serious scrutiny and urges him to probe it rigorously.'

'What nonsense!' snapped Michael. 'We do not have time for—'

'I think Isabel might be right,' interrupted Bartholomew urgently. 'Goda and Katherine both said that Joan was horrified when she discovered the comb was stolen – more than either would have expected from a woman who cares nothing for trinkets . . .'

'She explained why,' barked Michael. 'Her horse liked to be groomed with it. Isabel was wrong. Why would Joan hurt Paris? Or any of the victims?'

'Perhaps she does not like Frenchies,' suggested Cynric, who had been listening agog. 'Like lots of right-thinking folk. However, I can tell you that she collected Dusty from our stables about an hour ago, and was very agitated while she did it. I got the impression that something was badly wrong.'

351

'It is,' said Michael tersely. 'She is in a town that is set to destroy itself and anyone in it. Of course she was agitated – she has her nuns to keep safe.'

'I saw her not long after that,' put in Prior John. 'She told me that she was off to Lyminster, and when I remarked that dusk was an odd time to begin such a long journey, she suggested I mind my own business. Then she galloped away like a whirlwind.'

'But why would she—' began Michael.

'We can discuss her motives later,' interrupted Bartholomew shortly. 'After we have prevented a massacre.'

'*If* you can prevent it,' said John grimly. 'Joan was staying at the Spital, was she not? I imagine she guessed that the "lunatics" are really Frenchmen in hiding, and I have a bad feeling that she has not finished with them yet.'

'And I have a bad feeling that you are right,' said Bartholomew.

# CHAPTER 16

Bartholomew was glad when Heltisle's Horde was augmented by half a dozen Gilbertines, led by Prior John. The canons carried no weapons, so would be of scant use in a fight, but there was always the chance that the presence of priests would make a mob think twice about what it was doing. He glanced behind him, and noted that the six beadles were now down to five, as one had slunk away rather than face what lay ahead.

The glow from the Spital was brighter now, and he realised with despair that there were hundreds of torches – which meant hundreds of folk baying for 'enemy' blood. What could he, Michael, Cynric, five reluctant beadles and a handful of unarmed canons do against so many? Tulyet had been right: the Spital was already lost, and they should have stayed in the town, where they might have done some good.

'I still do not believe it,' Michael gasped as they hurried along. 'The culprit cannot be Joan. She is too bluff and honest for so sly a scheme. It seems to me that someone has gone to a lot of trouble to see her accused.'

'Katherine?' suggested Bartholomew. 'She is the Bishop's sister, and we all know how devious and ruthless he can be. Perhaps it runs in the family.'

As far as Michael was concerned, that was a worse solution than Joan. 'We only have Isabel's word that a comb *was* by Paris's body, and she was deceitful, as evidenced by her questionable dealings with Alice. Besides, there was no time for Joan – or anyone else – to reclaim the thing while Isabel lay insensible.'

'There was,' countered Bartholomew. 'When Isabel

353

swooned a second time – at the disturbing sight of a wantonly low-cut bodice – she was out for several minutes. If it was a repeat of her first episode, there would have been ample time for the killer to act.'

'I still do not believe—'

'And there is something else. We crossed Joan off our list of suspects because Goda said she could see Joan in the stables while she herself was in the kitchen. But did you check that is actually possible? I did not.'

'Nor did I,' said Cynric, who had been listening with unabashed interest. 'But I know the answer: you cannot see one from the other, because the chapel is in the way.'

'Goda lied,' Bartholomew went on. 'She did not mention seeing Joan when we first spoke to her – she only "remembered" during a second interview, by which time Joan had realised that she needed help.'

'There is a flaw in your argument,' pounced Michael. 'Goda claimed she could see the *shed* from the kitchen, too – which *is* possible, because I have a vivid recollection of a tray of cakes being carried from the kitchen when I was examining the burnt shed. But Goda made no mention of Joan slinking inside with a fancy French dagger – and remember that this was *before* anyone would have had a chance to bribe her.'

'Goda cannot have been gazing out of the door every moment that morning,' argued Bartholomew. 'At some point she would have looked away to put bread in the oven or fetch ingredients from the pantry. Or perhaps Goda did see Joan, but did not know it – she said the Girards "popped in and out". Well, one "Girard" may have been Joan in disguise.'

Michael remained unconvinced. 'But why would Goda lie? She cannot have known Joan well enough to warrant that sort of devotion.'

'She did not do it for friendship, she did it for money.

We know she was greedy – she coveted the dagger that killed the Girards, and she asked to be paid for answering questions. Joan capitalised on that avarice and bought herself an alibi.'

'He may be right, Brother,' said Cynric. 'Ever since the Spital murders, Goda has been flush with cash – new clothes, new shoes, new hair-frets. And that is suspicious, because the Tangmers are broke. She did not get her windfall from them.'

'No, she got it from the oils she stole from Amphelisa,' countered Michael.

'Not even the best oils would fetch the kind of money Goda has been laying out,' stated Cynric with great conviction. 'They—'

'But Goda began to sport these new purchases *before* Joan knew she needed an alibi,' Michael pointed out irritably. 'I repeat: Matt's logic is flawed.'

'Not so,' insisted Bartholomew. 'Hélène's milk was dosed with a soporific, and as I seriously doubt that Joan thought to pack some when she left Lyminster, it means she got it here – from someone with access to Amphelisa's supplies. I imagine Goda charged her a small fortune.'

'And may have blackmailed her about it after,' put in Cynric.

'Which means Joan knew that Goda would do anything for money,' Bartholomew went on, 'while Goda knew that Joan had deep pockets. A deal was made and we looked no further at either suspect.'

'Moreover, Goda *hated* the French,' said Cynric. 'I heard her say so several times. She would have had no problem looking the other way while Joan dispatched a few.'

'But people like Goda can never be trusted to keep their mouths shut,' continued Bartholomew. 'So Joan killed her, too. She is tying up loose ends, ready to return to her priory and her life as a servant of God.'

'What about Delacroix and his friends?' asked Michael archly. 'Are they to be forgotten in all this? I thought we had agreed that they were our most likely suspects.'

But Bartholomew was still thinking about Joan, and something else became clear to him. 'We have assumed it was Alice who told Norbert about the *peregrini* – that she guessed what they were on one of her visits to the Spital. But Joan and her Lyminster sisters also recognised them as displaced Frenchmen.'

'It *was* Alice!' snapped Michael. 'She betrayed herself by scratching.'

'Precisely! Joan knew that if she clawed at herself as she dispensed her treacherous news, everyone would assume that Alice was the guilty party. And we did.'

'Then what about the Rouen daggers?' pressed Michael. 'Joan said they were familiar. Why would she do that if she had been the one to wield them?'

'And has her testimony led us to the killer? No, it has not! What it has done, however, is make us think she is on our side, valiantly striving to dig solutions from her memory.'

'But why?' cried Michael. 'There has been no hint of Joan doing anything like this before. I would have heard if there were lots of unsolved murders around her priory.'

Bartholomew knew the answer to that, too. 'Because of Winchelsea. She was appalled by what she saw there, and Katherine said she is building a chantry chapel for the victims – a massive undertaking that reveals how deeply she was affected by the experience.'

'She was distressed by it,' acknowledged Michael. 'She mentioned it several times when we rode to the Austin Priory together. But—'

'She is avenging the victims by killing Frenchmen: Paris, Bonet, the Girards, Bruges and Sauvage. Although she made an erroneous assumption with the last two.'

'And tonight will see the remaining *peregrini* slaughtered,' finished Cynric. 'She will not even have to bloody her own hands, because our town will do it for her.'

When they reached the Spital and saw the baying mob outside, Bartholomew's heart sank. Spats sparked between the different factions – mostly scholars against townsfolk, but Maud's and Corner hostels were engaged in a vicious shoving match, while the bakers and the grocers harangued each other nearby. No one was listening to anyone else, and tempers everywhere ran high. There was no sign of Leger, and the scant troops Tulyet had spared to protect the place were under the less experienced command of a sergeant.

'I do not know where Sir Leger went,' the man said apologetically when Michael demanded an explanation. 'He just told me to take over.'

'He must have gone inside,' murmured Michael, and brightened. 'Maybe he has sneaked the *peregrini* out already.'

'Unlikely,' said Cynric. 'They would have been spotted.'

'Have you seen Prioress Joan?' Bartholomew asked the sergeant.

The man nodded to where the Trumpington road snaked south. 'She went that way an hour ago, like the Devil was on her tail. I called for her to stop – it was stupid, riding so wild with night approaching – but she ignored me.'

He hurried away when a quarrel by the gate resulted in drawn daggers. Perkyn watched him go with mounting alarm.

'I am not staying here to be cut down in my prime,' he gulped. 'I—'

'Stand your ground!' barked Michael, although the Horde had now dwindled from five to three. 'You will be quite safe as long as you follow my orders.'

'He will not,' whispered Bartholomew. 'There must be upwards of four hundred armed men here, all spoiling for a fight. You cannot reason with them, because they are long past listening, even if you could make yourself heard.'

'I disagree,' said Michael. 'They could have broken inside by now, but they hesitate out here. That means there is still a chance that we can persuade them to—'

'They are not "hesitating", Brother, they are thwarted,' countered Cynric, assessing the scene with a professional eye. 'The Spital was designed for this sort of situation – to repel folk who want to get at its lepers. The walls are high and the gates are sturdy, like a fortress.'

'So the people inside are safe?' asked Bartholomew in relief.

'Not safe,' replied Cynric. 'Just bought a bit more time. The defences *will* be breached tonight, and then the Spital and its inhabitants will burn.'

'But there must be something we can do,' said Bartholomew in despair. 'We cannot just stand here and watch innocents being butchered.'

'There is one thing,' said Cynric hesitantly. 'When I thought Satan was coming to live here, I made a thorough reconnaissance of the place, just to know what resources he would have at his disposal, like. There is a tunnel at the back . . .'

'A tunnel?' blurted Michael. 'Why would—'

'He just explained why,' interrupted Bartholomew shortly. 'The Spital was built like a fortress, to protect it from attack. Fortresses have sally ports, lest its defenders should ever need to slip out unseen.'

Cynric nodded. 'Unfortunately, the Tangmers cannot use it now, because the Spital is surrounded by hostiles. Anyone creeping out will be caught and killed.'

'Are you *sure* they did not leave earlier?' asked Bartholomew, hopefully. 'Before there were so many besiegers?'

'Quite sure,' replied Cynric. 'I can see one of them from here, watching us from the top of the wall. They are in there all right.'

'So if this sally port cannot help us, why mention the damned thing?' demanded Michael curtly.

'Because they *could* use it *if* we make sure they are not seen sneaking out,' explained Cynric. 'In other words, if we create a diversion for them.'

'Two diversions,' corrected Bartholomew. 'One for us to get inside so we can round them up, and one to bring them out and spirit them away.'

Cynric gaped at him. '*We* cannot go inside! What if the defences are breached while we are in there? We would be torn to shreds.'

'It is a risk we must take,' said Bartholomew. 'How else will we explain the plan?'

'But they are French, boy,' objected Cynric. 'The villains we fought at Poitiers.'

'We did not fight women, priests and children,' argued Bartholomew. 'Or the Tangmer clan, whose only crime was to offer sanctuary to people in need.'

'You may have fought the Jacques, though,' muttered Michael acidly. 'Unless they were too busy rebelling against their aristocratic overlords to defend their country at Poitiers.'

'Jacques?' pounced Cynric, his eyes alight with interest. 'Some are *Jacques*? Why did you not say so? I have no problem helping brothers who stand against oppression.'

'Good,' said Bartholomew, too desperate for Cynric's help to confess that the Jacques were no longer in there. 'Now, show us this tunnel before it is too late.'

As Cynric led the way cautiously through the shrieking besiegers, Bartholomew saw the Welshman was right to predict that it was only a matter of time before the Spital's defences were breached. At the front, a determined but inept gang of townsmen was trying to set the gates alight, while all along the sides were folk wielding axes, picks and hammers. At the same time, a number of resourceful scholars were busily constructing makeshift ladders, ready to scale the walls.

Then they reached the back, and Bartholomew felt hope stir within him. No one was there, because the whole area was choked with brambles, so that reaching a wall to batter at was impractical. But even as he drew breath to point this out, a mass of bobbing torches signalled the arrival of more rioters, all eager to find a hitherto unoccupied spot where they could stand and howl abuse.

'Stupid Tangmer!' spat Cynric, as the newcomers began to bellow at the strangers inside. 'He could have made it out earlier, but it will be ten times harder now that Isnard and his friends have arrived.'

Bartholomew peered into the gloom and saw it was indeed the bargeman and his cronies who had laid claim to the back wall. All had drunk themselves into a frenzy of hatred, and the vile words and threats that spilled from their mouths shocked him to the core. He wondered if he would ever see them in the same light again.

He glanced behind him, and saw that the last of the Horde had vanished, leaving just him, Cynric, Prior John, Michael and the six canons. His stomach churned. The plan's success depended on no one noticing what he was about to do, which would be all but impossible with so few helpmeets. If just one man looked across at the wrong time . . .

'Right,' whispered Cynric, stopping near a particularly dense thicket of brambles. 'Tell us the plan. I hope it is a good one, or your Frenchies will die and the Tangmers with them.'

Everyone looked expectantly at Bartholomew, who scrabbled around for inspiration.

'The canons must holler that they have spotted a spy, then make a show of running after him,' he said, thinking fast. 'The mob will scent blood and join the chase, leaving the rest of us to slip into the tunnel unseen.'

There was silence as the others regarded him in consternation. He did not blame them. There was a lot that could go wrong, and he was not happy with it himself, but it was all he could devise on the spur of the moment.

'But no one will believe us!' gulped John. 'We are men of God – the rioters will know we are not in the habit of flying off after some hapless soul like a pack of savages.'

'You are not,' agreed Cynric, eyes narrowed in thought. 'But Isnard is. Make sure he hears when you raise the alarm, and he will do the rest.'

'Yell as loudly as you can,' Michael instructed the Gilbertines, his voice unsteady with agitation. 'It would have been better with more men to help, but . . .'

'Do not worry, Brother,' said John, grimly determined. 'We know what is at stake. You can rely on us to do what is necessary.'

'Then let us begin,' said Cynric.

Bartholomew had no real hope that the diversion would work, because John was right: who would believe that the gentle, kindly Gilbertines would bay for the blood of strangers? But Cynric had the right of it, and bigotry saved the day. Isnard was livid at the notion that the enemy might be escaping right under his nose, and his bellows of rage drowned out all else. Within moments, the canons were leading a demented, screaming mass of drunken zealots over the fields at the back of the Spital, Isnard swinging after them on his crutches.

'Now, follow me,' Cynric hissed to Bartholomew and Michael when they had gone.

He ducked into the brambles and was immediately lost from sight. Bartholomew did likewise, Michael at his heels.

It was almost pitch black without the rioters' torches, but they could just make out a rough, winding path through the foliage.

'Someone has used this today,' whispered the book-bearer, although how he could tell in the dark was beyond Bartholomew. 'Sir Leger on his horse probably, which means he *is* inside, waiting for the best chance to lead his charges out. Good! Let us hope he has them assembled, so they will be ready to go at once.'

'I think we might have made a tactical blunder by sending the rioters across the fields,' blurted Michael suddenly. 'Because they will be coming back – empty-handed and furious – in exactly the direction that we will be taking the *peregrini*.'

'There is a concealed track,' whispered Cynric. 'Leger must have used it safely today, or someone would have noticed him riding back here and disappearing – and the Spital would be in flames already.'

They reached the wall, where a short, steep slope led down to an arch that was almost invisible in the gloom. Cynric slithered towards it and began to wrestle with a gate. Bartholomew followed, helping the less-agile Michael and marvelling that Leger had convinced a horse to make the journey.

'How did you find it?' he whispered, thinking that it would never have occurred to *him* to explore briar thickets in search of hidden entrances.

'By being thorough,' replied Cynric, 'which was important when I thought Satan was going to live here. But we can discuss this later. Now, get inside. Hurry!'

'You first,' said Bartholomew, regarding the gate and the passage beyond uneasily. He could see nothing but blackness. 'You have done it before.'

But Cynric shook his head. 'I had best stay here, ready to create the second diversion, which *must* be done properly, or you will all be killed as you come out. Prior John cannot do it, because even Isnard will be suspicious if he tried the same thing twice.'

It was a good point, although Bartholomew was dismayed to learn that Cynric would not be there when he ventured inside the Spital. The book-bearer was much better at anything that required sneaking around in the dark than him or Michael.

Heart pounding, and expecting at any moment to hear a screech to say they had been discovered, he stepped into the tunnel, one hand on the wall as he made his way along it. It was damp and stank of mould. The ground descended sharply, then began to rise again as they passed under the wall's foundations. Then his groping hands encountered another door. He grasped the handle and pushed. It opened, and fresh air wafted around him.

He emerged behind a compost heap, near the blackened rubble of the shed. Cautiously, he peered around, hoping desperately that the *peregrini* would be waiting there, but nothing moved.

'It should have been me left behind to handle the second diversion,' grumbled Michael, brushing dirt from his habit. 'I am not built for creeping about in underground passages. I am not a ferret.'

Bartholomew motioned him to silence, then crept forward cautiously. Two lamps burned near the gate, while more were lit in the chapel, but other than those, the Spital was in darkness. Moreover, there were no sentries on the wall or patrolling the grounds to raise the alarm in the event of a breach.

'The Tangmers were standing guard when we arrived,' he whispered. 'Cynric saw one of them. Now they are not. Does it mean they escaped while we were walking about outside?'

'I think we would have seen them,' said Michael worriedly. 'But look how many lamps blaze in the chapel. I have a bad feeling that they aim to claim sanctuary.'

'But they will not get it!' gulped Bartholomew in alarm. 'In Winchelsea, the parish church was set alight with dozens of people locked inside – the *peregrini* and the Tangmers will suffer the same fate if they are caught in there. We have to get them out!'

He began to stumble across the uneven ground towards it, Michael at his heels. They reached the hall and aimed for the chapel's main door, but it was locked. No one answered their frantic knocking, so they hurried to the side entrance in the hope of making themselves heard there. It was open. Bartholomew stepped inside and immediately smelled burning. He grabbed a lantern and ran into the chancel, coughing as smoke swirled around him.

'Where are they?' demanded Michael, peering around through smarting eyes. 'And what is on fire?'

'Amphelisa's workshop,' rasped Bartholomew as he started down the nave. 'I told her the chapel was not a good place for it. It is too close to those great piles of firewood.'

'*Unseasoned* firewood,' rasped Michael, 'which is why there is so much smoke. We—'

He faltered when a figure appeared through the swirling whiteness. It was a large Benedictine nun with a wet scarf over her nose and mouth. She had exchanged her black cloak for Amphelisa's old burgundy one, which was so impregnated with spilled oils that Bartholomew could smell them even over the stench of burning.

Behind her were three men, all armed with crossbows. Their faces were also masked, although Bartholomew recognised Leger's fair hair, and thought the other two were knights from the castle.

'Why could you two not have minded your own business?' growled Joan crossly. 'I suppose you used that wretched tunnel to sneak in.'

'How did you know about—' began Michael.

'I had a good look around when I was billeted here,' replied Joan briskly, and shook her head in exasperation. 'I had no wish to kill you, but now I have no choice.'

'I will do it,' offered Leger helpfully.

# CHAPTER 17

There was silence in the chapel, then Bartholomew leapt at Leger, in the hope that a swift assault would give him a vital advantage. It was a mistake. With indolent ease, Leger twisted away, and Bartholomew went flying from a casual blow with the crossbow. It did him no harm, but he landed in a place where the smoke was much thicker, simultaneously blinding him and rendering him helpless from lack of air.

'Put them with the others,' he heard Joan order. 'Quickly now.'

'Why?' demanded Leger. 'I can shoot them down here.'

'It is a chapel,' snapped Joan. 'A holy place. Now do as I say. Hurry!'

Bartholomew tried to scramble away when the knights came, but they knew how to handle awkward prisoners. He and Michael were bundled through Amphelisa's smouldering workshop and up the steps to the balcony. As the door was opened, an almighty racket broke out. Children sobbed, women screamed for mercy, and old men wailed in terror. Bartholomew and Michael were shoved inside so roughly that both fell. The clamour intensified.

'Silence!' roared Joan. 'Or you will be sorry.'

'*This* is a holy place, too,' Michael reminded her as the din petered out. 'Part of the chapel. If you spill blood up here, you will be damned for all eternity.'

'Who said anything about spilling blood?' asked Joan shortly.

Bartholomew sat up, acutely aware of the snap and crackle of the fire below. Smoke oozed through the floorboards. He blinked tears from his stinging eyes, and saw the *peregrini* and staff huddled at the far end. So were the Jacques.

'You think burning people alive is acceptable, but shooting them is not?' breathed Michael. 'Please, Joan! Think of your immortal soul!'

'I *am* thinking of it,' snarled Joan. 'Which is why I must avenge Winchelsea. It would be a far greater sin to pretend it never happened.'

'It is not for you to dispense justice!' cried Michael. 'It—'

'Who will, then?' she demanded tightly. 'The survivors of Winchelsea? All the fighting men are dead. The King? He is too busy with his war. Mother Church? She brays her horror, but her priests lack the courage to act.'

'Not them – God,' said Michael. '*He* will punish the guilty.'

'Quite,' said Joan. 'And I am His instrument, doing His will.'

'He does not want this!' Michael was shocked. 'And your actions will only compound the atrocity. Murdering more people will not make it better.'

'On the contrary, those whose loved ones were butchered by French raiders will take comfort from it. They said so as I helped them bury their innocent dead.'

Michael indicated the *peregrini*. 'They also lost loved ones that day. Delacroix's brothers were killed defending Winchelsea.'

'They are spies,' stated Joan uncompromisingly. 'They wrote to the French, advising them when best to attack Winchelsea. The Mayor told me personally. It is *their* fault the slaughter was so terrible and they will pay for their treachery today.'

Her eyes blazed, and Bartholomew knew Michael was wasting his time trying to reason with her. Meanwhile, the smoke grew denser with every passing moment, and her prisoners were already struggling to breathe.

367

'You cannot be party to this, Leger,' shouted Michael, snatching at straws in his desperation. 'You are a knight – your duty is to protect the weak.'

'My duty is to protect England from the French,' countered Leger. 'Which is what I *am* doing. Besides, you may have forgotten Norbert, but I never shall.'

'Norbert?' blurted Michael. 'What does he have to do with it?'

'He was murdered in that skirmish by *foreign* scholars. And since Tulyet refuses to take a stand against them, I have joined ranks with someone who will.'

He nodded to his fellows and they prepared to leave. Bartholomew was in an agony of tension. He *had* to stop them! Once the door was locked – and he was sure Joan would have the only key – their victims' fate was sealed. There would be no escape from the flames.

'Joan *used* Norbert,' he yelled, hoping Leger would turn against her if he knew the truth. '*Deceived* him. It was not Alice who told him that the Spital harboured French spies – it was Joan. She deliberately misled him by aping Alice's scratching.'

'But French spies *are* hiding here,' shrugged Leger. 'And Norbert would not have cared which nun the information came from – just that she was right.'

'You will not live long once you leave,' warned Bartholomew, opting for another strategy. 'Like Goda, you will be stabbed to tie up loose ends. And if you want proof, look at Joan's shoes – stained with the oil that spilled as she chased Goda around this—'

Eudo tore at Joan, bellowing his rage and grief. Leger shot him. The big man thudded to the floor and lay still.

'I did chase her,' admitted Joan, regarding the dead man with a chilling lack of emotion. 'But I did not kill her – she had grabbed a knife from the kitchen and she fell on it as we raced around. Her blood is not on my hands.'

'Paris,' said Michael, declining to argue semantics with her. 'You killed him for—'

'For being French,' spat Joan. 'And his death is *your* fault – I would not have known he even existed if you lot had not made such a fuss about him stealing someone else's work. And as for that spicer – well, he had to die after he had the audacity to inform me that the Dauphin only did in Winchelsea what English soldiers do in France.'

Most of the prisoners were on their knees or lying down, gasping for air. Only Delacroix remained stubbornly upright, glaring defiance through streaming eyes.

'And the Girard family?' asked Michael. 'I assume you could not bring yourself to knife the little girl, so you put a soporific in her milk.'

Joan winced. 'It was cowardly of me.'

'Yet you helped to rescue Hélène. Were you not afraid she would identify you?'

'One nun looks much like another to children. And as for pulling her from the shed . . . well, suffice to say that I was caught up in the moment.'

'How did you stab four adults with such ease?' asked Michael, casting an agonised glance at Bartholomew, begging him to act while he kept her talking. 'Two were Jacques – experienced fighters.'

'Experienced fighters who turned their backs on a nun,' said Joan shortly. She opened the bag she carried over her shoulder and began to rummage about inside it. 'Now, enough talking. I am—'

'Bruges and Sauvage were next, even though neither was French,' persisted Michael.

'I pray that God will forgive my mistake.' Joan pulled two daggers from the bag and dropped them on the floor, where they joined a number of others already lying there. 'I collected these after Winchelsea, when I vowed that a French life would pay for every English one. Today will see that oath more than fulfilled.'

369

'You only found one of the batch she left when she dispatched the Girards,' put in Leger gloatingly. 'You might have had answers a lot sooner if you had been more thorough.'

Michael ignored him and continued to address Joan. 'And when these weapons are found, I suppose you will have a flash of memory, which will "prove" that the *peregrini* killed Paris and the others.' His expression was one of deep disgust.

Joan inclined her head. 'Although your Junior Proctor will have to act on my testimony now, given that you will not be in a position to do it.'

'Wait!' shouted Michael desperately, as she turned to leave. 'You cannot do this!'

Joan paused and regarded him thoughtfully. 'Before I go, answer one question: how did you guess it was me? Not from that stupid comb I dropped when I dispatched Paris? I had a feeling that Abbess Isabel recognised it before I managed to reclaim the thing. Is that why Alice took it from my bag? To give to her, so she could be certain?'

'Yes, and Isabel has told everyone her suspicions, so you can never return to Lym—'

But Joan was already sweeping out, Amphelisa's cloak billowing around her. The soldiers followed, and the door slammed shut behind them.

For a moment, the only sounds were the growing roar of the flames below and footsteps thumping down the stairs. Then the Jacques released bellows of rage and ran at the door like bulls, kicking and pounding on it with all their might. But the wood was thick, and Bartholomew knew it would never yield to an assault, no matter how determined. The other adults began to wrap cloaks and hats around their faces and those of the children.

'Tangmer!' shouted Bartholomew. 'Is there another way out?'

'No – we never imagined one would be necessary,' gasped the Warden, his face ashen.

'We lied,' whispered Father Julien, who was on his knees, hands clasped in prayer. 'And this is God's judgement on us.'

'Lied about what?' demanded Michael.

'The dagger that killed the Girards,' said Julien. 'Of course we recognised it – they are made all around Rouen. But if we had admitted it, you would have accused us of murder . . .'

It was no time for recriminations, so Michael went to help with the children, while Bartholomew conducted a panicky search of the balcony. But Tangmer was right: there was only one way in or out, and that was locked. Three of the walls were solid stone, while the fourth was the wooden screen designed to keep lepers away from the healthy. The screen was sturdy, and would not be smashed without an axe – which they did not have.

Yet it did flex when Bartholomew thumped it in frustration. He examined the way it had been secured to the wall, and saw someone had been criminally miserly with the nails. There were plenty to anchor it in place where it met the knee-high wall at the bottom, but there were only a few at the sides, and none at all along the top.

'Help me!' he rasped, kicking it as hard as he could. The Jacques joined in and so did Tangmer, but their efforts were more frantic than scientific, and were aimed at the wrong spots entirely. Then Michael approached.

'Stand back!' he shouted.

He trotted to the back of the balcony, lowered his shoulder and charged, gaining speed with every thundering step. He struck the screen plumb in the middle, so hard that Bartholomew flinched for him. There was a screaming groan as the wood tore free at the top and sides, although the bottom held firm. Then the top flopped forward in a graceful arc to land with a crash on the nave floor below.

Michael was moving far too fast to stop, so his momentum carried him over the wall and out of sight. Horrified, Bartholomew darted forward to see that the screen now formed a very steep ramp, down which Michael was dancing, arms flailing in alarm. The monk reached the bottom and staggered to a standstill.

'I meant to do that,' he lied. 'Now bring everyone down. Hurry!'

No one needed to be told twice. They slid and scampered down the screen like monkeys, grateful that the smoke was less dense below. Confident no one would escape, Joan had not bothered to lock the side door, so everyone was soon outside, coughing and gasping in relief. The Jacques began to scout for signs of their would-be killers.

'We can douse the flames,' rasped Tangmer. 'Save our chapel.'

'No,' barked Bartholomew. 'You must leave *now* or the rioters will—'

He faltered when there was an urgent yell from Delacroix. The townsfolk had finally succeeded in setting the gates alight, and were hammering through the weakened wood with a battering ram.

'To the tunnel!' shouted Bartholomew, hoping Cynric would be able to stage a second diversion with very little warning.

He began to lead the way, aware that the besiegers' howls had changed to something harder and darker now that victory was within their grasp. He had no doubt that anyone caught inside the Spital would be cut down, regardless of who they were. There would be regrets and shame later, but that would not help those who were dead.

Then there was a crash, and the gates fell inwards. The

rioters poured across them, screaming for blood. In the vanguard were Heltisle's Horde, their faces twisted with hate. The *peregrini* children whimpered in terror.

Bartholomew stopped running and turned to face them. It was too late to lead anyone to safety now. He picked up a stick from the ground and prepared to fight. Michael came to stand next to him.

'We nearly did it,' the monk whispered, his voice heavy with regret. 'Just a few more moments and we would have been away.'

Suddenly, there was a rumble of hoofs, and Joan emerged from the stables on Dusty, the three knights at her heels. Their appearance through the drifting smoke was distinctly unearthly. All wore cloaks that flapped behind them and masks that hid their faces. Seeing the gate down, and knowing it would be easier to escape that way than coaxing their nervous mounts back along the tunnel, they thundered towards it.

'Like the four horsemen of the apocalypse,' muttered Bartholomew, sickened to know they would never face justice.

'With Joan as Death,' said Michael. 'It is an apt analogy.'

But as the Prioress approached the gate, a spark from the burning chapel landed on the cloak she had taken from Amphelisa. There was a dull thump as the oils in it ignited. Suddenly, she was no longer a person, but a mass of bright, leaping flames. She screamed in horror and pain, and Dusty, terrified by the inferno that raged so suddenly above him, took off like an arrow. Those in his path scattered in alarm.

Then there came an unmistakable voice from behind them. It was Cynric, who had grown increasingly alarmed by the length of time Bartholomew and Michael were taking, so had come to find out what they were doing.

'Satan!' he howled. 'It is Satan, straight from Hell!'

'He is right,' yelled Isnard. 'Margery said he was coming to live here. Well, here he is!'

'Run!' screamed Cynric at the top of his lungs. 'He wants our souls!'

Joan was burning more brilliantly than ever, and gave a shriek of such agony that it did not sound human. Heltisle's Horde turned and raced back through the gates. Their panic was contagious and within moments the Spital was empty, scholars jostling with townsfolk to hare towards the safety of home.

In the distance, louder and shriller than the wails of the mob, was Joan's voice, as Dusty bore her in the opposite direction. Bartholomew ran to the gates and looked down the road after her. She blazed for what seemed like a very long time before the flames finally winked out of sight.

# EPILOGUE

It was surprisingly easy for Michael and Tulyet to restore the peace following the events at the Spital. Word spread fast that Satan had appeared in the form of blazing Death, and most people fled to the churches, where their priests urged them to pray for deliverance.

Once they had begged the Almighty for mercy, few felt like risking His wrath by indulging in another skirmish. They emerged subdued when dawn broke the following morning, and most went about their business quietly, lest they attracted the wrong kind of attention. A few hotheads declined to give up, but Michael's beadles and Tulyet's soldiers quickly rounded them up and locked them away until their tempers cooled.

As soon as it was light enough to see, Bartholomew and Michael went to look for Joan, to retrieve her body before anyone guessed the truth and decided to resume the assault on the Spital. They found her by the side of the road, still smouldering, but identifiable by her size and the Lyminster ring-seal on her finger. They also found Dusty. The horse had managed to throw his rider before she had done him any serious harm, after which he found a quiet woodland glade and began to denude it of grass.

Joan's nuns collected her charred remains, and arranged to take them home. Michael could not imagine how they would explain what had happened to her in their official report – he was not sure what to say in his own. Magistra Katherine assumed command, and seemed much more comfortable in the role than Joan had ever been.

Leger and his two cronies did not get far either. Their

plan had been to ride straight to the King and denounce Tulyet as a traitor, but the road south was so badly rutted that they were forced to dismount and walk. The call to arms meant the whole country was alert for suspicious activities, and three warriors slinking along in the dark shocked the villagers of nearby Trumpington into action. The next day, they presented a trio of arrow-studded corpses to Tulyet, and informed him that the French army was now minus three of its spies.

Bartholomew returned to his teaching, determined his lads would learn all they could humanly absorb in the last few weeks of term. At the end of one busy day, he went to the orchard to read his lecture notes ready for the following morning. An apple tree had fallen years before, and provided a comfortable bench for anyone wanting peace and quiet. The sun was low in the sky, sending a warm orange glow over the town, and the air smelled of scythed grass and summer herbs. Michael joined him there.

'I am keeping Dusty,' the monk announced. 'He should have a rider worthy of him.'

'I suppose he deserves some reward for carrying "Satan" away from the Spital,' said Bartholomew. 'Cynric adores him for it, so he will certainly be well looked after here.'

'Yelling that Joan was the Devil was impressively quick thinking on his part,' said Michael. 'Such a ruse would never have occurred to me. It saved our lives.'

Bartholomew laughed. 'It was not a ruse – he believed it. Thank God for superstition!'

'I had a letter from Father Julien today,' said Michael, closing his eyes and tipping his head back to feel the setting sun on his cheeks. 'The nuns of Ickleton were delighted to accommodate him and his flock in exchange for me ridding them of Alice. The *peregrini* are safe now.'

'But for how long?' asked Bartholomew worriedly. 'Perhaps another mob, buoyed up by ignorance and misguided patriotism, will assemble, and they will be forced to run again.'

'Ickleton is well off the beaten track, and no one ever goes there. They will live dull but peaceful lives eking a living from the land. Julien says they are all grateful and very happy.'

'Even Delacroix? I cannot see him being content to wield a spade for long.'

Michael smiled. 'He also mistook Joan for Satan and plans to take the cowl – to make amends for all the vile things he did in the Jacquerie. Incidentally, it was conscience that brought him and his friends back to the Spital that night – they realised it was wrong to leave the others alone, so they returned to help them.'

'The Spital,' mused Bartholomew. 'What will happen to it now? It is only a question of time before someone decides to punish Tangmer and his family for hiding Frenchmen.'

'The Tangmers have made their peace with a public apology and an offer of free treatment for all local lunatics. As no one knows when such a boon might come in useful, both the town and the University have promised to leave them unmolested.'

'A public apology?' echoed Bartholomew in disgust. 'For offering sanctuary to people fleeing persecution? We should commend their compassion, not force them to say sorry.'

'It was an expedient solution, Matt. Besides, Tangmer's motives were not entirely altruistic. It transpired that he charged the *peregrini* a fortune for the privilege of hiding with him, although Amphelisa still labours under the illusion that they paid a pittance.'

They were silent for a while, thinking about Joan and the havoc she had wrought with her warped pursuit of vengeance. Eventually, Bartholomew spoke.

'So she stabbed Paris, Bonet, the Girard family, Bruges

and Sauvage with blades left behind after the raid on Winchelsea, although Bruges was from Flanders and Sauvage just happened to have an unlucky name. Then she dispatched Goda to ensure her silence, and aimed to murder the *peregrini* and the entire Tangmer clan in the chapel.'

'And de Wetherset brained Wyse to "prove" that I am incapable of keeping the peace. Orwel guessed it was him from what he learned in the Griffin, so de Wetherset murdered him as well. And I sealed poor Abbess Isabel's fate by claiming that she could identify the culprit.'

Bartholomew winced. 'His actions beggar belief! What will happen to him?'

'I sent him to Ely, to face an ecclesiastical court. Unfortunately, he hit Meadowman over the head with a stone and escaped en route.'

Bartholomew regarded him in dismay. 'Meadowman is dead?'

'No, thank God – just very embarrassed. I imagine de Wetherset will flee the country now. It is unfortunate, but at least his exploits will never become public, as they would with a trial. The town would go to war with us in a second if they ever learned the full extent of what he did.'

'And Heltisle is dead, of course. He bled to death after de Wetherset slashed his arm. I could have saved him, but he refused to let me.'

'You were right about Aynton, much as it irks me to admit it. Since the crisis, he has worked tirelessly for peace, and has done much to soothe ragged tempers.'

'Will you summon Suttone back now? His resignation must be invalid, given that Heltisle forced him out by sly means.'

'I offered to reinstate him, but he wrote to say that he is happier away from the turbulent world of University politics. He told me the nature of Heltisle's threat, by the way: a promise to fabricate evidence "proving" that Michaelhouse is full of heretics.'

Bartholomew was bemused. 'Why did either of them think people would believe such an outrageous claim?'

'Because Heltisle intended to base his allegations on your controversial approach to medicine, Clippesby's mad relationship with animals, William's worrisome fanaticism, and my association with a bishop of dubious morality. It would have been extremely difficult for us to refute his charges, given how cunningly he aimed to weave truth with lies.'

Bartholomew winced. 'I see.'

'But as regards a new Chancellor, Aynton has agreed to take advice from me, so I have arranged for him to be elected next week. I think he and I will do well together.'

Bartholomew was torn between amusement and despair. They had been through hell because some scholars felt Michael had accrued too much power, and now there was to be yet another of his puppets on the throne. Nothing had changed except some new graves in the churchyards. It all seemed so futile.

'Will you appoint a new Junior Proctor to replace Theophilis?' he asked.

'Eventually. I suppose I should have been suspicious of someone with such a glorious name. "Loved by God" indeed!'

'Aungel thinks he chose it himself,' said Bartholomew, recalling a conversation held when the Junior Proctor had been writing down other scholars' opinions about Clippesby's thesis, almost certainly with a view to passing them off as his own.

'Aungel is right – Theophilis' real name is John Clippesby, and – irony of ironies – he changed it because he did not want to be confused with a lunatic. But in his defence, he did not steal the letter you wrote to me outlining Norbert's confession, and he was innocent of betraying me to the triumvirate.'

'So who did take the letter?'

'No one – it had fallen behind my desk. But trying to filch Clippesby's ideas was a low thing to have done, like snatching sweetmeats from a baby.'

'Not entirely. It transpires that Theophilis is the one who was taken advantage of – every time Clippesby mentioned a text that he thought might be relevant, Theophilis raced off to read it. Then he reported back on what he had learned, thus saving Clippesby the trouble of ploughing through it himself.'

Michael laughed. 'And Clippesby certainly bested Heltisle over selling his treatise. Bene't College insists on honouring the contract, in the hope that we will overlook the fact that their erstwhile Master tried to cheat the University's favourite genius.'

They were silent for a while, each thinking about the events that had so very nearly destroyed the University and the town that housed it. Then Bartholomew brightened.

'I had a letter today. Matilde and my sister are coming home tomorrow. I have missed them both.'

Michael smiled contentedly. 'So all is well at last. You are to be reunited with your loved ones, I shall soon have another malleable Chancellor, all the nuns have gone home, I now own a magnificent horse, and Michaelhouse prospers beyond its wildest dreams.'

'It does?'

'The Pope has given the Chicken Debate his seal of approval, so the demand for copies will soar. Not only will we be paid every time one is sold, but we are on the verge of international fame. It is high time – our College is a good place, and I am glad its future is assured. You may be leaving us, but we will survive.'

Bartholomew was delighted to hear it.

\* \* \*

De Wetherset was not really equipped for life as a fugitive in the Fens. He had grown soft and fat from easy living in the University, and hated sleeping in the open like a beggar. But it was better than being paraded as a criminal, as he was sure that Michael had amassed more than enough evidence to see him convicted by the Bishop's court.

He grimaced. He had been right to try to claw power back from the monk, although he realised now that he should have done it gradually, rather than racing at the problem like a bull at a fence. But he had been impatient for change, and ever since his pilgrimage to Walsingham, he had been imbued with great energy and ambition.

Now all his plans lay in ashes, and he was not sure what to do. Every fibre of his being screamed at him to avenge himself, but he had no idea how to go about it. Should he slip back to reignite the trouble between University and town that he had so carefully stoked up? Or go to Avignon, to give the Pope his own version of events?

He winced as he moved the foot that his so-called friend Heltisle had stabbed. He had refused to let Bartholomew examine it again, preferring instead to hire Doctor Rougham. Bartholomew had warned Rougham that slivers of the pen might still be in the wound, but Rougham had scoffed his disagreement. Unfortunately, Bartholomew had been right, because the wound was festering and it hurt like the Devil.

That night, de Wetherset fell into a fever, and when a Fenland fisherman found him two days later, he was gibbering in delirium. The fisherman had heard that the Spital took local lunatics in for free, so he carried him there on his boat. Tangmer and Amphelisa accepted the new arrival politely, and rewarded the good Samaritan with a bowl of stew and a penny. The fisherman went away, happy in the belief that he had done the right thing.

'Well?' asked Tangmer, staring down at the writhing,

gabbling ex-Chancellor. 'Here lies the author of all our troubles. Should we help him or let him die?'

'We should help him,' said Amphelisa. 'But he will never fully recover from the madness that afflicts him now, so we shall instal him in our most secure cell. Later, when his fever abates, he will doubtless claim that he is sane, but all lunatics do that, do they not?'

Tangmer blinked. 'You mean we should keep him here for ever? Locked up like a dangerous madman?'

'He *is* a dangerous madman. Why else would he have killed Wyse, Orwel and Abbess Isabel, or stirred up hatred between his University and the town – hatred that almost saw us destroyed? This is the best place for him, husband, and we shall keep everyone safe from his wicked machinations for as long as he breathes.'

'Well, then,' said Tangmer softly. 'Let us hope he lives for a very long time.'

# HISTORIC NOTE

The Hundred Years War was an uncertain time for England and France. The Battle of Poitiers in 1356 had dealt the French a serious blow – their king was captured and carried back to England as a prisoner – but the resulting peace was uneasy. To show England that France was not yet ready to concede defeat, part of the Dauphin's army staged lightning raids on the English coast. Two of these targeted Winchelsea, which was much easier to reach from the sea in the fourteenth century, although it is inland now.

The first attack was in 1359, while townsfolk were at their Sunday devotions. The church door was locked and the building set alight, an act of savagery that became known as the St Giles' Massacre. The second incursion came a year later, when some two thousand men, according to some sources, slaughtered the port's inhabitants, and looted and burned its buildings. Robert Arnold was Mayor of Winchelsea at about this time, and Valentine Dover was a burgess.

This second raid sent alarm rippling through England. There was an immediate call to arms, where every male aged between sixteen and sixty was ordered to prepare himself for war. Meanwhile, the regular English army marched south to Paris, leaving a trail of death and destruction in its wake. This campaign ended with the Treaty of Brétigny in July 1360, although that was by no means the end of hostilities, which rumbled on for the rest of that century and half of the next one.

The war with England was not France's only problem. In 1358, there was a popular uprising known as the

Jacquerie. It was disorganised and chaotic, and fell to pieces when its leader was captured and executed. After his death, the aristocracy embarked on a programme of vicious reprisals that displaced a huge number of people, many of them hapless innocents. Some doubtless did try to find safety across the Channel.

Thomas de Lisle, Bishop of Ely, was in self-imposed exile at the time. He had been accused of several criminal acts, including murder, kidnapping, theft and extortion, and rather than risk conviction in a court of law, he had legged it to Avignon, where he threw himself on the Pope's mercy. There was a Katherine de Lisle who became Prioress of Lyminster some time before 1370, but her relationship with the Bishop is uncertain. Her predecessor was Joan de Ferraris, who last appears in the records in April 1360.

The Bishop's incumbency was marked by a number of unsavoury disputes. One was with Alice Lacy, Prioress of Ickleton, and followed a visitation by Isabel of Swaffham Bulbeck (Isabel was actually a Prioress, but I promoted her to Abbess to avoid too many nuns holding the same title; similarly, Katherine de Lisle was never *Magistra*).

Isabel discovered 'various enormous defects' and evidence of loose morals at Ickleton, and her report to the Bishop saw Alice immediately deposed. However, Alice did not go quietly. She returned to her priory in a terrible rage, breaking down its doors and helping herself to its treasure. When the Bishop's agents tried to stop her, she threatened to cut off their heads. She was eventually excommunicated.

There was no *conloquium* of nuns in Cambridge in 1360, although there was a Benedictine convent called St Radegund's on the road known then as the Barnwell Causeway. Remnants of the foundation can still be seen in Jesus College today.

Other people in *The Sanctuary Murders* were also real.

Richard de Wetherset did return for a third term as Chancellor in 1360. He was succeeded by Michael de Aynton (or Haynton). The Master of Bene't College was Thomas Heltisle, and other scholars in the University at this time included Baldwin de Paris, Jean de Bruges, Walter Foxlee, John Smith and William of Koln (Cologne). William Shropham was Warden of King's Hall, and William Pechem was Prior of the Franciscan convent.

By 1360, Ralph de Langelee had stopped being Master of Michaelhouse. Evidence is sketchy, but it seems Michael (de Causton) took his place. Other Michaelhouse Fellows in the mid-fourteenth century included William (de Gotham), John Clippesby and Thomas Suttone. There was also a William Theophilis, who had arrived by 1369, when he also became a proctor. John Aungel, Thomas Mallett and John Islaye were later members of the College.

There were three hospitals in the Cambridge vicinity. One was the Hospital of St John the Evangelist, which later became St John's College. Another was the Hospital of St Mary Magdalene of Stourbridge, the chapel of which still stands today. And the third was the Hospital of St Anthony and St Eloy, or Eligius, which stood on the corner of Trumpington Road and what is now Lensfield Road. It was founded in 1361 by Henry Tangmer (who had a kinswoman named Amphelisa), and although it was technically a 'lazar house', leprosy was in decline by the fourteenth century, so the likelihood is that it was for people with a variety of skin conditions, or perhaps even those with mental health problems. Regardless, its relatively isolated position suggests that the residents were kept apart from the general populace. It was often referred to as the Spetylehouse or Spital. It later became an almshouse, and was only demolished in 1837.